THE ASH GROVE

Further Titles by Margaret James from Severn House

THE GREEN BAY TREE
THE SNAKE STONE

THE ASH GROVE

Margaret James

SEVERN SH HOUSE

This first world edition published in Great Britain 1995 by
SEVERN HOUSE PUBLISHERS LTD of
9–15 High Street, Sutton, Surrey SM1 1DF.
This first edition published in the USA 1996 by
SEVERN HOUSE PUBLISHERS INC of
595 Madison Avenue, New York, NY 10022.

British Library Cataloguing in Publication Data

James, Margaret
Ash Grove
I. Title
823.914 [F]

ISBN 0-7278-4855-0

Typeset by Palimpsest Book Production Limited,
Polmont, Stirlingshire
Printed and bound in Great Britain by
TJ Press (Padstow) Ltd, Padstow, Cornwall.

Chapter One

The early morning mist was cool, soft and hazy, but when this had cleared it was sure to be yet another hot day. Too hot, in fact, even to consider doing any work.

So, while their tutor's assistant was setting out their inkwells, chalks and slates, and while Mr Fenton himself thumbed through the Latin grammar in search of that morning's lesson, Owen Morgan and his cousin Rayner Darrow were privately agreeing that this sunny summer Monday in the blazing June of 1797 should be a holiday.

"Shall we go to Foxley Woods?" asked Owen. He and Rayner had skirted the rose garden, leapt across the ha-ha, and were presently crossing the water meadows. "Or shall we go to the Blue Pool?"

"Let me think." Rayner considered the options. Strictly out of bounds to the boys – for neither Foxley Woods nor the Blue Pool were on Ellis Darrow's land – discovery in either of these places would certainly result in a thrashing from Mr Fenton. They might even be punished by the Squire himself.

So Rayner, who at ten years old seemed younger in many ways, and especially fearful of defying his father's authority or risking his displeasure, looked doubtful. "Why don't we just go fishing?" he suggested. "In the brook?"

"*Fishing*?" His cousin Owen, who was the same age, to the day in fact, for the boys shared the same birthday, laughed this idea to scorn. "Catching minnows and stickle-spines, only to throw them back in again? That's baby's play!"

"But we might get some perch today. Or chub. Or grayling, even." Rayner enjoyed fishing. He was good at it, too. "Why don't we—"

"None of them make good eating, so what's the point? Come on, Rayner," urged Owen, his soft, Welsh lilt more hypnotically seductive than ever now, "don't be so dull. If we slip into Foxley Woods, we could have an adventure. We might even spot Henry Summers."

"Yes! We just might." Brightening, Rayner grinned. For Henry Summers, a notorious poacher whom local landowners and magistrates had long been trying to tangle in their own nets, was the scourge of every sport-loving squire in the district. Twice arraigned, he had twice been let off scot-free, for upon examination the evidence against him had proved too flimsy for even an attempt at a conviction. For some reason, even subpoenaed witnesses had become strangely tongue-tied when confronted by the villain in the dock. . .

As the richest, most important landowner in the area, Rayner's father Ellis Darrow was also chairman of the local Bench. A scrupulously fair and honest magistrate, who knew perfectly well that Henry Summers was as guilty as Judas Iscariot himself, he would never have condemned a man on hearsay or unsubstantiated report. But, all the same, it was one of the Squire of Easton's life ambitions to have the fellow convicted, sentenced and suspended from the highest gallows in Warwickshire.

Rayner was only too aware of this. "If we should come across *him*," he murmured, "my father would wish to know all about it. He would need to know everything—"

"To be sure he would," agreed Owen. Ingenuousness itself, he smiled. "Well, then?"

"Let's go." His conscience clear – for, far from bunking off lessons, the squire's son and heir was now investigating the activities of a dangerous felon – Rayner followed Owen Morgan across the fields and into Foxley Woods.

* * *

By ten o'clock the summer mist had cleared completely, and an orange sun burned in a sky the colour of the bluebells which were only just beginning to fade.

In the woods, however, it was cool and damp and green. Pretending to be painted savages, two dark-eyed, dark-haired little boys crept through the undergrowth, now and then startling a rabbit or putting up a pheasant – which rose, wings whirring in angry indignation, from an ill-concealed nest.

Reaching a natural clearing, they found themselves standing on the mossy banks of the stream which fed the springs of drinking water on Squire Darrow's estate. Here, a recently fallen tree had created a dam, behind which was a deep, dark pool of brown water. "Shall we swim?" suggested Owen.

"Well—"

"I shan't duck you." Ever the man of action, Owen was already half undressed. "I'll not hold you under."

"You promise?

"I promise!"

"Oh." Still, Rayner was doubtful. But the water looked so cool and inviting. Rayner, on the other hand, was sticky, sweaty and uncomfortably hot. "Oh, very well," he agreed.

"Good man." Owen grinned.

Two years ago, Owen had taught Rayner to swim. After a fashion. In the cold, grey waters of the artificial lake on his father's estate, Rayner had gasped and choked and spluttered, had dog-paddled out of his depth and almost drowned, while Owen laughed at him, then hauled him back to the shallows. Then he had tricked his shivering, terrified student into floundering out of his depth again, and again, and again.

But this little pool did not seem to pose any great dangers of that kind, so today Rayner shrugged off his clothes and followed Owen's example, shivering not with dread but with pleasure as the brown water lapped his shoulders. Then, as Owen grabbed his legs and pulled him under, the water closed over his head.

A good two miles from the southern boundary of the Easton estate, Foxley Woods was the private property of Mr Nathaniel Graham, who had bought the land the previous autumn, but actually come to live in the refurbished manor house only six weeks ago.

A keen preserver of game, who fancied himself the equal in cunning and guile of any poacher throughout the length and breadth of Warwickshire, on buying the estate Mr Graham had immediately set about defending his spinneys, coppices and pheasants with a ferocity which was almost mediaeval in its zeal. Hundreds of spring-guns, always primed and loaded, lurked in the lush summer undergrowth, pointing their lethal bolts at all unwary trespassers or casual passers by. Cruel iron man-catchers, each quite capable of taking a leg off at the thigh, skulked in even the greenest of dells.

Because of this, Rebecca Darrow had forbidden both her son and her nephew to enter any part of Mr Graham's estate. This prohibition had been seconded by her husband, who had hinted that defiance of the ban would result in a beating, administered not by their tutor but by the Squire of Easton himself. So, naturally, the boys trespassed on Mr Graham's trap-infested land as often as they dared. Discovering a new man-crusher, and springing it with a stick, was the undoubted highlight of any day.

Tiring of trying to do any serious swimming in so confined a space, and by now nicely cooled off, the boys clambered over the dam. "Come on, then," said Owen, hauling himself into shallower water, "let's go and see if we can find some eggs."

"But we're not allowed to disturb—"

"Oh, for God's sake! We'll only take one or two, for our collection." Owen grinned. "There were half a dozen nests back there, in the spinney."

So the boys forded the stream, stirring up mud and gravel to such an extent that, had he observed them, Nathaniel Graham would have suffered a bilious seizure at the very least. Dawdling along the banks, Owen and Rayner threw stones into the shallows. They poked sticks into the mud. Then, in a little clearing, they discovered some fresh, pink mushrooms – or at any rate, what they decided *ought* to be mushrooms – so they sat down and ate them, all the while dabbling their feet in the fast-flowing stream.

As they ate, they realised they were in fact very hungry. Fortunately, Owen always had food in his pockets – for Bethan Davies, his former nurse, who nowadays worked in the kitchens at Easton Hall, kept her erstwhile charge well supplied with pastries and cakes. It was rumoured she intended to make him as fat as she was, and if Owen hadn't been so fidgety and energetic, she would no doubt have succeeded in her attempt.

Splashing back to the place where they had left their clothes, Owen and Rayner began to ransack Owen's greasy pockets. But, as they did so, they heard the goblin's wail.

Rising, then falling, then rising again, it was the cry of a soul in torment. Pleading and beseeching in an agony of loss, it made the flesh creep and the hair stand on end.

"Oh, God!" Frozen in mid-rummage, Rayner grew pale with dread. "Owen, is it—"

"The *bwbach*!" Owen's face grew paler still.

Now, the boys stared all around, first into the green opacity of the trees, then at one other. Hurriedly, they dressed, pulling on shirts, breeches and waistcoats in crumpled haste. Abandoning their picnic, they took to their heels, not caring that Rayner's stockings had been left on the bank, nor that Owen's neckerchief, incriminatingly embroidered with his initials, still lay in the mud at the water's edge. They had to get away!

Crashing through the undergrowth, in their panic hardly knowing where they went, the trespassers soon found themselves in the deepest, densest part of the wood. Fighting their way through thickets of bramble and thorn, their faces were scratched and their clothes ripped to shreds in minutes.

But, in spite of this, they kept going. Bethan Davies's bedtime stories, which invariably featured all manner of malevolent fairies and evil spirits, were so much a part of them that even as great big boys of ten they were terrified of ghosts, goblins and witches. They would have faced any number of spring-guns, and braved whole serried ranks of man-catchers, rather than confront that awful, howling thing back there in the wood.

But confront it was exactly what they were obliged to do. Stumbling out of a particularly dense thicket of hazel saplings, most of which they'd damaged in their flight, they came face to face with Mr Graham's head keeper. At his side was a young woman. Her bony knuckles showing white, she held fast to the wrist of a scruffy little red-headed girl.

"Well, gentlemen!" Stephen Hurst grinned. Reasonably assuming he must be the last person on earth these particular trespassers could wish to meet, the keeper folded his arms. "To what do we owe the pleasure of *your* company this fine day?"

The boys gaped at him. Appalled, but also immeasurably relieved, they found they could not speak.

The red-headed girl was squirming like a ferret. A rather anaemic ferret, however – for, apart from the scarlet weals of a recent slap which incarnadined her left cheek, her tear-stained face was ashen. She squirmed again. But then, as the boys stared at her, she seemed to realise the game was up. She was outmanoeuvred, outclassed, outnumbered hopelessly. So, her struggles became less violent. Miserably, despairingly, she sniffed. Then she wiped her nose on her sleeve.

Clucking irritably, the woman poked her between the shoulder blades. Then she glanced sharply at the keeper. "Do you know these creatures?" she enquired.

"I do indeed." Still, the keeper grinned. But then, pursing his lips, he blew down the barrel of his gun, which he now tucked under his arm. "I reckon we should all go back to the footpath," he said.

"All of us?" Eyeing the two boys, the woman grimaced in disdain. "Even these little villains here?"

"They're no villains, ma'am." The keeper met Rayner's eyes. "May I have the pleasure of making the introductions?" he demanded. "Or shall I leave that to one of you?"

Rayner shot an enquiring glance at Owen, who was staring resolutely at his feet. Obviously, his cousin intended to remain dumb. If he'd had any sense, Rayner might have done likewise. But then, generations of good breeding triumphed, and *noblesse* obliged. Looking up again, the heir to the Easton estate forced a polite smile. "I am Rayner Darrow," he began, bowing to the woman courteously. "I am the son of Ellis Darrow, of Easton Hall. This my cousin, Owen Morgan."

"So, Mr Darrow – Mr Morgan – you're aware you are trespassing on private property?" The woman smiled in return, but hers was a bitter smile. "There are severe penalties for trespass, you know."

Indeed, Rayner did know. So he said nothing more.

"I'll see you to the path." Tired of all this messing about, Stephen Hurst began to lead on. "Mind you keep to the way, now," he advised. "There are traps all over this part of the wood, and an encounter with one of those fellows will do you no good at all."

To illustrate his point, at one of the forks in the path the keeper broke a branch from an overhanging oak tree, thrust it into the undergrowth, and let the trap concealed there bite it. The branch broke easily.

"That could have been your leg." The keeper shook his head. "Clean as a whistle, eh?"

Four days later, Owen and Rayner were summoned to Ellis Darrow's study, where the squire harangued them at great length on the evils of trespass, truancy and general disobedience. Then he came to the question of punishment.

Rayner clenched his fists in anticipatory dread. Involuntarily, Owen's own gaze was drawn towards the collection of canes in the tall Indian jar, which stood by his uncle's desk. Never yet used as offensive weapons, they were only biding their time. Today would surely see one of them make contact with his shrinking frame.

But this was not to be. "I have decided you will not be beaten," continued the Squire of Easton, his brow furrowed and his expression grim. "Instead, your allowances will be stopped until Michaelmas Day. Your hours of study will be doubled. On Sundays, you will attend divine service morning and evening, until such time as some improvement is seen. Both in your general behaviour, and your demeanour towards those in positions of authority and trust."

Ellis Darrow looked from one wretched miscreant to the other. "Well? Do you have anything to say for yourselves?"

"No, sir." Humbly, Owen hung his head.

"No, sir." Rayner followed his cousin's example. "Thank you, sir."

"Then you may go," said the squire.

"Damn Stephen Hurst!" cried Owen, as the door of his uncle's study closed softly behind him. "Damn him to hell, the tale-bearing swine!"

"Hush!" Fearfully, Rayner glanced behind him. If his father heard Owen cursing, the boys' allowances would be stopped until All Saints' Day. Mr Fenton would be authorised to use his cane after all.

But still Owen ground his teeth and swore to get even, one day.

As it happened, it was most unfair to blame Stephen Hurst – who had, in fact, forgotten all about his encounter with two juvenile trespassers on his master's land. A chance remark by Isabel Graham, that she had met some other children in the woods, followed up by a request that they might be invited over to the house to play, was responsible for the story coming out, and reaching the Squire of Easton's ears.

But Rayner and Owen were not invited anywhere. The rest of that long, hot summer of 1797 was passed mostly indoors, chafing and fidgeting under the watchful eye of their tutor. Rayner's sisters Jane and Maria were invited to meet their new neighbours; while they anxiously examined Isabel Graham's gowns, fearful lest they should discover the trimming and stitching were superior to the embroidery on their own, Rayner had his head bent over Caesar's *Gallic Wars* or Cicero's *Orations*, while Owen was getting great gobbets of the Scriptures by heart.

Or trying to.

Mr and Mrs Nathaniel Graham, lately arrived from Richmond, Virginia, had long-established family connections throughout the whole of Warwickshire. So it was only natural they should have decided to settle there.

Scions of an ancient Royalist family still staunchly loyal to the Hanoverian kings, Nat Graham's ancestors had done well for themselves in the New World, but Mr Graham himself had found he was a fish out of water in the new Republic of the United States. Increasingly cold-shouldered by his Anglophobe, anti-monarchist neighbours, he had finally sold his tobacco plantations and emigrated to Canada. But republican ideals poisoned the air there, too. So the Graham family decided it was time to come back home.

Isabel Graham, an only child with a penchant for company and excitement, had quickly discovered that these tastes could hardly be indulged in the green solitude of Warwickshire. After that first encounter in the woods, Isabel was driven to seek out the gamekeeper again. Following him around the coverts and obliging him to talk to her, she was delighted to discover from Stephen Hurst that the two young gentlemen recently apprehended in the hazel thicket had female relations. "What are their names?" she demanded, excitedly.

"Miss Darrow and Miss Darrow again, of course," replied the keeper, who knew his place.

"I mean, their Christian names!" Crossly, Isabel twisted a strand of her startlingly red hair, round and round and round. "Well, Hurst?"

"Miss Jane and Miss Maria, I believe." As Isabel fidgeted about, then trod squarely on yet another clutch of pheasant's eggs, Stephen Hurst sighed. "Had you better not go back to the house, Miss?" he suggested, wishing he could wring this tiresome creature's skinny little neck. "I'm sure your nurse is wondering where you are."

To his surprise and delight, Isabel complied. Then, after some hours of pestering her mother, who was reclusive, and preferred reading her Bible to seeing company, she eventually persuaded Mrs Graham to invite Mrs Darrow and her daughters to Haddesdon Manor.

The Squire of Easton's lady received this invitation with pleasure. While hardly a gadabout, Rebecca Darrow had no objection at all to evaluating another woman's choice of furniture, fittings and upholstery, and she looked forward to finding Mrs Graham's colonial taste far inferior to her own. So, after having sent her husband to wait on Mr Graham and formally sanction the acquaintance, she ordered the carriage. To the manor Mrs Darrow and her daughters duly went.

At fourteen, Jane Darrow was already a young lady. Once a tree-climbing, mischief-making daredevil of a tomboy, who liked nothing better on a frosty morning than to ride to hounds, or steeplechase across open pastureland, this summer her love of country pursuits had suddenly given way to a consuming interest in fashion, flirtation and finery. Recently nothing but a grubby little hoyden, of whom her nursemaids had despaired, all of a sudden she had become an irreproachably hygienic, fastidious child-woman, who could spend all day putting her hair up and taking it down again. Soon, she would be on the look-out for a husband.

Although only eleven, Maria was mature and sensible far beyond her years, so was her elder sister's preferred companion and confidante. Introduced to nine year old Isabel Graham, who was still a child in manners, dress and appearance, it was perhaps inevitable that the Darrow girls should find her tiresome in the extreme.

So the visit was not a success, and they were not long in the carriage going home again before the squire's daughters began to pick over their new neighbour's many faults and failings, then to magnify these tenfold.

"She's even younger than Owen and Rayner," complained Maria who, as the nearer in age to Isabel, had been asked by her mother to make a special effort to be pleasant to the child. "In fact, she's just a baby, in thought, word and deed. An excessively spoiled and backward baby, too. My dear Jane, do you not agree?"

"Most certainly," agreed her sister, who was thinking of bonnets and trimming. "I never saw such a brat."

"But my dear Maria! My dear Jane!" Rebecca was shocked. "How can you be so cruel? So very unkind?"

"My dear ma'am, I'm sorry to offend you, but I speak only the truth." Maria shook her head. "The little fool can neither read, write, nor cipher. Indeed, she can hardly make herself understood in common speech, for she drawls and snuffles so."

"Her bedchamber is so full of dolls and other silly playthings," added Jane, "which I'm sure my sister learned to despise *years* ago, that one can't find a place to put one's feet. I trod on a doll – indeed, I broke it. I couldn't help it. But Isabel didn't care. She has so many toys that the loss of one makes no difference at all to her."

All the way home, Jane and Maria muttered to one another about Isabel Graham's childishness and stupidity.

In spite of their mother's reproachful stares, they resolved to have nothing more to do with her until she was a little more grown-up. They treated their little brother and their cousin with the casual indulgence accorded to their kittens, puppies and other pets. But Isabel was too boring even to be a pet.

Alighting from the carriage, Rebecca went into the house. But, noticing Owen and Rayner dawdling near the dovecote, talking to the man who looked after their mother's beloved peacocks, turtle doves and other ornamental birds, the sisters decided to accost them. Correctly supposing the boys to be temporarily released from the bondage of what was these days almost perpetual study, Jane and Maria enticed them into the rose garden. There, they told them all about their day.

"She said she was already acquainted with you." Flicking fastidiously at a speck of dust on Owen's lapel, Jane raised her eyebrows and smiled, in arch enquiry. "So, my dear Owen, pray enlighten us. When were you introduced?"

"I don't know what you're talking about." Threatened with a beating if he were not word perfect on a set chapter of the *Acts of the Apostles*, to be repeated to Mr Fenton later that evening – and well aware that he wouldn't be, for learning by rote was not his forte – Owen was inclined to be sulky. "What do you mean, introduced?"

"To the young lady who met you trespassing – how shocking, dear Owen, could it *really* have been you, lurking in the undergrowth like a common poacher – on her father's estate?" Maria also looked arch.

"She had run away from her nurse. There had been some disagreement over a flannel bodice, I believe, so she was taking a ramble all by herself. But the gamekeeper found her, and warned her out of the woods."

"*That* was Miss Graham?" Disgusted, Owen sniffed his disdain. "I'd supposed she was the keeper's daughter. Or some urchin from the village."

"Why did you think that?"

"Well – she looked a sight. Her gown was torn and filthy. Her hair was all elf-locks. Her face was as dirty as a gipsy's. My aunt says Miss Graham is supposed to be beautiful. But that girl was a fright."

"As ugly as sin," agreed Rayner.

"Red as a carrot, lank as a skinned rabbit, and freckled as a toad." Owen grinned. "If that girl's a beauty, I'm a Chinaman, and Rayner here's a Red Indian brave."

"Miss Graham is an heiress." Jane looked from one boy to the other. "My mother says she will bring her husband forty thousand pounds. Yet more when her father dies. If I were you, John Rhys Owen, I would court her good opinion directly, beauty or not."

"*I* don't mean to live off a wife!" retorted Owen, indignantly. But then, he grinned. "I shall make my own fortune," he declared. "I'll marry whom I please – I shall wed the Great Sultan's daughter herself, if I so choose. Rayner here can take the skinny, freckled thing."

"I'd sooner shoot myself dead."

"What a pair of fools." Maria clicked her tongue. Well aware that it was desirable to marry for love, and would be wicked indeed to court a rich woman merely for her money, if she were Owen Morgan she would even now be resolving to fall for Isabel Graham. To seek her good opinion in return.

Fortunately, where looks were concerned, Jane Darrow and her sister Maria took after their mother. Fashionably fair-haired and pale-skinned, they presented a complete contrast to their dark-haired, dark-eyed brother and cousin.

Their sweet, heart-shaped faces were undeniably pretty. Their figures, too, were light and slender, and beautifully accentuated by the high-waisted gowns then in fashionable favour. Possessing rank, money and breeding – for these days it was conveniently forgotten that their mother had been a manufacturer's granddaughter – they were the best matches in the district.

Or they had been. Over the next few months, however,

it became depressingly clear that their stars were to be eclipsed by an even brighter sun. As Owen and Rayner had observed, strictly speaking, Isabel Graham was no beauty – no beauty at all – but an heiress such as she needed only a regular number of arms and legs to be lauded far and wide.

Common report soon talked her up, and in due course her anaemic, ginger looks were universally agreed to be as lovely as those of an angel. As for her own voice, which was certainly peculiar – a strange, Southern drawl, it was almost incomprehensible to the natives of Warwickshire – this was quickly decided to be an additional charm. She was pronounced delightful by all.

Soon, she and her parents were on regular visiting terms with all the families round about, especially the family at Easton Hall. For it was from Rebecca Darrow, who was as devout and God-fearing a woman as Mrs Graham herself, and as reluctant to stray into frivolous company as she was, that Isabel's mother hoped to learn all about her neighbours and their ways.

Isabel became better acquainted with the Easton children. Maria and Jane learned to tolerate her, while Rayner, the baby of the family, came to understand the benefits of having someone younger and less well-educated than himself about the place. Someone whom even he could patronise and impress.

But perversely, for he gave her no encouragement at all, it was Owen whom Isabel appeared to like best. She sought him out, hearing him speak nonsense with great deference, and watching fascinated as he showed off, as he turned cartwheels across the manicured lawns which surrounded the beautiful Elizabethan manor house, or climbed one of the great oaks in the grounds – and all too often fell out of it, as well. But on these painful occasions, he would always laugh Isabel's concern to scorn. Dusting himself down, he would sooner have died than admit he had wrenched his ankle or sprained his wrist.

Born in South Wales and brought up with Gower Welsh as his first language, Owen's English was every bit as distinctive as Isabel's own. But now, catching the rhythms of his speech, she began to mimic him, his Celtic lilt being grafted most uneasily on to her Southern drawl.

She was infected by his bluntness, too. "God, there's messy," she observed one fine morning, as she examined Maria's not very successful sketch of the new marble fountain in front of the house, which was playing for the first time that summer. "It's entirely wrong by there, look – all crooked it is!"

"My dear Isabel, what can you mean?" Laughing good naturedly, for she knew she was no Hogarth, Maria turned to look at the child. "Do you presume to find fault with my perspective, perhaps?"

"No. But this bit where the water's supposed to be coming from is awful." Critically, Isabel frowned. "Looks like a bottle with sticks poking out the top, so it does."

The American brat was Owen Morgan incarnate! Maria nearly choked.

Just at that moment, Owen himself appeared on the terrace. "What you laughing at, then?" he demanded, suspiciously.

"Nothing, dear Owen. Nothing at all." Still grinning, Maria took his hand. "Look at my picture," she invited. "See this bit by here. Does it strike you as peculiar, now?"

"God – I don't know!" Narrowly, Owen observed her. He knew he was being teased, but for the life of him he could not see the joke.

Neither, apparently, could Isabel. For she too stood there quite perplexed, every bit as puzzled by Maria's sudden mirth as Owen was.

Later that day, Owen was taking a short cut through the small physic garden which his aunt had established in a sunny corner. Here Rebecca grew sage, rosemary, borage and a host of other medicinal plants, to be used in infusions and ointments in the home.

Observing someone sitting on a bench, he realised it was Isabel. Permanently at a loose end, for she appeared to do no lessons of any kind, nor did she ride, draw or even read for pleasure, he presumed she was waiting for Maria to finish her piano practice. Or for Jane to accompany her on a walk.

In the bright sunshine, he noticed, her red hair glowed like fire. Picking a couple of marigolds, used in the making of poultices for wasp stings, he looked from the flowers to Isabel, then back again. Her hair was exactly the same golden orange as the flower petals. It shone just as brightly as they did. For the first time ever, he saw beauty in Isabel Graham.

Just then, she glanced up. She saw him.

"Good morning," she began, smiling. Today, she was dressed all in white, which suited her. "Just waiting for your cousins, I am."

"Oh." Embarrassed, Owen looked down at the flowers in his hand. Whatever had possessed him to pick *them*? Only girls picked flowers! He blushed furiously.

But Isabel did not notice, for she was eyeing the marigolds. "Pretty, they are," she observed. "Lovely they look, shining in the sun."

"You think so?" Owen shrugged. "Here you are, then," he muttered, thrusting the flowers straight at her, "you have them."

She beamed at him. Accepting the marigolds, she clasped them to her heart, inhaling their sharp, pungent scent. "Thank you," she said.

"Well, I didn't want them did I?" Owen scowled at her, fixing her with his large, dark eyes. "They should have called you Marigold," he observed.

"You think so?" Isabel shifted along the bench. "Sit down," she invited.

Owen sat.

"Talk to me," said Isabel.

"What?"

"Talk to me! I know – tell me all about yourself."

Drawing up her knees and making herself comfortable in the left hand corner of the bench, Isabel continued to smile at him. "You're an orphan aren't you? You were born in Wales. Is that far from here?"

"Miles away. Hundreds of miles!"

"Oh." Isabel looked suitably impressed. "What happened to your parents, then? Why did you come to live in Warwickshire?"

"I – I can't talk about any of that." For a moment, Owen closed his eyes. Then, jumping to his feet, he left her. He ran off to find Rayner, while Isabel stared after him in astonishment, wondering what on earth she'd said.

Chapter Two

That golden summer of 1797 was not without its winds and gales, its sudden tempests, nor its storm clouds edging inexorably over the far horizon. In the countryside, outbreaks of rick-burning, machine-smashing and cattle-maiming alarmed every man in England with property to protect. But in the towns, things were even worse, causing beleaguered manufacturers to mutter constantly about the Jacobins, radicals and free-thinkers who were undermining the very foundations of civilised society.

All the same, riots in nearby Birmingham, where the Darrow family owned factories turning out firearms and ammunition for the everlasting French wars, took Rebecca Darrow completely by surprise. Born Rebecca Searle and the granddaughter of a manufacturer, she had grown up in that dirty town, and thought she understood the mood of her own workforce through and through.

"If there's work to be had, and good wages to be earned," she protested, as she learned that the hands were on strike yet again, "surely the men should be content?"

She looked from her manager to her chief clerk, then back again. "Do these fellows not realise the damage they cause? Can they not understand that if they bankrupt *me*, they will also ruin themselves? That we shall all starve?"

"They don't see it like that." The manager sighed. "These days, the working men feel their power. They see they can hold their employers to ransom, so they do."

"What do they ask for this time?"

"Higher pay for those on piece work, an increase in

wages for men tied to the flat rate, and a reduction of one half-hour in labour each working day."

"So I am to fund their idleness," observed Rebecca, sourly. "Very well. Leave it with me. I shall speak to my husband this evening. Tomorrow, I shall let you know what we wish you to do."

That particular dispute was settled amicably enough. But, as Rebecca had expected, only a few more weeks went by before there were more stoppages, more complaints, more demands for higher wages and a shorter working week. It was the same everywhere. The words revolution, insurrection and insubordination were on every manufacturer's lips.

Those dog days of summer, however, which seethed with sedition, radicalism and all kinds of discontent and unrest, were eventually succeeded by cooler autumn ones. Masters and managers hoped the tempers of the factory hands would cool, too. But for many manufacturers, the damage was done. One evening in the September of 1797, as Ellis and Rebecca sat together in Ellis's study, looking over the quarterly accounts from the largest of their manufactories – which Rebecca's grandfather Jeremy Searle had founded as a little button works, but which now occupied a site spreading over four acres of valuable real estate – Rebecca removed her spectacles, rubbed her aching eyes, and shook her head.

"Terrible," she murmured. Heavily, she sighed. "This is all quite dreadful. Our profits are almost negligible. Thanks to strikes and stoppages, this quarter we've lost the equivalent of at least twenty working days. I'm tempted to sell up. Put every single hand out of work. How would they like that?"

"I don't think selling up is an option. For one thing, who would buy?" Ellis closed the ledger. "We must continue as before," he said.

"Continue to lose money hand over fist, is that what you mean? Continue to be dictated to by a mob, by a rabble who understand nothing but their own greedy ambitions?

Who, in their foolishness, would pull down the very fabric of the commonwealth upon all our heads?"

"I mean, we must speak to the managers," replied Ellis. "They must spy out the troublemakers, see they're dismissed, then deal fairly with the grievances of the rest."

"Grievances!" Rebecca snorted in derision. "They have no grievances. Or at any rate, they have no little complaints worth that hard name! My dear Ellis, if you could only listen to yourself. Just recently, *you're* beginning to sound like a radical, too."

"Change must come, Becky. The winds of revolution blow fiercely these days. All we can hope to do is weather the storm." Ellis opened a drawer in his desk. "Now, my dear, before you go on to accuse me of being a Jacobin or a Paineite as well as a radical friend of the mob, may we change the subject for a moment? You see, the letters have arrived."

"Indeed? When did they come?"

"This morning. They were brought from the post office in Warwick, by special courier."

"These are the original documents?"

"No. Merely copies. But, as you will see, that does not signify at all." Taking out the batch of papers, Ellis spread them across his desk. "While you and the girls were out paying calls, I took the opportunity to glance through them."

"What did you discover?"

"I think they tell us most of what we need to know."

"Then, may I?" Rebecca nodded towards the papers.

"Yes, of course. Is the light satisfactory over there?" Ellis moved a candle or two. "Prepare to be astonished," he murmured. Then he picked up a book, and turned away.

Rebecca began to scan the sheets. Transcribed in a fine legal hand, all was neat, clear and easily legible, and half an hour later she had read everything, from the plain, matter-of-fact description of the terrible events themselves, to the witnesses' statements, the summary of the trial, and the newspaper report of the subsequent execution.

As she set this last sheet aside, she shuddered. Then she glanced up at her husband. "Should you be in possession of all this information?" she enquired. "Here, for example, names are named. Here, witnesses are brought forward, cautioned, then quoted at length. My dear Ellis, I would have thought even you—"

"You're right, of course. Strictly speaking, I have no business to see this material at all." Ellis laid his book face down on his desk. "The witnesses' statements in particular are highly confidential. But Mr Bellingham, who is currently chairman of the Swansea Bench, is aware of my personal interest in the case. He knows that, as a magistrate myself, I fully understand the need for discretion. He sent me these papers on the understanding I should show them to no other living soul. That after reading them, I should put everything in the fire."

"I see." Rebecca frowned. "In that case, perhaps you should not have shown them to me."

"My dear Becky! You and I are one. If not actually in flesh, then in spirit, certainly." But now, taking the papers, Ellis began to fold them into quarters. Then, one by one, he fed them to the fire.

"What will you say to Owen?" asked Rebecca, as she watched them burn.

"Need I say anything?" Ellis looked up from his labours. "Will it enrich his existence, to know that his father was a common felon? That he died butchered like an animal, after breaking half the laws of this land?"

"No, but—"

"That his mother met her death at the hands of those men who were her husband's closest associates? Nay, his very partners in villainy? That Jacob Atkins is himself now rotting in a convicted criminal's grave?"

"Maybe not." Rebecca stood up. "But there are so many loose ends! So many doubts, so many queries still unresolved!"

"What do you mean?"

"According to Mr Bellingham, Jacob Atkins's son Michael – whom many of the witnesses quoted maintain was his father's right-hand man – was not involved in either of the murders, nor in any of the other crimes. During his trial Jacob Atkins insisted his son knew nothing about the death of Lalage. Nor that of her husband, nor of anyone else. Consequently, Michael Atkins was never even interviewed. Let alone brought to trial. All the same—"

"Mr Bellingham examined Jacob Atkins many times," observed Ellis. "Always under oath. My dear Becky, the man was on trial for his life. Why should he have lied?"

"I don't know. But what if he did?" Rebecca began to pace the room. "Well," she murmured, "at least we can now piece most of it together. After you and your sister Lalage had – what shall we say? A disagreement?"

"Disagreement!" Ellis grimaced, his face working painfully. "Becky, Lalage tried to kill you! She—"

"That's of no consequence now," interrupted Rebecca. "Well, then. Lalage left Warwickshire in the company of her husband, Alex Lowell. Widowed, she subsequently married a certain John Rhys Morgan, a farmer from North Gower, who was also a smuggler and dealer in contraband.

"Lalage gave birth to Owen. Some years later, John Rhys Morgan was arrested on suspicion of some sort of villainy, and died at the hands of the military while attempting to escape."

"As Bethan Davies told us."

"Yes, indeed." Rebecca kept pacing. "At your instigation, Jacob – or Jack, as Bethan will have it – Atkins is investigated. Nothing is established against him. But then, three years later, a servant of the family is dismissed without wages or a character. He goes to the authorities and lays information that his master is involved in the trading of contraband. He also insists, under oath, that he was present on the occasion of Lalage

Morgan's death – which he maintains was suicide under duress."

"Yes." Ellis winced, as if in pain. "So he did."

"But before your sister died – before, in fact, she ever met any members of the Atkins family, let alone accused them of procuring her husband's death – she asked her housekeeper Bethan Davies to take her son away. To convey him safely to England. To his own uncle's house."

"God knows why," muttered Ellis.

"You still think it strange?"

"Given that Lalage hated both you and me, and that I detested *her*, I am indeed surprised that my sister saw fit to entrust her only child to us."

"But Ellis, she loved you once! As children, you were devoted. When I first knew you, you loved *her*."

"Don't speak of that."

"But, Ellis—"

"Please, Becky!"

So Rebecca let the matter drop. "Should we not tell Owen anything at all?" she demanded, anxiously.

"As I said before, I don't think there's anything he needs to know. He is aware that his father is dead – Bethan Davies told him so, and he believes her. He assumes his mother is also in her grave.

"In spite of this, he seems to be a happy child. His cousins love him, and he loves them. You, my dear, are his second mother – and a rather better friend to him than his first ever was, I strongly suspect. Speaking for myself, I – well, I can tolerate him."

"Yes. But all the same—" Rebecca protested.

"Why cloud his days with sorrow? Why burden him with knowledge which can be of no benefit to him, now or in the future?"

"Perhaps you are right." Considering, Rebecca nodded. "Yes, dear Ellis – I'm sure you're right."

So it was agreed. Owen was told nothing of Mr Bellingham's letter, and if he noticed that his aunt and uncle were unusually silent and abstracted for the next few days, he appeared to think little of it, let alone assume it had anything to do with him.

Bethan Davies, for many years the Morgan family's devoted housekeeper and Owen's own nursemaid, was getting old. Formerly hearty and energetic, if somewhat stout, over the past twelve months she had become progressively less active, for she was shorter and shorter of breath. In consequence of this, she had slowed down considerably, and these days she spent most of her waking hours sitting at the kitchen table, making vast quantities of exquisite pastries, puddings and pies, of which she herself consumed a substantial share. Her weight had therefore ballooned, and she was now almost grotesquely obese.

But Owen still loved her. Still the child visited the kitchens daily, to see his old nurse, to sit down beside her and chat to her in the Gower Welsh which was his own first language, but which he was nowadays rapidly forgetting. Much to Bethan's distress. "These English relations of yours," she muttered sourly one chilly October morning. "They'll turn you into a Saxon yet. When *I'm* dead and buried, you'll forget you're a Welshman at all."

"But you're not dead yet, Bethan," observed Owen cheerfully, as he scooped up another handful of fat, purple raisins and began to stuff his face. He grinned at her. "How old are you, anyway?"

"One and twenty and a day." Reaching for the big jar of raisins, Bethan took a few herself, then munched thoughtfully. "Tell me, now. Is it the maids-of-honour your aunt likes best? Or does she prefer the honey and cinnamon tarts? I can never remember."

"She likes both equally." Owen's dark eyes sparkled with greed. "So make a batch of each, why don't you?"

"I might." Bethan pinched his cheek. "You and your cousin will undertake to deal with any leftovers, then?"

“Of course.” Again, Owen grinned. “We’re still growing, Bethan. We need our nourishment!” Helping himself to a couple of crystallised figs, the child stood up.

“Lessons now, is it?” demanded the nurse.

“Yes. All day.”

“Be off with you, then.”

“I’m going.” Regretfully, Owen took himself off.

Later that day, as Owen wrote out a fair copy of a Horatian ode, Bethan was taken ill. A scullery maid found her slumped at the kitchen table where, blue in the face, she was hardly able to breathe.

Hastily summoned, the local apothecary shook his head. She was an old woman, he said. Her heart was not strong. He could prescribe nothing but beef tea, warm blankets and complete rest.

So now Bethan took to her bed. For a few days, she seemed to rally. But then, she contracted a chill. The infection settled on her lungs. Neither the best medical care, nor the most wholesome diet, nor even regular visits from the local minister himself, could avail. In the course of a cold November night, she died peacefully in her sleep.

Told the following morning, by the woman who had been detailed to sit up with the invalid at night, Owen was at first silent and disbelieving. But then he became wildly, furiously angry. Glaring at the bearer of the bad news, he cursed her roundly, fortunately for his own hide, in a language she did not understand.

Hastily summoned, Rebecca sent everyone else away. “Come, Owen,” she said, opening the door of her own private sitting room. “Come and sit with me.”

But neither hot chocolate served in a silver mug, a dish of his favourite almond sweetmeats, nor the company of his kind, unfailingly motherly aunt could comfort someone as bereft as Owen felt. When Rebecca offered to embrace him, he literally pushed her away. When she reminded him that Bethan was now in heaven, her sufferings at an end, he cried that his were only just beginning. Far from drawing consolation from religion, between sobs Owen Morgan uttered some of the most terrible blasphemies Rebecca had ever heard. Cursing and swearing, he announced that he did not even believe in God. There was only the Evil One, and he it was who had taken Bethan away.

"Pray for forgiveness, Aunt?" he demanded, as Rebecca tremulously suggested he should take back those last, hasty words, and go down on his knees at once. "I shall never say my prayers again, for as long as I live!"

So, seeing he was not disposed to be consoled, and attributing his reckless blasphemies to his early upbringing rather than to a naturally bad character, Rebecca decided he would be best left to himself for a while. "Go and walk in the knot garden," she advised. "Put on your greatcoat and muffler, then take a little exercise by yourself. But before you leave me, dear Owen, hear me for just one moment more."

"Ma'am?"

"There is nothing to be gained from railing against your Maker. On the contrary." Rebecca clasped his cold hands in hers. "My dear child, I know you are distressed, that you feel your heart is broken. But do not fail this test! Try to resign yourself, to—"

But she did not finish, for now Owen broke away, muttering something inaudible – but, Rebecca was afraid, it was almost certainly profane, probably in the extreme.

As he left the room, Rebecca sighed. She loved her nephew dearly. But these days she feared for him, too.

Too lazy, or too indifferent to his own comfort even to think of fetching his greatcoat, Owen merely buttoned his jacket, then went out. Crossing the park, he walked through the ornamental wooded area planted for the squire and his lady's pleasure, then went into the wilderness beyond, where he kicked stones along the far shore of the lake.

He did not appear at dinner time. Nor at tea. As the

afternoon light was fading, Rebecca became concerned. She sent the other children out to look for him.

It was Isabel, on a visit to Jane and Maria while her parents were in London on business, who found him. Lying under a wizened apple tree, he was half buried in the long, yellow grass of the biggest, most overgrown of the orchards.

"Owen?" For a long, terrible moment, she feared he was dead. Nervously, she touched his shoulder. "Owen!" she repeated, her voice shrill with alarm, "Owen, please get up! Or at least speak to me!"

Owen did not move a muscle. But he did condescend to speak. "Go away," he said.

Never one to do as she was told, Isabel crouched down beside him. "Why are you lying here?" she enquired. For, she did not begin to understand the significance of the old servant's death. No one had thought to explain to her, and by now she had forgotten all about it, anyway. "Why are you crying?"

"I'm not crying!" Owen stifled a sob. "Go *away*!"

So Isabel sat down. Patiently, she waited for her companion's gulpings and chokings to subside.

Eventually, they did. Now, Isabel thought, we will get some sense out of him. But it was not to be. Owen was too chilled to talk. In fact, he was half frozen. His hands and face were blotched with cold, here being an angry red, there an unpleasant, grey-ish blue.

Isabel, on the other hand, was warmly wrapped up in a voluminous cloak. Belonging to her mother, it was richly lined with the most costly of American sables – and, wonderfully generous in cut, it was easily large enough for two smallish children to share.

So, slipping it from her shoulders, Isabel laid half of it across Owen's prostrate body, while she rearranged the other half to cover herself. "It's not because of Bethan, is it?" she asked casually, stabbing wildly into the dark. On the other hand, she reasoned, nothing else untoward had taken place that day. “It’s not just because Bethan’s dead?”

But it appeared it was exactly that. At the sound of the name, Owen’s stifled sobs redoubled their intensity. Soon, they became howls. Astonished, Isabel stared. “So was Bethan very important to you?” she enquired, trying to understand. “Was – was she your nurse, maybe?”

Lifting his face for a moment, Owen nodded. Then the tears began to flow again.

Isabel’s small, white hand patted Owen’s darker one. “I once had a nurse,” she observed, offhandedly. “In Virginia. Her name was Elegant.”

“Elegant?” Lifting his head again, Owen stared at her in disbelief. “What a stupid name!”

“It’s not stupid at all! It suited her exactly.” Remembering, Isabel sighed. “She was very tall. Very thin. Elegant, in fact.”

“No servant is elegant,” muttered Owen. “No—”

“She was a beautiful, purple black.” Now, Isabel was in a world of her own. “So black! Her skin was like dewberries. Shiny, and blue-black. I loved her more than anyone. But I loved Benedict, too.”

“Benedict?”

“Her son. My foster brother.”

“Oh.” In spite of himself, Owen found he was intrigued. “So what happened to *your* nurse?”

“My father sold her.”

“Sold her?” Puzzled, Owen sat up. “How could he sell her? She wasn’t a sheep. Or a horse.”

“She was a slave. Slaves can be bought, and sold. Just like cattle, in fact. Didn’t you know that?” Sometimes, thought Isabel, these English people proved to be astonishingly ignorant. “It was my mother who wanted her sold.”

“Why?”

“*I* don’t know. As if they’d have explained to me!” Casting her mind back, Isabel frowned. “In fact, it was very strange. You see, I thought my father liked her. He certainly liked Benedict! He used to take him on his knee and croon to him. Give him sugar candy, when he never gave any to me.

"So anyway, Mr Hemming from Deepwater bought Elegant, and took her to Louisiana. But she caught a fever there, and died."

"How do you know?"

"They told me." Helplessly, Isabel shrugged. "I kept asking when she was coming back, you see. So anyway – when they told me Elegant was dead, I nearly died too. I made myself so sick . . ."

Isabel gulped. She knuckled her eyes.

"What happened to Benedict?" asked Owen, solicitously.

"Oh, he came into the house, to learn to be a valet." Again, Isabel shrugged. "But soon after that, we left Virginia anyway. We went to live in Canada. My father wanted to take Benedict with him, but my mother forbade it."

"What became of him then?"

"When we sold the plantation he was sold too, along with all the other slaves."

"Oh." Digesting the novel idea that even people could be bought and sold, Owen almost forgot his own unhappiness. In any case, he had no tears left. He stood up, brushed himself down, and handed Isabel her cloak. Together, they walked back to the manor house.

From that day forward, Owen tolerated Isabel rather more readily than he'd been used to do. For he and she shared a secret sorrow. His Aunt Rebecca loved him, his cousins were his friends, it was true – but only Isabel understood what it was to mourn. To be acquainted with grief.

Chapter Three

The bells rang out to welcome the new century. In churches and chapels throughout the land, the people prayed for forgiveness of their sins and deliverance from their enemies.

On the whole, however, they weren't unduly concerned about the latter. Napoleon Bonaparte was merely the most recent of a long line of foreigners – invariably French in origin – intent on subduing the island race, and no ordinary Anglo-Saxon would have given any more for the upstart Corsican's chances than for those of his predecessors.

Napoleon was a bogeyman, that was all. A name to conjure with when children needed to be subdued or frightened off to bed. Indeed, nursemaids and mothers from Cornwall to the northernmost isles regularly informed their infant charges that if they were naughty, or refused to go to sleep, Boney would come and get them. "Then, when he catches you," they would add, "he'll gobble you all up. While you're still alive!"

At thirteen, Rayner and Owen were far too old to be taken in by this nursery nonsense. They were not afraid of the French, whom they'd been taught from birth to despise. As every red-blooded Englishman knew, the French were snail-eaters and effeminates, to the very last man.

Having also been taught the rudiments of mathematics, English grammar and Latin syntax at home, soon Rayner would be ready to go away to school. His father had been to Harrow, and Rayner was to follow in his footsteps. As for Owen – it was generally felt that an orphan with no property to inherit nor, indeed, prospects of any kind, was hardly worth educating at all.

"They've said nothing to me." Lying on the daisies under one of the great oaks in the park, Owen and Rayner were sorting marbles and having a private conversation, keeping a wary look-out for pests like Isabel Graham the while. Morosely, Owen sniffed. "So I suppose when *you've* gone," he muttered, "I shall be sent about my business directly. Given a half-sovereign and a loaf of bread, then told to be on my way."

"Nonsense." Rayner grinned. "There's no reason why you shouldn't come with me. Look – I'm sure Mr Fenton would recommend it. He thinks very highly of your learning and application, so he's certain to tell my father how clever you—"

"Don't be ridiculous."

"Don't *you* be a fool to yourself! You write a beautiful clear hand. Your command of English grammar is perfectly proficient. You can spell, and in Latin and mathematics, you're miles ahead of me. You probably always will be."

"Maybe." Owen shrugged. "But what of it? You are the heir. You are to be squire here. I, on the other hand, am a poor relation. A charity child, who has nothing, save what your father chooses to give.'

"But my father has always been generous. He—"

"He hates the sight of me. He hides it well, I agree. But, all the same, I feel it."

"What foolish nonsense!" Rayner laughed. Then, playfully, he punched his cousin's shoulder. "My father is severe with everyone, save my mother and the girls. It's just his way."

"Is it?"

"Of course it is. Owen?"

"What?"

"Would you like to go to school with me?"

"I – well, yes. I think so."

"Then I shall tell my father. I shall ask him to send you to Harrow, too."

"As you wish."

"As *I* wish? Don't you want to come?"

"Of course I do." Jumping up, Owen grinned. "Yes!" he cried, rather more cheerful now, "I'll come! You and I together – what a pair of fellows we'll be! We'll make perfect fools of the ushers! Run rings round the masters! Our names will go down in history."

"Sir?" Having sought the interview without more ado, ten minutes later Rayner stood in his father's study. A pleasant, south-facing room overlooking the rose gardens, Rayner could never feel at ease here, for he was only ever summoned hither when he was to be reprimanded. Or – very rarely – whipped.

His father was so reserved. So unbending, so stern. Grey-haired, harsh-featured, he was also the tallest man Rayner knew, and the easy relationship which the child had always enjoyed with his plump, blonde, pretty little mother had somehow never been even remotely possible with this great, gaunt crag of a man, who never laughed, seldom smiled, and whose features seemed almost permanently set in a coldly forbidding frown.

Rayner screwed his courage to the sticking point. "Sir, in September I am to go to school."

"So you are." Irritably – or so it seemed to Rayner – the Squire of Easton glanced up from the paperwork which was spread all over his desk. His quill remained poised, in mid-air. "Well, child? What of it?"

Rayner drew a deep breath. "May Owen go with me?" he asked.

"Owen." Ellis frowned. For a moment, he appeared to consider the request. But then he spoke. "There's no need for that," he replied.

"No need, sir?"

"None at all." Observing his son to look somewhat mulish now, Ellis Darrow sighed. "Do you not see how it is?" he demanded. "You do not? Very well, then. Allow me to explain.

"You, Rayner, are the heir to a large estate. At school, you will mix with the heirs to other fortunes, with the sons of gentlemen, who will be your friends and form your acquaintance for the rest of your life. Their interests will be yours. Their incomes will be commensurate with your own. From among their sisters or other female relations, you will choose your wife.

"Owen, on the other hand, is poor. He has no prospects, he will inherit no property. In short, he will be obliged to make his own way in the world. So, sending him to a great public school would be both unwise and unkind. He would be educated far above his station, and learn no lesson so well as envy of his betters, and dissatisfaction with his lot in life."

"But, sir! You—"

"Rayner, *you* forget yourself!" Ellis glared. "Have I not made myself plain?"

"Perfectly, sir. But—"

"Then there is nothing more to say."

"But he is your own nephew!" Shaking in his shoes – for no one, save occasionally Rebecca, ever presumed to question the judgement of the squire – Rayner met his father's startled gaze. "Owen may have no property," he went on, recklessly. "He may indeed be without prospects, save those you are willing to open for him. But his talents and birth surely fit him for a gentleman's education? If he knows nothing, moreover, if he meets nobody – if he has no learning, if he makes no friends – how is he to make his way in life?"

"Rayner, I expressed a reluctance to send Owen to Harrow. I was not proposing to turn him out of my house!" Ellis shook his head. "You sincerely wish your cousin to go with you to school?"

"Yes, sir. I do."

"In spite of understanding my reservations in the case?"

"Sir, I know you have Owen's best interests at heart. But I feel—"

"I shall think about it." Ellis managed a faint smile. "Rayner, your concern for Owen Morgan's welfare and happiness does you great credit. I only hope he returns your regard."

"Well?" demanded Owen, as Rayner opened the door of the old nursery, to find his sisters and cousin anxiously awaiting his return from the fray. "What did he say to you?"

"That he would think about it."

"Oh?" Maria frowned. "What is there to consider, pray?"

"Since Owen is poor and has no prospects, my father is anxious not to educate him above his station in life."

"Stuff and nonsense! What can he be thinking of?" Jumping down from her seat on an ancient, ink-stained desk, Jane shook her ringlets in disgust. "*I'll* go and talk to him. If you like."

"Would you?" Owen dared to look hopeful. Jane was her father's darling. If anybody could persuade him to do anything, it was she. "Will you go now?"

"Certainly." Jane gave Owen a hug. "Don't look so anxious," she went on, gaily. "He'll get no peace until he agrees, so he might as well give in gracefully. Preferably today."

So Jane went to see her father, who never denied her anything. Fifteen minutes later, she was back in the nursery, well pleased with herself. "He wishes to speak to the pair of you," she said.

The squire was standing at the window, gazing out towards the park. "I have decided that since you both appear to wish it, you shall go to school together," he said.

"Thank you, sir!" Delighted, Rayner beamed.

"Thank you," echoed Owen. Too much in awe of his

uncle to smile, he merely nodded his own gratitude. Then, assuming he was dismissed, he turned to go.

"Just one moment." Walking away from the window, Ellis sat down at his desk. He looked from one child to the other, then fixed his gaze on his nephew. "Well, Owen," he began calmly, "since you are here, we may as well discuss one other matter now. I had meant to speak to you later this evening, but – I have been making enquiries about your father's relations, you see."

"Sir?" Owen was astonished. He hadn't known his father had any kin.

"I find you have another uncle living," continued the squire. "He is an apothecary, practising in Cardiff. Just recently, I wrote to him. You may be interested to see his reply."

"Thank you, sir. I would." Owen accepted the proffered letter. He began to read.

"My dear Mr Darrow," wrote David Morgan, "many thanks for yours of the 12th instant. You may imagine my feelings on receiving the same! I can only say, may heaven bless you for your goodness, and keep you in happiness and prosperity for the rest of your days.

"As you will appreciate, the death of my brother and the disappearance of his wife and child were heavy blows for me to bear, especially since these were the only relations I had in the world. After my brother's demise, I made many enquiries into the fate of Mrs Morgan and her son, but I could discover nothing. They had vanished, apparently without trace. For a long time I was most desolate, and only the consolations of religion and philosophy kept me from total despair.

"But enough of that. I write today both to thank you from the bottom of my heart, and to inform you that I myself, although not a rich man by any means, am certainly prosperous enough. An apothecary by trade, I am in a comfortable way of business in the town here. I have my own hearth, my own home, and am in debt to no man.

"Believe me when I say my heart is open – more than open – to the child. Might you therefore permit him to visit me? I would of course pay his travelling expenses, and furnish him with all necessities during his stay here.

"I hope to hear again from you very soon. In the meantime I remain, my very dear sir,

"David James Morgan."

Looking up again, Owen blinked owlishly. It was as if he couldn't quite believe the evidence of his own eyes. "But, sir – how did you come to find Mr Morgan?" he enquired, eventually. "How did you learn—"

"Quite by chance." Having had time to think about it, Ellis now decided Owen need not be told everything. He need not, for example, know that David Morgan had been mentioned to the squire by Bethan Davies herself – mentioned on several occasions in fact – but since Bethan had no idea where the man was to be found, Ellis had told her not to speak of him to Owen.

So it had been several years of diligent detective work, aided by Ellis's fellow magistrates in South Wales, which had finally tracked him down. Or at any rate, had located a David Morgan, apothecary, of Cardiff, who was the right age and apparently came from North Gower.

Further discreet enquiries suggested that David Morgan was a respectable man, having no criminal connections, and certainly no record of felony on his own account.

"Well, Owen," continued the squire, "as you see, Mr Morgan is anxious to make your acquaintance. I therefore intend to write and suggest you go on a visit. If this is acceptable to you."

"Indeed it is, sir." Owen was still somewhat bewildered, and presently he blinked again. He could not even begin to stammer his excitement. Or, for that matter, his thanks.

But Rayner could. Enchanted by the romance of it all, he now wondered if he too might have undiscovered relations lurking in distant shires, who might one day invite *him* for a surprise holiday. "Well done, sir," he said, beaming. "Very well done indeed!"

"Thank you, child." Ellis almost smiled. Almost. His conscience smote him cruelly now. For, he had traced Mr Morgan not with a view to enriching Owen's existence, but to getting rid of him altogether.

For the boy was growing so like his mother Lalage! Much taller, slimmer and better-looking than Rayner would ever be, Owen's regularly handsome features, his graceful carriage, his everyday demeanour – even his facial expressions, especially the be-damned-to-you look in his large, dark eyes – were his mother's own, so much so that Ellis felt sick at the sight of him. If only David Morgan would take a fancy to the boy, and propose to play a part in his upbringing, this would be deliverance indeed. The answer to Ellis Darrow's most fervent prayer.

By late June, the final preparations had been made. It had been agreed that Owen should spend two months in Cardiff, returning to Warwickshire in the middle of September, in order that he and Rayner might travel together when they went off to Harrow later that fall.

Jane and Maria, not to mention their dear friend Isabel Graham, had been as thrilled as Rayner to discover that Owen had a long-lost uncle whom he was now going to visit – travelling post, and all alone, as if he were quite grown-up – in the wilds of darkest Wales.

"Dear Owen! How excited you must be!" Watching her cousin sorting books and clothes, and offering plenty of good advice as he packed then re-packed his couple of valises, Jane finally slid from her perch on the window-seat and went over to help him fold his shirts properly.

As they finished, and both straightened up, she measured herself against him. "What a great, stout fellow you're becoming!" she exclaimed, teasing him. "You're almost as tall as I am these days."

"Not quite." Turning her round, Owen stood against her, back to back. "Look in the glass." He nodded towards the fireplace. "I've some way to go yet."

"Nonsense. There's only an inch or so in it." Jane turned back to him. Shaking her head, she sighed. "My dear little cousin," she whispered, "how pretty you were once! How charming, how sweet! But nowadays, you grow lantern-jawed and hideous. Indeed, you're almost a man."

"Well, you're already a woman." Owen smiled at her. "Soon, you'll be married. You'll have children in the nursery, servants to scold, a husband to please – every care in the world, in fact. You'll have no time for little cousins at all."

"I shall always have time for you."

"I doubt it."

"It's true!" Charmingly, Jane pouted. "Anyway – I shan't be married for years yet. My father is too jealous to allow it."

This, unfortunately, was no more than the simple truth. At seventeen years of age, Jane Darrow was a good-looking, fair-haired girl who was regularly talked of as a possible bride for Squire This or Sir Somebody That – but who also had a father as possessive as a Turk and as fearsome as a wounded grizzly bear. Recently out, she was invited to a far greater number of balls, routs and assemblies than her parents were either able or willing to attend; she received much more than her fair share of attention and admiration, but she had not yet been made any offers of matrimony.

Not that she cared. She was enjoying herself far too much to worry about that. For these days, she was learning to be enchanting. To be bewitching. In short, to flirt. At every opportunity, she practised the arts of seduction and coquetry – and now, fluttering her eyelashes prettily, she smiled at Owen. "Write to me," she said.

"*Write* to you?" Surprised, her cousin stared. "But – what shall I say?"

"Oh, I don't know! Yes, I do. Just tell me everything!" She laughed at him. "I do so love to receive letters!" she cried, shaking her curls. "Look – I'll make my father frank some covers for you. Then, you'll have no postage to pay. I'll furnish you with paper, a set of pens – and a penknife, and some powder to make ink!"

"It's not the expense of postage which concerns me," said Owen. "I don't begrudge that at all. But I shall bore you, I'm sure."

"Nonsense," smiled Jane. "Now, my dear Owen, listen to me. I wish to know everything. No matter how trivial a circumstance seems to you, rest assured that the details of it will be perfectly fascinating to me. So – describe your uncle, his home, his profession, his servants, his patients. Everything!

"As for your good self, leaving your home here in Warwickshire – or should I say, returning from exile in a foreign land to your own native heath – what a great adventure that will be! How interesting everything will prove! How novel, and how strange!

"Indeed, I am positively consumed with envy. My dear little cousin, you *must* let me know how you get on."

Now, realising she was getting somewhat carried away, Jane paused for breath. But still her eyes sparkled like sapphires in the snow. Still, her complexion glowed. Owen looked at her. "I'll write to you," he promised.

Then, taking her by the shoulders, he pulled her towards him. Impulsively, he kissed her cheek. "Will you write to me?" he asked, looking into her eyes, darkness meeting light.

"Of course I shall," Jane replied.

Two days later, Owen had gone. Sitting alone in the old schoolroom where Owen and Rayner had spent many a tedious hour, Jane traced a set of initials her cousin had carved on his desk. She had always been fond of him, it was true. But this ache – this pain in her heart – was more severe than any mourning for the absence of a mere cousin should ever have been . . .

Owen's journey through the green heart of England was uneventful, not to say disappointingly dull. Although their way lay through deep, dark forests, no desperate highwayman appeared from among the oak trees to demand the passengers' valuables and gold. The horses were unsporting beasts who never bolted once.

So, sitting in a jolting, malodorous stagecoach, a fat widow's umbrella handle sticking into his side, and a farmer breathing beer fumes into his face, while a dissenting clergyman prosily addressed his captive audience on the flaws in the doctrine of original sin, Owen had plenty of time to reflect on the romance of his mission, and feel thoroughly homesick for Warwickshire.

Very soon, travelling post in the company of disagreeable people became a way of life. He slept for much of the way. But then, on the fourth day of his journey, he woke to find himself in the market place in Cardiff. The widow had already climbed out, and a short, stocky, dark-haired man in gold-rimmed spectacles was peering anxiously into the darkness of the vehicle. As Owen gaped at him groggily, the man took the child's hands in his.

"Owen Morgan? I knew you at once!" Now, the man positively beamed at the child. "Oh, God," he cried, "dear God, you're so like your mother, it's as if she was born again!"

Owen blinked once, twice, then made as if to climb out of the coach. The man helped him totter down the steps. Then, standing the boy in the sunshine, David Morgan stepped back and gazed. "Such a woman," he whispered, as the tears came into his eyes. "So tall, so straight, so beautiful! I tell you now, I never saw her equal. Never, in all my born days. No wonder my poor brother lost his heart to her!

"Well now, child – where's your luggage? These two pieces here?" David Morgan glanced round. "Daniel? Can you manage those by yourself? Very well then, boy. Let's go." So, giving Owen no chance even to speak, let alone ask any questions, David Morgan talked on, leading the child to his house while his manservant Daniel brought up the rear.

The apothecary's house was only a short distance away, down a dark, shadowy alley which branched off the market square of the sleepy little town. The uncle, nephew and servant entered through the apothecary's shop, an Aladdin's cave of wonder in which laden shelves held a hundred or more glass bottles, each filled with a different-coloured liquid, each of which sparkled and shone – and where rows upon rows of ceramic pots proclaimed they held tincture of this or oil of that.

Upon a dark slab of counter lay pestles and mortars, balances and weights, razor-sharp blades and long-handled spoons, while the air was heavy with the scent of spices, herbs and floral essences of all kinds.

A confirmed bachelor, David Morgan was looked after by Daniel and Susannah Elias, a middle-aged married couple who had no children of their own and who tended to treat their somewhat absent-minded, kindly master as if he were the son they'd never had. So, they were as delighted as could be to have a real, live child to cosset. They made Owen as welcome as the dawn.

"Here's your bedroom." Leading him up a narrow, winding staircase, Susannah showed Owen into a small, white-washed chamber which contained a bed upon which reposed layer upon layer of bright red Welsh blankets. There was also a large, black chest of drawers made from solid Welsh oak. "Now, if you're ever cold in here, just say. Daniel will make up a fire directly."

Cold? In the middle of summer? Bemused, Owen shook his head. At Easton Hall, fires were lit from November to March only, unless somebody was ill.

The visitor was made very welcome, and soon felt himself at home. For, among these people, there was no stiffness.

No reserve. A few days after his arrival, Owen sat with his uncle in the shop, watching while the apothecary prepared tincture of opium for general sale. At last, he had screwed up enough courage to ask the question to which he'd wanted to know the answer for years. "Uncle?" he began, "What became of my parents?"

"Your parents, dear child? I wish I could tell you. Pass me those bottles, will you, boy? Thank you." Now, as he surveyed the row of little glass phials, into which he was about to decant the laudanum, David Morgan sighed. "I made enquiries, of course. I discovered this little circumstance, I learned that little fact. But try as I might, I never found out precisely what occurred."

"Will you tell me what you *do* know?"

"But it's not pleasant, child!" David shook his head. "It's not a pleasant tale at all."

"Pleasant or not," rejoined Owen, "John and Lalage Morgan were my parents. I have a right to know what happened to them."

"That's true enough, I suppose." Carefully, David stoppered the flask of laudanum and placed it on a convenient shelf. Taking off his spectacles, he rubbed his eyes. "Your father was a good man," he began, relaxing on to a stool. "Always remember that. He was a loving brother, a gentle husband, and I'm sure he was a kind father to you."

"Yes," agreed Owen. "He was very kind indeed."

"Ah! So you remember him well?"

"I *try* to remember." Owen shrugged. "But I've lived in Warwickshire for so long, that nowadays remembering anything from that time is like peering through a mist. All the same – there are certain things I recall quite clearly. Being carried on his shoulders, for example. Being taught to swim."

"What about your mother? Do you remember her?"

"Not well. But sometimes, I think I see her face. Especially in dreams."

"Also, when you look in a glass." Meeting Owen's

large, dark eyes, again David sighed. "Well, then," he said, "here's what I know. I make no judgements, mind. I speak no ill of anyone. I tell you the bare facts only, and let you draw your own conclusions thence.

"So. As you're aware, John Rhys Morgan was a farmer. A prosperous one, too. He'd inherited a generous freehold. He had his own herds, his own flocks, enough land – more than enough, in fact. Indeed, he should have been content.

"But he was not. Men have needs, you see. Some need liquor, some need women, some need drugs like this tincture of opium here. Often, it's no matter, no matter at all."

"But?" prompted Owen, gently.

"But *your* father needed danger. Excitement. He liked to defy authority – he wanted to be his own master, and have no one say him nay. When he was still a very young man, he became involved in the trade of contraband.

"I begged him to give it up. Especially after he married your poor mother, most especially when I heard he was to become a father for the first time. But he would not listen to me. He hated the Saxons, he said, the dirty Saxons who robbed and taxed and oppressed poor Welshmen. He would defy them until his dying day.

"I could never make sense of that! He'd married a Saxon, after all. She was the moon in his sky. Even his partner in crime, whose name he did mention to me once, but which I cannot now remember, was an Englishman."

"But one sympathetic to the plight of poor Welshmen, perhaps? A good friend, though from Saxon stock?"

"Perhaps." David shrugged. "Good or bad, it's of no consequence now. So, one day, when you were six or seven years old, my brother was arrested on suspicion of dealing in contraband. He was to be taken to Swansea, to be examined by the magistrates there – or at any rate, that's what I was told. But he died before he ever arrived in Swansea, at the hands of the military."

"How did you find out?"
"Oh, the story was in the newspapers. Just a little mention, at the bottom of a page it was. The Excise congratulated themselves on the capture of a notorious smuggler, who happened to have died in the arresting officer's custody.
"The man's land was to be confiscated. He'd had a wife and child, but they had run away – or so it was rumoured. At any rate, they'd not been seen or heard of since the arrest." David sighed again. "A reward was offered, for information as to their whereabouts. But the woman was never found. Nor was her child."
Sharply, Owen drew breath. "Do you think my mother may still be alive?" he whispered.
"I don't know, child. I honestly don't know." With a corner of his cuff, David dabbed at his eyes. "But after all this time, I doubt it. Well – if she had survived, surely she would have come forward, in order to claim you?"
"Maybe, or maybe not. You see, she and my uncle did not get on."
"Indeed? Why was that?"
"I don't know. I did once ask my cousins. But they are as ignorant as I am." Owen shrugged. "I do know that my mother married young, long before she met my father. Her first husband was a certain Mr Lowell, a near neighbour in Warwickshire. But later, after my uncle and his sister had quarrelled, the Lowells moved to South Wales, where Mr Lowell died. His widow married my father."
Owen looked down at his finger nails. "I doubt if my uncle approved of the match. But even if he did, I cannot suppose a Welsh farmer would have been welcome in the drawing rooms of Warwickshire."
"But they are good to you?" Anxiously, David searched Owen's face. "These Darrows, child – are they kind?"
"Very kind." Reminded of the people he loved best, Owen smiled. "My aunt and cousins could not be kinder – in fact, they are my best friends. I don't think my uncle

likes me much. But maybe I'm wrong. He's distant and reserved with everyone."

"Perhaps, then, he's that species of man."

"What do you mean?"

"The ancient philosophers described the human race in terms of four kinds of personality, or humour. These are, the choleric, the sanguine, the melancholic, and the phlegmatic. These old ideas are not so much in fashion now, but personally I think there is a great deal of truth in what the ancients said.

"Your uncle, for example – maybe *he* is naturally melancholic. He is distant and reserved because he cannot help it. He was simply born that way."

"Maybe," Owen agreed. "But—"

"Is he actually unkind?" asked David, warming to his theme. "Is he cruel, perhaps? Is he unjust?"

"No. Never. In fact, he seems over-anxious to behave honourably towards me."

"I'm very glad to hear it." David stood up. "Well, child – I've told you everything I know. As you've seen for yourself, it's all ancient history, buried so deep in the past that I feel we should let it lie. Do you agree?"

"I suppose so." Owen shrugged his compliance.

"Excellent. So now, instead of being gloomy, let us be happy that in spite of your early misfortunes, you have found friends to love you. To look out for your welfare, and help you on your way." David put on his spectacles. He looked crafty. "Tell me, Owen – what do you think of the apothecary's trade?"

Owen was, in fact, fascinated by his uncle's work. He loved to sit in the apothecary's shop, that ill-lit sorcerer's cave of countless wonders, watching David Morgan measure powders, count drops, distil and pound and mix miscellaneous ingredients into an amazing variety of healing salves, tinctures and balms – which could then, it seemed, cure almost every ill the flesh was heir to. Except a broken heart.

So, delighted to observe that the boy was indeed interested in his work, David taught Owen to make various simple ointments and emulsions. To pronounce the Latin names of the dozens of ingredients he used in his secret art, and to prepare the raw materials of nature for conversion into medicines of all kinds. Owen learned how willow bark, pounded and powdered, could be used as an extremely efficient specific against marsh ague. How foxglove leaves, infused in quantity, were astonishingly effective in cases of dropsy and breathlessness.

David Morgan had a large practice, and soon the child was accompanying the apothecary on his visits to patients, standing deferentially behind his master while David described the malady, then prescribed the cure. David himself observed that his female patients especially tended to brighten more or less immediately when the apothecary took his handsome young assistant along on a visit.

"You seem to be a tonic in yourself, child," David told him, as they left the house of an aged hypochondriac, for whom David had been prescribing vividly coloured placebos for the past decade. "You've done Mrs Evans more good in five little minutes, than I and all my drops have in five whole years."

"Maybe she'll get better now, then," suggested Owen.

"Oh, my dear child – there's no chance of that!" Shaking his head, David grinned, hugely. "We'll be called upon every other day from now on. Just you wait and see."

When at last September came, Owen found he did not want to return to Warwickshire. Well, he did – and yet he didn't. A regular correspondence with Jane kept him in touch with the doings of everyone at Easton, and as he read her letters he found he did miss them all.

But, here in Cardiff, he was employed. Here, he was useful. He wondered if the Squire of Easton had been right – if going to Harrow *would* be a waste of time, especially since he had now decided he would like to become an apothecary.

"Will you write to my Uncle Darrow this week?" That fine late summer evening, apothecary and assistant sat quietly in the shop, preparing a batch of salves. Now, Owen looked anxiously at his Uncle Morgan. "Would you ask the squire if I could perhaps live with you just a little while longer?"

"You wish to stay here, in this house, with me?" Behind his spectacles, David's eyes were bright. "You wish to be my assistant, and take after me?"

"Yes, I think I do." Confident that David Morgan would welcome the suggestion with open arms, Owen grinned. "I would like to be an apothecary. Also, I feel at home here. I think it's where I belong."

So David wrote to Ellis Darrow proposing that Owen should stay in Cardiff and attend the local grammar school there, while learning the apothecary's trade.

Readily – rather too readily, in David Morgan's private opinion – Ellis Darrow agreed.

So Rayner went to Harrow alone.

Chapter Four

The school at which Owen Morgan was the newest pupil was a very small foundation. Taking only twenty boys, these lads were mostly the sons of tradesmen and manufacturers, from Cardiff and the Vale of Glamorgan, and the areas round about.

Although this was a grammar school offering a traditional English education, Owen's masters did not spend too much time on the classics, reasoning that Greek and Latin would be of little practical use to the shopkeepers and ironmasters of the next generation. Instead, the boys were taught to express themselves clearly in the English language, to understand accounts, and to write a fair, round hand.

Thomas Taliesin, a dark-eyed, dark-haired boy from the Valleys, was the first to pick a fight with the new boy, the first to have his nose bloodied in the process, and the first to decide that Owen Morgan was a good fellow.

This was perhaps inevitable, for the two of them had a great deal in common. An orphan like Owen himself, Thomas's parents had died of septic quinsy within a week of one other, leaving him the notional ward of an ancient aunt who kept fifteen cats and a house-trained pig, but who found the idea of sharing her rambling old house with a thirteen-year-old boy insupportable.

She had scoured the newspapers and weekly periodicals until she found an advertisement for a cheap school a fair distance from her home. So Thomas, and two other boys whose relations didn't want them, were permanent boarders at the school, and sat at the headmaster's own table. Fortunately, Mr Dryden's wife liked boys, and was a very good cook, so they didn't do too badly.

As Owen soon realised, Thomas was a braggart, a liar and a thief. He stole regularly from shops and market stalls, and was not above offering the proceeds of his thievery for general sale, in the school yard. There was a fortune coming to him when he was twenty one. Or so he said. In the meantime, while he waited for his ship to come in, his shoes were down at heel, his linen ragged and his cuffs frayed.

But he wore his highwayman's hat with a jaunty air, he grinned and whistled and played the most outrageous practical jokes, and Owen was inclined to like him.

"You are allowed out on Sundays, aren't you?" demanded Owen one Friday dinner time, as he and Thomas washed off the blood, after one of their play-ground spats.

"Who's asking?" enquired Thomas, gingerly investigating the damage to his nose, upon which Owen had landed a punch.

"We could go swimming, maybe." Owen grinned. "Do you swim?"

"Like a bloody fish, man." Offended, Thomas glared. But then he grinned, too. "We'll go up to the old claypits, shall we? I'll teach you to dive."

As well as learning to dive, Owen learned to blend into the scenery of rural Wales. Little by little, he felt he was becoming Welsh again.

But, although he and David nowadays slipped easily into Welsh from English, and just as easily back again, Owen found that at school the speaking of Welsh was not encouraged at all. There, the language of instruction was English. Indeed, most of the pupils came from families whose only language was the Saxon tongue, and of the twenty scholars in the little school, only Thomas and Owen himself knew more than a few words of the ancient Celtic their forefathers had spoken

– and even they had learned two completely different dialects of that.

But, in spite of this, they soon realised they could have private conversations which no one else understood. In a bastard version of the most beautiful language in the world, they discussed their hopes, their dreams, their plans for the future. Both orphans, both sharp and clever, both supposing themselves effectually cast off by their rich but heartless relations, who would certainly live to regret their cruelty, it was perhaps inevitable that Owen and Thomas Taliesin should become great friends.

"But you're not absolutely set on becoming an apothecary, are you?" demanded Thomas one recreation, as the two of them sloped across the school yard muttering to one another in a rough approximation of the language their parents had taught them. "You don't honestly mean to spend your life mixing salves for winter chilblains, or balm for cradle cap?"

"Why should I not?" Owen grinned. "The relief of suffering is a noble calling," he declared, parroting David Morgan. "The alleviation of pain—"

"Don't give me that cant." Extravagantly, Thomas yawned. "Apothecaries! Healers of the sick! Quacks and piss prophets, more like. Every man Jack of them, one and all."

"Oh, yes? What about you, then? What will you be?"

"A rich man." Thomas kicked a stone across the yard. "I shall become a manufacturer. An ironmaster, with my own foundries, my own mills, my own workshops. I'll have a thousand men under *me*. All obedient to my behest."

"Where will you get the cash to finance an undertaking like that?"

"I'll seek out a wealthy fool, and persuade him to invest. I'll offer him profits beyond calculation, merely for sitting on his backside and signing his name." Thomas sighed. "I can't wait to be a man. To leave this dismal little town. To strike out on my own!"

* * *

In those first years of the nineteenth century, the population of Cardiff was a little over a thousand souls. David Morgan was one of three apothecaries in the town, but his practice extended far into the countryside round about. His patients were usually farmers and their families, the better-off sort of peasant, and servants. But, such was his reputation, the gentry also consulted David Morgan – although in cases of serious illness, a physician from Monmouth or Chepstow would be called in.

Not that this was worth the expense. Not in the least. The physician might be an Oxford or Cambridge man, might style himself Doctor and know the Latin for any organ or bone you cared to name – but his practical skills would be minimal. Whereas although he was merely an apothecary, and merely licensed to dispense drugs, David Morgan's understanding of physiology, pharmacology and obstetrics was second to none.

So it was David who taught Owen the rudiments of anatomy, how to set bones, how to treat burns, and how to recognise the symptoms of common ailments in both children and grown men.

Full of intellectual curiosity, and blessed with a highly retentive memory, Owen absorbed information like a sponge. "Perhaps we ought to send you to college after all," murmured his uncle, as he watched Owen at work one Saturday afternoon. "We could make a physician of you, maybe."

"I don't think so." Carefully counting drops, Owen added them to the specific against the gout, which he was concocting under David's watchful eye. "I wouldn't want to spend my days fawning on the aristocracy. Or haunting the anterooms of the great."

"You wouldn't need to, child." David grinned. "Talented as you undoubtedly are, and with good looks to boot, the great – the ladies especially – would be beating a path to your door!"

* * *

The year turned, then turned again. Faithful to his promise, Owen wrote regularly to his cousin Jane, and received her replies. These occasionally enclosed a flowery little note from Maria, hoping he was well. Sometimes, even Isabel Graham wrote to him, slipping her highly-scented, hot-pressed letters inside Jane's.

Isabel's letters were longer than Maria's, but not very interesting for all that. As he opened her latest offering, he saw that today's epistle was no exception to the general rule.

'My dear Owen,' he read. 'I hope you are quite well. Last week, Papa bought me a new pony. She is a dappled grey and her name is Twilight. The weather here is very bad. It rains constantly. I do not know when I shall get out to ride. I am very well. My parents send their kindest regards.'

Yawning, Owen tossed this exciting intelligence aside, and began to read the letter from Jane. Having sanctioned the correspondence between the two cousins, Jane's parents saw no need to censor it, so she could write about whatever she pleased – and she did. Furthermore, she was a natural correspondent, who, if given a sheet of paper and a pen could bring a rout, a ball, or a dinner party to gloriously vivid life. She described people she did not like with a delightfully malicious wit, and always concluded her long letters with, 'my parents send their best love. As, of course, do I.'

Best love. Owen did not doubt that Rebecca loved him, loved him dearly in fact, as much as she loved her own son. But Ellis? Well – he obligingly franked these fat, bulging letters, so that David did not have to pay the carriage costs. That was something, Owen supposed. Ellis also paid for his nephew's education, which was much appreciated, since Owen loved school.

Jane reported that Rayner, on the other hand, hated Harrow. Bored by lessons, and loathing all forms of physical activity or the organised sport in which the famous public school distinguished itself, he was frequently beaten, either for failing to hand in his preparation or for letting his side down. Those few letters Owen received from his cousin seemed to underline this lack of progress, if not the unhappiness of the person who had written them. For Rayner's handwriting would have disgraced a little child just learning pot-hooks, any ability to express himself fluently or amusingly was sadly lacking, and his spelling was a disaster area.

"So much for a superior education," Owen would reflect, turning back to Jane's closely-written paragraphs. Although *she* had had no formal education at all . . .

One day, seeing the latest of her bulky manuscripts sticking out of Owen's school bag, Thomas Taliesin snatched it and began to read aloud, for the edification of the whole class. "No, let me," he begged, as Owen tried to grab it back. "It's damned intriguing. I want to know what happened next."

So Owen let him read Jane's account of a very grand ball, during which her friend Martha Dennison had danced a whole two dances with a man she had afterwards learned was a notorious philanderer – nay, had risen from the bed of his latest mistress only an hour since, in order to attend that very ball! The mistress had arrived later, dressed to kill, and given poor Martha some very black looks.

Then, at tea, Jane had overheard some scandalous details of an affair between the county's most senior MP and the local magistrate's pock-marked but apparently highly desirable young wife. Then, best of all, a clergyman the worse for drink had poured his bowl of white soup into a lady's lap, whereupon the lady had violent hysterics and her husband knocked the parson down, to the delight and horror of the distinguished company.

"Hand it back now," said Owen, as Thomas laughed heartily and pleaded to be allowed to go on. "The rest is private, so give it to me."

But Thomas merely turned over the page. Then, of course, he saw the signature of the correspondent. "This is from a woman!" he cried grinning, a mad baboon incarnate. "Morgan has a woman! She sends him her best love! She—"

"Does she, by God? What's her name?" demanded John Friar, chortling delightedly.

"It's Jane." Thomas Taliesin cackled like a demented hen. "She is Morgan's dearest Jane. She's his darling, precious—"

"She's my cousin!" Snatching the letter, Owen glared. "She sends me news of home, that's all! She's *not* my precious, nor my darling—"

"How old is she?" interrupted John Friar.

"Seventeen. But—"

"Quite grown up! Is she pretty?"

"Yes, she is. But I—"

"Morgan's blushing!" Thomas Taliesin was beside himself with delight. "Look at him! He's bright red!"

"Come along, Morgan." John Friar shook Owen by the shoulder. "Spill the beans. This cousin of yours – is she an heiress?"

"I have no idea."

"You must have. Is her father rich?"

"Yes. But he also has a son. So his daughters may never be—"

"Are you going to marry her?"

"Of course not. I told you – she's my cousin. Besides, she's much older than me."

"Cousins may marry." Thomas Taliesin looked wise. "Well now, boys – if *I* had a cousin, daughter of a rich man, who sent me her best love at the end of a nice long letter like this, *I'd* propose to her directly, let her be ten, twenty years older than me! I'd—"

"Shut up, Taliesin." Still red in the face, Owen glared. "Shut your mouth now, or I'll break all the teeth in it and push them down your throat."

"You and whose army?"

"Taliesin, I'm warning you!"

"Come on, then." Thomas Taliesin grinned. "Let's see who's the better man! Tell you what, Morgan – if I knock you out, will you permit me to make my addresses to your dear cousin Jane? After all, *I'm* not her near relation. *I've* no objection to mounting an old nag – provided her saddle bags are full of gold. I—"

Owen lunged at him. The other boys pushed back the desks, and settled down to enjoy the fight.

"You were the victor, I hope?" murmured David Morgan mildly, as he mixed calendula and orange flower water, in order to make a salve for Owen's split lip and blackened eyes.

"I think so. But it was a close run thing." Easing off his torn and filthy jacket, Owen winced. "I'm afraid my shoulder may need strapping," he whispered. "It's very sore."

"Let's see, then." David examined the joint. "Ah, yes. Dislocated, it is. Hold still."

As his uncle manipulated the bones and tendons, Owen's eyes filled with tears. One by one, they began to spill over. Soon they were trickling in dirty runnels, all down his face.

"Be brave," adjured David, as he worked. Deftly, carefully, he eased the joint back into alignment. "There – it's done. Sleep on your back tonight."

"You don't wish to strap it up?"

"No. At your age, the less interference with the flesh, the better." David met his nephew's mournful gaze. "So what was it all about?"

"He insulted my cousin Jane. He called her an old nag, and said he wouldn't mind mounting her. He—"

"So you felt obliged to defend the lady's honour." David shook his head. "So for you, it will be women."

"What do you mean?"

"For your father, it was danger. For you, it will be the opposite sex." David sighed. "From now on, I suppose I shall be seeing this sort of mess regularly."

"I shan't get into fights." Slipping off his high stool,

Owen winced again. "I had to hit him this time. But I don't enjoy getting hurt. I don't like pain."

Two years into the new century, the coming of peace with France meant that, for intrepid English travellers, continental holidays were possible again. Jane wrote that the Darrow family hoped to spend that summer in Europe, touring France and perhaps moving on to Italy in the autumn.

Her parents and Maria were greatly looking forward to going abroad, but Rayner was being very awkward about the whole thing. "He protests he has no desire whatsoever to be among 'frogs'," continued Jane, "for he understands very little of their vile language, has no opinion of their much-vaunted cuisine – preferring roast rib of beef with a decent gravy to horrid foreign messes any day – and he despises their simpering manners entirely."

In Rayner's juvenile opinion, moreover, the Peace of Amiens was a sham. England and France were natural enemies. As soon as the Darrows set foot on French soil, war would break out again. His parents and sisters would be arrested, imprisoned, and would end their days on the scaffold, as victims of Madame Guillotine.

Grinning, he'd added that he understood his father's policy. The poor squire was more or less obliged to snatch this chance to get the family abroad, for where else would he find husbands for his daughters? After all, Jane and Maria were so hideous that no sane Englishman would look at either.

"Be assured, dear Owen," said Jane, "that *I* wish as much as ever Rayner does that he could stay at home. But my father is adamant. Travel is to broaden Rayner's mind. It must needs refine his coarse sensibilities, too. My dear Owen, travel would have more chance of refining a Berkshire hog than of improving my dear brother, who is – alas – grown up into a booby, and one of the most oafish, lumpen kind, dear to us though he is and ever will be.

"But now, something occurs to me. I wonder if he

could come and stay with you? Might your uncle allow it? Would you ask him? You would be doing everyone a favour – everyone except, perhaps, yourself! But you were always fond of Rayner, and he loves you dearly, so I'm sure he would be delighted to see you again."

By the same post, David received a letter from Ellis Darrow. His daughter Jane, he wrote, had recently allowed him to glance over a specimen of his nephew's correspondence, and Ellis had been impressed by what he'd read. Now, he congratulated David on the boy's good sense, marked ability to express himself fluently, and excellent orthography. He must be attending a very good school.

While not mentioning his son's reluctance to join the family party to France, Ellis continued that he would like to ask David a favour. Would it be possible for Rayner to visit his cousin, and stay for a month or so? The boys had been close friends during childhood. As young men, they were surely curious to see each other again. Did David not think they might enjoy spending some time together?

Owen was all for it. So David wrote back by return, inviting Rayner Darrow to visit and stay for as long as he pleased.

Rayner stepped out of the coach and gazed all round the market place. Then he saw them. Two tall, good-looking boys of about his own age, they were eyeing the naked ankles and calves of a girl who was setting out a fruit and vegetable stall. He walked up to them, then tapped one on the shoulder. "Owen?" he hazarded.

The boy spun round. "Rayner!" With a yell pleasure, Owen swept his cousin into the most crushing of bear hugs, then drew back to look at him, beaming all over his face. "Tom," he said then, to the boy lounging at his side, "this is Rayner. Rayner Darrow, my long-lost Saxon cousin from wildest Warwickshire!"

"Indeed? You surprise me. Come now, Morgan – peas in a pod could hardly be more alike!" Thomas Taliesin grinned. Extravagantly, he bowed. Then he held out his hand. "Thomas Taliesin, at your service," he said.

Rayner bowed too. "Rayner Darrow, at yours," he replied.

Owen hooted with laughter. "You two belong in Bath," he jeered. "In the Assembly Rooms, with the famous Mr Nash."

"So? He was a Welshman, exactly like you. Born and bred in Swansea." Tom threw an arm around Rayner's shoulders. "Well, man? Where's your luggage, then?"

"They're unloading it now. That trunk and the three valises are mine."

"Very well. Leave them with the ostler here. Owen will send Daniel for them later."

The three boys went to David's house, where Tom was always welcome, and where Rayner was made so straight away. Sitting at the kitchen table, planting their huge adolescent feet on the clean rush matting, they ate half of Susannah's weekly bake at a sitting, then went out again, to explore the town.

Rayner was well provided with cash, so his first stop was at the livery stables, where he hired a pony and trap, reserving these for his own exclusive use for the next fortnight, as he meant to see the district in style. If any of his proposed jaunts appealed to Owen or Tom, he added, they were welcome to join him. All their costs – meals, accommodation at inns, whatever – would be at Ellis Darrow's kind expense.

By that evening, all three lads were firmly in each others' confidence. As they lounged on settles in the local pot house, eyeing up the landlord's daughter, and trying to decide if she would be a worthwhile proposition, Rayner casually revealed that actually he'd already had *his* first woman.

"Actually worth having, was she?" demanded Thomas Taliesin, nonchalance incarnate.

"What?" Rayner dragged himself away from his study

of the barmaid's charms to frown at Tom. He muttered that he supposed so. Although, he confessed, he felt that apart from the fact that it relieved congestion, there was nothing much else to recommend it. In short, Rayner pronounced, women were a waste of good drinking time. He beckoned the barmaid over once again.

"Do you drink a vast deal?" enquired Owen, as he raised his foaming tankard to his lips.

Rayner grinned. "Of course," he replied. "It's expected of me. At Harrow, you know, we have fellows who can down a bottle of port in three minutes flat – and still stand! I'm working towards that."

"When you leave school, what will you do next?"

"The old fellow wants me to go to college." Rayner pulled a face. "We're going to have harsh words about that, I fear."

"Why don't you want to go? *I* would!" Thomas grinned. "I know! You could take Owen along with you. He could be a sizar."

"A what?"

"A scholarship man. Don't you Saxons know anything? Look, take Morgan here. Then at least you'd have some decent company."

"It's certainly a thought." Rayner considered the notion. "It might even be fun, if Owen were there too. But forget the charity boy idea. I'll speak to the old devil about paying Owen's fees. We'll see what he says to that."

"Please don't ask the squire." Owen frowned into his beer. "Your father doesn't like me," he muttered. "He never has, and he never will. I'll make my way in the world without his grudging aid."

"But you could pay him back," argued Thomas. "When you make your fortune, you could return his cash with interest."

Owen laughed. "Tom here is going to be a rich man," he explained. "He's to become a great manufacturer, who will set the whole of South Wales afire."

"I shall indeed." Now, Thomas Taliesin looked crafty.

He glanced towards Rayner. "Are your sisters well?" he enquired.

"They're in excellent health. In splendid spirits, too. They're quite beside themselves at the thought of going to Paris." Rayner grinned. "God, Owen – you should see Maria! These days, she's powdered, painted and bedizened like nothing on earth. She costs my father a fortune in silks and satins. She intends to catch a duke, you see. Or an earl, at least."

"What about Jane? Does she aspire to a coronet?"

"I doubt it. She's certainly no fine lady." Rayner shrugged. "Oh, she's neat and pretty, I grant you that readily enough. But she isn't showy, you see. Not at all. My father expects to marry *her* off to an embryo bishop, or some such whey-faced fellow.

"But if he could keep her in Warwickshire, I expect he'd settle for a mere country gentleman. Provided he had a steady six or seven thousand a year, of course."

"Oh." The idea of Jane married off made Owen feel most uneasy. "How is Isabel?" he enquired.

"She's exactly the same," replied Rayner. "Scrawny, ginger, freckled. No bosom before, no backside behind. As hideous a girl as you could expect to see, if you rode for a whole summer day. It's a good thing she'll be rich."

David Morgan's own childhood had been delightfully carefree. He had been allowed to ramble where he liked, do pretty much as he pleased, in fact – and now he saw no reason at all why three young lads of fifteen should not spend the summer roaming the countryside. Provided they didn't get up to too much mischief, of course.

There was security in numbers, he reasoned. Whereas he would have felt very uneasy about one boy of that age wandering off alone, surely three of them together would be safe enough?

So, that summer, Rayner, Owen and Thomas went roving. Whenever they came across an ironworks, a row of blast furnaces set into a scarred and pitted hillside, or any kind of manufactory, Thomas spied out opportunities and explained how, when he came into his inheritance or met a wealthy fool, he would make his fortune. He drew sketches and plans and day-dreamed about getting rich.

Rayner looked out for women. For, in spite of his assertion that they were useful only in that they helped to relieve congestion in a man, he also appeared to enjoy their company. In fact, Owen realised later, his cousin wasn't particularly interested in taking girls to his bed. Instead, he liked to have their attention; their admiration; their fawning adulation and fascinated regard, as they hung on every word he said.

He was not to be disappointed in South Wales, for he was of course the major attraction wherever they went. His dark good looks, aristocratic bearing and expensive clothes assured him this welcome attention. The landlords of the inns where the boys put up often assumed Rayner's two companions were his servants, and one would sometimes draw Owen or Thomas aside to remark that there was a very handsome lady in the Green Chamber or the Rose Room this evening. Would their master like to make her acquaintance, perhaps?

At whatever kind of inn they chanced on of an evening, pot house or superior coaching establishment, it was never long before, well primed with porter or best ale, Rayner and Thomas began to show off, Thomas impressing the older men with his knowledge and ideas, and Rayner fascinating their wives and daughters. Usually, Owen merely listened to all this palaver, secretly laughing at them both. But sometimes he walked out into the cool summer night, to take a breath of cleaner, fresher air.

One evening, as he strolled back from a walk to a pretty little river near the inn, he noticed a girl taking some packages from a private coach. He'd seen her earlier, in fact. She was a lady's maid. Her mistress, a fat, middle-aged widow, looked very well off. Perhaps he should try to interest her in one of Thomas's lunatic schemes . . .

The girl nodded to him. "Good evening," she began, an attractive Welsh lilt lending additional charm to her low, rather husky voice.

Owen decided she must be a country girl. A native Welsh speaker, perhaps, too. So he replied in Welsh – and was delighted when she spoke to him again in his own native tongue.

"You're with the young English gentleman, aren't you?" she enquired. Sweetly, she smiled at him. "Are you his valet? Or his footman, maybe?"

"That's right." By now, Owen was used to being mistaken for a servant. "I'm his valet and footman combined," he replied.

"Then I hope he rewards you accordingly. Were you looking for someone just now?"

"No. I merely stepped outside for a moment, to breathe in some night air."

"Oh, I see. Well, then—"

"Don't go in yet." Owen looked into the girl's face. He saw that she was pretty, very pretty indeed. Dark hair framed her face, escaping from under her cap and curling charmingly round her ears. Dark eyes sparkled in the moonlight. Full, red lips curved in a delightfully sensuous smile.

She was probably older than he. Eighteen, at least. He knew her mistress had retired for the night. Perhaps she would like to take a short stroll? "Would you like to walk down to the waterfall?" he enquired.

"Will your master not miss you?"

"No." Owen smiled. "He's engaged at dice. He won't get up again until he's lost everything in his pockets and pledged his mourning rings besides."

So the girl took his arm and together they walked away from the inn.

There was a full moon, so the path was well lit and there was no fear of stumbling in the dark. "What's your name?" asked the girl.

"Owen Morgan."

"I'm Betty Taylor." The girl sighed. "Well – Betty's not my given name, of course. My mistress calls all her maids Betty."

"What is your given name?"

"Dilys."

"I prefer that."

"So do I."

Reaching the waterfall, Dilys sat down on one of the boulders near the water's edge. She patted the stone next to her, so Owen sat down as well. She smiled at him. "You may kiss me, if you wish," she said.

He did wish, very much. So now, hesitantly, he kissed her cheek. It was the first time he had ever kissed a girl who wasn't also a relation, and it felt very strange – but very exciting, too. He kissed her again.

"Oh, for goodness' sake! Not like that!" Shaking her head, Dilys turned towards him. She put her arms around his neck, then kissed him squarely on the mouth. "How old are you?" she enquired when, a minute later, she drew away.

"Seventeen," he lied.

"Get away with you." She laughed. "I must go back now. But I'll see you tomorrow evening, maybe."

The following evening, Dilys met him outside the inn and led him down the path, past the waterfall and into the woods beyond. Sitting down in a grassy glade, she pulled Owen down beside her, then kissed him, opening his mouth with hers. Then she placed his hands on her breasts, encouraging him to massage them while her own fingers fluttered to and fro across his lap, lightly stroking his private parts. "Is that nice?" she whispered.

Nice? It was wonderful. But Owen found he could only squeak in reply.

So she kissed him again. Hours – or maybe it was merely a few minutes – slipped by. Then, suddenly, Dilys stopped stroking his lap and drew back a little. But this was only so she could pull up the skirts of her gown.

"You may look," she said, lying back on her elbows. "You may touch me. You may even kiss me, if you wish. But you may go no further than that."

Astonished, Owen merely stared at her. So she took his hand and showed him what to do. "Just there," she murmured. "That's right. In fact, it's bliss."

It took a little practice, but soon Owen found he could do it. He could actually perform a miracle. In the space of a few minutes, he transformed a self-assured, rather bossy little woman into a shuddering, wild-eyed, moaning animal, who groaned and gasped and clawed at him as if she were drowning, and he the only creature who could save her – which, at last, he did.

He hadn't known he possessed such astonishing power.

But she had power, too. Now, he had no choice but to go on, to—

"No, my dear. We mustn't." She clung to him. She was almost in tears. "I'd like to, in fact I'd love to, but if you get me with child—"

"Oh, Dilys! Please let me! I'll be so careful!"

"Hush. This is almost as good." She undid his buttons, then took him in her hands, and worked on him. When his release came, he literally sobbed with relief. He thought he must die of it.

They walked back to the inn hand in hand. "We go on to Brecon tomorrow," she said. "I shan't see you again."

He gaped at her. He had to see her again! At this particular moment, he wanted to marry her. "Give me your address," he said. "I can write to you then."

"Write to me?" Her eyes grew round. "You know how to write a letter?"

"Well, of course I do."

"I can't even read." She hung her head. But then, she looked up at him. "You're a lovely young man," she said. "You'll meet dozens of other girls – most of them prettier and all of them cleverer than me."

"I doubt that. Oh, Dilys—"

"I'll remember you, Owen Morgan." Sadly, Dilys smiled at him. "I was the first, wasn't I? To touch you, I mean?"

"No!" Owen reddened. But then he admitted it. "Yes," he said.

"How old are you really?"

Owen shrugged. "Fifteen," he muttered, crossly. "But I—"

"A mere child." Dilys gave his hand a comforting squeeze. "I'm twenty two. Engaged to be married. I'm going to wed my mistress's butler next spring."

Jane and Maria looked out of their hotel window and down into the busy street below. Paris was fascinating. So exciting! To two country-bred English girls on their first trip abroad, it even smelled delicious, although some of the component parts of that smell were extremely unpleasant, to say the least.

Maria's hired maid had finally finished her lady's hair and gone on her way. "Well?" demanded Maria.

"You look wonderful." Jane smiled. "But my father will say you're too fine."

"He's just an old misery. *He* would have all the women in England dress as Quakeresses. Like you and Mama, in fact." Maria sighed. "Why don't you let Sophie do your hair for you? Style it *à la Parisienne*? You don't need to wear your gowns quite so loose, either. Tight sleeves would show off your arms, and a narrow bodice would become you very well."

"Would it?" Doubtfully, Jane frowned. Today, in spite of long sleeves which came down to her wrists, her sister's creamy shoulders and bosom were almost naked, on display for all the world to admire. Before going out, her father would insist that *she* put on a scarf, or even oblige her to exchange her lovely new gown for a more modest one, which left rather more – or in fact, everything – to the beholder's imagination.

Chapter Five

Rayner was proved right. The Peace did not last. By the May of 1803, England and France were at war again.

It had been strange, being at peace. It had also been rather unsettling, what with factory workers throughout the land suddenly being put on short time, or even thrown out of work altogether, and with bands of unemployed labourers roaming the countryside begging, poaching, thieving and worse. Surely, people murmured, being at war with France was the natural state of things?

The years were slipping by. Leaving school, Rayner was packed off to Oxford, where he learned to drink, swear, fornicate and gamble in earnest, like the red-blooded English gentleman he most assuredly was. Perpetually short of cash, and almost permanently in debt, he frequently found himself wondering how soon he might reasonably expect to inherit. How many years more might the old fellow last?

Sitting in her study one spring morning, Rebecca happened to glance at the calendar. Soon, it would be Rayner's birthday. Owen's, too. "They'll both be nineteen," she mused, astonished that time could have flown by so rapidly. "Quite grown up! In fact, if not in law."

Jane was almost twenty-three years old. These days, she was universally acknowledged to be the best catch in the district. After Isabel Graham, of course. A young, healthy, extremely pretty woman, whose father doted on her and would no doubt give her at least twenty thousand pounds on her wedding day, she would probably have a yearly allowance of a good two thousand. If not more.

Courted and flattered by everyone, Jane herself seemed to favour Charles Harding, the eldest son of a local landowner who had good prospects and a rich uncle in Northumberland. Childless as he was, it seemed likely he would make Charles his heir. Nothing definite had been said, but nowadays both sets of parents went out of their way to be civil to one other, and complimentary about each others' most delightful children.

Rebecca found herself thinking about orange blossom and wedding clothes. How many bridesmaids should there be? For the match would definitely be a desirable one. So now, perhaps, those preliminary, tentative moves should be made.

First, there must be a gesture of good intent. Maybe, this summer, the Darrows might give a ball? Rebecca had never organised a ball, but she was confident that she could.

"Ellis?" At dinner that day, after everyone had been served and the servants had withdrawn, Rebecca laid her small, white hand upon her husband's sleeve. "Ellis, my dear? What do you think of our giving a small party this summer? I was wondering about having a little ball – just the neighbours and a few friends – for Jane?"

"What does Jane think of that?" Meeting his favourite daughter's steady, blue gaze, Ellis smiled at her. "Well, my dear? Should you like it?"

Jane smiled in return. "If you and my mother are so kind as to consider it," she began, "I'm sure I should be delighted—"

"But of course she'd like it!" Excitedly, Maria threw down her napkin. She clapped her hands in glee. "In fact, she'd simply adore it! You'll invite the Hardings, naturally. Charles will engage Jane for every dance. Then, during the *Boulangeries*, Charles and Jane will slip away. He'll take her hand, drop down on one knee, and then—"

"Maria, please!" Jane was blushing scarlet now.

But Maria was not to be silenced. "When shall it be?" she demanded. "Not for six weeks, at least. We must wait until the roses are out. Until the evening air is heavy with their fragrance, until the jasmine and honeysuckle entwine. Until Charles Harding's courage is screwed to the sticking point!"

"Indeed?" Laughing at her younger daughter, Rebecca shook her head. "I shall consider some dates in May, I think. The evenings should be quite balmy then."

"But not *too* balmy!" Maria laughed, too. "We don't want everybody wandering about outside, do we? Queering the pitch for poor Charles. Getting in his way."

Rebecca chose her date, marked it down in her private diary, then began to make her guest list. Realising Rayner would be at home that weekend, she decided to invite a friend or two for him.

But which friends should she select? Rayner's boon companions were louts. They drank, swore and gamed like heathens. Ellis loathed them all.

Perplexed, Rebecca chewed her pen. But then, in a flash, it came to her. She would invite Owen Morgan! He had been away from Easton for almost six years, and in all that time Ellis had never once suggested asking the poor boy to stay.

But, whatever Ellis thought, Rebecca now decided she would like to see her nephew again. So she wrote out the card.

"Shall we invite your cousin Owen?" she asked artlessly, when Jane and she sat down to afternoon tea, later that same day. "We could ask him to come on a short visit, perhaps? To coincide with the party, maybe?"

"That's a splendid idea!" Meeting her mother's eyes, Jane smiled. "He could keep Rayner in line, too. Prevent him and his horrible friends from becoming too drunk and disorderly."

"Yes, indeed." At the thought of Rayner and his

cronies, Rebecca shook her head in dismay. But then, she brightened. "Jane, my dear?"

"Yes, Mama?"

"I wish to ask you something, and I mean to do so plainly. We all know Mr Harding likes you, and I believe you like him. My dear – you know what I'm about to say. If Charles should propose to you, do you mean to accept him?"

Jane coloured. "I wouldn't wish to presume," she began. "I like Charles Harding, certainly. I think he likes me. But, my dear madam – I don't know if he's thought of marriage. I—"

"Your father and I would be very happy to see you settled." Rebecca patted her daughter's hand. "We like Charles very much. We feel that if any man could make you happy, Charles Harding would be he. That's all I shall say."

Opening the double doors to the grand saloon, which had once been the great hall of the Elizabethan mansion, and even now took up almost half the ground floor of Easton Hall, Owen Morgan gazed all around. Such splendour, he thought. Such opulence! Such banks of hot-house flowers, such long tables, all spread with snowy linen and gleaming silver plate. The apothecary's snug little home, clean and cosy and smelling always of beeswax, lavender and sweet herbs, seemed merely poky when compared with all this.

"So, Owen," Ellis had said earlier that day, "I understand you are to follow in your uncle's footsteps, and become an apothecary. A worthwhile calling indeed. Also, one eminently appropriate to your situation in life. How do you get on?"

"Very well indeed, sir. I enjoy my work very much."

"I'm glad to hear it. Very glad."

Owen had itched to get away, for time had not softened Ellis Darrow's manner at all. Still stiff, still formal, still as cold as charity, he'd regarded his nephew with a cool, suspicious frown and seemed reluctant to talk to him at all. Although he himself had sought the interview.

But Rebecca, Jane and Maria had been delighted to see him again. Of that there was no doubt at all! Jane had declared herself overjoyed to see him looking so handsome and so well. She had hugged and kissed him like a sister. Indeed, the memory of her soft, warm lips yet remained.

Embracing him, Rebecca had called him her own dearest nephew, and remarked amazedly on how big and good-looking he'd grown. "I believe you must be at least three inches taller than Rayner," she'd declared, gazing up at him, squinting narrowly and pretending he was out of focus at such a great height. "My dear child! You're the image of your uncle! Of course, you don't need *me* to tell you that. You have only to look in a glass."

"I only hope I don't resemble the miserable old devil in character, too," Owen had observed. But only to himself.

The room was filling nicely now. Ladies and gentlemen talked and laughed, engagements for the first two dances were sought, and chaperones made themselves comfortable in easy chairs placed well away from draughts.

Dressed in his best clothes, but still painfully aware that he must nevertheless look very much the poor relation, Owen prowled the perimeter of the room. Dodging past a huge vase of lilies, he suddenly stopped dead in his tracks. That redhead over there! It wasn't – it couldn't be Isabel Graham? Rayner had told him she was still a scrawny thing. A green-eyed minx with crooked teeth and horrid, blotchy freckles. A skinny little jade.

So who was this voluptuous creature with glowing auburn curls, a creamy complexion only lightly dusted with the palest of freckles, and eyes like emeralds?

The creature saw him. A second later, she stood before him. "Owen Morgan!" she cried, beaming. "Can it really be you?"

"Good evening, Miss Graham."

"My dear Owen! Don't be formal. Not with me." Impulsively, Isabel hugged him. Standing on tiptoe, she kissed his cheek.

But then, as she let him go again, Rayner appeared at her side. The look he gave Owen was far from cordial. "What's all this?" he enquired.

"Rayner, my dear! Don't be jealous." Charmingly, Isabel laughed. "I was merely expressing my pleasure at seeing your handsome cousin again. Hasn't he grown? He's so tall! Much taller than you'll ever be."

"Is he?" Rayner looked at his cousin, who reddened. "Do be quiet, Isabel," he muttered. He met Owen's gaze. "As you can see, she's become a terrible flirt."

"Have I?" Coyly, Isabel smirked. Then she strolled away.

Owen shook his head. "I'm sorry," he began. "For a moment, I thought I'd done something awful. I imagined you and Isabel must be – well—"

"Engaged? Good God, no." Rayner shuddered. "She'd like to be, I'm sure. My father would be all for it, and so would hers. But they wouldn't have to live with her, nor take her to bed!"

Finding Owen standing idle, merely talking to Rayner, Jane dragged him away to be introduced to Mr Harding, who was apparently her particular friend. "You'll like Charles," she promised. "He's clever, he's amusing, and he's kind."

So he might have been. But as far as Owen was concerned, Charles Harding proved to be nothing but a short, sandy-haired individual with no special charm, whose mild, hazel eyes looked vacant, whose chin was weak, and whose soft, girlish mouth gave the impression of a peevish nature. He shook Owen's hand firmly enough, however, and said he was delighted to make his acquaintance.

Jane was satisfied. Charles Harding was proverbially

shy, and she was pleased to see he was making an effort, for her sake if not for Owen's own. "Well now, my dear Owen," she declared, "since you are guest of honour here tonight, and the ball is given for me, I think it fitting that I should dance the first two dances with you. Charles? You won't mind that?"

"No, indeed." Politely, Charles Harding bowed. "As it happens, I wish to discuss something with Mr Dyer, of High Cross. It's a business matter, and would merely bore you. So – you dance with your cousin. I'll take his place a little later, if I may."

So Owen and Jane took up their positions in the set.

Owen was not an experienced dancer. But, naturally graceful, he was light on his feet, and by following Jane's lead and taking the nod from her, he managed very well. As they made their way down the dance, she smiled at him. "You're doing splendidly," she whispered.

"I am?" Owen wasn't so certain.

"To be sure." Jane touched his arm. "Miss Fraser thinks so, too. She was pointing you out to her friend, just one moment ago. Now, they're both admiring you!"

"They're observing me, you mean. Laughing at me for a clumsy, unfashionable poor relation, and hoping I'll be caught out."

"Don't be so foolish. You look perfectly presentable. Quite handsome, in fact! As for being clumsy – your dancing is far superior to that of a good few couples in this set, I may tell you that now."

"You're very kind. But then, you're always kind to me."

"You think so?"

"Of course I do!" Increasing the pressure on Jane's fingers, Owen smiled his gratitude. "When I lived here at Easton Hall, you were kindness itself. Then, when I left this place, you wrote to me. You kept the Hall and its inhabitants alive for me. I shall always be grateful that you took so much time to remember your poor cousin, sent so far away."

"My dearest Owen, that was no hardship. You know how much I love you!" Jane's blue eyes were wide. "You know you were my favourite child. My infant protégé, my own special pet."

"I'm not an infant now," Owen began. "I—"

"No, indeed. You've grown up into a very fine young man. You're doing well in the world. We're all extremely proud of you."

"All? Even your father?"

"Yes, indeed. In fact, he's so impressed by your industry and application that he talks of sending you to university, in order to take a doctor's degree. You could practise as a physician then."

"I see." Owen frowned. "Would he do this for my sake? Or because it would be more acceptable to Squire Darrow's pride, to have a physician in his family?"

"What do you mean?"

"If I am obliged to earn my own living, your father would prefer me to follow a gentleman's profession. As opposed to a mere working man's trade."

"Owen! That idea is both unworthy of you and unfair to my father. He thinks only of you. Of your present happiness, and future good."

"Does he?"

"Certainly." Jane herself frowned now. "You mustn't be ungrateful," she murmured.

"I hope I'm not." Chastened, Owen bit his lip. "I'm sorry," he muttered. "I'm behaving like a lout."

"A lout is something *you* could never be." Candidly, Jane met Owen's eyes. Again, she smiled. "I must dance with Charles Harding now," she said. "Why don't you go and rescue Rayner?"

"I'm sorry?"

"You could dance with Isabel Graham, perhaps?"

The party was over. As the last few guests shrugged on

their cloaks, as the last carriages were called and bowled away into the early hours of the morning, yawning servants began to clear up the debris and mess.

"Did he say anything?" Rubbing her tired eyes, Maria put her head round her sister's dressing room door. "Jane?"

"Thank you, Susan. That will be all for tonight." As her maid bobbed then left the room, Jane frowned. "I wish you wouldn't talk like that," she murmured. "Not in front of the servants, anyway."

"I'm sorry." Maria plumped herself down on the other half of her sister's stool. "Well?"

"He was very attentive. He complimented me excessively, both on my dancing and my looks. In fact, he was charm itself. But—"

"He did not speak." Pouting, Maria sniffed. "Stupid man."

"Maria, you must not call Charles stupid!"

"If the cap seems to fit—"

"Maria!"

"We all watched you dance with Owen." Plucking at a ribbon in her bodice, Maria sniffed again. "Well, all I can say is, if I were Charles Harding, and if *I* had seen you dancing with a young, handsome gentleman whose admiration was so obvious that even a child might have discerned it, *I* would have made sure of my prize tonight."

"Maria, what can you mean?"

"Don't be deliberately obtuse. The whole room was buzzing with it!" Maria stood up. "So much so that I would have thought the voice of suspicion might have whispered something into even Mr Harding's half-deaf ears!"

Before retiring to bed, Jane had kissed Owen goodnight. The warmth of that kiss, the perfume of her breath, and the awareness of her body so close to his had disturbed him so much that he felt light-headed at the mere recollection of it.

Standing on the terrace, leaning on the balustrade, he sighed. For the first time in his life, he was aware of a delicious pain, which was no pain at all. Of a pleasant ache which did not gripe, but rather soothed instead.

Could this be how it felt to fall in love? Owen thought it more than likely. He sighed again. He went to bed thinking Charles Harding was a very lucky man.

The following morning, during a very late breakfast, a note was brought in for Jane. In it, Charles Harding presented his compliments to her and to her family, and told her that the party had been charming. Both he and his parents had enjoyed themselves very much indeed.

He was writing now to inform Jane that, unfortunately, news had arrived that morning which obliged the family to make a short visit to a relation in the north of England. The Hardings would leave Warwickshire today, but hoped to be back by the end of the month, when Charles would look forward to seeing Jane again. Until that time, he was hers most affectionately, etc, etc.

Handing Rebecca the note, Jane shrugged.

Reading over her mother's shoulder, Maria sighed. "Great booby," she muttered.

"I beg your pardon?" murmured Rebecca, who was still reading.

"Nothing, Mama." Maria shook her head. "Well, no one can say he lacked opportunity. But the whole county will agree he lacked sense."

Sitting at the other end of the table, where Rayner was boring him with tales of undergraduate life, Owen had heard very little of this exchange. Later, however, meeting his cousin walking in the rose garden, he ventured to speak to her. "Is anything amiss?" he enquired.

"What did you say?" Narrowing her eyes against the bright sunshine, for she had forgotten to collect her parasol, Jane looked up at him. "I'm sorry, Owen?"

"Is something the matter?" Sitting down on a convenient bench, Owen did not know if he wanted Jane to sit beside him, or go on her way. "Is anything wrong?"

"No, of course not." Sitting down, Jane began to twist a ring on her little finger, round and round and round. She stared fixedly into the middle distance. "Why should there be?"

"When that note was brought in at breakfast time, I wondered if its contents had alarmed you. After reading it, you looked rather upset."

"On the contrary. I was not upset at all. You imagined that."

"Oh." Clasping his hands before him, Owen looked down at the ground.

Although Jane was sitting at the other end of the bench, a good twelve inches away from him, Owen found he was very conscious of her now. Out of the corner of his eye, he could see the hem of her gown. He could discern the thread of silver in the weave which, glinting in the sunlight, dazzled him. Mesmerised him, in fact.

Suddenly, urgently, he needed to know. So he cleared his throat, and asked her. "Have you become engaged to Mr Harding?" he enquired.

"No, I have not." Irritably, Jane plucked at the lace on her sleeve. "I'm not engaged to anyone."

"Do you expect to be?"

"I suppose so. In due course."

"Do – do you love him?"

"Does that matter?" Jane turned, to look her cousin full in the face. "It would be a splendid match for me! It would—"

"This splendid match. Do you desire it?"

"Why should I not?" Jane shrugged. "I like Charles, certainly. More to the point, my parents like him, too. As for *his* parents – I'm sure they would welcome the connection unreservedly."

"Why is that?"

"I'm young. I'm healthy. When I marry, my father will give me twenty thousand pounds."

"I see." Owen held his cousin's gaze. "Jane, are you being forced into this?"

"Of course not!" Jane shrugged. "My parents merely wish me to be happy. I, in turn, feel I owe them—"

"Oh, Jane!" Reaching for his cousin's hand, Owen held it. "Don't marry him unless you like him!"

"I *do* like him! I told you so just now. I—"

"But you don't love him. Does he love you?"

"He – I don't think he even considers—"

"You can't possibly marry a man who does not love you!" Owen's grip became stronger. "A woman about to become engaged should look happy!" he cried. "There should be a lightness in her step. A sparkle in her eyes. Her complexion should glow! But when you're with Charles Harding, you look as miserable as sin."

"That's not true. I—"

"I watched you last night," continued Owen, feverishly. "After we danced together, I observed you narrowly."

"Did you, indeed?"

"Yes, I did!" Owen was practically crushing Jane's fingers. "Going down the set with *me*, you were merry. You laughed and smiled. You even teased me a little – though kindly, I'll agree. But when you danced with Charles Harding, you were solemnity itself. You never spoke a word to him, you—"

"That was because I was concentrating on the dance, which was a new one. I needed all my wits about me, to —"

"I was so surprised I asked Isabel why you should look so grave."

"What did she say?"

"That I would look grave myself, if I were obliged to stand up with the greatest bore in all creation, who would glare and rebuke me if I put a single foot wrong."

"I see." Jane sighed. "Isabel does not like Charles."

"So it would seem. Does anybody?"

"Don't! Please, Owen – don't talk like this!" Jane blinked, then began to sniff. Searching for a pocket handkerchief, rummaging up her sleeves, on the bench and in her bag, she happened to edge a little nearer to her cousin – who, sorry for upsetting her, and anxious to offer comfort, slipped his arm around her waist.

She laid her head on his shoulder. Then, without quite understanding why, or how it came about, she raised her face to his.

His head spun. His pulse raced, and his heart thumped against his ribcage so hard that it hurt. Looking into her eyes, he saw himself reflected there. Last night, she had told him she loved him . . .

Her lips looked so soft, so rosy red that they reminded him of that special Turkish sweetmeat, of which his aunt had recently become inordinately fond. Might his cousin's lips taste of roses, too?

He had to know. So now, taking her in his arms, he kissed her.

To his great surprise, she let him hold her. She even kissed him back. But then, a moment later, she pulled away. "I'm so sorry," she began, her colour high. "I really don't know—"

"It was my fault." Blushing furiously, Owen rubbed his hot face. "Please forgive me. Believe me when I say I didn't mean to do that."

"Didn't you?"

"No! Well – I suppose I did. But you mustn't think I meant any harm. I just wanted to—"

"*I* wanted you to kiss me." Now, Jane looked deep into his eyes. "I wanted to know how it felt."

"Oh." Hardly able to believe what he was hearing, Owen stared at her. "How did it feel?"

"I don't know the words to describe it. Perhaps there aren't any. Owen?"

"Yes?"

"Do you love me, too?"

"I – I think I must." As Owen thought about it, he realised it was true. It had always been true, and he wondered how he could have been so foolish. So deliberately blind to the obvious, so obtuse. "What I do know," he said slowly, painfully, as haltingly as a lame man learning to walk again, "is that if you married Charles Harding, I should die of grief."

"What shall we do?"

"I don't know." Confused and perplexed indeed, for everything was happening so fast that he felt sick and dizzy, Owen shook his head. "If we tell your father, he will kill me."

"Don't be absurd! He wouldn't even think of such a thing."

"Maybe not. But he would hardly be pleased to learn you intend to give up all thought of Charles Harding, and marry Owen Morgan instead."

"But I haven't said I'll marry you. I—"

"Of course you haven't. You would not be so foolish." Now, his head clearing a little, Owen stood up. He began to pace up and down, like a barrister-at-law. "Let us consider the relative merits of Mr Harding and Mr Morgan," he began. "First, Mr Harding. Personable, healthy and rich, he is a very fine young man. He is also the sole heir to a valuable, unencumbered estate in the English Midlands.

"As for Mr Morgan – well, he is poor. His prospects are not good, for his happiness and prosperity depend upon the goodwill of two uncles. One is a rich man, who does not like him. The other is a man whose ability to procure Owen Morgan's advancement lags far behind his desire to accomplish it."

"What nonsense you talk." Jane herself stood up. "Owen, *do* you wish to marry me?"

"I—"

"Set aside all that stuff about your poverty and dependence. Leave my expectations and position in society out of the calculation. Take my hands in yours. Do you want *me*?"

"I do." Owen looked into her eyes. "I love you with all my heart," he whispered. "I always have, and I always will. I would die for you."

"There'll be no need for that." Standing on tiptoe, Jane kissed him. "There it is, then. I shall speak to my father today."

"Should I not talk to him first?"

"I think that might be just a little unwise." Thoughtfully, Jane shrugged. "Your uncle is a just and honourable man – but it's a fact that he has no great affection for you."

"When will you go to see him?"

"Early this evening, after tea. He is usually at leisure then."

"So the storm will break about seven o'clock. At a quarter past, I shall be summoned to his honour's council chamber. There, I shall be told to leave his house at once, never to return."

"My dear Owen! Don't be so dramatic!"

"Do you honestly imagine he will greet your revelations with delight?"

"He loves me dearly. Why should he seek to destroy my happiness?"

"He won't see it as destroying your happiness. His concern will be to prevent you from throwing yourself away." Sorrowfully, for he could see the enterprise was doomed entirely, Owen shook his head. "Well," he murmured, "we have the rest of the morning, at any rate. Shall we go for a walk?"

"Yes," said Jane. "Let's. Show me the places you loved as a child. Take me where you and Rayner used to play."

So Jane and Owen walked in the woods, strolled along the margins of the lake, and dawdled across the park. Between kisses, they made plans. Jane saw no reason why her fortune should not be shared with Owen. Secure in the certain knowledge that she was her father's favourite child, she had no reason to believe he would deny her anything.

"I shall go and sit with my aunt," said Owen, when they

parted after tea, both having made rather lame excuses for missing dinner, so already in the squire's black books. "My darling, listen to me – is it wise to talk to him this evening? He's already annoyed with me."

"Don't be so faint-hearted." Taking advantage of the darkness in the corridor outside her father's study, Jane kissed her lover on the lips. "Where's my stout little fellow, who could climb any tree in the park? Who could swim across the lake and jump the ha-ha, like a little mountain goat?"

As always, Ellis was very pleased to see Jane. Drawing up his daughter's usual chair, he sat down again himself. "Is this a merely social call?" he enquired, lighting his pipe and puffing contentedly.

"Not exactly." Jane smiled. "Sir, I have reason to suppose that you will shortly receive a visit from a gentleman who has made his addresses to me."

"I see." Ellis smiled, too. "Have you discussed this with your mother?" he enquired.

"No, sir. I thought it better to speak with you first. If you approve of the business, then I will feel authorised to tell Mama."

Ellis looked at her. For a moment, regret that he must shortly lose her clouded his features. But then he smiled again. "My dearest child," he began, "I shall not deny that it will be most painful for me to give your hand in marriage to any man. But Mr Harding is a fine young gentleman—"

"He is indeed." Reaching out to him, Jane took her father's hand in hers. "But, sir – we are not discussing Mr Harding. It is of Mr Morgan that I wish to speak tonight."

"Owen?" Ellis gaped at her. "My dear child, what are you saying?"

"Merely this." Jane looked into her father's eyes. "Since Owen first came to this house, since he was just a little child, we have been friends. Then he went away –

but while he was living in South Wales, we corresponded regularly. We told each other our hopes and schemes. We opened our hearts—"

"You did *what*?" Ellis's pale face darkened. "I know you wrote to the boy," he muttered. "But in all my born days, I never imagined you discussed—"

"Sir, there was no impropriety!" Jane's expression was all candour, and her eyes were wide. "My mother herself read my cousin's letters to me. Every single one! *I* wrote to Owen in order to keep him informed of the doings of this family. As Mama agreed it was proper I should.

"My dear sir – Owen has been precious to me from the time he was a child. When I saw him again, I felt I was reunited with a cousin – almost a brother, in fact – and a friend. But these past few days have shown us that we feel more than mere friendship. Today, we declared ourselves, admitted to each other that we have fallen in love. So, since we have both attained years of discretion, we wish to marry."

"This is the work of a few days?" As Jane spoke, Ellis had grown pale again. But now, his cheeks were rekindled by the dull red of anger. "This creature has wormed his way into your affections in a matter of *days*? My dear Jane, you must have run mad. A person who has nothing to recommend him – no fortune, no prospects, no talents—"

"No talents?" Jane herself grew angry then. "Sir, how can you say such a thing? How can you be so dismissive, so unkind, so cruelly—"

"Does Owen know the extent of your fortune?" interrupted Ellis, testily.

"Yes, he does."

"Did he discover it before or after he made his proposals to you?"

"Before. But, sir – he has always known you would do handsomely by me."

"Now, he no doubt hopes to profit from my intent."

"Come, sir. Bearing in mind what you know of Owen,

that is hardly fair." Looking away, Jane shook her head. "You have never liked him," she murmured. "He is your own sister's child, but you have no affection for him, none at all. Why is this?"

"My sister and I were estranged," Ellis replied. "Owen's mother and I – child, this is all in the past! But if you knew what it costs me to look at my sister's son, you would pity me!"

"If you were in pain, of course I should pity you. But if you would explain yourself, I might also understand." Jane looked steadily back at him. "Does my mother know why you dislike Owen?"

"I forbid you to discuss this matter with your mother! If you so much as mention—"

"Then why did you take Owen in?" asked Jane. "If you hated my aunt, why did you offer her son a home?"

"I was brought up in the Christian religion. I understand my duty. Now, I shall expect you to know yours."

"Indeed?" Jane met his eyes. "I hope I have never given you any cause to think I don't?"

"No, you have not. So now, I shall expect you to act in accordance with my wishes."

"Do you mean I must give Owen up?"

"If you wish to be called my daughter, indeed you must."

"I see." Jane blinked rapidly. "Sir, I see I have taken you by surprise. I have upset and annoyed you, too. May we discuss this matter again tomorrow?"

Ellis shrugged. "There is nothing more to say."

"Sir, I—"

"My dear child – for so you are, and will ever be to me – don't persist in this folly! If you do, you will destroy your own happiness forever. You will also break your parents' hearts."

"I don't see how!" Jane met his eyes. "Sir, Owen has always behaved honourably by me – and, in spite of what has passed between you and me today, I still love him dearly. I believe he loves me. I hope you will not be so cruel or unjust as to hate him merely for loving where he cannot help it?"

"I hope I should never be unjust to anyone, for any reason at all."

"You will not send him away, or look unkindly on him?"

"Provided you and he accept that there can be no wedding – that your relationship can never be any but that of cousin and cousin – Owen is welcome in my house."

"May I go now?"

"You may."

Owen found Jane in the rose garden, sitting quietly in the dusk. There were no tears, but her pale face, and the way she clung to him, told him the news was bad.

"Was he very angry?" he asked.

"Yes."

"He forbade you to think of me?"

"He forbids us to think of marriage." Jane bit her lip. "But all the same, I shall defy him. If I must."

"You mean to run away?"

"Yes, if it comes to that."

"You mustn't." Owen hugged her. "My dearest Jane, consider. If you run away, he will hate you. He'll cut you off without a penny, and never see you again. But my darling, we're both young. I have no fortune, it's true – but I mean to make one."

"How?"

"I shall take up his offer of an education. I shall study hard, and at university I'll make friends who can be of service to me. So – I shall cultivate the right people. Learn to move well in polite society, and become a great physician, too. Give me five years, that's all. You'll see what I can do!"

"Shall I?" Jane looked at him. "You're so sanguine. But do you think—"

"In a way, your father is right. He thinks of your

happiness. If I had a daughter, on whom I meant to bestow twenty thousand pounds, and I discovered a penniless fellow was paying her particular attention, *I* should forbid her to think of him."

"But you're his nephew! He has known you since you were seven years old! He has no reason to think you anything but good and honourable."

"But I am still poor."

"He could do something for you, if he chose."

"He intends to support me through university. You said so yourself."

"That's generous of him." Jane sniffed. "His rents alone are six or seven thousand a quarter. When he married my mother, she brought him factories in Birmingham, a flourishing ironworks, and an income of at least ten thousand a year. Yet he will do hardly anything for you. All because of some silly argument between him and your mother, which he won't even discuss. He always did bear grudges. Owen?"

"Yes?"

"Do you know why they quarrelled? Did your mother ever speak of it?"

"No, never. I did not know of the Darrows' existence until my father died, and Bethan told me I was to come here. Why not ask your mother about it?"

"My father expressly forbade me to ask my mother anything. So it appears we must remain in ignorance." Jane stood up. "I shall not take supper tonight."

"Would it be wise for me to stay away?"

"If you are hungry, go and eat." Jane began to walk towards the house. "Even *my* father could not be so mean as to deny you the right to approach his table. Even he will hardly suspect you of mercenary designs on his potted meat or cold souse," she said bitterly.

It was as if someone had died. Maria and Rayner sympathised with the lovers but, too afraid of their father's wrath to take their side in public, they did their commiserating behind closed doors.

The servants knew everything. They all liked Owen and would have been delighted to hear a wedding had been arranged, but for the moment they crept about warily, biding their time and hoping for the best – whatever that might turn out to be.

The only person in the household who was not in the least bit afraid of the squire was his wife. Valiantly, Rebecca tried to pretend nothing was amiss. "My dear Owen," she would say as he came into dinner, "pray be seated. Will you have some soup?" Then she would motion to the butler to serve the guest first. Simmons would nod to the footman, who would then glance nervously at the squire.

But Ellis would say nothing at all.

Jane hated mealtimes now. The carefree chat of previous dinners and breakfasts and afternoon teas had been replaced by frosty silences and awkward pauses, which were harmful to the digestion and gave one heartburn in earnest.

"I have decided to go back to Cardiff," announced Owen, as he and Jane strolled by the lake one morning, about a week after their tumultuous declaration of intent.

Jane sighed. "So eager to leave me?" she whispered, miserably.

"I'm not eager to leave *you*." Owen took her hand. "But it is hardly pleasant for *me*, to be in a house where my presence is only tolerated, and that grudgingly."

"You're loved by most of us! There's only one person who merely tolerates you."

"That person happens to be master here."

"So you're running away."

"I am returning to Cardiff to sort out my affairs. To arrange my attendance at university, where I mean to begin this October."

"My father is still to pay your fees?"

"Yes. He called me into his study to tell me so. He was cool towards me. But he was neither insulting nor unkind."

"Oh, Owen! What shall we do?"

"We must wait." Owen clasped both her hands in his. "I make no demands of you," he said. "I extract no promises. You are a beautiful, eligible young woman who, while she remains single, is certain to be courted. If you meet a man of fortune whom you like, and if you feel able to return his regard, I shall understand.

"For my part, I shall always love you. To prove this, I shall work hard, remain constant – and try to show your father that, although I have no fortune and no special talents to recommend me, I have done my best to deserve you."

"I'll never love anyone else." Jane smiled up at him. "Never."

Owen kissed her. "Then all we need to learn is patience," he said. "Come. Let's go back."

They saw the servant running towards them. "Mr Morgan?" Out of breath, the footman bowed. "Miss Darrow, I beg your pardon – but his honour requires Mr Morgan's presence in his study. At once."

Chapter Six

The visitor stood in Ellis Darrow's study, gazing out of the window and across the park. As Owen entered the room, he turned, and Owen saw a well-made, middle-aged gentleman with skin burnt the colour of fine mahogany, and a patch over one eye which gave him the air of a pirate king.

"My dear Owen." Today, to his nephew's great surprise, Ellis was almost friendly. "Thank you for coming so promptly. Here is a gentleman whom I particularly wish you to meet."

The squire glanced towards his guest. "Mr Hickson, this is Owen Morgan. The young man of whom I was speaking just now."

"Mr Hickson?" Owen held out his hand.

"Mr Morgan." Firmly, George Hickson shook it.

Then they both looked at Ellis Darrow, who sat down and motioned to his guests to be seated too. "I see I must explain," he began. "Well, then. Here it is. My dear Owen, Mr Hickson here was a particular friend of your mother's first husband, Mr Alex Lowell."

"Alex and I were at school together. We went on the Grand Tour together, too." George Hickson rubbed his one remaining eye. "He was a good fellow! A splendid fellow, in fact. The best friend, the dearest—"

"Quite so." Cutting short this fulsome praise of Alex Lowell, Ellis met Owen's interested gaze. "Were you aware that your mother married twice?" he enquired.

"I knew my father was her second husband, certainly."

Owen shrugged. "But she never spoke to me or anyone else of her first."

"Then how did you know of his existence?"

"He was buried in the local churchyard. My father's herdsman was also sexton there, and it was one of his duties to tend Mr Lowell's grave."

"I see." Ellis cleared his throat. "Well, now. Mr Hickson here is an East India Company merchant. These days, he is a district magistrate, too. But some years ago, in his capacity as broker-in-ordinary to the Company, he was charged to manage some investments for Mr Lowell.

"Unfortunately, there was some misappropriation of funds, and Mr Lowell lost a great deal of money."

"Not because of *me*, sir!" George Hickson's rheumy eye blazed. "Sir, you must not allow this young fellow to believe *I* was responsible for—"

"No, indeed." Ellis looked down at his desk, then up at his nephew again. "Well then, Owen. To cut a tediously involved and complicated story short, here is what happened. More or less.

"Mr Lowell was a gentleman's son and heir, who on his father's demise inherited a large estate here in Warwickshire. A very wealthy man, he invested a substantial part of his fortune in East India Company stock.

"In the prime instance, Mr Lowell's investments were managed by Mr Hickson here, initially through an agent in London, but then in Calcutta by Mr Hickson himself. They brought Mr Lowell a very handsome return. Then, however, Mr Hickson's superiors decided he might benefit from a change of situation and air, so he was sent up country to direct the affairs of a tea plantation, in the Himalayan hills.

"His responsibilities in Calcutta devolved on a Mr Jarvis, to whom Mr Hickson also entrusted Mr Lowell's affairs."

"But Greville Jarvis was a blackguard!" Mr Hickson ground his teeth in rage. "A scoundrel of the first order! A thieving, rascally—"

"Yes, indeed." Ellis flashed Mr Hickson a glance which Owen understood meant the squire would tolerate no more interruptions. He hoped Mr Hickson understood it, too.

"Mr Jarvis was a clever villain," continued the master of Easton Hall. "He feathered his nest at the expense of others, it's true – but for many years, he left no trace whatsoever of his own deceit. All the same, he ruined Alex Lowell.

"Some years later, Mr Lowell and I managed to recover some little part of the original investment, but the bulk of it remained lost. I believed for ever. That is, until Mr Hickson came to call on me today.

"For, when he finally returned to Calcutta and observed the conduct of Mr Jarvis, Mr Hickson became suspicious. He was instrumental in initiating the enquiry into that person's affairs. In doing so, he recovered a large percentage of Mr Lowell's cash."

"But, in the meantime, my friend was ruined!" George Hickson looked ready to burst into tears. "My dear Mr Morgan, only picture the scene! In their despair, Alex and your poor mother left Warwickshire. They retired to the decent obscurity of South Wales. There, Alex Lowell died – of a broken heart!"

"But my mother survived their misfortunes," observed Owen. "*She* married again."

"Poor lady." Dolefully, Mr Hickson sniffed. "What else could she do?"

Politely, Ellis coughed. "Owen," he began again, "Mr Hickson returned to Warwickshire in the hope he would be reunited with Mr Lowell, and be able to tell him face to face that his fortune is restored. But, since Mr Lowell is dead and left no direct heirs, this fortune will probably pass to a distant cousin, presently living in Leicestershire.

"Nowadays, however, Mr Hickson occupies a very senior position in the government of Bengal. His official purpose in coming to England is to recruit likely candidates for service in the East India Company. My dear Owen, would you be interested in going out to the East?"

"To the East?" Owen thought for a moment, certain of his need to process this rush of unexpected information both swiftly and efficiently. He dredged his memory for what he knew of India – which, he had to admit, wasn't very much.

But he liked the idea of travel and adventure. Liked it very much, in fact. He needed to make his fortune. This offer suddenly seemed a heaven-sent opportunity to do exactly that. "I think I would be very interested indeed," he replied.

Jane did not share Owen's enthusiasm at all. "He means to get rid of you!" she interrupted tearfully, as Owen was right in the middle of telling her just how rich and successful he was going to be. "He will pay your passage out East without a single murmur of complaint. But only because he intends you to die of malaria when you get there!"

"Nonsense." The more Owen thought about Mr Hickson's proposals, the more he liked the sound of them. While he did not intend to emulate the devious Mr Jarvis and go in for wholescale rapine and corruption, from talking at length with Mr Hickson he understood that an ambitious, intelligent young man with a flexible attitude to life could do very well in the East. "I'll make my fortune," he declared. "I'll become as rich as Croesus himself, you'll see. Then I'll come home and marry you. If you'll wait for me?"

"I'll wait." Miserably, Jane shook her head. "You need have no fears on that score."

"Oh, darling!" Owen took her in his arms. "Don't look so sad!"

"I must be sad." Jane began to cry again. "The person I love best in the world wishes to leave me."

"I shall hate to leave you! But don't you see what a wonderful opportunity this will be for me?"

"So what has become of your ambition to be a famous physician, consulted by the wealthy and courted by the great?"

"I must set that scheme aside," said Owen. "This new project offers far more scope for advancement, for making my fortune, than becoming a doctor could ever do. Darling, I'm young, I'm healthy, I have a certain native wit. I must succeed!"

"Will you write to me?"

"Of course I shall! Every single day. I shall keep a journal, which I'll copy out for you and send you piecemeal. You shall know everything – the hour at which I wake, what I do all day, when I lie down again to sleep."

"I shall do the same." Taking his face between her hands, Jane looked deep into Owen's eyes. "But this will not be a correspondence between children. You must open your heart and mind to me, and I shall do likewise for you."

"But what if your father—"

"This will be no concern of his. Our letters will be private. I shall speak to my mother, and convince her that now I am of age, it would not be at all proper for her to overlook my correspondence. I'm sure my father will abide by her decision."

"My aunt has always been my friend."

"She loves you. As do my brother and sister. Whatever my father may think or say, you must never doubt that the rest of us love you dearly, and will always wish you well."

Maria and Rayner did not – could not – love Owen as much as Jane did, but they were certainly very fond of him. When George Hickson's proposals became known to them, they were delighted. Rayner offered his sincere best wishes, and Maria laughed with pleasure at the prospect of Owen growing rich.

"Although you will not be nearly so handsome when

you come home," she cautioned him, as she glanced towards the leathery old gentleman who was their father's favoured guest, and who enlivened their dinner time conversation considerably with his travellers' tales of the distant East. "My dear Owen, pray keep out of the noonday sun! I hate to think of your beautiful complexion becoming so weathered and red that Jane will faint with horror when she sees you again."

"I shall wear a broad-brimmed hat at all times," promised Owen, solemnly.

That night, as the family took supper together, Mr Hickson was persuaded to explain the mysteries of suttee, the horrible heathen practice whereby widows were obliged to immolate themselves on their late husbands' funeral pyres. "It's a most barbarous custom," concluded Mr Hickson, as he finished his account of the Maharajah of Mirzagarh's funeral, which he himself had personally attended, as the representative of the Governor of Bengal.

"Barbarous," agreed Ellis.

"Absolutely," murmured Maria, shuddering gracefully.

But Jane merely shrugged. Burning to death must be a terrible way to die – but a voluntary suttee no doubt possessed a certain tragic nobility? Surely, a sacrifice like that must inspire an almost religious awe? If a woman had truly loved her husband, moreover, was it not natural that she should wish to be at his side, even at the gates of death and hell?

"But nine out of ten women are forced into it," Mr Hickson was saying now, as if he had read her mind. Lugubriously, he sighed. "Poor creatures, they have a dreadful choice. Death in the flames, with honour. Or a despised and dishonourable widowhood, during which they are treated like dogs and universally reviled. India is no place to be a woman."

"But must her lot always be a cruel one?" enquired Rebecca earnestly.

"Yes indeed ma'am, it must." Mr Hickson grimaced.

"Even as infants, little girls are married off to hideous old men, who proceed to get them with child before they're barely out of childhood themselves. If they bear daughters, it's ten to one those unfortunate babes will be taken from them, and destroyed."

"But that's murder! That's—"

"It's the custom of the country, ma'am. Girls are a drain on the family resources, you see. They must be kept in purdah, which is an expensive business all round, and when they grow up, they need to be found husbands. They must have dowries, too.

"To most families, daughters are a curse, not a blessing. Every woman in India, from the maharajah's bride to the lowest sweeper's wife or village tyrant's concubine, prays night and day to bear sons."

But Ellis was no village tyrant. Neither his intense dislike of Owen, nor the dismay he'd felt at his daughter's recent, most unwelcome revelations, had resulted in the issue of unreasonable edicts, in his forbidding Jane and her cousin to speak to one another in private, or even to meet alone. Indeed, now he had made himself plain, the squire counted on their obedience to his command. Jane knew her duty as a daughter, he was sure of that.

As for being in love with Owen – although he did not doubt her sincerity, Ellis was confident that if the boy went out to India for a few years, his place in his daughter's heart would be usurped. It must be!

After supper, the family group broke up. Jane and Owen disappeared, to take their favourite walk along the north shore of the lake. "Would you burn yourself alive for me?" asked Owen idly, as he skimmed a pebble across the broad expanse of water, and watched it skip and jump across the mirror of glassy grey.

"Yes. I think perhaps I would." But then, in spite of herself, Jane shuddered. "Although I'm sure I should be horribly afraid, and disgrace myself excessively, by screaming and crying like a child."

“That would be perfectly understandable.” Owen frowned. “I shall be most interested to observe this system in operation,” he said.

“You may observe part of it here,” muttered Jane. “At Easton Hall itself.”

“Where young women are of no account, you mean? Where they are instead mere chattels, to be used as bargaining counters, or disposed of at a father’s whim?”

“Exactly.”

“That’s nonsense. You are your father’s favourite child. Far from wishing to dispose of his elder daughter, he wants only the best for *you.*”

“Does he?” Jane shrugged. “He thinks I’m a fool,” she murmured. “That you’re a mercenary rogue, after my dowry and whatever else you can get. Why else, he reasons, should any man want me? How great would be *my* value, if there were not so many sacks of gold stacked up behind me, as an inducement to his lust?”

“Oh, Jane!” Owen shook his head at her. He took her hands in his. “When I return from India, I shall be so rich that you will not need a dowry! I shall also be of age. So, if your father still forbids us to marry, we’ll go to church anyway.”

Rayner would be sad to see Owen leave. He was even a little jealous, for while Owen would sail the high seas and see the splendours of the Orient for himself, Rayner was obliged to moulder in a dreary Oxford college. Or sojourn in the damp green fields of Warwickshire, learning how to manage the Easton estate – which would one day be hung like a great, heavy millstone around his own unwilling neck.

Foolishly, he had missed *his* opportunity to travel – and now the war with France seemed likely to drag on forever, he despaired of even visiting mainland Europe, let alone seeing the wonders of the East.

Owen left Easton Hall early on Tuesday morning. He would go to Cardiff to take leave of his uncle, then travel on to Avonmouth to catch the packet boat round the coast. "I *shall* write to you," he promised Jane, as they took a private and highly emotional leave of each other in a secluded part of the rose garden. "I *shall* come home."

"I shall be waiting." Jane blinked back her tears. She did not want his last memory to be of his sweetheart crying. "Dear Owen, take care. Remember, you are not your own man now. You belong to me."

After Owen had gone, Jane did not burn herself alive, but she certainly made a sort of suttee of herself. She accepted no invitations to dances, balls or routs, nor would she give any afternoon parties or musical evenings for her many friends. She became, in effect, a recluse.

Charles Harding turned his attention to Maria. After some weeks of dogged persistence and unfailing good humour on his part, he managed to convince her that she was by no means second best. Only his parents' outdated notions of what was due to seniority had persuaded him to pay diffident court to Jane.

He liked Jane very much, he said. He respected her, too. But it was pretty, elfin Maria whose charms had ensnared him. She, and she alone, whose beauty and goodness had pierced his heart.

"My dearest Maria," he concluded, as he gazed earnestly into her clear, blue eyes, and wondered how much her father would give her for pin money, "will you make me the happiest of men? In short, will you marry me?"

Mr Frederick Harding was a hard-headed farmer. He had no time at all for modern, romantic nonsense such as this. But, seeing the elder daughter had run mad and was not to go to market after all, Charles's father told his son to pull on his top-boots, climb into the sty, and try to get the other sow by the ear. While he himself approached Ellis Darrow on the subject of his second child.

Mr Harding and the Squire of Easton were both good businessmen who liked to feel they'd got a bargain. They also delighted in all the haggling, feinting and palaver which preceded any deal. After the requisite amount of prevarication and discussion, therefore, a bargain was struck. The Hardings got Maria and all her personal property – gowns, jewellery and other feminine bits and pieces – plus fifteen thousand pounds, most of it in Government stock. In addition to this, the squire undertook to provide his daughter with pocket money for the next ten years, or as long as he lived, whichever was the shorter period.

On the day the wedding was celebrated, Owen's first letter to Jane finally arrived. From then on, great fat parcels came regularly. They smelled of spices and indigo, of dust and heat, and warm, baked earth. Their contents were more precious to her than anything else, either on land or sea.

"Well?" demanded Rebecca, as Jane folded her latest letter and lay back on the sofa, smiling a beatific, almost unearthly smile. "How does he get on? What does he say?"

"He is well. He sends us his love." Surreptitiously, Jane wiped away a tear. "He says he misses me."

Jane read her letters again and again, learning them by heart. She lived for their coming, and when a parcel arrived for her, she would be cheerful and talkative for several days. But then, she would relapse into a world of her own, not going out, not seeing anybody or doing anything but peruse her private papers over and over, and write whole volumes in reply.

The Darrows' neighbours shook their heads and sighed. Who would have thought that pretty, charming Jane Darrow would turn into a species of anchorite? Become a mad, melancholy, mooning thing?

Six long years went by.

Chapter Seven

George Hickson was nearing the end of his active life. Old and tired, his constitution grievously weakened by the recurrent fevers, agues and debilitating night sweats which plagued most Europeans in this dreadful climate, his mind was weary, too.

These days, he took no pleasure in his official duties. None at all. Promoted to senior district magistrate of a large province, he was constantly called on not only to give judgement, but also to hear appeals, something he had once enjoyed, as he cut through the cats' cradles and tangles of Oriental non-logic with his sword of Anglo-Saxon common sense.

Just recently, however, listening to a native or whole family of natives loudly rehearsing their grievances – sitting, in fact, through the interminable rigmarole of an Indian court case – merely gave him a headache.

So, he meant to retire. To leave all this to his deputy. As he thought about it, he smiled. Taking Owen Morgan under his wing had been the best thing he ever did. Childless – for after being widowed twice, he decided he could not bear the idea of bringing yet another Englishwoman to this hostile land, to pine and die in the heat and dust, and had solaced himself instead with women from the bazaar – he felt that in Owen, he had at last found a son.

He would have liked a grandson, too. "What do you say to asking the Waterstones over tomorrow evening?" he suggested craftily, as he and Owen sat on their verandah one sultry dusk, drinking their first sundowners, and watching the sky dissolve into a glorious pageant of purple, gold and scarlet fire. "Nazim Shah has mended the oven, so he could concoct one of his special dinners. Afterwards, I'm sure the ladies would be happy to sit out on our verandah here. Delighting in the sunset, and watching the officers play polo on the maidan."

"Well, Miss Julia Waterstone would certainly like that." Owen grinned. "She's had her eye on Major O'Sullivan this past twelvemonth or more."

"She's also had her eye on you." George Hickson shook his head. "Why don't you like her? She's a fine figure of a woman. Only twenty eight or nine. Not *that* much older than you."

"No, but—"

"Don't tell me. I know what you're about to say. You're already spoken for. Yes?"

"Yes."

"Damned shame." George Hickson sighed. While staying in Warwickshire, he hadn't even realised that Owen and Jane were especially fond of one other, let alone as good as engaged. But later, observing that great, fat packages of letters were regularly exchanged between the two continents, and that whenever he received a packet, Owen was particularly cheerful for several days, he had asked if there were a lady in the case.

Owen had simply replied that the letters were from his cousin Jane, whom he hoped one day to marry. If her father would allow it. It wasn't until several years had gone by, however, that he told George Hickson the full story.

"The old fellow may come round." This evening, George was in a sentimental, mellow mood. "After all, you've done very well for yourself out here. You may not be as rich as a rajah – but you must be worth at least ten, fifteen thousand pounds nowadays."

Owen agreed that indeed he was. For, on his arrival in India, he had applied himself not only to the study of law, but also to the arcane sciences of bribery and corruption. He had realised, without having to be told in so many words, that in the East nothing could be done without recourse to *baksheesh*.

But although he readily accepted presents and tips, for the past six years Owen Morgan had – unlike some of his fellow Europeans – trodden the difficult path of the foreign overlord with honour and integrity. In doing this, he had astonished many of his peers.

Even more astonishingly, he had kept away from native women, too.

"That daughter of the padre fellow, eh? She and her Mama arrived here last Wednesday, from up country. She's a pretty little thing, wouldn't you say?"

A week later, George was trying again. "Why don't you ask her if she and her parents would like to go with us and the Forresters in a party, to see the Blue Fort at Andrapur?"

"You ask her, if you wish." His quill pen poised, Owen was searching through the great volume of paperwork which permanently littered his desk. "I'm afraid I haven't any time to spare."

"Why? What are you doing?"

"Preparing the prosecution's case for that assault and battery business. If the clerks are to have the papers on Tuesday, I need to get my submission done by the weekend."

"But what's the tearing hurry?"

"When I arrived here, I inherited a mess. I wish to leave everything in order for *my* successor." Owen leaned back in his chair. "George, I've decided to go home."

"I see." Lugubriously, George Hickson shook his grizzled head. "That makes two of us."

"You're not thinking of retiring?"

"Yes. But not to England. It's too damned chilly for old bones like mine." George grinned. "I've bought a little place up in the hills, and I shall go there. I'll take a couple of creatures from the bazaar – nice clean girls, you understand, but orphans or outcasts or some such – and live out my days in peace and solitude."

"In your own personal Shangri-La?"

"Precisely." The district magistrate's remaining eye grew misty. "I'll do a little fishing," he continued. "A little writing, maybe. A little walking here and there. All that sort of thing."

"It sounds delightful."

"*I* think so." Again, George Hickson grinned. "So what about you? Shall you go back to *Belait*? To renew your siege to Miss Darrow and her cruel Papa?"

"I intend to write to my uncle," agreed Owen. "To ask if I may visit the family in Warwickshire." Thoughtfully, he tapped a pencil against his teeth. "George, would you perhaps write to him, too? He has a high opinion of your good sense. So, if you could persuade him that I have worked hard and waited patiently, he might be disposed to reconsider—"

"He damned well ought to be!" George grimaced. "Apart from the odd lapse now and then, you've lived like a monk out here. A man would think you had taken holy orders. If ever constancy deserved recognition, then you should have it, and be rewarded with Miss Darrow's pretty hand."

The voyage home, on a heavily-armed British warship carrying sixteen guns in addition to a full complement of civilian passengers, seemed interminable. It was hazardous and terrifying, too. A fleet of French privateers stalked the solitary British vessel all the way to the Maldives. Then, storms in the Indian Ocean rent the rigging and tore the sails to tattered shreds. A series of squalls off the Cape Verde Islands made Owen vow that if, by the grace of God, he made it to *Belait*, he would never venture from dry land again.

A violent gale in the Bay of Biscay almost succeeded in sending the gallant little frigate to the bottom of the sea. But finally, as the Captain had promised it would, the ship rounded the coast of Brittany and entered the English Channel.

"Come, sir. Will you have a sight of Albion?" A jaunty young midshipman, who had just come off the watch, offered Owen the use of his telescope.

Owen accepted the offer readily. Now, spying green hills and rolling pastureland, he found he wanted to weep. For at last, at long last, he was home.

England was so beautiful! So clean and wholesome. So impossibly, gloriously green. As the coach sped on its way through the southern counties, as acres of pasture and meadow, woodland and common and heath were spread out before him, dozing in the soft summer sunshine, Owen knew he had done the right thing. He had been exiled long enough, and had earned the right to come home.

Very early one Thursday morning, he crossed the county boundary into Warwickshire. An hour or two later, as he stepped from his hired chaise, and gazed up at the front elevation of Easton Hall, the tears came into his eyes once again. He must have been mad! How else could he have even considered leaving this lovely place, with its dear inhabitants, its beloved woods and fields and groves, and so many happy memories? But then he recalled that one inhabitant was not so dear.

He sighed. But then he squared his shoulders resolutely. He had worked hard, striven faithfully, and if his uncle was still disposed to dislike him, there was nothing more he could do.

"Owen? Great God in heaven! It *is* you!" The small, fair-haired woman who came running down the grey stone steps of the manor house was beside herself with delight. Her dressing gown flapping undone, she threw herself into her cousin's arms. Beaming up at him, she hugged him, then kissed him, and then she hugged him again.

"Maria?" Blinking and completely bemused, Owen gazed down at her. "It *is* Maria, isn't it?"

"Yes, of course! But isn't this shocking?" Still smiling, Maria shook her head. "Here am I, a respectable married woman, embracing a man who is not her husband, and in full view of the servants, too. I'm not even dressed!

"But today, you see, I woke at dawn. When I heard the chaise, I thought my imagination must be playing tricks on me. All the same, I glanced out of the window – and there you were, looming out of the morning mist!"

"It *is* rather early," Owen agreed. Coming to himself, he took his cousin's hands in his, then stepped back to look at her. "Well, now. Are you and Mr Harding here on a visit?"

"Not exactly. I'm staying here with the girls, while Charles is away on business."

"But is the rest of the family at home?"

"Oh, certainly. They're all still abed, of course. But if I go and tell them you've arrived, they'll be up betimes. Have no fear of that!"

Disengaging her hands, Maria linked her arm through her cousin's. "Dear Owen!" she cried, dashing away a tear. "It's *wonderful* to see you here again! Come. Let's go inside."

So now Maria, these days Mrs Charles Harding and the mother of two fair-haired, hazel-eyed daughters, led the weary traveller into the entrance hall of the manor house.

There, yawning footmen were shrugging on their jackets, house dogs stretched and gave themselves rousing shakes, and bleary-eyed maidservants were just beginning to go about their daily tasks. As Mrs Harding led a good-looking, smartly-dressed young gentleman through the vestibule, then up the stairs, dogs and servants stared, in horrified disbelief. What could the young lady be thinking of? More to the point, what would the squire say?

"But that's Mr Morgan," murmured a footman, who was carrying a tray of silver from the butler's pantry to the breakfast room. "It's young Mr Morgan, come home again!"

"Owen Morgan?" demanded the housekeeper. "Little Owen Morgan, who made his addresses to Miss Jane?"

"The very same. But grown-up, and made his fortune by the look of it!" exclaimed the cook, delightedly.

By seven o'clock, the whole house was wide awake, and buzzing with the good news.

Owen was welcomed with open arms. Rebecca wept, then beamed, then wept again, embracing and kissing him like a mother all the while. Even Ellis greeted him cordially, and shook him by the hand. But Jane merely hugged him in silence, her heart too full to speak.

Rayner was not there to greet his cousin, for he was making a tour of Scotland in the company of his wife and parents-in-law. Two years ago, he had finally married Isabel Graham, the 'little freckled thing' who had grown up to become the undisputed belle of Warwickshire.

But Owen hardly so much as marked their absence, for he had eyes only for Jane. "I was so afraid you would pine," he said, as they walked in the rose garden, hand in hand, their fingers entwined. "I worried lest you might grow thin and pale. But these days, you're even lovelier than you were before."

Jane blushed, then laughed. "There's rather more of me to *be* lovely," she admitted, somewhat ruefully. "I am too fond of sweets and pastries for my own good."

"You're beautiful." Owen smiled at her. Seeing her look so pretty, observing that her complexion glowed and that her eyes were bright, did his heart good.

Everybody noticed the change in him. Everybody saw it, and remarked that Owen himself looked older, much older in fact. There were fine lines on his forehead now. The crow's feet were spreading inexorably about his large, dark eyes. But maturity suited him. It gave some distinction to his features. Rubbing away the childish roundness of his cheeks, it revealed the fine bone structure he'd inherited from his mother. Nowadays, he looked even more like the squire.

* * *

"My aunt looks tired tonight," observed Owen, as he and Jane took a last stroll before retiring to bed.

"I'm afraid Mama has not been well of late." Jane sighed. "My father has consulted physician after physician. All have examined her, of course, and talked with her at length. But none can identify a particular ailment or complaint.

"Their consensus seems to be, that her fatigue is the result of a constitutional weakness. Something which needs no treatment but rest and freedom from care."

"That's what medical men always say, when they cannot tell what causes those symptoms the patient has described." Sighing too, Owen shook his head. "She seems cheerful enough, however. In herself."

"She's delighted to see you." Jane hugged him round the waist. "As are we all, of course. Even my father welcomes you home again."

The following morning, after breakfast, Jane and Owen were the last to leave the table. As they dawdled over a third or fourth cup of chocolate, they were joined by Maria again.

"Those wretched children!" she complained, plumping herself down in her father's chair. "I have no patience with them! They defy their nursemaids, are disrespectful towards their governess – and are so saucy with *me* that I positively itch to smack them, hard!

"But here is the conundrum. When they are with their Aunt Jane, they are as meek as little mice. As good as even the purest gold."

"Shall I go up and see them?" offered Jane. "They may air their grievances then. Though their demands are never so unreasonable, we will doubtless reach an amicable compromise."

"Oh, leave them to howl." Crossly, Maria sucked her teeth. "Let Betty and Martha sort them out. As they are paid to do! Have you asked him yet?" she demanded, meeting Owen's eyes.

“I’m sorry?” murmured Owen, smiling.

“Don’t be deliberately obtuse.” Unappeased, Maria glared back at him. “He can hardly persist in his obstinacy now. At any rate, he cannot pretend you are just a child, who does not know his own mind. Or a heartless fortune-hunter, who seeks to dazzle and entrap a young and foolish girl.”

“Maybe not.” Owen shrugged. “I shall not speak to the squire yet,” he said. “You see, I mean to leave Warwickshire before the end of next week.”

“What do you intend to do then?”

“I’d thought of going down to Bristol.” Taking Jane’s hand in his, Owen held it. “These days, you see, I understand commerce. I can afford to buy shares in cargoes to China, the Indies, the Americas. In due course, I might even become a shipper myself.” Owen glanced back towards Jane. “Would your father let you become a merchant’s wife?”

“I don’t see why not. *He* married a manufacturer’s grand-daughter. He has interests in trade on his own account.” Jane herself shrugged now. “He’s done very well out of the French wars and the resulting blockades. Although he’d sooner die than admit it, to be sure.”

“Ask him today,” urged Maria. She shook her cousin by the wrist. “Dear Owen, why lose any more time? He spoke to you very pleasantly this morning. These days, he is almost disposed to like you. Strike while the iron is hot, I say.”

“Should I?” Considering, Owen bit his lip. “My dearest Jane, what do you think?”

“I think my sister is right,” Jane replied.

“Very well.” Owen stood up. “If you both deem it advisable, I’ll seek an interview. I’ll ask him today.”

Ellis invited his nephew to be seated, which was in itself a very good start. So, without any prevarication, Owen grasped the nettle. He asked for Jane’s hand in marriage.

Ellis pursed his lips. For a long moment, he considered. Finally, he spoke. "If you mean to support a wife," he began, "you will need a sufficient income. What assets do you possess?"

Quickly, Owen explained. "I am not a *rich* man," he concluded, modestly. "But I am at least well-circumstanced. I could maintain a wife and family in perfect comfort and respectability."

"How?"

"I have invested in a wide range of securities, and from these I derive a good income. It is more than sufficient for my own needs, so – so I—"

"Go on."

"Well, sir." Owen met his uncle's unwavering gaze. "I ask for nothing of yours!" he cried. "All I want is Jane as my wife! My cousin's fortune is *not* an issue here, so if you are disposed to withhold—"

"But it would not be an encumbrance, either." Heavily, Ellis sighed. "Your aunt thinks most highly of you," he muttered, as if to himself.

"I love, esteem and admire her," rejoined Owen. "She has been a second mother to me."

"While to her, you are as dear as her own son."

Ellis stood up. "Very well," he said. "Would you ask Jane to come and see me?"

"You mean, you give your consent?"

"I wish to speak to my child." Ellis opened the door of his study, then ushered his nephew out. "I need not call a servant," he added, drily. "You doubtless know exactly where my daughter is to be found."

Jane was beside herself with happiness. Flinging herself into Owen's embrace, she laughed, cried, laughed again, then burst into a flood of tears.

By the time Owen had at last kissed all these away, she was a little calmer. "He says we must wait for Rayner and Isabel to come home," she said. "Well, of course we must. Rayner will be your best man."

"Shall you ask Isabel to be matron of honour?"

"Yes. She and Maria will share that duty, while Catherine and Louise Harding will be bridesmaids."

"I see. So this is to be a rather grand affair?"

"Of course. My father can afford to entertain the whole county. So he shall." Jane hugged Owen again. "How everyone will stare!" she cried. "They had me marked down for an old maid, you see. Owen?"

"Yes?"

"I'm almost thirty." Sitting down on a bench, Jane bit her lip. "Is that too old to begin a family?"

"Of course not! My mother was at least that when I was born. You shall have two, four – six children!"

"Three boys and three girls."

"Maybe."

"I can't believe it's all going to happen." Jane began to sniff again. "We've suffered so much," she wept. "There've been so many years of waiting, waiting, waiting! Owen, did you keep my journals?"

"Of course I did. I kept them all. I preserved them in amber, every single page."

"Did you read them over and over?"

"Yes, then over and over again. I know them by heart."

"Did you always mean to return?"

"Of course! Every evening, when I looked towards the setting sun, my thoughts turned to you. Now, I said to myself, she is drinking her chocolate and planning her day. Soon, she will be up and dressed, ready to pay a morning call. Oh, my darling! You can't imagine how much I longed for you!"

"I thought of you, too. Constantly."

"I know you did. Jane, has your father heard from Rayner today?"

"Yes, he has. They expect to be in Warwick on Friday evening."

"So the banns can be published, and the wedding could be about a month from now." Owen hugged his fiancée to his breast. "Well, Mrs Morgan? How do you like the sound of your new name?"

"Jane Morgan. It sounds plain but honest." Ruefully, Jane shook her head. "Will you be ashamed to go to church with such an old woman?"

"What old woman? You look hardly twenty five."

"Nonsense. You say that to flatter me. *You* look at me with the eyes of love. But the rest of the county does not."

"I don't care what the rest of the county does, thinks or says. The opinions of a pack of booby squires do not interest me in the least."

"Just as well." Jane became serious now. "I told my mother we would sit with her for a while this evening," she said.

"How is she today?" asked Owen.

"A little better, I think. Less feeble, less tired. There's one blessing, anyway – her body may be weak indeed, but her mind is active as it's ever been." Standing up, Jane began to walk towards the house. "She means to invite your uncle to stay."

"That's kind of her."

"Then, after we are married, my father intends to take her for a holiday. To the Lake District, then to the coast. The latest physician recommends it, she looks forward to it, so I'm sure it will do her good."

"I do hope you're right."

"You don't think it's a good idea?"

"I don't know." Owen shrugged. "Since my return, I have observed your mother narrowly. From these observations, and from what you have said, I have deduced that the problem must be her heart."

"It is failing, you mean?"

"I hope not. But it's certainly weak. Undue exertion, a sudden shock, a fright – any of those might prove fatal to one in my aunt's delicate state."

"Have you spoken to my father about this?"

"Of course not. He retains the services of eminent physicians. He would despise the opinions of a half-trained apothecary." Owen shrugged. "In any case, I may well be wrong."

"All the same—"

"As her physicians say, my aunt needs rest, a wholesome diet, and freedom from anxiety. If she is careful, she could live for many years yet."

"You're sure of that?"

"Perfectly." Encouragingly, Owen smiled. "We can play our parts, can we not? In fact, my dear Jane, Maria was telling me only this morning that *you* have relieved my aunt of her cares with regard to the factories in Birmingham. You now oversee the management of those yourself. Is that not correct?"

"My father and I direct their affairs between us."

"So you have taken a great burden from your mother's shoulders, and educated yourself in the process. You will be of inestimable value as the wife and partner of the most ambitious merchant adventurer Bristol has ever seen, will you not?"

"I hope to be." Jane shrugged. "Poor Mama," she whispered, wretchedly.

"Don't fret about this." Owen took Jane's hand in his. He would not let her be sad! For he had come home to be happy. Not to mourn his aunt.

Chapter Eight

The holiday in Scotland had not been a success. The weather, of course, had been awful. The roads, such as they were, turned to mire in the rain, bogging down both carriages and baggage wagons up to their axles, and causing the drivers to swear like military men. The inns were variously grubby, dirty or downright filthy, and the service therein universally execrable. Rayner and Isabel arrived home tired, cross and irritable, at odds with everyone and everything.

Although he tried, Rayner could not like his father-in-law, whom he considered a dull, colonial bore. Mr Graham loved to shoot, but Rayner hated all field sports, and he had bitterly resented being obliged to spend whole days trudging damply through the Scottish mists, looking for animals to kill. Isabel found her mother's company equally tedious.

As for the young couple, they were no longer in love, and these days they often found themselves reflecting that they did not even like each other very much.

Their home, a gracious, modern house once the property of the Lowell family, but acquired by Ellis Darrow some years since, had been their wedding gift from the squire. Isabel had natural good taste and, lacking any other occupation, she had fitted the place up so beautifully that it was now the envy of all her friends, and admired county-wide. It wanted only a brood of children to make the idyll complete. No children had been forthcoming. But Isabel was young and strong, Rayner was hearty, and there was plenty of time yet.

*   *   *

Invited over to Easton Hall, the young couple found everyone fizzing and buzzing with energy and happiness. Even Rebecca seemed bright-eyed and vivacious, and was up and busy just like in the old days, before she became ill.

"Your Mama is brought back to life with a vengeance," observed the young Mrs Darrow, as she watched Rebecca practically flirting with her handsome nephew, and playfully tapping his arm with her ivory fan. "It's just as I've always maintained. There's nothing wrong with the old biddy. She merely suffers from boredom and *ennui*. As who would not, married to that tedious old man?"

Rayner made no comment. Nor did he deign to smile. This annoyed his wife extremely, for these days the belle of Warwickshire also fancied herself as something of a wit. She liked to have a receptive audience. At supper that first evening, therefore, she regaled the company with droll accounts of her doings north of the border. She extolled the beauty of the glens, but then expatiated at length on the ferocity of the mosquitoes, which seemed to infest every single one.

"They're the most diminutive little brutes," she admitted, as she removed one long glove to display a row of great red weals, which disfigured her white flesh.

She glanced towards Owen. "You're laughing at me now," she pouted. "Well, perhaps you have reason! In India, I dare say, the mosquitoes are as big as sparrows. Or even speckled hens!"

"They are certainly rather fearsome beasts," agreed Owen, smiling. "But they never bothered me."

"How fortunate for you. They would doubtless have eaten *me* alive."

Drawing on her glove again, Isabel leaned back in her chair. Thus, her beautiful figure was displayed to the best advantage. The diaphanous evening gown, high-waisted and cut rather lower than any respectable matron might have thought proper, clung to each and every firm and rounded curve. They were moulded like Grecian marble. Indeed, statuesque was a word which might have been coined especially to describe Isabel.

The freckles had disappeared completely. "But that's all owing to the judicious application of Gowland's Lotion," whispered Maria to Owen, who sat next to her at tea. "Two years ago, she was absolutely mottled."

"Well," thought Owen, "she's not mottled now!"

As far as Owen could see, Rayner was more or less indifferent to his wife's charms. While even Ellis Darrow's gaze was drawn again and again to his beautiful daughter-in-law, Rayner himself was more interested in quizzing his cousin about India. He wished to know all about the domestic lives of the maharajahs, and he was completely enthralled by the gory details of a tiger hunt.

Owen enjoyed telling traveller's tales. So now, his dark eyes sparkling and his features animated, he gave an account of a royal wedding, of a fabulously wealthy rajah to two sisters from a neighbouring state. A natural storyteller, soon he had his audience in the palm of his hand. Even Ellis stopped reading the newspaper, and listened, entranced.

When Owen came to describe the dresses and accoutrements of the two brides, Isabel's green eyes became quite round. "Diamonds as big as walnuts?" she whispered. She glanced down at her own little rings. "Rubies like hen's eggs?"

"Yes, indeed." Owen smiled at her. "The poor princesses were quite weighted down with jewels and cloth of gold. They could hardly stagger along."

Isabel's eyes glowed with greed. She smiled back at him. "Were the princesses particularly beautiful?" she enquired. "I ask, because I have heard that some of the native women in that country are exquisite."

"I'm afraid I cannot satisfy you there. I never saw a woman of the respectable sort without her veil." Owen shrugged. "Most women in that part of the world spend their entire lives in purdah. They are occasionally taken out, usually in a litter or bullock wagon. But even then they are heavily shrouded and veiled."

"So you hardly ever saw a female face?"

"I encountered many bazaar women, of course. Also sweepers, servants, nursemaids and the like. Some of *them* – the young ones especially – were extremely pretty."

"Did you meet any English women?"

"One or two. They were usually the wives of senior officials. Now and again I was introduced to somebody's niece, or daughter."

"To any niece or daughter in particular?"

"Oh, Bel!" Hugely, Rayner yawned. "Do stop teasing him! Owen, she wants to hear you admit you were unfaithful to my sister."

"Rayner, I protest! Of all the defamatory, slanderous—"

"I never saw any woman who could equal Jane, in India or anywhere else." Taking his cousin's hands in his, Owen held them. "The whole time I was away, I thought constantly of her. I remembered all of you, of course. But she was never out of my mind."

Owen had arranged for a consignment of Indian silks, cottons and calicoes to be delivered to Easton Hall. When they arrived, Jane, Maria and Isabel fell upon them with delight, unrolling bale after bale and trying the fabrics against one another, draping them and criticising the various effects.

Maria wished her sister to be dressed in the very height of fashion on her wedding day. So, although their own perfectly competent local seamstress was busy stitching wedding clothes for everyone else, Maria insisted that Jane should go with her to Birmingham, to visit the town's finest dressmaker and there to order her wedding gown, some exquisite underclothes, and a scarlet riding habit of the best Yorkshire cloth. The day after the Indian silks had arrived, therefore, the sisters ordered the carriage and drove into town.

Isabel had intended to go with them. But that morning, she woke with one of her headaches. So she sent a note over with the boot boy, pleading indisposition.

Jane and Maria were not unduly upset. Isabel was a fidget and a meddler, who advised and interfered and argued all the time. They would get on much better without her.

After spending the morning languishing in bed, by afternoon Isabel felt better. She ordered the barouche-landau, then drove over to Easton Hall, meaning to sit with Mrs Darrow for an hour or two.

But when she arrived, she was informed that Rebecca was resting. Ellis had gone fishing with Mr Graham, while Rayner had called in but disappeared again about some business of his own. Mr Morgan also was out.

Isabel decided to take a stroll in the gardens. By the time she had walked herself into a stupor of boredom, the others might have returned.

She met Owen coming from the direction of the stables. "Mr Morgan!" Delighted to see him, she beamed. "Oh, isn't it close?" she demanded, fanning herself. "So horribly, *stiflingly* hot! Although I dare say this heat is nothing at all, when compared with that of India."

"I must admit, the day seems only pleasantly warm to me." Owen smiled back at her. How pretty she was! Today, she wore a white muslin gown with a scooped but modest neckline and very short sleeves, which became her beautifully. Her creamy skin looked soft and dewy, and her coppery hair shone.

"Have you finished your walk?" he enquired.

"I thought I had." She linked her arm through his. "But now you are here, I could be persuaded to take another turn through the rose gardens. Provided we stay in the shade, of course."

"Of course," Owen agreed.

"Tell me some more about India," she said, as they strolled.

"What do you wish to know?"

"Anything. Everything! I love a story, you see."

So Owen told her tales of danger. Of horror. Of narrow escapes and difficult journeys. Of splendour and squalor, and of magnificence she could hardly begin to imagine.

"But I spent much of my time poring over files and documents," he admitted, as she shook her head and sighed over his description of the wonderful Turquoise Palace at Azrapur, where golden fountains gushed sea green water, and where even the servants were dressed from head to foot in a hundred shades of blue. "I sat in my office scribbling, and positively sweltering in the heat. While the monkeys quarrelled in the peepul trees, and my servant swished the punkah to and fro, to and fro."

"Even that sounds romantic to me," whispered Isabel. She glanced up at her companion. "How alike you and Rayner are!" she cried, shaking her copper curls and sighing again. "Well, of course, you always were very similar. But whilst you have grown tall and handsome, he's merely grown stout."

"He was always rather more stocky than I."

"Nonsense. He indulges himself at the table. So, naturally, he has become fat. His passion for sweetmeats far exceeds his lust for cards and dice."

"Don't mock my cousin."

"He's *my* husband. I shall mock him all I please."

But, after pouting crossly for a few moments, Isabel smiled again. How pleasant it was, to stroll in the gardens of this lovely house with such an interesting, good-looking young man! How fortunate, too, that her headache had disappeared . . .

Owen had been riding. He smelled of stables, of horseflesh, and of clean but perspiring human being. Isabel sniffed greedily. It was such a long time since she'd smelled a man! For Rayner was so lazy and fastidious that all *he* ever smelled of was Hungary water and fresh linen. Exactly like a woman, in fact.

Leaving the rose gardens, they entered the laburnum walk. Here, the trees were in full summer leaf, so concealed the walkers completely. Bees buzzed contentedly, and butterflies fluttered to and fro in the limpid green shade.

Half way down the avenue, Isabel's lace shawl caught on a branch, tugging the neckline of her gown awry and revealing one creamy shoulder in all its ivory beauty. "Please," she murmured softly, "can you help? The fringe is tangled, you see."

"Don't pull, then. You'll tear it." Carefully, Owen went to work. Easing the silken threads from the branch, one by one by one, he eventually shook the shawl free. He held it out to her.

Helplessly, she smiled. She had no free hands, for her parasol was in one, and her net purse in the other. So Owen had no choice but to go to her and drape it round her shoulders himself.

The sun filtered through the leaves and branches, casting a cool, somewhat eerie light on the people below. Isabel's skin was as white as milk anyway, but in this light it had an almost greenish tinge, a cool, marmoreal hue.

Owen looked at her. Standing stock still, Isabel wore a half-smile, of the kind seen on the faces of nymphs or goddesses in classical statuary. He drew a deep breath. He wanted so much to touch her! Just once.

He gazed into her cool, green eyes. Still, she smiled at him. "Of course you may," she said.

Uncertainly, wonderingly, he reached out to her. He stroked her face. He was surprised to find it warm and yielding.

"Go on," she whispered.

He could not help it. He kissed her, very lightly, on the lips.

He started back at once. Surely she would strike him now? Scream, even? But no. Instead, she closed her eyes. Dropping her parasol and purse, she wound her white arms around his neck. "I knew, of course," she whispered, murmuring into his ear. "I knew the very moment I saw you again."

"What did you know?" he demanded softly, afraid to break the spell.

"I want you." She kissed him, opening his mouth with hers. "You want me."

"No!" Coming to his senses, Owen pushed her away. His heart pounding, his brain on fire, he strode off down the laburnum walk, leaving Isabel standing there.

That evening's conversation was insipid and dull. In Birmingham, Maria had overspent her allowance, so she was fretful and irritable. Owen was almost completely silent, and Jane was tired, disinclined to chat. Feeling stronger today, Rebecca had come downstairs for the whole evening, but at nine o'clock she rang for her maid and the party broke up.

Pleading a headache, Owen also took himself off to bed, where he spent a sleepless night. By the morning he realised that the world had tilted. He was in love with his cousin's wife.

He loved Jane, it was true. Respecting her, admiring her, he would probably even have died for her. But she had never inspired the kind of racked and reckless longing which Isabel Darrow had kindled in his heart!

Lying on his stomach, actually in pain, he pictured Isabel's white shoulders. Then, he recalled the kiss, remembering the taste of her lips and how her little pointed tongue had flicked back and forth across his teeth. Such a kiss – and so unlike the chaste kisses he had exchanged with Jane that those decorous embraces surely deserved a completely different name.

Owen was not without experience of women, or of the world. He had lost his virginity to a servant when he was just seventeen. In India, he had even visited brothels. There, half-caste women, European in dress and manner but truly Oriental in every other way, had taught him how to give a woman pleasure, as well as find it for himself. There had been a brief affair with the wife of an army officer, too. Mrs Sydenham had been a complaisant mistress, and he had learned a great deal from her.

But this intolerable ache in his heart, and the feeling that he was burning alive and nothing could put out the fire, was new to him.

He knew Rayner went to Warwick every Wednesday morning, to meet his friends at a little private club. Here, they drank, gambled and swore like the blades they'd secretly have liked to be. But for a few hours only, before they went meekly back to their comfortable lives and tedious rural obligations on their country estates.

So now, telling Jane's maid that he was going out for an hour's exercise, which he hoped would blow the lingering remnants of last night's headache away, Owen borrowed a black mare and rode over to call on Isabel.

"I knew you would come," she said, as she took his hand and led him indoors. "It's as if I have in my hand an invisible silken thread. It's wound about your heart. When I twitch it, you must pay heed to me."

"Must I?"

"Oh, yes." Isabel smiled up at him. "I've sent my girl to Warwick, to buy ribbons for my new gown. The kitchenmaids are busy cleaning the silver. The footman is on an errand for Rayner."

"Where is Rayner?" asked Owen, half hoping that his cousin was at home, after all.

"He's gone to Warwick, too." Taking Owen into her private sitting room, Isabel closed the door. She turned the little gilt key. Then, she pulled off the muslin cap which covered her hair. Shaking loose the coppery strands, she began to unlace the bodice of her gown.

"Not here!" began Owen, panicking. "Isabel, for God's sake not here!"

"No?" Isabel's gown was gaping open. She wore no shift or stays. "You wish me to cuckold your cousin in his own bed?"

"No!" Turning away, Owen folded his arms. Tears came into his eyes. "I don't want you!" he cried. "I don't – I mean, I *can't*—"

"But of course you can. That's why you came."

"On the contrary. I came here to apologise. To tell you how sorry—"

"Nonsense." Isabel's voice was like melting honey. "Turn round," she whispered.

"I think I should leave."

"Owen!"

The urgency in her voice made him start. He spun round. He met Isabel's great, green eyes, which flashed like emeralds on fire. Then, of course, it was too late.

They reclined on the floor of Isabel's charming sitting room. Both naked, they were nevertheless perfectly comfortable, for they lay on a soft Turkish carpet and an Indian throw. "I'd thought you might be a virgin," murmured Isabel, offhandedly.

"*Did* you?" Offended, Owen frowned.

"But of course, that was stupid." Creamily, Isabel smiled at him. "A man like you, so handsome, so clever, so infinitely desirable – you must have lost your innocence a long time ago."

Owen made no comment.

Isabel took his hand in hers. She laid it on one breast. "How fortunate it is," she mused, as she encouraged his fingers to massage her, "that we discovered it in time."

"Discovered what?"

"That we adore one other, of course. How fortunate, too, that only one of us is married." Isabel stroked Owen's shoulder. "How beautiful you are," she sighed. "So smooth, so brown, so strong. Rayner is white, hairless and fat. Just like a woman, in fact.

"God, he disgusts me! In bed, he grunts and groans like a sow in farrow. He pushes and he heaves—"

"Bel, we must not hurt Rayner or Jane."

"I can't see how hurt is to be avoided."

"If we are careful—"

"You don't still intend to marry her?" Isabel sat up. A wild-eyed, wild-haired fury, she glared at him. "You can't wed her now!" she cried.

"But, Bel—"

"I shall leave Rayner. My parents will cast me off, it's true. The Darrows will certainly be baying for *your* blood! But I have a little money of my own – and you have a fortune."

"A rather small fortune."

"You have enough." Leaning towards him, Isabel brushed his lips with hers. "Do you love me?" she whispered.

"Yes." Owen hung his head. "Against my will, against my inclinations, against my honour, I do."

"Then we will go away together."

"But how—"

"We'll find a way." Isabel kissed him again. "Promise me one thing."

"What is that?"

"You will not marry Jane."

Chapter Nine

As the family was finishing dinner, Owen made his excuses and left the table. He went into the drawing room and lay down on a sofa. Closing his eyes, he tried to go to sleep.

Only a few moments later, however, he became aware of someone sitting by his side. All tender concern, Jane was stroking his hand. "Owen?" Anxiously, she smoothed his hair back from his forehead. "What's wrong?"

"Nothing!" Starting guiltily, Owen stared at her. "Nothing at all. Why should there be?"

"It's just that you look like a little boy who's been caught with his hand in the jar of sugar candy." She smiled at him. "What have you been doing today?"

"Nothing much." Owen shrugged. "I went for a hack on Gryphon, as you know. I called in to see Rayner. But he wasn't there."

"He always goes into town on Wednesdays. But surely Isabel was at home?"

"Yes, she was."

"So at least you were given a dish of tea."

Owen took a deep breath. The urge to confess – to tell the whole story, then go down on his knees and beg Jane's forgiveness – was overwhelming.

But then he remembered what he would be confessing. He had betrayed his fiancée, cuckolded his cousin, and debauched his cousin's wife. Rapidly, he blinked. "I still have a headache," he began. "I—"

"Let me bind it for you, then."

"No. That old-fashioned remedy does no good at all.

In fact, it does considerable harm." Owen drew another deep breath. "I used to get this sort of thing in India. If I lie down for an hour or two, in a darkened room, I expect I shall improve by and by."

Owen was downstairs again by tea time. Relatively composed now, he found he was able to look his cousin in the eye without blushing in shame. But when Maria remarked that Rayner and Isabel were expected for supper that same evening, he grew pale. His tea slopped in the saucer. He thought he might faint.

"He wasn't well this morning, or yesterday." Jane looked anxiously into Owen's eyes. "Mama? What do you think?"

Rebecca felt her nephew's pulse. "Racing," she murmured. "My dear Owen, you're not at all well. Shall I send for Dr Henchard?"

"It's nothing. Indeed, it's nothing at all." Owen tried to smile. "I do know what I'm talking about," he continued, valiantly. "My dear aunt, you forget that I spent many years in an apothecary's house, learning his trade. Believe me – this slight indisposition may be troublesome, but it will soon pass."

"Well, if you're quite sure." Rebecca was still concerned. "I shall mix you some of my special powder," she said. "Just a teaspoonful, in a glass of water. You shall drink it down."

That evening, Isabel looked so ravishing that Owen's fever returned in earnest. But he tried to control it. He avoided her society, and at supper he contrived to sit as far away as possible from his cousin's wife.

After supper, Rebecca proposed cards, and Ellis agreed to play. Jane and Maria had muslins and chintzes to talk over, Charles Harding and Rayner were still sitting over their port, discussing business, and Isabel had her needlework. Owen alone had nothing to do. So, excusing himself, he went for a walk.

As he strode off through the dusk, he became steadily more confident that he had got the better of this – this fit of temporary insanity. He would put that morning's work behind him, he resolved, and never think of Isabel Darrow again.

But then, he heard someone call his name. To his dismay, he realised Isabel had followed him. Catching his hand, she strolled at his side. Then, taking him down a mossy byway, she led him towards a little temple which Ellis had built many years before to serve as a summer house – but which was nowadays hardly ever visited by anyone, so it had become green and damp with decay.

The lovers met one another's gaze. "Please, Isabel!" cried Owen, as they stood in the warm summer twilight, "please go away!"

Isabel stood her ground. "Have you told her what happened this morning?" she enquired.

"I've said nothing." Owen looked away. "Nor do I intend to."

"Then the task will fall to me."

"Isabel, you mustn't." Owen was aghast. "You can't!"

"Can't I?"

"No. Isabel, what passed between us this morning was lunacy! We were both mad, and—"

"You mean to forsake me?"

"For God's sake, Isabel! You're married! I myself am engaged, to a woman whose love for me is the most unselfish, the most tender—"

"You're engaged to a nun." Isabel's pretty mouth puckered in scorn. "Yes, I admit she waited for you. Of course, *you* flatter yourself that she hungered for you, too. You imagine all those years of self-denial were as painful for her as they were for you."

"Isabel, don't mock Jane. She—"

"I know all about it, you see. I've even heard extracts from the journals. The famous Indian diaries – those daily affirmations of undying love, sent on their way across thousands of miles of ocean, damp with salt water and lover's tears." Isabel was positively sneering now. Her expression was sour with disgust. "Those passionate epistles. Those frantic, reckless—"

"Isabel, be quiet."

"She read them aloud, you know. To everyone. We all heard about the pig-stickings, the tiger hunts, the weddings and funerals, and so on. How fascinating, I used to think, as I yawned behind my fan. How astonishing, how wonderful that dear Owen should actually find the time to *do* all that. Let alone write such nonsense down!

"I used to wish she would read out the more personal passages. But these were censored, of course. Or at least, I hope they were! For surely your letters did not consist entirely of anecdote and badinage? You did at least conclude with how much you longed for her? How even your deepest sleeps were made restless, by the remembrance of her last sweet embrace? How you yearned to hold her in your arms, to part her soft red lips, and—"

"Isabel! I will hear no more of this!"

"No?" Isabel shrugged. "Very well. But tell me this. Before you went away, did you have her?"

"My God! How can you even think of asking such a thing?"

"You must tell me!" Isabel's emerald eyes glittered brightly. Greedily, she licked her lips. "Did you put your mark on her? Make her your own?"

"Jane is a respectable, modest woman! I would never have compromised her like that. She—"

"So you left her a virgin, and a virgin she remains." Isabel tossed her head. "How many years did she wait for you?" she mused, apparently talking to herself. "She has been courted, you know. Many came after you, sniffing round the squire's ankles, anxious to bed that twenty thousand pounds. All were turned away.

"But what of Jane herself? She had no reason to expect you would be true – or even return at all. Disease, injury, the rigours of a hostile climate, the likelihood that a fine-looking fellow like you would find another woman to replace her – all these possibilities must have crossed her mind. The chances of even seeing you again were not great. But she was faithful. Why?"

"Because she loves me!"

"No." Isabel's eyes sparkled in the twilight. "Because she is afraid! My dear Owen, she has known you from early childhood. You are her baby cousin, her infant favourite, her own little pet. You foolish creature, she doesn't want a husband at all. She wants a child!"

"Don't." Owen shut his eyes. "She wants a husband," he whispered.

"Nonsense. You want a mother, and she wants a son." Now, lasciviously, Isabel rubbed her bosom against his arm. "Have you seen her breasts?"

"Isabel!"

"You have not. I doubt if you ever will." Spitefully, Isabel laughed. "When you are married, she will muffle herself in white flannel before shc cvcn approaches the nuptial bed. Once there, she will bear your brutish passion with the kind of Christian fortitude she has been bred to understand is expected of her. If she should happen to conceive, she'll be—"

"Isabel, I don't wish to hear this."

"Then why don't you leave me?" Sitting on one of the stained marble benches at the entrance of the little temple, Isabel smiled at him. "Go on. Run away. Scuttle back to your nun."

Owen looked at her. But he did not move.

"Struggle if you must," said Isabel. "But remember, this is not all my doing. You don't want that frozen virgin! You want *me*."

"Let us suppose you are right. What should I do about it?"

"Tell Jane the truth."

"Do you think I am so forgetful of the obligations of friendship, of affection, that I would hurt her so cruelly? That I would humiliate her, expose her to—"

"Marry her, then. Marry your nun, your modest, respectable woman, who loves you so well."

"I shall."

"I see you must." Isabel sighed. "Very well. Let today see the first and the last of what you choose to call madness. But to which I would give a much kinder name!

"Before you go, however – before I return to my suet pudding of a husband, and you prepare to wed your immaculate bride – let me take something I can treasure. Something to console me, through the long and dreary days ahead. Give me one last kiss!"

Owen looked at her. Her eyes sparkling, her lips already parted, she smiled at him.

He knew he was lost.

"There," she said, half an hour later. Lying supine beneath him, contentedly she sighed. "You may go now, if you choose. But before you commit yourself irrevocably – before you marry your middle-aged virgin – remember the pleasure *I* gave you tonight."

Owen gazed down at her. White as the marble on which she lay, here and there her flesh was grazed and scraped and red. He had, he reflected, certainly put his mark on Isabel.

"We could go away together," she was saying now. "To the Indies, to any of the Colonies. Even to the New World!"

But then, suddenly, she began to cry. "Oh, my darling," she wept, "pity me! For you, I am prepared to lose my family, my friends, my reputation – everything! I ask so little in return."

"On the contrary, you ask far too much."

"No!" Isabel's sobs grew harder. "All I desire is that you release a woman who does not want you anyway!"

"How do you know she doesn't want me?"

"Has she ever kissed you?"

"Of course she has."

"I mean, do her lips tell you of her longing for you? Do they give you her heart and soul? Does she devour you, and can she be satisfied? Or are her kisses the sort she might with perfect propriety offer a sister, a brother, a friend?"

Owen was silent.

"I thought as much." Through her tears, Isabel smiled. "Of passion she knows nothing. Nothing at all."

Owen buried his face in his hands. "I can't," he whispered.

"You can," she said. She pulled him close to her. She kissed his ear. "You want me still. Come inside me again."

Hours had passed. The long summer twilight had faded and the sky was full of stars.

"I shall not marry her." Lying spent and exhausted on the cold marble floor, Owen was hardly conscious of the naked woman at his side. "There. Are you satisfied now?"

"You will leave this place?"

"Yes."

"May I go with you?"

"No, you may not!" Sitting up, Owen groped for his clothes. "But rest assured, I'll tell her tonight."

"Excellent." Isabel stood up. She began to dress.

When they reached the gardens which surrounded the Hall, Isabel took Owen's hand. He tried to shake her off, but she held him tightly, her long, thin fingers digging into his flesh.

Evidently, they had been missed. As they approached the gravel sweep, they saw Rayner and Charles Harding coming from the direction of the stables, both looking anxious and tired.

Rayner saw them first. His cry of relief brought all the others running. But then, as he took in his wife's bedraggled appearance, his features clouded over. "Have you had an accident?" he asked. All concern, he reached for Isabel's hand.

But she pushed him away. Imperiously, she glared at Owen. "Tell them," she said.

"Isabel, I can't! Not yet. I—"

"Tell them!"

Owen looked round the assembled throng. These people were his family! His friends. He felt sick and ill, faint and nauseated by the almost obscene cruelty of what he was about to do.

"I cannot marry Jane," he muttered.

"What?" Ellis Darrow gaped at him. "What did you say?"

"I cannot and will not marry my cousin Jane." Owen hung his head. "I have behaved shamefully," he went on. "I have forfeited any right to address a modest, respectable woman, and I therefore ask my cousin to release me from any obligation to her."

"Good God!" Ellis looked murderous now. "Will you come inside, sir?" he demanded.

"No, sir. I cannot."

"So, in addition to dishonouring my daughter, you will defy me?" Ellis was ashen. "I say again, will you step inside?"

"No." Owen bit his lip. "I shall never enter your house again."

Rebecca looked ready to faint. "But, Owen!" she cried. She would have gone to him, embraced him even, had not Ellis held her back. "My dear Owen, will you not explain?"

"Perhaps my wife should do that." Rayner took Isabel by the wrist. He could smell her now. See her lips were bruised and swollen, hear the soft rasping of her breathing, feel the pulsing of her thumping heart. Her gown was stained and torn, and so haphazardly fastened that it was plain she had dressed herself. She had the look of a cat with the cream. Contented, fed, she was a woman sated, who could ask for no more.

"Take that creature home." The look Ellis gave his daughter-in-law would have frozen boiling oil. "Go now!"

Rayner dragged Isabel away. But Owen merely stood there. His misery and distress were so evident that, while she could hardly support herself, still Jane pitied him. "Oh, darling," she whispered. "Owen, my dearest – why?"

But he would not look at her. Instead, he met Ellis Darrow's gaze. "I shall write to Jane," he muttered. "If she wishes, she may keep the contents of the letter to herself. Or she may make the matter public.

"But whatever she decides, I would like her to know that she cannot think any worse of me than I do of myself."

Then Owen turned to leave. His footsteps crunching on the gravel, he walked away from Easton Hall.

Maria was the first to notice Rebecca's pallor. To see her stumble, then fall. "Mama!" She caught her mother by the elbow, trying to support her. "Mama? Lean on me!"

But Rebecca did not seem to hear her. As if her bones had turned to jelly, she collapsed, slumping unconscious against her husband's chest.

"We must get her to bed, directly!" Her face blanched by fear, Maria rang for Rebecca's maid. Then, taking her mother's hand, she chafed it. "Oh, God!" she wailed.

"What is it?" demanded Ellis.

"Help me to take her up." Maria looked ready to faint herself. "Sir? You must help me!"

Rayner and Isabel had gone home. So now, Charles Harding was asked to ride over to Warwick, and bring Dr Henchard back with him post haste. While he was gone, Jane and Maria put their mother to bed.

Ellis sat at his wife's bedside. His face a gaunt, grey mask, he held her hand in his. Neither speaking nor moving, he waited for the physician to arrive.

Concerned and anxious to help, the servants crowded round the doorway. But when they observed the look on the squire's face, they did not dare make a sound, let alone enter the room. While Maria gave ineffectual orders and rang down for tea, smelling salts, hot poultices – for anything and everything, in fact – Jane sat beside her father.

Watching her mother's face, she was alarmed to see how pale it had become. Even in the soft glow of candlelight, it was waxen. In fact, it was almost green. "Sir?" she hazarded, fearfully.

"What is it?"

"Will you please pass me that looking glass?"

"What? Oh. Here." Releasing Rebecca's hand, Ellis reached for the glass. But then he realised why his daughter had asked for it. "She can't be," he muttered.

But, held to Rebecca's lips, the glass remained clear. "Oh, sir!" Jane choked back a sob. "My dear father, I'm so sorry! Her heart—"

"Leave me." As Jane tried to take his hand, Ellis pushed her away. "Go!"

Jane had little time to grieve for her mother, much less to think of herself and her own personal sorrow. Now, she feared that having just lost one parent, she must shortly lose the other, too.

For a while, she was so afraid for his sanity that she hardly left her father's side. Defying established convention, and thereby scandalizing the whole neighbourhood, she even attended the funeral. For she was sure that if she let him out of her sight, Ellis Darrow would do something terrible, either to himself or to someone else.

"Sir?" she began, the morning after they had buried Rebecca in the family vault at Easton St Nicholas, "sir, may I speak?"

"What is it?" Ellis had not eaten for three days. His face was a dirty yellow-grey. His eyes were bloodshot and his lips a livid blue. "Well, child?"

"My dear father, will you not take just a little nourishment? Some soup, maybe? Some gruel, or broth?"

"I want nothing." Ellis looked at her. "*You* loved the

creature," he muttered. "You, my favourite child, you even wanted to marry him!"

"Sir, I—"

"She's won." Ellis ground his teeth in rage. "The hounds killed the vixen, it's true. But the cub lived, to complete what she had begun."

"Oh, sir!" Sitting down beside him, Jane laid her soft hand upon her father's arm. "Owen knows he has done wrong," she whispered. "I think he must surely feel it."

"Do you, indeed." Ellis shrugged. "Did he write to you?"

"Yes," Jane replied. "He sent a short note."

"What did the creature say?"

"He blames himself for everything. He exonerates Isabel absolutely. He wishes me well and happy."

"Is that all?"

"On that day, he says, his eyes were opened to defects in his own character, of which he was completely ignorant before. He says also that I am far better off without him."

"The last observation is just." Ellis scowled. "Oh God!" he cried, "I wish you had never met him!"

"Sir, he has behaved very badly. I shall not deny that. But I am sure – nay, I am certain – that he suffers now."

"Suffers!" Ellis glared at her in scorn. "He's probably forgotten he ever did anything amiss! He's just like his mother. Feelings of compunction, remorse or repentance are all strangers to him."

Jane did not agree. But she thought it better not to say so, or at any rate just now. "Sir," she began, "I never did learn why you disliked his mother."

"Did you not? Then, I shall tell you." Reaching for Jane's hand, Ellis held it. "As children," he began, "Lalage and I were very close. Perhaps rather *too* close. Although, of course, nothing actually improper ever passed between us.

"When I married, Lalage took it upon herself to be

extremely jealous of your mother. In fact, she hated her. She envied her beauty, her goodness, and she especially hated the fact that Rebecca had conceived you easily, when Lalage was childless herself.

"You have heard, of course, that just before you were born, there was a terrible fire here at Easton Hall. The story goes that a pair of ruffians whom, as the local justice I had sent to prison for poaching, returned one night to take a dreadful revenge.

"But that was not the case. My sister had paid the men to burn my home. She knew I was away from Easton, and was not expected back for a week or more. Her intention was, that you and your mother should perish in the flames."

"Oh, God!" Horrified, Jane looked at him. "Sir, is this mere hearsay? Or proven fact?"

"It is fact. My sister admitted as much to me."

"So then?"

"I told Lalage I never wanted to see her again. So, she and her husband left Warwickshire and went to live in South Wales. Alex Lowell died there, and Lalage remarried.

"Her second husband was a Welsh criminal. A murderer, a thief – in short, a ruffian of the very basest kind – he was eventually arrested on suspicion of dealing in contraband. He died in military custody. My sister subsequently took her own life."

Ellis closed his eyes. "That creature," he whispered, "was the result of their union."

Rebecca's will was proved, and her executors set about their appointed tasks. In addition to her personal effects, it was discovered Rebecca had had a small annuity, inherited from her grandfather. This, unusually, was at her sole disposal, and was not to revert to her husband on her death.

The obvious beneficiaries would have been her three children. But her son and daughters would be well provided for out of their father's estate. So, aware that Ellis was under no obligation to provide for him, and was in fact most unlikely ever to do so, Rebecca had bequeathed almost all she possessed to her dear nephew, John Rhys Owen Morgan.

The attorney hardly dared meet the squire's gaze. "We shall of course contest this," he observed carefully, as he collected his papers together. "Although his aunt's bequest was unconditional, Mr Morgan's recent conduct does not seem to warrant—"

"No." Ellis stood up. "Find the creature, pay him what he is owed, and make an end of it. Do not mention the matter to me again."

Chapter Ten

David Morgan was most surprised to see his nephew, especially since he had just finished making the final preparations for his own journey into Warwickshire. "Well, child?" he demanded, as the travel-stained, miserable creature sat down at his uncle's table, buried his face in his hands, and began to sob like a baby, "whatever's all this?"

But all Owen would mutter was that the wedding would not take place. Then, he burst into tears again. His uncle shook his head. Rising to his feet, he shuffled off to concoct a soothing cordial. This, he would oblige his nephew to drink.

In his time, David Morgan had treated many a fit of bilious melancholy. He well understood that, in most cases, fresh air, exercise and a change of scene were the best remedies. Assuming that poor Owen had been jilted by an unfeeling hussy, even though she might be a lady born and bred, he exhorted his nephew to bear up, be a man – and to remember that, if he still had a mind to marry, there were kinder maids than Jane Darrow anxious to be wed.

But Owen was not to be comforted. So, after watching his nephew mope and pine for a fortnight or more, David decided to call reinforcements to his aid.

Thomas Taliesin, seven years married to a pretty, bright-eyed schoolmaster's daughter, and the father of four strapping sons, had realised his ambitions to succeed in the world of commerce. He had found a wealthy fool or two, persuaded these persons to cough up some cash, and become an ironmaster. He had worked hard, laboured long, and nowadays his forges produced the best bar iron, and his two foundries turned out some of the finest castings to be had in all of South Wales. Wishing to expand his range of operations, he needed more investors in his company.

Owen had plenty of capital to spare. So why, David reasoned, should he not venture some of it in his friend Thomas's growing concern? Or in some other industrial enterprise, such as a mine or a factory? "Here in South Wales," observed David Morgan, "there are certainly plenty of them, from which you might choose."

"I'll think about it," muttered Owen, but most ungraciously.

"You do that." Sagely, David nodded. "Have you replied to Thomas Taliesin's letter?" he enquired.

"No. But I'll get round to it soon."

"You mind you do." David met his nephew's sullen gaze. "You need to get out and about, boy," he added. "Activity! That's the thing."

A month after Owen had returned to South Wales, he received a letter from his uncle Darrow's attorney-at-law, informing him that he was a beneficiary under his late aunt's will. But, far from being delighted by this sudden windfall, the shock of Rebecca's death almost killed Owen, too. He took to his bed, saying he didn't care if he never rose from it again.

"Mourn her if you will, child," murmured David, as he sat at his nephew's bedside and sighed his sympathy. "Remember her goodness, and pray for the repose of her soul. All that is right and just. But for God's sake! Don't torment yourself into an early grave! Surely your dear aunt would never have expected you to grieve like this?"

Owen said nothing. So David wrote again to Thomas Taliesin, this time inviting him to stay, in the hope he would bring his nephew back to life.

"How much did the old lady leave you?" demanded

the practical Mr Taliesin, as he sat by the invalid's side.

"What? Oh – the bequest." Owen shrugged. "I am to receive an annuity, of seven hundred a year. The attorney suggests I cash it in."

"What would you get if you did?"

"Almost four thousand pounds." Owen turned his face to the wall. "I've a mind to give it all away," he muttered. "To endow an asylum or hospice, for the care of the melancholy mad."

"Don't be so foolish." Encouragingly, Thomas clapped his friend on the shoulder. "Take the money for yourself!" he cried. "Invest it in industry! Make it grow! Then, you can feather your own nest – and endow your foundation, too."

"Perhaps." Indifference incarnate, Owen sighed. "Very well. I'll consider it."

Two days later, Thomas went home. A week afterwards, he sent Owen a brief note, inviting him to supper the following Thursday evening, and offering him a bed for the night. For Thomas was expecting a guest, a fellow ironmaster, whom he suggested Owen might be interested to meet.

"I'm not going at all," muttered Owen, as his uncle asked if would hire a horse, or take the apothecary's own pony and trap.

"*Duw annwyl*, give me patience!" David glared. "You *will* go," he declared. "You're looking forward to it tremendously, in fact. So, if you feel you cannot put pen to paper, telling Thomas Taliesin as much, I shall write the letter myself."

"Mr Owen Morgan, of Cardiff. Mr Michael Atkins, chiefly of Pontypool. But also of Swansea and the Vale of Glamorgan, not to mention all the areas round about." Thomas beamed from one friend to the other. "Pray sirs, do be seated. Mrs Taliesin will be down again directly. Or so she tells me!"

Owen sat down. Accepting a dish of tea, he glanced again at the other guest, who was regarding him with the polite interest and mild curiosity of a man who made new acquaintances almost every working day. "You are a manufacturer, I believe?" he began. Not because he cared one way or the other, of course, but because he thought he ought to find something to say.

"A manufacturer, an ironmaster, a philanthropist – Mr Atkins is all these, *and* much more!" Complacently, Thomas Taliesin shook his head. "Owen, my boy, if you would be an industrialist yourself, you could do no better than hear Mr Atkins on the subject. Indeed, you should hang on every word he has to say."

"My dear Thomas, your tongue runs away with you." Indulgently, Mr Atkins smiled. "Mr Morgan, I am indeed a manufacturer. But, as our host implies, I have other interests, too."

Owen was just about to ask what these were – but then, the door of the drawing room was thrown open wide. "My dear Mrs Taliesin!" At once, Mr Atkins rose to his feet. "A pleasure. As always! I trust I see you well?"

Mrs Taliesin blushed. "Mr Atkins," she murmured. "I'm so sorry to have kept you waiting. One of the children, you see—"

"No matter, dear lady, no matter!" Mr Atkins beamed. "Well? I trust all is now in order?"

It was. The party went in to dinner.

A fair-haired, handsome gentleman in robust middle age, Michael Atkins proved to be well-mannered, well-informed, and to have plenty to say for himself. Obviously an Englishman, he had something of the arrogance and complacency of most of the breed. But his general air was pleasant enough, and he was clearly no fool, so Owen had no objection to hearing what he had to say.

"Mr Morgan has been in India these six years," explained Thomas, as Mr Atkins left off talking about his own particular concerns, and began to discourse on the state of the nation and the growing divisions between masters and men. "So he has seen nothing of the recent upsurge in radicalism, which threatens the established order. Nay, which bedevils all trade and industry! Nor has he observed how the morals and manners of the labouring classes have decayed."

"Has he not?" Shaking his head, Mr Atkins smiled. He turned to Owen. "So, Mr Morgan," he began, "you are a traveller, recently returned to your native heath. What brought you to South Wales? Have you relatives here?"

"Yes," replied Owen, "I have indeed. In fact, my nearest relation lives in Cardiff."

"Is the gentleman involved in industry, or trade?"

"Not exactly. My uncle is an apothecary. He has a large practice in Cardiff and the countryside round about."

"Have you no closer family?"

"Alas, no." Owen shrugged. "My parents died when I was a child. My uncle brought me up." Well, he thought, this was true enough. Apart from his family connections in Warwickshire, which were lost to him forever, he had no other kin in the world.

In spite of being somewhat preoccupied, Owen paid close attention to much of what Thomas and Mr Atkins had to say, and on the whole the evening went very well. Asked by Mr Atkins if would care to visit one of his manufactories some time in the near future, he accepted the invitation readily.

"The domestic goods market," explained Mr Atkins, as he ushered his visitor from the forge and into the machine shop, where bought-in castings were being drilled and punched and bored. "The tinning and japanning industries, the non-ferrous metal trades – these are the coming thing."

"I see." By now half-deafened by the relentless banging and clanging of metal on metal, not to mention half-blinded by smuts and sulphurous, burning dust, Owen gazed all around the modern pandemonium which was the machine shop. Here, he found himself absolutely marvelling at the energy of the smoke-blackened hobgoblins, who laboured so diligently in this hellish atmosphere. He also wondered if his own headache would ever go away.

But soon enough, Mr Atkins led him out of that demon's den and into fresher air. As an ironmaster in the Vale of Glamorgan, he continued, he had done very well out of the French wars. But these would not last forever, and a manufacturer who applied himself to nothing but the production of artillery and cannon would find himself bankrupt when peace was declared.

Therefore, Mr Atkins had opened a new manufactory here in Pontypool, and was beginning to diversify into household wares – fire-irons, grates, fenders and the like. Perhaps Owen would like to inspect the casting sheds now?

Owen agreed that he would. For, to his own great surprise, he found he was becoming interested in all this.

So, in spite of his headache and the ringing in his ears, Owen enjoyed his day out. He left the factory in Pontypool very thoughtful. He felt something had clicked neatly into place. At last, he thought, he'd found his occupation. He would become a manufacturer, too.

"He's a pleasant fellow," observed Owen, as he and Thomas Taliesin sat together enjoying a light supper a few days later. "He's plain-spoken, cordial, and he seems honest, too. I feel I could do business with him."

"Indeed, you might go much further and fare far worse." Thomas poured more Madeira. "I've been one of his suppliers for a good six months now, and I'll tell you this for nothing. He pays his bills regularly. Cash on the nail, and he doesn't quibble over trifles, either. Not like some."

"How long have you known him?"

"Three years. Four, maybe." Thomas raised his glass. "Yes, I'd say Mr Atkins was as straight as a die. Honest as the day is long – which is remarkable, when you come to consider it."

"How so?"

"Well. I would not bear false witness against my neighbour. So, if I tell you what I've heard, it is between you and me only. Is that agreed?"

"Most certainly."

"Well, then. He's a widower. His unfortunate wife, whom he married quite late in life – he must have been forty, at least – was apparently something of a catch. Rich, beautiful and virtuous, too. But she died in childbirth. He lost her, and the infant as well."

"Poor fellow."

"Poor fellow, indeed." Thomas refilled Owen's glass. "But there were those in the metal trades who murmured it was no more than justice and due retribution, all round."

"Retribution?" repeated Owen. "For what?"

"For his manifold sins and wickednesses. You see – during the last century, before he was involved in his present occupation, our Mr Atkins was a mere country gentleman. He came from an ancient line of English squires, living in Pembrokeshire, I believe – or at any rate, in one of those little outposts of Saxon autonomy dotted here and there throughout rural Wales.

"His father was a farmer, and a magistrate. But he dealt in contraband too. Times were violent then, and it seems old Mr Atkins was implicated in the deaths of at least two Excise men. For this he was arraigned, convicted and hanged. There were those who whispered that our friend was as deep in that business as ever his father was. But, even when he was on trial for his life, old Mr Atkins refused point blank to implicate his son."

"What do you believe?"

"I don't know that I believe anything in particular. Of course, one doesn't go up to a man and enquire! But, as you say yourself, Michael Atkins seems to be an honest man. His business associates speak well of him, and his word is undoubtedly his bond." Thomas looked thoughtful. "The seed does not necessarily carry the taint of the parent plant."

"I suppose not." Owen had the grace to blush.

"It was a long time ago," continued Thomas, reflectively. "Twenty years or more. If our friend does have anything on his conscience, there's been time enough for him to repent.

"Indeed, in some ways he *does* behave like a penitent. He supports an orphanage near Swansea, and he endows the foundling hospital in Bridgend."

Mr Atkins was delighted when Owen visited him again and asked if he would be interested in going into partnership, or at least in making a deal. For as it happened, said Mr Atkins, he knew just the thing that might suit.

His new factory had a constant use for a particular type of iron casting, which he could not readily manufacture himself. In the past, he had dealt extensively with an ironmaster who had made exactly the kind of thing he wanted. But eighteen months ago, Mr Heatherwood had died intestate, leaving a strong-minded widow and her five sons to squabble amongst themselves.

Unable to agree on the division of spoils, the family had allowed the business to decay. Lawsuits looked likely to bring them all to the brink of bankruptcy. What if Owen were to step in, offer them cash – which Michael Atkins was certain they would take – and become an ironmaster himself?

"The site of the works is an excellent one," continued Mr Atkins encouragingly. "A ready supply of coal, iron-ore and limestone is to hand. An idle workforce would welcome a new employer with open arms."

If Owen would undertake to produce what he wanted, moreover, Mr Atkins would undertake to buy, and also recommend him to other manufacturers throughout the region.

Owen decided this was a heaven-sent opportunity. For some weeks now, he'd been considering various business ventures in the north of England. But if he became an iron-founder here in South Wales, he'd be near enough to Cardiff to visit his uncle. Nowadays, David Morgan's chronic shortness of breath and bad colour seriously alarmed his nephew, who did not relish the thought of losing virtually the only kin he had left in the world.

He decided to take a look at the Heatherwood Works.

Hiring a horse from the livery stables, Owen set off across the valley. On the northern rim of the South Wales coalfield, he found the site.

But if he'd expected to be inspired, he soon realised he was doomed to be disappointed that day. Overgrown – in fact, near-derelict – the place was desolate. The sight of crumbling, roofless casting sheds, a boarded-up foundry, and an empty forge in which yellow dandelions and rosebay willowherb grew in wild profusion, did nothing to raise his already sinking spirits. As he poked about the rubbish, as he took in the squalor and wholesale decay, his enthusiasm for Michael Atkins's scheme evaporated into thin air.

His dream of becoming an ironmaster had been an idle one. This was not for him, after all. He was about to turn his horse's head for home, when he heard somebody call his name.

"I thought we said Wednesday!" gasped Thomas Taliesin, as he clambered over a jagged boundary wall and stood there in his greatcoat, breathing hard, and desperately trying to recover his wind.

"*We*?" muttered Owen, ungraciously.

"Of course." Thomas grinned. "You did intend to come here with me, I assume? Well – there's no sense in looking round this sort of place all by yourself, is there?"

"Isn't there?"

"Of course not! What will you see? Nothing but ruination, desolation and decay."

"What do *you* see?"

"Well, now." Thomas gazed all about. "It's a good site," he observed. "There's plenty of coal to hand. Not to mention ironstone outcrop, over there in the hills. Transportation of goods would be a problem, mind. There's no canal, so you'd need to use pack-mules, and they don't come cheap.

"But if you could sell cast iron at twenty six pounds a ton – and there's no good reason why you should not – you wouldn't fail to make some sort of profit. In the end, that is."

"But could I make the type of castings Mr Atkins wants here?"

"Oh God, yes!" Thomas grinned. "You've got a decent foundry look! No problems there. There's a forge, too. Of sorts. So you could make bar iron, as well.

"But let's begin at the beginning, shall we? Have a look at the furnaces. See how long it would take to put them back into blast, and get you in business again."

The Heatherwood Ironworks was typical of many small operations to be found in South Wales, in that it did not specialise. It was neither foundry, forge nor mill, but all three – and more. Anything the customer wanted, Heatherwood could attempt to provide. For here, the raw materials extracted from the hills round about could be processed to make pig iron, which could then either be sold, re-melted to make castings, or further refined in the forge to make wrought, or bar iron, for which there was a limitless demand, both in England and throughout the world.

Thomas Taliesin strode through the casthouse and gazed up at the hillside, into the side of which were built two blast furnaces. Alongside these were calcination kilns, and a building to house a steam-engine, which provided the blast. This was empty, for the machine itself had been sold for scrap months ago.

The furnaces were old. Peering up these great, dark chimneys, Owen's heart sank even more. Even he could see the firebricks were crumbling, and would need to be replaced. Ducking out of the hole in the side of the south furnace, he gazed up at the leaden sky above. "It's getting dark," he observed. "Time to be on our way."

"Don't be too eager." Thomas laid a restraining hand on his sleeve. "Let old woman Heatherwood sweat it out a few days longer. She'll drop the price a bit further then."

"What?" Owen gaped at him. "You don't imagine I'm going to buy this place?"

"You'll be a fool if you don't." Thomas grinned. "I know it looks terrible at present. The words millstone and neck, not to mention hopeless and liability, spring readily to mind.

"But by the time you've put these furnaces into blast, got the forge working and the foundry on song, together with a hundred men scurrying about the place, you'll think differently, believe you me. Come on, man. I'll help you. Give you the benefit of my sound judgement and good advice. Will you give it a go?"

Owen considered. He looked at his friend, standing there four-square and confident on the windy hillside. Could Owen Morgan be an ironmaster, too?

Suddenly, he knew he could. He could bring Heatherwood back to life. "I'll see my lawyer tomorrow," he replied.

"There. You've done it!" Thomas Taliesin shook Owen by the hand. "So now, I bid you the most hearty of welcomes to the most exclusive of clubs."

"Thank you." Owen grinned. "But, Tom – I hope you don't think I intend to tread on *your* toes?"

"No, indeed. In fact, I've taken steps to ensure you could not."

"So you and Mr Atkins set all this up between you?"

"In a manner of speaking." Thomas grinned too. "Nowadays, he's doing so well that he needs far more castings than I can produce. That is, unless I supply his factories only – which I wouldn't wish to do. It's the eggs-in-one-basket notion, you see. I always fight shy of that. So then I thought, why not divide the pickings between us? Why don't we both grow rich?"

The contracts were signed. The deal was done. So now, needing somewhere convenient to live, Owen took out a lease on a substantial, stone-built, plain but perfectly adequate house, not far from the ironworks themselves.

Neither large nor spacious, Cwm Dhu was nevertheless quite big enough for a bachelor and two or three servants. In many ways, moreover, it reminded Owen of his childhood home, with its painted mortar floors and stencilled plasterwork, its lofty gables and its dark little rooms, each leading in and out of the other.

"Do you think you'll be happy here?" asked David, as he gazed all round the bare, stone-flagged kitchen, and shook his head very dubiously indeed.

"Why should I not?" Owen shrugged. "This place is snug enough. It's weatherproof. I agree it's small, and rather bleak. But it's all I need."

"Is it?" David sucked his teeth. "I wonder. I had you down for a family man. A husband and father, with children playing round you, and a babe on each knee."

"Oh." Again, Owen shrugged. "I doubt if I'll even marry," he murmured. "Let alone father children. I've been a bachelor too long to desire any changes nowadays."

As Michael Atkins had promised, as soon as it was known Heatherwood was back in business, the orders came rolling in. So, the buildings were repaired. The first furnace was put into blast. The day this was tapped and a lazy stream of molten iron came snaking out, flowing smoothly into the sand moulds which lay ready and waiting, was the day Owen realised that for once in his life he had got something completely right. This business was for him. He *was* an ironmaster!

"A beautiful sight." A workman from the casthouse

stood at Owen's side. He shielded his eyes from the heat and glare. "Eh, master?"

"Beautiful," Owen agreed.

Having decided that as master he would take an active part in running the place, Owen dispensed with the services of a manager. Instead, he appointed his foremen, they found hindsmen, and everyone got on with the job in hand.

Country-bred and gently-reared though Owen had been, he found that once he got used to them, neither the nostril-searing heat, the constant dancing smuts, the dirt nor the stench of iron-founding appalled him in the least. Instead, he was fascinated by the whole magical process of turning ore and limestone into fat, dormant pigs, or gleaming metal bars. In fact, he was like a child with an enormous, enchanting new toy.

The workforce – men, women and children alike – had a good opinion of him from the start. For Owen was one of them. He even spoke their own language, albeit with a strange, peculiar inflection which they put down to his having spent time among the heathen in foreign climes. The hot Indian sun had obviously addled his brain. But at least he was not an incomer. A Saxon who would milk their country dry, then leave its indigenous population to rot.

Owen visited his uncle regularly. These days, David was hoarser and croakier than ever. But, in spite of this, he would not give up his pipe of tobacco, even though the smoke made him wheeze and choke like a dying frog.

One evening, as nephew and uncle sat together, a tap on the door was followed by the manservant entering the snug little sitting room, where there was always the best fire. "It's a woman," said the servant, without preamble. "She's asking to see Mr Morgan, at once."

"Tell her to step into the shop, then." It was very late, and David was tired. Resignedly, he sighed. "I'll be out directly."

"I beg your pardon, sir – but it's Mr Owen Morgan she wishes to see." The servant sniffed his distaste. "She's so ragged, unkempt and dirty that I told her if it was relief she needed, she should take herself off to the poorhouse. But she would not be denied."

"I'll see her." Owen rose to his feet. "After all, she may have travelled a very long way. Perhaps one of my men is sick, and she's a wife or daughter come to seek my aid."

Chapter Eleven

When she saw Owen, Isabel broke down, bursting into tears of both exhaustion and relief. "Oh, God!" Gulping and sobbing, she threw herself into his arms. "Oh, great God in heaven! I thought I would never find you! But now I have, I don't think I can even bear to look at you, in case you—"

But then her sobs choked her, and for a few minutes speech was an impossibility.

The servant had said she was ragged and dirty. Now, Owen realised, she was starving too. Her shoulders were bony, her arms like sticks, and her lovely face quite gaunt with need. While not exactly in tatters – for no one of any sense or education would have mistaken Isabel Darrow for a beggar, or a tramp – her shoes were down at heel, her shawl dirty, and her gown torn.

As she clung to Owen and wept, David Morgan came into the shop. Having heard Isabel's hysterical crying, he confidently expected to find a patient *in extremis*, desperate for his aid. But instead, he found his nephew being half-strangled by a lunatic in a shabby silk gown. At a loss, he stared. "Well, then? What ails the girl?" he demanded irritably.

With some difficulty, Owen extricated himself from Isabel's embrace. "This lady is not a patient," he began. But then, he bit his lip. Some kind of explanation was necessary. But what? "She's an old acquaintance of mine," he said.

"Oh?" Not in the least impressed, David sniffed. "May I know when and where you were introduced?"

"This is Mrs Darrow," muttered Owen. "She is my cousin Rayner's wife."

"Your cousin's wife?" Glancing again at Isabel, who was still weeping and whose face was stained with dirt and the tracks of previous tears, he shook his head. "Oh. I see."

Owen frowned. "What do you mean, you see?"

"I mean, I understand perfectly now. It all makes sense. Your sudden departure from Warwickshire. Your arrival here, with straw in your hair and your linen not changed for a week. Your wedding not to take place after all. Then, your dear aunt dead of a seizure, but you yourself not permitted to stand by her grave."

Grimacing, David shook his head. "Everything awry," he muttered. "The family at Easton suddenly incommunicado. You behaving like a dog that's been whipped for stealing the mutton from the kitchen spit."

"Uncle, I—"

"Save your breath, child. Whatever the explanation, I don't wish to hear it. Not this evening, at any rate." David touched Isabel's shoulder. "Well, young lady," he continued, "you had better come into the parlour. I'll have the abigail make up a poultice for your feet, and I myself will fetch you a cordial. While I do that, you can explain yourself to your friend here. After he's locked up, that is."

Isabel was most unwilling to let Owen out of her sight, even for a moment. But, when he promised that after he had locked up the shop, he would join her in the parlour straight away, she consented to be led into that snug little room, and to sit by the fire there.

A minute later, Owen was sitting down himself. "Well, Isabel?" he began.

"Don't look unkindly at me! I can't bear it!" Her tears having temporarily abated, Isabel began to cry again. "Oh, God!" she sobbed. "God and all the saints in heaven, I wish I were dead!"

"Come, Isabel. You *must* speak to me. What on earth has happened?"

"Can't you guess?" wept Isabel. But then, she made some attempt to control her tears. "Very well," she muttered. "I'll attempt to enlighten you. I'll begin at the beginning, shall I?"

"Please do."

"You remember that after we had – after you'd told them you had changed your mind about marrying Jane, the squire ordered Rayner to take me home?"

"Yes."

"Well, as soon as we arrived there, he told my maid I'd had an accident, and to put me straight to bed. You may imagine how I passed that night! The following morning, my husband came to see me. He sat down on a hard chair, and read me a lecture on sin." Isabel's soft mouth twisted angrily. "God," she hissed, "he's so like his father! Such a cold, unforgiving, self-righteous, puritan saint! Ever preaching the desirability of sobriety, chastity and moral rectitude. But ogling my breasts the while!"

"What exactly did Rayner say?"

"He told me I had behaved abominably. I had forfeited any right to the society of decent people, and I would be an outcast for the rest of my days. Then he asked if I intended to repent."

Viciously, Isabel gnawed her lower lip. "So much cant! I know *he* visits brothels! I've smelled them on him! So anyway, I told him that although he might call me a whore, he was nothing but a hog. As for his sister, she was a nun. Which was hardly surprising, coming as she did from a holy pair like the Darrows, who no doubt suffered nothing so impure as carnal knowledge to pollute *their* wedded bliss! Whose children were conceived by the Holy Ghost. Born of the Virgin Rebecca—

"He slapped me hard then, across the face. I think I must have fainted. Later that morning he was sent for, and I learned his mother had died during the night. The shock had killed her, they supposed. Owen, I know how tenderly you loved your aunt. I'm sorry to give you pain."

"What happened next?"

"He shut me up in the house. He locked me in my bedchamber, in fact. I suppose I wasn't a prisoner, not exactly – but I was forbidden visitors. Not that I'd have had to turn them away, for by then everyone knew what had happened, and no respectable matron would have come near me, for I would have polluted her by my very presence. My maid brought me all the news. Of course, the servants' tongues never stopped wagging, of that you may be sure.

"Even my mother would not see me. In fact, my parents let it be known that they had disowned me. Rayner could cast me out, and I might die in a ditch for all they cared. I was no child of theirs."

"Oh, Isabel! That's terrible." In spite of himself, Owen was moved. He had expected Rayner to forgive his wife. He'd assumed things in Warwickshire would soon get back to normal. Jane would forget him, and eventually marry a better man than he. "Isabel," he began gently, "what do you mean to do now?"

"I don't know!" Isabel's tears were ready to flow again. "I just wanted—"

"How did you manage to get away from Rayner?"

"I bribed my maid to leave my door ajar. I gave her my silver needle-case, with the laudanum bottle secreted in the lid. She'd always coveted it, you see. I had a few guineas in my escritoire.

"I travelled post, then when my money ran out I begged my passage. I hailed wagons, farmers' carts, tradesmen's drays – anything. Oh God! It was horrible!"

"How did you find me?"

"I knew your uncle was an apothecary. Maria happened to mention his circumstances once, and astonishingly enough I had remembered the facts. So when I was set down in the market place, I enquired at the inn, and was directed here."

Now, David himself entered the little parlour. He brought with him a jug of something flavoured with sweet herbs, camomile, and honey. Pouring a glass, he handed it to his guest. "Drink it all," he said.

Meekly, Isabel accepted the glass. She began to sip. Then, David's maidservant, Sarah Hughes – who frequently assisted at those minor operations and surgical procedures which, as a licensed apothecary, David Morgan was legally permitted to perform – removed Isabel's ragged shoes, and washed her feet. Carefully, she treated all the blisters and scrapes which disfigured Isabel's soft, white skin.

"Thank you," said Isabel, when the maid had finished. "You're very kind."

Sarah smiled in acknowledgement. She stood up. "Will you have something to eat, ma'am?" she enquired.

"I'm not hungry." Isabel stifled a yawn. "But I'm so weary, I could sleep for a week."

"Where may she sleep?" asked Owen.

"She must have the maid's room," replied David, decisively.

"What about Sarah?"

"She and Bronwen will share a bed in the scullery." David reached for the candle. "Come along, young lady. I'll light you upstairs."

"Thank you, Mr Morgan." Isabel struggled to her feet. Then, reddening, she hung her head. "But before I go to bed," she murmured, "I have something of a rather delicate nature to say to your nephew here. I—"

"Very well." David handed the candle to Owen. "My nephew shall light your way."

The maid's room was small, but clean and warm. To Isabel, who had spent a week on the open road, it looked like a bedchamber in a palace.

"I'll leave you, then," said Owen. He placed the candlestick on the washstand. "Sarah will bring your tea, about seven. But if you need anything in the night, do please—"

"Owen?"

"Yes?"

"Thank you for your kindness. Thank you for taking me in, and for giving me a roof above my head tonight."

Owen shrugged. "I feel responsible for you," he said.

"Yes. I believe you do." But then, Isabel grimaced, as if in pain. "All the same, our just and charitable society being what it is, no one would have blamed you if you'd felt no concern at all. If I had been found dead in the gutter a stone's throw from your door, nobody would have called *you* to account."

"Maybe not. But I should have reproached myself."

"That is because you're a good man." Isabel reached for his hand. "Stay a moment longer. Close the door."

"Isabel, I don't think—"

"I need to say just two words."

"Well?"

"Touch me." Taking his right hand, Isabel placed the palm against her stomach. "Don't you feel him quicken?"

"Quicken?" Owen stared at her. "Isabel, what are you saying?"

"He kicks and bucks like a baby antelope! My dear Owen, I'm carrying your son."

There was nothing for it but to take her to the little house near the ironworks and introduce her to the two servants there as Mrs Morgan, their master's wife. Of course, David's own servants' chatter made the circumstances of the alleged Mrs Owen Morgan's arrival in South Wales, torn and bleeding and looking for all the world like a tinker born and bred under a hedgerow, except that she wore a grubby silk gown, general currency for miles round about. Everyone agreed that it was a rum business.

Very rum indeed.

For a while, Isabel was happy. Relief that she was not to be turned out – for indeed, Owen now had a spare bedchamber fitted up specially for her, and engaged a maid to look after her – and gratitude that she was allowed to take his name, so could therefore meet the gapes of local people with a bold, level stare of her own, made her tractable and pleasant.

For a time.

But then, she began to fret. She had nothing to do all day, and was consequently extremely bored. Recovering from her ordeal on the highways and byways of England and Wales, she found she had plenty of energy, but nothing to expend it on.

"Go walking," suggested Owen, when she grumbled that she had spent all one particular afternoon watching sooty raindrops slide down the window panes, and almost died of boredom as a result, "take some exercise. In the fresh air."

"What fresh air?" Contemptuously, Isabel sniffed. "If I so much as poke my head outside the front door, I begin to sneeze. My bonnet is covered in smuts in an instant."

"But if you go just a little further down the valley, you'll find the air is clear."

"If I go down the valley, I shall then be obliged to climb the mountain. If I have a mind to come home again, that is. In any case, I am presently in *no* condition to scramble about amidst rocks and scree."

Isabel pouted for a few moments longer. But then, she smiled. Going over to where Owen sat, she wound her white arms around his shoulders. She kissed his face.

"Don't do that," he murmured.

"Why?" Isabel kissed him again. "You do need me," she whispered. She ran her long, thin fingers through his hair. "Why pretend to hate me, when you know you love me still?"

Owen merely sighed.

So, encouraged, Isabel slid her fingers under the neck-band of his shirt. She shook off her cap. Strands of her coppery hair stroked Owen's face.

Pregnancy had not diminished Isabel's appetite for sex in the slightest. Indeed, if anything, this had increased. So, after a token resistance, Owen allowed her into his bed. He let her seduce and beguile him all over again.

She was determined to bewitch him, and she did. Now, she even had an ally, for inside her the unborn baby wriggled and squirmed and demanded attention as imperiously as ever his mother did. Owen watched fascinated as little elbows, fists and knees pummelled and punched and kicked, lying safe beneath the soft blanket of Isabel's milk-white skin.

Tracing the child's ghostly outlines, watching the baby twist and turn and then, as if exhausted, come to rest, Owen realised he was still mad. He was still in love with his cousin's wife. But, more than that, he was beginning to love her for herself. She had been so brave. So selfless. She had given up everything to be with him . . .

She was also generous, and kind. Sated herself, she was always careful to make sure he was completely satisfied, too. One evening, realising he was still awake, she touched his arm.

"What is it?" he murmured.

"You're very restless," she said.

"I was thinking." Wearily, he rubbed his tired eyes. "There's a problem at the works. We can't get one of the furnaces properly into blast. There's something wrong with the big steam engine, too – but I don't know what it can be."

"Well, you need your sleep." Isabel took his hand in hers. "I could relax you," she whispered.

"Could you?"

"Of course." Sitting up, she slipped out of her nightdress. She pushed the bedclothes aside.

Until he had carnal knowledge of Isabel, Owen had assumed that English ladies of *her* class and breeding were delicate, fastidious creatures. A wife tolerated her husband's lust simply because it was expected of her. If she meant to be a mother, sexual congress was a tribulation she was obliged to bear. Only the lower orders and professional whores understood the giving and receiving of pleasure for its own sake.

But then, he reasoned, Isabel wasn't English anyway. Although her ancestors had lived for generations in the green heart of Warwickshire, Isabel was an American by birth. Perhaps that accounted for it? The hot sun of Virginia had warmed her cold Anglo-Saxon blood.

So now, he lay supine, letting her hands and mouth work their magic on him.

"How do you know about these things?" he asked later when, good for nothing, his problems at the ironworks completely forgotten, he lay exhausted by her side.

"My nurse taught me," she replied.

"Your nurse?" Owen was astonished. "But how—"

"Don't look so shocked. It wasn't like that." Tossing back her copper ringlets, Isabel smiled. "My nurse was a passionate woman. She was very desirable, too. She had at least seven children, two or three of them my father's own. But her other lovers came from all over the estate.

"Her duties as my nurse were not burdensome, so she had plenty of opportunity to amuse and divert herself. To divert others, too! She visited all over the plantation, in fact. Whenever she paid a call, she would sit me in a corner of the cabin with my dolls, throw off her shift, then go to work.

"When we left Virginia, I forgot all about those interesting outings of mine. But when I was first married, something triggered memories of that time." Isabel shook her head. "I thought all grown-up women behaved thus. I imagined it was part of the contract, that a wife should give her husband pleasure. But Rayner did not agree. The first time I did, or began to do – for indeed, I was abruptly forestalled – what I have just done for you, my husband was disgusted. He said I was behaving like a harlot."

Bitterly, Isabel sighed. "*He* knows all about them, of course! As God is my witness, I do not traduce him in the slightest when I tell you he's had experience of dozens, if not scores!"

"*Has* he?" Owen was amazed. He had dismissed Isabel's earlier insistence that Rayner frequented brothels as demented raving. "Are you quite sure of that?"

"Most certainly!" Isabel replied.

"But – Isabel, how did you learn of it? Surely he did not tell you to your face?"

"Oh, the whole county knows! Rayner and Charles Harding are bywords in Easton, and the area round about. For a while, my maid was intimate with Mr Harding's manservant. That fellow has a mouth as wide as the entrance to Hades itself.

"All the same, nobody speaks of it in public. Maria pretends she knows nothing about it, nothing at all. Owen?"

"Yes?"

"You're so kind. So honest. Not a hypocrite, like Rayner and his friends. I was right to come to you."

"Yes, I think you were."

"We will be happy together, won't we?"

"I hope so." Contentedly, Owen yawned. Now, he would certainly go to sleep.

But with no calls to make, no friends to chat with and no occupation to keep her busy, for much of the time Isabel was not happy at all. She was too bored to be content.

The servants did the routine housework, of course – but although in rural Wales, it was perfectly permissible for a mistress to take charge of her own kitchen, Isabel thought it beneath her even to enter the servants' hall. All she would do was order meals. Lacking any skills in practical needlework, she could not make baby clothes, nor mend household linens. So she simply had nothing to do.

As her girth increased, and she became clumsy and lumpish, her temper became uncertain in the extreme. The imperfections of the house, which she had once thought charming, were a constant irritation. Her bedchamber was too poky, the stairs were too steep, and the sitting room too dark.

Her diet was unsatisfactory, too. "I am sick of mutton," she complained, as a hash of onions, potatoes and meat was placed before her, for the third day running. "Is there never any beef or pork to be had in this Godforsaken place?"

"The Welsh eat mutton." Owen was hungry, and not disposed to quarrel with his victuals, even if these were stodgy and badly dressed. He passed Isabel the pepper. "So, Isabel – if you are to live in Wales, you must learn to like it too."

Isabel scowled at him. Dropping her knife and fork on her plate, she called for some cheese and celery, instead. Then, having chewed a stalk or two and rejected the cheese as maggotty, she announced she was going for a walk.

But whenever she went outside to take a breath of fresh air, she was never able to find any. Up on the mountainside or down in the valley, it made no difference. There were smuts, smoke and dust everywhere.

Passing to and from the ironworks, the workmen and their sluttish wives stared at her. They never spoke, but merely nodded and grinned, like the simpletons they were. Not understanding their outlandish language, Isabel had no intention whatsoever of learning it, so it annoyed her extremely that Owen himself would jabber away to anybody and everybody in a tongue as foreign to Isabel as Ancient Greek. But his offer to teach her some Welsh was rejected with scorn.

"You could go on a visit to my uncle, if you like." Owen had had a busy day at work, and expected an even busier one tomorrow. A third furnace had been built and was to be put into blast, a new steam engine was to be installed, so he was as excited as a child with a new toy. "It's a long round trip, I agree. But you could stay overnight, couldn't you? If you spent a day or two in Cardiff, you could look out some linen for the child."

"There's none to be had in Cardiff," retorted Isabel, crossly. "I shall have to send to Manchester for all that."

"Then, sit and chat with my uncle."

"Your uncle!" Isabel snorted her disdain. "Who in her right mind would wish to spend even an hour in the company of that foolish old man?"

When Owen came home the following evening, grubby and tired but triumphant, Isabel's mood had not improved. "You look like an artisan in that filthy coat," she grumbled. "You smell quite disgusting. I hate the stink of engine oil and coal dust, and you reek of both."

"I'll go and wash, then." Owen was happy tonight. The new engine was working perfectly, the processes were on song, and since the war in Europe had intensified, orders were flooding in. "I'll do it now, while you make tea."

"Pray do." Isabel glared at him. "Whatever his faults, Rayner at least always looked the gentleman."

All that evening, it was the same. Prodding and goading, sneering and provoking, Isabel longed for a quarrel, but Owen was too tired to oblige her. She was still grumbling when he fell asleep in his chair.

The following day, she was sullen from dawn to dusk. That evening, she wanted sex.

"I *do* love you," mumbled Owen, as he turned over and attempted to go to sleep. "But I worry that we might hurt the child." He yawned. "Oh, darling! Let me sleep! I'm so tired tonight."

"Tired," pouted Isabel. Spitefully, she pinched his arm. "You cruel, unfeeling brute. What you mean is, you're tired of me."

"Nonsense." Owen closed his eyes. But now, he found he was thinking of Jane. Dear Jane! The kind of woman a man would always be glad to come home to. The tranquil, soft-voiced creature any sensible man would be delighted to call wife.

"You're thinking of her again." Isabel's rather shrill, sharp voice cut like a blade, right into the dream. "You're remembering your virgin nun."

Owen knew this was a guess – that she could not see

into his heart or his mind – but still he started, a guilty thing surprised. "Don't, Isabel," he muttered. "You give me a headache when you go on so."

"I hate this place." It was breakfast time. Isabel had made tea, but she had forgotten to warm the pot, the water had not boiled, so now she passed Owen a scummy cupful of weak, greyish broth. "It's so poky," she grumbled. "So drab. When I remember my own house, how light and airy it was—"

On and on she went, and she was still complaining when Owen left for work.

He returned home very tired. Having spent much of that day in the heat and dust of the casthouse, his head already ached, and when Isabel began to memorialise her fine linen sheets, her beautiful gowns, and her little lap dogs who would certainly be pining for their mistress, he found he could bear it no longer. "Why don't you go back to Warwickshire, then?" he cried.

"What?" Startled, Isabel stalled in mid-grizzle. "What did you say?"

"You heard me." Owen closed his tired eyes. "Beg Rayner to have you back. Ask him to overlook the awkward fact that you're big with another man's child. There's a more than even chance he might."

"But Owen, I—"

"He's been schooled from childhood in the art of turning the other cheek. Of forgiving those who trespass against him. If you grovel enough, he might take you in."

"Do you mean that?" Her eyes wide, Isabel stared at him. "Do you actually—"

"Yes, indeed." Deliberately misunderstanding her, Owen ploughed on. "Rayner's not a vindictive man. So, if you abase yourself, if you lie in the dust and lick his boots, he'll probably raise you up and forgive you everything."

"Owen, do you honestly wish me to go back to Rayner?"

"Do *you* wish it?"

"Sometimes, I think I do." Isabel was sniffing hard.

"When you haven't spoken to me properly for days together, when I long and long for some pleasant conversation, I do. Whatever his failings, Rayner was always sociable. He loved to chat."

"Well, I am an only child. My parents died when I was very young. I have spent long periods of my life in my own company, so it's only natural that I should be somewhat self-absorbed."

"I think you've grown to hate me."

"I've grown to hate the fact that you can be so tiresome!" Owen was angry. Why couldn't Isabel leave him alone? Why did she need to be entertained all the time, night and day?

For, there was more than an element of truth in what she said. He didn't actually hate her, he couldn't hate poor Isabel – but she did annoy him. Also, he didn't desire her. Not any more, not while she was so fat and ungainly, with the blue veins standing proud on her legs, her ankles swollen, and her once beautiful bosom bloated and heavy as lead.

"He might take me," she was saying now. Miserably, she sniffed. "After all – there's a chance this could be Rayner's child."

"What?" Owen came out of his reverie with a start. "What did you say?"

"I said, this baby could be Rayner's."

"Oh? But you told me he—"

"He was a boring, disagreeable lover. He gave me no pleasure in bed. But he was not incapable."

"Oh. I see."

"What a mess it all is." Awkwardly, Isabel rose from the sofa. Collecting the tea things together, she sighed. "Do you still love *her*?"

"I—"

"Of course you do. You think of her constantly. You even dream of her. You say her namc in your sleep."

"Isabel, I have known her from a child. I have always loved her."

"More than you love me?"

"Oh, Isabel!"

"Answer me!"

"I love her face. Her voice. Her manner. I love her quiet serenity, and I love her grace. Wherever she is, there is also peace."

"But where I am, there is discord."

"Those last words were yours, not mine." Owen met Isabel's great, green eyes. "You know I love you!" he cried. "That I will always look after you. Yet you cannot leave me alone. You will not let me rest. Sometimes, Isabel, it's as if you want to goad me into saying I hate you. You drive me to distraction!"

"I gave up everything for you." Isabel was weeping bitterly. "I abandoned my husband, who loved me dearly. For your sake, I became an outcast. A wanderer on the face of the earth."

"You're being perfectly ridiculous now."

"I offer you everything, and all I want in return is a little affection." Isabel went to stand beside him. She stroked his shoulder, then slid her hand inside his shirt. "Owen?" she whispered.

But Owen was not moved. Early the following morning, he had to see Mr Atkins. He would need a clear head if he was to talk business. Isabel, on the other hand, never left her bed until well past noon. "I'm going to bed now," he said. "I don't wish to disturb you with my muttering, so I shall sleep in the small dressing room."

"Then you turn your back on me? I am carrying your child. I need your company, yet you—"

"You told me yourself that the child might be Rayner's. Go to him, tell him so. Just think, Isabel. That boy could be the heir to half of Warwickshire."

"You're so cruel!" Isabel clutched at the back of a chair. She swayed, then she fainted, and Owen was obliged to call her maid.

Chapter Twelve

"Please, Owen! Don't go!"

"Isabel, I'm not needed here. I'm only getting in my uncle's way."

"But I'm so frightened!" Isabel grabbed at Owen's hand. Pincer-like, her fingers dug into his flesh. So he was obliged to stay, although while the examination went on, he studiously looked the other way.

When Isabel had fainted, Owen and her maid had sat her up, wafted smelling salts under her nose and waited patiently for her to come round. Then they'd put her to bed. Thinking it best to remain with her that night, Owen had lain down beside her, only to be woken at two in the morning by a woman convinced she was in labour.

She wanted David Morgan now. Although she had previously dismissed him as a foolish old man, she both liked and trusted him, and had more or less obliged him to agree to be her midwife, when the time came.

So, duly sent for, he came. Roused from his sleep by a boy on a donkey, he got up, dressed himself, then rode for miles along bad roads and across pathless heathland, reflecting that it was just as well the moon was bright.

Concluding his examination of Isabel, he rolled down his shirt sleeves and reached for his coat. "Cover her now," he told Isabel's maid. "Make sure she's warm, and try to keep her quiet." He turned to his nephew, who stood sullen and awkward, as near to the door as he could possibly contrive to be. "Come downstairs," he said.

David led Owen into the parlour. As they entered that

cosy little room, the Dutch clock on the dresser was striking seven, and Owen picked up his jacket. "I must go," he began. "The men will be expecting me early today. We're taking delivery of—"

"Sit down." As he spoke, David himself sat down. Rummaging in his pocket for a notebook and pencil, he wrote out a prescription. "Have the housemaid make up a quart of this, in the proportions I've specified. It should calm her, at any rate."

"I sincerely hope it will."

"Do you?" Glancing up at his nephew, David frowned. "You young fool," he muttered. "Don't you know anything?"

"I beg your pardon?" Offended, Owen glared. "What exactly do you mean by that?"

"Isabel," said David carefully, "is a woman."

"Yes, I had noticed."

"Don't be saucy with *me*, boy!" But then, sighing, David folded his arms. "Women," he began, "pregnant women especially, are not like you or me. Poor things, even the best of them are blind to reason. Deaf to common sense. Sometimes, I think the Almighty was laughing in his sleeve when he created our mother Eve. He enjoys the joke still.

"So, women cannot help their God-given natures. They *must* be hysterical. Do you understand me? The very word means pertaining to the womb – which, as even you must know, is the source of all the ridiculous fancies and foolish notions every woman entertains."

"Indeed?" Owen yawned. He hadn't time to listen to this apothecary's cant. "Mr Atkins will be waiting for me," he muttered. "I must—"

But David caught his wrist, and held him. "Isabel is near her time," he continued. "Her womb is stretched almost to bursting, and releasing evil humours into every part of her body. It's no wonder she's fidgety as a cat on a stove! Starting at her own shadow. Raging like a wounded tigress about nothing at all. So—"

"So I must let her abuse me? Sit patient and forbearing while she shrieks and scolds and calls me a brute?"

"While she's with child, you must. Be compliant. For, after childbirth, you will see the flow of hysterical humours abate. The limited powers of understanding God gave her poor sex will be restored."

"Thank heavens for that." Sulkily, Owen shrugged. "I do try to be kind," he muttered, "even when she's being unpleasant to me. What more can she expect?"

"You must be kinder still. Give her whatever she wants – within reason, that is." Ruefully, David smiled. "Do you take my meaning? It will be worth your while, believe you me. Afterwards, she'll be so docile that you won't even recognise the harridan who spoiled your comfort at dinner time."

"Oh." Owen sniffed. "Is there anything else?" he enquired sarcastically.

"Don't argue with her. In her condition, it's a waste of breath. So, if she wants to abuse you, let her rant." David picked up his hat. "I would guess it will be another ten days or so. No more. I'll come back next week, and see how she goes on."

Isabel accepted the sleeping draught. After drinking it down, she fell into a deep slumber, and stayed in bed for the rest of the day. Curiously enough, but perhaps because she was quiet and rested, when Owen himself went to bed he found he did desire her.

David had been right. Afterwards, she was calm and placid. Grateful, even. She kissed him and said she loved him dearly. That night, her labour began.

There was no time to summon David, so a woman from nearby Cwm Mawr was called in, instead. Clean, efficient and knowledgeable, she calmly coached a terrified Isabel through an ordeal during which her patient screamed and howled and cursed her Creator to the ends of the earth, crying out that she wanted to die.

"Never again," wept Isabel, as her daughter came into

the world. The midwife cleaned her up and muttered to the lady's maid that she'd never known such a carry-on. Never, in all her born days. This birth had been an easy one!

"She has your eyes." Later in the day, Isabel had become calmer. Taking the baby from its cradle, she held her daughter close. "Dear Owen, do look! They're yours absolutely. In colour, shape, *and* set! Isn't it astonishing?"

"Astonishing," Owen agreed, privately reflecting that this child was most certainly a Darrow. From which side of the family, however, he would not care to speculate.

But at least Isabel was happy now. "Look at her little hands," she was murmuring, as she counted the fingers, and examined each tiny pink pearl from one to ten. "She's perfect."

"Perfect." Owen smiled. He stroked the baby's cheek. The great rush of protective love which he felt for this tiny, helpless scrap of humanity had taken him completely unawares.

When Isabel's milk came in, she neither groaned nor complained, nor did she demand that the midwife bind her breasts in order that they might not stretch or sag. Instead, she bore the discomfort with cheerful fortitude. "Of course I shall feed her," she insisted, as she and her daughter tried to get the hang of the thing. "It's becoming quite the fashion nowadays."

"Oh, well. If it's the fashion!" Owen ruffled her hair. He glanced at the baby. "She seems to know what to do, at any rate."

A girl from the village in the valley came in to help with the baby. Having eight brothers and sisters of her own, she was quietly expert at changing linen and cleaning up mess. In fact, she understood all those mysteries which a fine lady like Isabel could not possibly be expected to comprehend.

Invited to visit and stand godfather, David took his

niece in his arms and talked to her. "Of course she's beautiful!" he murmured. "What do you say, my precious? Oh, certainly! Of course you're clever. Charming, too."

Then he glanced towards the child's parents. "What will you call her?" he enquired.

"Honor." Owen shrugged. "It's Isabel's choice. I favoured Sarah. Or Elizabeth."

"We'll have her baptised Honor Elizabeth, then." Complacently, Isabel smiled. "Will you stay a week longer?" she asked David. "It's so comfortable and pleasant when you are here."

It was as well David did stay. A slight fever, which Isabel had been running for a day or two, worsened that night. Soon, the new mother lay delirious, by turns burning hot, then freezing cold, and totally incoherent throughout.

"Don't despair." Mixing a cordial, which he would then try to dribble down his patient's parched throat, David gave Owen's hand a comforting squeeze. "She'll get the better of this, I'm sure. So don't you make yourself ill, fretting needlessly."

"What shall we do about Honor?"

"Find her a nurse, of course. That's something you could see to now."

So, a wet nurse was duly found, and Honor was properly nourished. Soon she became so chubby that Owen called her his little air balloon, insisting that if a careless pin pricked her, she would pop.

Isabel, on the other hand, was now painfully thin. Recovering from the fever, she remained so pale and transparent that Owen still feared for her life. "I think we should send for her mother," he said, as he and David sat at supper together that evening. "I shall write to Mrs Graham tonight."

"Well, child – as you think best." David sighed. "But do you imagine her mother will come?"

"She might." Owen shrugged. "Mr Graham is hard and unfeeling, it's true. But his wife is neither unforgiving nor unkind. She would wish to see her child and granddaughter, I'm sure."

Mrs Graham came. On her arrival, she went straight upstairs to Isabel's room. When she came down again, Owen understood that she had forgiven her daughter unconditionally. She had probably done so long ago. As far as her husband was concerned, his erring child was dead and buried. But to her mother, the daughter was as dear as ever she'd been.

"You should take her away from this place." Sitting down to dinner with Owen and his uncle, Mrs Graham looked from one to the other. "The air here is so foul, and the situation so unhealthy, that I fear for Isabel's safety if she remains here indefinitely."

"Could you leave the works to its own devices for a month or so?" asked David. For he agreed with Mrs Graham. "I know your livelihood is here, but Isabel is surely more precious to you than cold castings and insensate iron bars?"

"Yes, she is." Owen nodded. "I'll take her to Brighton," he declared. "She would like that."

"Yes, indeed." Mrs Graham brightened visibly. "There, she will breathe pure air. Feel a clean breeze against her cheeks. A little sea bathing would set her up for ever, I'm certain of it."

Owen found he liked Isabel's mother. "Will it be difficult for you, going home?" he asked, as they strolled through the scrubby little garden surrounding the house, one Sunday morning in late June.

"My husband thinks I am in Bristol, visiting friends." Mrs Graham sighed. "Well, of course he thinks nothing of the kind. But this is the fiction with which I chose to present him, and which he chose to accept."

"I see. Forgive me for asking, but is Mr Graham a kind husband to you?"

"Kind enough." Sighing again, Mrs Graham shook

her head. "Mr Morgan, I was born into a relatively impoverished family. My father worked hard, but he was on the whole unsuccessful in life. He died a bankrupt, and was buried in a pauper's grave.

"Poor white trash – that's what I was called by Richmond society, when Mr Samuel Heathcote Graham's son took a fancy to me, and married me in defiance of both his family and his friends."

"But you were happy together?"

"Yes, at first. You see, I was a strong, healthy creature then. Confident I could produce any number of fine, strapping sons. But after Isabel was born, I became very ill. The doctor told my husband that there could be no more children. That if he valued me at all, we should sleep apart for the rest of our days.

"I have no fortune, talents or skills of my own. So, if my husband were to cast me out, where would I go? Abandoned by him, I would simply walk the streets until I found a convenient gutter in which to starve."

Compared with the dirt and squalor of industrial Wales, Sussex was the Garden of Eden. A paradise on earth. Brighton itself was perfectly beautiful. Clean, white, impossibly elegant architecture delighted the eye. The sun sparkled on the playful blue waves, and the pretty gardens which stretched all along the seafront invited the visitor to linger and inspect at leisure.

Growing stronger every day, Isabel was happy there. Her baby was contented and thriving. A little sea bathing, together with daily visits to the warm brine bath, had done the new mother a world of good. Her lodgings, situated in the most fashionable part of town, were comfortable, spacious and clean.

Every day, the little family walked on the Steyne, where they watched detachments of Guards in scarlet uniforms on elaborate manoeuvres, or smartly parading up and down. Observing these casually elegant displays of military might – mere playing at toy soldiers, or so it seemed to the untutored eye – no one would have guessed that just across the Channel lay a great army, patiently waiting to invade. To subdue the island race for ever.

But then again, there was no real cause for anxiety – for, as every red-blooded Englishman was well aware, *he* was the equal of at least fifty foreigners, who were all cringing, frog-eating, Papist slaves.

Isabel loved driving, so every other day Owen hired a barouche or a chaise, then took her and Honor for a ride along the strand, or across the Downs.

"Do you ever wish you had gone for a soldier?" enquired Isabel one fine morning, as she and her little family bowled along in a smart, new barouche, letting the sun kiss their faces and the wind tangle their hair. "Do you see yourself in a scarlet coat, with epaulettes of gold?"

"Not at all." Driving past a military encampment, where serried rows of tents stretched into the distance for as far as the eye could see, Owen shook his head. "I'm a coward," he explained. "Those brave fellows yonder laugh at sword-thrusts. They go into battle with their heads held high, and bear their injuries with a fortitude *I* could never summon to my aid! You see, I don't like pain."

Owen and his family arrived back in South Wales relaxed and contented, well pleased with the world and one another. Owen had benefitted from a much-needed rest, and Honor had enjoyed having the undivided attention of two people instead of just one. Isabel had gained some weight, her face had recovered its peachy bloom, so when she looked in a glass she could remark with satisfaction that she was, once again, a very beautiful woman.

She was a happy woman, too. Looking round the little house, which she could see would not seem half so poky if redecorated in plain, pale colours, Isabel declared her intention of putting the past firmly behind her. From now on, she would be a model wife and perfect mother. She would learn to bake, brew and darn stockings, she would keep poultry, and she would salt her own pork, beef and bacon. She would love and care for Honor and Owen for the rest of their days.

Owen was both relieved and a little annoyed to learn that in his absence the furnaces had been in blast, the foundry on song and everything else on full steam ahead: in fact, that while he was away his workers had, on the whole, got on quite well, without either his guiding hand or his pastoral care.

But there was bound to be a pile of correspondence in his little office, which would certainly be needing his attention – so he left Isabel unpacking while he walked over to the counting house. There, he found his clerks had dealt with all routine enquiries and orders, but there were still a few matters outstanding which needed his personal yea or nay.

"Now then, Mr Morgan, I'm sorry about this," began his chief clerk, as he laid a sheaf of papers requiring his signature upon his master's desk. "Since this was directed to the works, we opened it. But when I came to glance over it later, I discovered it was a private letter to you."

"No matter, Henry." Owen took the letter in question from his clerk's hesitant hand.

As he looked at it, he felt hot, then cold, then hot again. Indeed, he thought he might faint away. For, the handwriting was so familiar, and the consequent associations so dear, that his heart contracted at the sight of it.

"What is it?" asked Isabel, gently. For Owen had returned from the foundry not bright-eyed and garrulous, as she'd expected, but silent and abstracted. Indeed, he seemed to be on the very edge of tears. "Owen, my dear?"

He handed her the letter. "It's from Warwickshire," he said.

"Is it bad news?"

"See for yourself."

"Very well. Let me sit down. Then I'll read."

'My dear Owen,' began Jane. 'You will, I am sure, wish to be informed of a melancholy event which took place here recently, for it concerns one of your nearest relations – although not one dear to you.

'On Friday evening last, my father was taken ill, with chest pains and breathing difficulties. For three days he insisted that at his age, such little indispositions were only to be expected. That these symptoms meant nothing, and would soon pass.

'On Tuesday he was no better, however, so I called in his physician. He prescribed drops, blisters and hourly cupping. But by then, the illness had taken a firm hold on your uncle's constitution. On Thursday morning, he died.

'I have lost the best friend I ever had, or expect to have, in the whole of this wide world. I fear my grief is insupportable. I doubt my tears will ever cease to flow. Indeed, I am so desolate that I think my heart must break.

'My dearest cousin, I have known you from a little child. You have a kind heart and your nature is generosity itself. Nowadays, you have many claims upon your charity. But, all the same, I hope you will find some time to think of me, and remember me when you pray.'

She signed herself Eleanor Jane Darrow. Merely that. Looking at his cousin's signature, Owen realised he had never known Jane was actually her second name.

He felt sick with misery. To receive such a letter containing such news was bad enough. But the gentle tone of the writer, innocent of all reproach or bitterness, somehow made it worse.

He wanted so much to go to her! To kiss and comfort her, to hold her in his arms and shut out all the world. But then, he remembered, she had her sister and brother to keep her company. In fact, she would be surrounded by kind people all of whom loved her dearly. She would hardly miss *him*.

“Do you wish to go and see her?” asked Isabel, who just recently could often read his mind.

“If I did, would you be upset?”

“I should not be very happy about it. But I understand that it is something you might need to do.”

“Yes.” Owen looked at her. She held his daughter in her arms. Poor Isabel, he thought, she had no one but the baby and himself. He knew he could not go to Warwickshire.

Owen tried to put the whole business out of his mind. Determinedly cheerful, he kept himself busy. He threw himself into the further development and expansion of the ironworks. He played with the baby, and strove manfully to be a kind, affectionate husband to Isabel.

But his heart was not in South Wales. Three days after he’d received it, Isabel found the letter under his pillow. Stained with tears, it had obviously been read and re-read, then read again.

Sensibly, she left it where she’d found it, and never mentioned it to Owen at all. Instead, she tried to be a perfect mother and a good wife. For these days, she understood just how much Owen had given up, for her sake.

Chapter Thirteen

That autumn of 1813 faded into winter. The year turned. Soon enough, the snow and sleet of January and February gave place to milder weather conditions, and the greys and browns of winter were gradually replaced by the fresh greens of early spring.

One sunny Friday morning in March, as he and she walked in the knot garden at Easton Hall, Rayner looked at his elder sister critically. He did not like what he saw. She looked so tired! Pale, listless and wan, she wore her weariness like a garment, a heavy, shapeless shroud of dull, black worsted, which weighed her down, and made her every step drag almost painfully.

But she refused to rest, saying she wanted – indeed, needed – to be kept busy. Rayner feared that far from merely keeping busy, she was literally wearing herself out.

For, after the death of her mother, she had virtually taken over the management of the Birmingham factories, going into town three days a week to speak to their managers, to discuss new projects, and to find yet more ways to increase profitability.

After her father died, however, Jane began to spend six days a week there, breathing in the smoke and fumes of the great industrial city, and suffering its extremes of heat and cold, its near-deafening clangour by day, and its lonely silence in the watches of the night. Rayner feared for her health, and said so.

She heard him patiently, then shook her head. "Don't

ask me to slow down," she said. "I must keep myself occupied."

"All the same, you could take some time off. You might enjoy just a little recreation, now and then."

"No." Jane turned away. "If I'm idle, I start thinking. If I think too much, I fear I may run mad."

"Did you ever write to him?" enquired Rayner a few days later, as he and Jane sat together in the dining room at Easton Hall, lingering over a gloomy supper, and all alone save for one other.

"Yes." Jane shrugged. "I scribbled a short note."

"How did you know where to direct it?"

"Mrs Graham's maid mentioned to my Sarah that her mistress had been to visit them. After Isabel was confined, you understand, she became very ill. Owen sent for her mother. I simply asked Mrs Graham where they lived."

"I see."

"But that reminds me. My dear Rayner, I've been meaning to ask you this for a long time. Now you are Squire of Easton, where do *you* intend to live?"

"I don't really know." Looking up from his cheese and fruit, Rayner let his gaze wander all around the dark, panelled dining room. Lit by at least three dozen large, white candles, it still seemed dismal, and gravely forbidding. "I haven't thought about it much."

He reached for his sister's hand. "What about you?" he asked. "Do you wish to stay here at Easton Hall? Or would you consider coming to live in my house, to keep me company?"

"I think I should prefer to stay here. For the time being, anyway. If you don't mind."

"Stay as long as you please. Look – if you wish, I'll make the old place over to you. Lock, stock and barrel. How about that?"

"*You* are the squire, Rayner!" The reproach in Jane's voice was gentle, but unmistakeable. "Surely, *your* place is here?"

Perhaps. But, as he rode home through the damp twilight, Rayner decided there was no way he could go back to live in that old mausoleum. Even to oblige his beloved sister Jane. He had never liked Easton Hall, which was an old-fashioned, Tudor manor house not at all to his modern taste.

After a disastrous fire, it had been rebuilt using up-to-date methods of construction and draughtproofing, but it was still a gloomy place, full of shadows and ghosts. So, although it was admittedly much warmer in winter than many a newer house, Rayner had long since decided he preferred his own home, with its large windows, light and airy rooms, and lofty plastered ceilings, which reflected rather than absorbed the candle light.

"Rayner? What's the matter?" asked Jane. It was Lady Day, the beginning of the financial and legal year, and she had called on her brother expressly, to seek his permission to buy a piece of land adjacent to one of the factories. Here, she thought, they might build some houses for the foremen and their families. "I know we will need to mortgage a farm," she'd continued. "But when I spoke to Mr Harris about it, he told me that would be a small price to pay. These days, land in Birmingham doubles in value every couple of months. The time to buy is now."

"I wasn't querying your judgement. Not at all." Rayner shook his head. "You should have been the son," he sighed. "You're the one who understands commerce. You exhaust yourself in the management of the factories and the estate. But all that simply bores *me* to tears."

"I have to keep busy. You know why." Narrowing her eyes, Jane looked at her brother appraisingly. Long past noon, he was still in his dressing gown which, straining at the seams, strove valiantly to meet across his belly. This was of a magnitude not often seen in a man still in his twenties, and not otherwise fat. "Perhaps," she went on, "*you* should take some exercise, too. But anyway, what's making you so gloomy today?"

“I was thinking of my father and mother.”

“Oh.” Jane looked down at her mittened hands. Still clad in the deepest of mourning, these days she was far too thin for unrelieved black to become her, and she looked like a witch. But she evidently did not care. “What were you thinking?” she asked, carefully.

“That it was wonderful how they managed to live together so happily, for so long. They never quarrelled, did they? Nor fought, nor hurt each other in any way.”

“Why should they have quarrelled? They loved one other.”

“Loving someone hardly guarantees he or she will make you happy. Or content.”

“No.” Jane sighed. “Oh, Rayner!” she cried, “I miss my father so much! I still talk to him, you know. Every day, I consult his wishes, or ask his advice.”

“You were his favourite child.”

“He was my dearest friend.”

“More dear than—”

“Owen?” Jane glanced up. “Yes. Even more dear than Owen.”

“Even when—”

“Oh, yes. Of course.” Sadly, Jane smiled. “When Owen and I first asked his permission to marry, and he refused it, I knew what you and Maria thought would happen next. You expected me to sulk and grumble. To exclaim against his cruelty, and try his patience night and day.

“But although I complained and wept on Owen’s shoulder, in my calmer moments I understood. He refused to allow it because he loved me. He knew Owen and I could never be happy together, even if we were miserable apart.”

Rayner frowned. “You’re quite sure of that?” he demanded. “Maria and I were equally convinced that you were made for one another. Though the disparity in your fortunes was a difficulty, to be sure.”

“To my father, that was the least of it. The fact is, he thought Owen feckless and unprincipled.” Plucking at the lace on her cuff, Janes sighed. "When my cousin returned from India, he tried to see improvement. Perhaps he tried too hard, for he saw amendment and change where there was none.

"But you see – he could not admit that Owen was shallow, and weak! He could not let himself doubt that I would be able to respect my husband! For he knew that if I ceased to respect and honour, I would also cease to love."

"Ah." These ideas gave rise to some most uncomfortable reflections, and Rayner thought it wise to change the subject. "I intend to let Easton Hall," he announced. "Unless, of course, you have decided to live there permanently?"

Jane merely shrugged. "I don't much care where I live," she replied.

"Do you not? Then come to live here, as my companion."

"I – I don't think I would wish to do that."

"Why on earth not?"

"Rayner, you know I love you dearly! But don't you think our characters and tastes are rather too different for us to live together amicably, day after day after day?"

"Perhaps." Rayner bit his lip. He knew perfectly well what his sister meant. These days, his home was sometimes little more than a boarding-house-cum-brothel, for to assuage his loneliness he frequently had large parties of friends to stay, amongst whom were actresses, the better sort of women of the town, card-sharps, gamblers and drinkers. In their squalid but lively company, Rayner ate, drank and diced, and forgot his many cares.

"I would like to buy my own house, I think," his sister was saying now. "In fact, I have recently heard of one which might be the very place for me."

"Oh? So tell me – where is this place to be found?"

"It's near Easton Hall. On the toll road to Dereham Bridge, to be precise."

"Let's go and look at it, then!" Rayner grinned. Now,

the empty afternoon stretching gloomily ahead of him was offering an outing, a diversion, a treat. "Let me throw on my clothes, and we'll go. Cromford?" Jane's brother poked his head out of the drawing room door. "Where *is* the man? Cromford, I say!"

So, while Rayner's valet dressed and powdered his master into respectability, Jane ordered the carriage. Brother and sister climbed in, and off they went.

"How did you hear of this place?" demanded Rayner, as they bowled along.

"Quite by accident." Jane shrugged. "Last week, I had occasion to visit one of the cottagers, whose daughter is sick. I arranged for my maid to send over some jellies, jars of soup and other nourishing things, then I asked Mrs Adamson if they still had sufficient fuel to keep a fire burning in the poor girl's chamber. For I know that at this time of year, stocks do tend to be low.

"John Adamson said that was no problem. The rector had told him he could fell the old apple trees in the orchard of The Ash Grove."

"I see. But does the owner of the place not object?"

"The house is empty. The freehold belongs to the rector of Dereham Wells. He may do as he wishes with his own apple trees."

The Ash Grove turned out to be a small, square, lime-washed cottage, in a village a mile or two beyond the northern boundary of the Easton estate. Originally built for the rector's elderly, widowed mother, since her death it had been sadly neglected. The roof had sprung a dozen leaks, the plaster was stained, and the woodwork was rotting quietly but inexorably away.

As Jane and Rayner entered the cobwebbed vestibule, Rayner stumbled against the banister. It collapsed. Clearly, the stairs were unsafe. So they confined their explorations to the ground floor, where they found mouldy panelling, damp carpets, and mouse droppings everywhere.

But, quite obviously, the house had once been pretty. Once, this decaying ruin had been a cosy home. The latticed windows were grouped charmingly in large, light bays, and in the little parlour, some once beautiful Chinese wallpaper hung in dusty shreds. Parts of it still retained its original colour and texture. Might it be saved?

Leaving the house, Jane walked in the garden. Closing her eyes, she saw herself here in summer time, tending her roses, tying her vines, cutting flowers for the house.

Or even bending over her beehives. Netted and gloved against attack, a smoke canister ready in her hand, she watched while the gardener's boy abstracted the dripping, golden combs.

She would grow currants, she decided. Plant raspberries and gooseberries, make jams and jellies, chutneys and preserves. She would take in orphan girls, and train them to be dressmakers, or lady's maids. She might even—

"Jane?" Rayner touched her hand. "This place is derelict," he whispered. "It needs so much—"

"It could be repaired."

"But only at great expense! For what you would spend on this ruin, you could bespeak a beautiful new house."

"Why?" Jane turned to him. "I like this one," she said, firmly. "In fact, I like it so much . . ."

"I see." Shaking his head, Rayner smiled. For today was the first time since Ellis had died that Jane had shown any real interest in anything personal to her.

Now, however, animation brightened her sapphire-blue eyes; a flush of excitement kindled her pale cheeks. "When were you hoping to move in?" he enquired.

"As soon as possible," Jane replied. She thought for a moment. "How long would repair and refurbishment take?"

"I'll speak to George Robbins, in the office at Easton Hall." Catching some of his sister's enthusiasm, Rayner's dark eyes glittered, too. "I'll ask him to get over here first thing tomorrow, and give his opinion. But *I* would imagine the work could be done fairly speedily. Within three months, this place could be habitable again."

"Excellent!" Jane actually smiled. "Then I'll speak to the Reverend Mr Fowler today. I'd thought of offering him two hundred pounds. Does that seem reasonable to you?"

"Offer him a hundred and fifty first. But look, I'll speak to him, shall I? Jane, listen!" For, seeing Jane was about to object that she could arrange the purchase of a small house without *his* officious interference, Rayner placed an index finger against his sister's lips. "I know you are perfectly capable of negotiating with the parish priest," he continued. "But let me do this! It will distract me – and, God knows, I have as much need of distraction and employment as most men."

On the way back to Easton Hall, Jane relapsed into silence. Obviously, she was thinking hard. "Choosing chintzes already?" teased Rayner. "Laying down carpets, and selecting pots and pans?"

"No. Not just yet." Jane turned to him. "Do you think of her?" she asked. "Do you miss her still? If she were to come to Warwickshire – if she sought an interview, then went down on her knees and implored your forgiveness – would you take her back?"

"No." Rayner shrugged. "What about you? If he arrived here abject and wretched, if he prostrated himself at your feet, would you pardon him?"

"No, I would not."

But now, brother and sister glanced away. They could not look one another in the eye without blushing the deepest of scarlets. For each knew perfectly well that the other lied.

Rayner instructed lawyers, summoned builders, and retained a surveyor on site. Expert opinion estimated that basic repairs to the cottage, which was fortunately quite structurally sound, could be made by Easter. The place would be perfectly habitable by late May.

"So, in the meantime, we will take the holiday I have

dreamed of," he declared, banging his fist on his desk in triumph. "There will be no time for you to mope or reflect," he added hurriedly, well aware that his sister was about to object. "We will be constantly on the move, so all those new sights and sounds will engage your attention continually.

"As for the factories and the estate – we employ managers and bailiffs, do we not? They can earn their wages in earnest, while you and I are away."

"But where shall we go?" demanded Jane, bemused.

"We'll tour the West Country. We'll reconnoitre the area round about the Mendip Hills, we'll explore Somerset, and Devon – we'll maybe even go as far as Cornwall, if we choose."

"How will we travel? Post?"

"*Post*? Certainly not!" Rayner shuddered gracefully, in patrician disgust. "We ourselves will take the smaller barouche, while your maid and my valet can travel with the luggage, in my father's old coach." Shaking his head, Rayner grinned. "They should enjoy that."

"But if we take two carriages, and two sets of horses, our expenses will be great."

"No matter." Rayner grimaced, in fastidious distaste. "I have a horror of sharing my travelling accommodation with servants. One can hold no intimate conversations, nor even relax in comfort, with their great, lubberly feet planted in one's way.

"Now, I have made a study of the country through which we shall pass. The roads vary from quite dreadful to tolerable enough. Bearing this in mind, I thought that instead of travelling through Gloucestershire, we could go down the Wye Valley and cross the Severn at Newport. Thus, we might explore the Vale of Glamorgan *en route*. We could visit some parks and gardens in Monmouthshire and South Wales."

"South Wales?" Jane met her brother's eyes. "Would that be such a good idea?" she enquired, somewhat doubtfully.

"Well – I know you would not wish to encounter a certain person on your travels. No more would I! So, we shall not be calling on Mr Morgan and his family, of that you may be perfectly sure."

"All the same—"

"Jane, I will not have my pleasures circumscribed by anyone! Let alone by the likes of him!"

"But—"

"My dear sister, listen to me. When Mama died, and my father was so distracted that we had fears for his sanity, I took it upon myself to write the usual letters. Then I cleared out my mother's desk, and also wrote to everyone with whom she had corresponded within the previous five years.

"A Mr Lloyd of Pontypool was among those correspondents. He wrote me the most charming letter in reply to mine. Apparently, he was quite devoted to Mama. More to the present purpose, however, he extended a cordial invitation to her children to call upon him, at any convenient time.

"If you look over the maps, you will observe that Pontypool is very well placed for a break in our journey. I propose to write to Mr Lloyd, and ask him to give us shelter for a day or two, before we take the ferry to Avonmouth or Portishead."

"I see." Looking at the maps and plans which littered Rayner's desk, Jane saw her brother was quite right. Pontypool would indeed be a convenient half way house. "Very well," she agreed.

To Pontypool, therefore, they would go.

Chapter Fourteen

"The image of her! The living, breathing image! Forgive me, my dear young lady. Do forgive me." Hauling an enormous yellow handkerchief from the depths of his coat pocket, Mr Evan Lloyd dabbed his overflowing eyes. "I'm a very old man," he continued, as if by way of explanation. "At my time of life, tears come so easily. But, my dear Mr Darrow – surely she was not yet fifty?"

"She was fifty two," replied Rayner, who was now sniffing just a little himself.

"No age! No age at all." Mr Lloyd blew his nose hard. "But there's one blessing, at any rate. You two poor creatures still have each other. You were never married, Mr Darrow?"

"No," replied Rayner, firmly. "Never."

"Nor likely to be, I fear." Lugubriously, Mr Lloyd sighed. "When a man has a pearl of such price for his mother, he well understands the fact. He'll never even set eyes on the woman to equal her! Believe me, sir. I speak as one who knows."

He turned to Jane. "I meant no offence to you, Miss Darrow," he said. "If any woman was ever as lovely, as accomplished and charming as the late Mrs Darrow, you are she."

Mr Lloyd did not flatter Jane. She did indeed look well. Today, she and Rayner had driven along the Abergavenny to Newport road with the cover of the barouche folded away, and she had caught the sun. Consequently, her cheeks were quite pink. Animation and interest had struck sparks into her clear, blue eyes.

Also, she had at last left off full mourning. So, instead of unremitting black, she nowadays wore the mauves, purples and greys so well suited to all of her fair colouring.

Mr Lloyd's house was large, rambling, and very old. Originally a farmhouse, it retained the lofty ceilings, in which the great iron hooks for smoking carcases still rather ominously remained, together with the enormous fireplaces, and the cold, stone-flagged floors common throughout all of South Wales.

Nowadays, however, this venerable barn was draught-proofed and weathertight. Comfortably furnished and well-appointed, Jane and Rayner had inspected it with growing satisfaction, and were complacently looking forward to their stay.

Leaving his guests in their own private quarters, in order that they might wash their faces and tidy their hair, Mr Lloyd shuffled off to harangue his servants about supper. Then, collecting Jane and Rayner in an old-fashioned gig, he drove them over to his extensive tin plate works, the ugly sprawl of which began not five hundred yards from his own front porch. They would like to see the rolling mills and burnishing shops, he was sure.

At this delightful prospect, Rayner began to yawn uncontrollably. But Jane, who sat beside Mr Lloyd, was interested enough to ask so many questions about the processes that he quite fell in love with her. "You are your mother born again," he told her, his old eyes filling with tears a second time.

"You intend to take the ferry from Newport to Avonmouth?" enquired their host, as they drove back to the house.

"Yes, indeed," Rayner replied.

"A sound plan, sir. A very sound plan indeed." Sagely, Mr Lloyd nodded his approval. "But it's a long journey. I fear it will tire your sister grievously. Will you not stay with me a full week? To rest up for the travails ahead?"

Rayner had no objection. During their tour of the house, they had passed through the dining room. There, he had noticed several bottles of excellent claret, sitting ready and waiting on the sideboard. In the kitchen, he had smelled what promised to be an equally excellent mutton roast. He and Jane agreed to stay in Pontypool for three days longer than originally planned.

On the afternoon following their arrival, Mr Lloyd informed them that he expected a dinner guest that day. A fellow manufacturer who owned an ironworks further up the valley, in addition to some factories and processing plants in the Vale of Glamorgan, Mr Atkins was a successful entrepreneur and a very wealthy man.

"I suppose in truth he is my competitor," conceded Mr Lloyd, as he concluded his brief biography. "I ought not to like him at all! But, heaven knows, there are opportunities for everybody in this part of the world. Rich pickings for all, both at home and abroad. I send *my* goods to America. To Bombay. I even have orders from as far afield as China these days!" The old man frowned. "Now, where was I?"

"You were speaking of Mr Atkins," smiled Jane.

"Ah, yes. So I was. Well then, he's a pleasant fellow. A widower, a little younger than I. He's still hale and hearty, though, and very good company." Mr Lloyd beamed. "So, you young people will enliven the party. We old men will do our best to entertain you."

Mr Atkins was announced just as Jane came back downstairs, formally dressed for dinner. In her favourite pale mauves and dove greys, today she looked charmingly pretty, and also very young. Indeed, with her soft, fair hair brushed back from her brow, then teased forward in separate strands to frame her face with silken tendrils, she looked no more than twenty five at most. Rayner would have been taken for her senior any day.

A tall, fair-haired, thick-set gentleman with disconcertingly light, almost colourless eyes which were themselves set off by very blond lashes and brows, Mr Atkins was well-dressed, well-groomed, and very expensively shod. His linen was immaculate, his cheeks beautifully shaven, and he wore a set of mourning rings on his fob.

"My dear Mr Atkins," cried Mr Lloyd, shaking him by the hand and drawing him into the room. "I rejoice to see you look so well. Now, then. May I present my guests? Here is Miss Darrow, and this is her brother Mr Rayner Darrow, from Warwickshire."

"Warwickshire?" For one split second, Michael Atkins looked as if he had seen a ghost. His brow contracted, the pupils of his eyes dilated, and his pale face grew even paler still.

But then, he recovered. He shook Rayner by the hand, bowed politely to Jane, and asked how each of them did. Jane and her brother responded in kind.

Mr Lloyd excused himself then, to enquire after the progress of dinner and supervise the drawing of corks. As Jane spread her skirts on the sofa, Mr Atkins sat down in a wing chair. "I once heard of another family by the name of Darrow," he began, evenly. "*They* lived near the village of Easton, also in Warwickshire."

"We are one and the same!" Complacently, Rayner smiled. Gratified indeed to learn that his family name and fame had spread so far, he was curious to know how Mr Atkins had chanced upon it. "How did you hear of us?" he enquired, eagerly.

"I cannot now recall." Blandly, Mr Atkins smiled. "I heard Mr Lloyd speak of you, perhaps? Yes. That must be it. Your parents and he are friends. Is that not so?"

"They *were* friends." Rayner sighed. "My mother and father died within a twelvemonth of each other, a year or so since."

"I'm very sorry to hear it." Michael Atkins looked at Jane. "Miss Darrow, a loss such as that must have been a dreadful one for you to bear."

"It was indeed, sir." Looking down at her hands, Jane bit her lip. The tears came into her eyes, and she found herself unable to say more.

But then, Mr Lloyd appeared again. Soon, he was followed by a very smart footman, who announced that dinner would now be served.

If Rayner and Jane had expected the two older men to talk of business, and exclude them from all but the most perfunctory conversation, they soon found their fears were unfounded. Mr Atkins was well-travelled, he had read widely, and he had formed opinions on almost everything. But these opinions were just, and eloquently expressed, and all in all he seemed a very sensible man.

He took particular pains to draw Jane into the conversation. Learning that she took an active part in the management of the family's business affairs, he spoke to her about the current state of trade. Then, he discussed agriculture with Rayner. Finally, he asked both brother and sister a great many questions about the Easton estate.

Always eager to boast of his great consequence and social standing, Rayner answered Mr Atkins's polite enquiries perfectly readily. "Do you know Warwickshire, sir?" he asked then, for Mr Atkins had smiled and nodded with great interest as Rayner bragged of the beauty of his parkland, the elegance of his house, and the extent of his rolling acres. "Do you have connections there yourself?"

"No. None." Mr Atkins dabbed his lips with a napkin. "But you see – I love to wander. In recent years, I have travelled extensively, all over the British Isles.

"I have passed through Warwick itself many times. It seems a pleasant spot."

"It is indeed." Rayner beamed. "Well, sir! Should you ever have occasion to pass that way again, be certain to call upon me. Your welcome will be most hearty, of that you may be sure."

* * *

The desserts were cleared away. The heavy silver plate was removed, and the cloth dusted free of crumbs. But as Jane rose to leave the gentlemen to their port, Mr Atkins frowned. Indeed, he seemed most reluctant to see her go. Turning to Mr Lloyd, he hinted that perhaps such strict adherence to etiquette was not really *de rigueur* this afternoon? Not among such good friends?

"Of course not." To Rayner's distress, Evan Lloyd waved the decanter and glasses aside. "Well then, Mr Atkins. Will you take tea or coffee today?"

But Michael Atkins did not hear him. He was too busy paying attention to something Rayner had to say.

So, the tea things were brought in. Although she was a visitor to the house, it seemed only natural that Jane should take command of the china and kettles.

"Will you take sugar, Mr Atkins?" she enquired. "Cream?"

"Thank you." Mr Atkins accepted his cup with a reverence more fitting to the receiving of the divine wafer.

Meeting Jane's pretty blue eyes, his own glowed.

Jane smiled.

Rayner grinned.

Mr Lloyd harrumphed and searched for his yellow handkerchief, snorting like a catarrhal dragon the while. Taking a flask of brandy from his waistcoat pocket, he poured a generous measure into his cup.

By the time the afternoon drew towards evening, the manufacturer and his guests were mellow and relaxed, and inclined to be the greatest of friends.

In spite of living in the heartland of industrial South Wales, Mr Lloyd had contrived to make an attractive garden in which to take a breath of air and a little exercise on a fine summer's day. Extending for an acre or so all around his house, this garden was surrounded by windbreaks of trees, which also muted the noise of industry from the works, and filtered the smog-laden air. So, after drinking their tea, the party took a turn through Mr Lloyd's shrubberies and parterres.

"You must find the landscape somewhat bleak here, in South Wales? After the luxuriance of Warwickshire, I mean." Smiling, Mr Atkins looked from Rayner, then to his sister, and then to their host, before finally letting his glance rest enquiringly on Jane. "Here, the grass is grey-green. The trees are sooty, and the air full of dancing smuts which can do nothing for your complexion. Or for your gown."

"No, indeed." Blushing in spite of herself, Jane met Mr Atkins's candid eye. "But," she murmured, "Mr Lloyd has made quite a little Eden here! In spite of the difficulties of cultivation and care, which he must encounter at every turn."

"He has certainly done his best." Touching Jane's sleeve, Mr Atkins directed her glance away from himself. "If you look to your left, you will observe he has even enticed the birds of the air to this pretty spot. Tell me, Miss Darrow. Is that a wren? Or a martin?"

"I suppose it must be a martin. Or maybe a sparrow. Do you not think it a little too large for a jenny wren?"

"I defer to your judgement. Your young eyes must certainly be better than mine." Sighing, Mr Atkins shook his greying head. "How pleasant it must be," he cried, "to have all one's faculties still intact! How delightful, to feel one's senses are still sharp and keen!"

Jane glanced back towards him. This man was certainly middle-aged. But he was still handsome! Still vigorous, still upright, still sensible and strong. There was no need for *him* to bewail deteriorating eyesight, or dwindling energy! If anyone could be said to be in the prime of life, Mr Atkins must be he.

As Jane strolled about the garden, listening with growing complacency to Mr Atkins's remarks and observations, her brother sat in the shade of a flowering cherry, idly talking to his host. "Have you and Mr Atkins known each other long?" enquired Rayner, as Mr Lloyd nodded in the warmth of the late afternoon.

"I beg your pardon?" Mr Lloyd shook his head. "My dear sir, do forgive me. Did you mention Mr Atkins?"

"I asked, if you had known him long?"

"Let me think." Mr Lloyd frowned. "I have known *of* him these ten years or more," he replied. "We have been intimate for at least two. Or even three."

"He seems a very amiable gentleman."

"He is indeed." Mr Lloyd nodded his agreement. "He is a philanthropist and benefactor to all. He has provided much-needed employment in the valley here, and he has also built a school for the children of local labouring men."

"So he is well respected hereabouts?"

"Well respected indeed. Well liked, too." Mr Lloyd grinned. "He seems to be much taken with your sister."

"I wish he might be." Rayner sighed. "My sister has suffered greatly of late. As well as losing both her parents, she has been ill-used by the most rascally, beggarly wretch – but I will not elaborate. Suffice it to say, I should be very happy to see her settled. To know she was loved and esteemed by a good and generous man, such as your friend Mr Atkins seems to be."

Mr Atkins did not finally take his leave until it was almost supper time. Indeed, Mr Lloyd pressed him to stay and take that meal with them, too.

But the visitor said this was out of his power. He must get back. As his hat and gloves were brought in, he shook Rayner's hand again – but this time he took Jane's, too. "My dear Miss Darrow," he murmured, compressing her small fingers in his much larger paw, "my dear young lady, I need not tell you how great a pleasure this afternoon has been for me. This truth must be self-evident! I hope we may meet again soon."

He turned to Rayner. "It is plain that, just recently, your sister has endured much suffering and distress. So, you will forgive me for observing that while it has been a privilege to meet you both, it has been more than a privilege to see her smile."

Jane blushed. "I have not passed so delightful an afternoon for a very long time," she told Mr Lloyd.

Michael Atkins smiled. He took up his hat. "My house here in Monmouthshire," he began, "is somewhat higher up the mountainside than Mr Lloyd's. Consequently, the air is clearer. Pure enough, in fact, to allow us to keep a little farm.

"Perhaps, Mr Darrow, you and your sister would like to see it? We have lambs, one or two foals, and kittens aplenty just now. My spaniel bitch has recently produced a very fine litter. If Miss Darrow would be so gracious as to inspect—"

Jane's blush deepened most attractively.

"Thank you. My sister and I would be delighted. Shall we say about eleven, tomorrow?" Rayner grinned. He was inclined to like Michael Atkins tremendously. Anyone who could make his sister smile must be his friend, and the man who could make her blush with pleasure must be a very extraordinary fellow indeed.

Chapter Fifteen

The drive up the valley was very pleasant. Provided one looked in the right direction, of course. For, on the one hand, there was desecration aplenty. Mine-workings, surface scourings and haphazard excavations defaced some of the most beautiful countryside imaginable, befouling the fair face of nature with the pits and scars of industry.

But if a man turned his eyes away from all this mess and squalor, he could gaze upon soft green pastureland and rolling hills, rising to rocky outcrops and clumps of wind-stunted thorn. These in turn were overshadowed by high, grey mountains, which made the scene laid out before brother and sister truly picturesque.

As their carriage bowled on to the gravel sweep lying before a rambling, lime-washed farmstead, Mr Atkins himself appeared at the door. Hatless, he was still in his shirtsleeves and waistcoat, and these, together with his old-fashioned corduroy breeches and well-buffed but ancient leather boots, ensured he looked every inch the bluff, honest, country gentleman.

"Well, Miss Darrow!" he exclaimed, handing Jane out of the little pony carriage which Mr Lloyd had lent them – for their own barouche was far too wide to squeeze along those narrow country lanes, without getting its varnish absolutely scratched to pieces – "you come betimes! Mr Darrow, a very good morning to you. Does not your sister look radiant? She's bright as the summer day. Fresh as the dew on the roses themselves."

Jane blushed from her neck to her cap. But she

was not displeased by such an effusive reception. Not at all . . .

Entering the farmhouse, the visitors were offered cake and wine, then invited to tour the farm. "You shall go dry-shod," promised the considerate Mr Atkins. "I have had the fellows lay straw along all the paths where we shall tread."

In the stable yard, Rayner and Jane met orphan lambs which by now had become quite tame, and were almost household pets. There was a new foal to admire, and also a soft-eyed Jersey cow with one crumpled horn, who daintily picked her way across the cobbles to take a closer look at the cornflowers on Jane's best bonnet.

A liver-spotted spaniel bitch, the proud mother of five fine puppies, came to rub her damp nose against her master's hand. "Good girl," murmured Mr Atkins, caressing her muzzle. Smiling, he glanced towards Jane. "She wishes to introduce you to her family," he said.

Inspecting the litter, Jane's particular attention was drawn to an inquisitive, bright-eyed little scrap who was completely white, except for some dark splotches on its pretty face. "This young fellow is perfectly charming," she observed, smiling her indulgence as the puppy frisked and gambolled around her skirts. "Or is he perhaps a she?"

Mr Atkins scooped the little creature up. "This is Blanchette," he said. Then, he offered her to Jane – who now submitted to having her face licked all over, as she held the warm, roly-poly bundle against her heart.

"Are you especially fond of dogs, Miss Darrow?" enquired Mr Atkins, as he watched his guest have her bonnet knocked awry, and her cheeks and forehead spring-cleaned yet again.

"Of some dogs," replied Jane, laughing as she dodged the over-zealous attentions of that busy, pink tongue. "I am nervous of bulldogs and mastiffs, to be sure. But Blanchette here is a delightful little thing."

"Then, do me the honour of accepting her," said her master, complacently.

Jane felt her cheeks glow. "But would she be happy to leave her mother?" she murmured. Embarrassed, she was extremely gratified, too. "Is she quite ready—"

"Oh, I think so." Mr Atkins grinned. He glanced towards the barn. "See for yourself," he said.

So Jane looked, and saw. Reclining on a bale of dry straw, the spaniel bitch watched her children play. But if one strayed out of her sight, she displayed no particular concern or motherly anxiety. Her duty towards them was done.

As for Blanchette herself, she was busy nuzzling up to her newest friend, and snickering and whimpering so charmingly that Jane could not help but love her. "Well, Rayner?" she demanded, turning to her brother. "Do *you* think I should take Blanchette away?"

"I fear you must." Rayner smiled. "Indeed, you owe it to her and to your host. The creature obviously loves you – and as for Mr Atkins here, he would be most undeservedly, nay cruelly wounded, if you were to reject his gift!"

So, the party went on, Rayner taking great care where he stepped, and Jane carrying Blanchette, not caring where she trod at all.

They looked all over the model farm, then inspected the dairy. "Are you a native of these parts, Mr Atkins?" enquired Rayner politely, as they entered the new byre.

"No, indeed," replied their host. "My family originally came from near Swansea, where my father was a farmer. I myself married a woman from the Vale."

He sighed. "But I am a widower now, and have been for fifteen years or more. Of course, my parents are long since dead – and I, alas, was their only child."

"Have you no children of your own?"

"I had a daughter. She died in infancy." Once more, Michael Atkins sighed. "But I hope to meet her again, by and by."

"I'm sure you will." Jane met his eyes. Pity made her own soft, and gently glowing. "I'm certain of it, in fact."

"Thank you, Miss Darrow." Mr Atkins cleared his throat. "How long do you stay with Mr Lloyd?" he asked her, changing the subject determinedly.

"We had intended to leave today." Shaking her head, Jane smiled. "But our friend will not hear of it. He insists we keep him company for at least a week."

"I'm very glad to hear it." Michael Atkins smiled back at her. "You see, Mr Lloyd dines here this coming Wednesday. I look forward to seeing you and your brother at my table, too."

At their departure, Mr Atkins took Jane's hand. He held it for at least twenty seconds longer than was necessary.

As their carriage swayed off down the lane, Rayner caught his sister's eye. "I think you have made a conquest there," he observed.

Jane nuzzled Blanchette. "I think I shall love her just as dearly," she murmured, blushing furiously.

"Don't deliberately misunderstand me." Rayner shook his head. "He seems a very pleasant fellow," he continued.

Jane's blush deepened. "He still mourns his wife," she said.

"He recalls her with tenderness, I agree. He preserves all the affection and respect due to her memory. But I would guess that after fifteen years, he might be willing to be consoled."

"He might," agreed Jane.

"Also, he's a rich man."

"My dear Rayner, he's a rich, *old* man."

"He's maybe twenty years your senior, to be sure. But he's hale and hearty, his teeth and colour are good, and his handclasp is strong. He is still an eminently marriageable gentleman."

"Perhaps."

"So there it is."

"No, Rayner!" Jane frowned. "I will not have you marry me off to a stranger! To a fellow of two days' acquaintance, of whom we know nothing at all."

"My dearest Jane! Of whom we know plenty! All of it good, as well." Shaking his head, Rayner grinned. "My dear sister! I wish I could have your dreams tonight."

As Jane lay in bed that soft summer evening, with Blanchette snuggled under the counterpane snuffling and snorting contentedly, she thought about what her brother had said.

Of course, Rayner was being both presumptuous and precipitate. He was meddling where he had no business either to give his opinions, or to interfere.

But – she *did* like Mr Atkins! He was polite, he was pleasant, he was generous, he was kind. The more she thought about him, the more she was inclined to prefer him to almost any young, foolish, necessarily fickle man. She looked forward to Wednesday quite composedly.

As it turned out, however, she did not have to wait anything like that long before she saw Mr Atkins. For at eleven the following morning, he waited on Mr Lloyd again.

Mr Lloyd took the card from the salver, and sighed. "I'm sorry, Mr Darrow," he said, getting up from the breakfast table, where he had been tarrying with his guest. "I interrupt our conversation with the greatest regret, of that you may be sure. But as you see, duty calls. Duty calls!"

The old man shuffled out of the breakfast room. Shrugging on his coat, he began to make his way to his office at the back of the house. Half way there, he came across Jane, who had breakfasted in her bedchamber and was now in the drawing room, playing with Blanchette. "My dear young lady!" The Welshman's face creased into a smile.

But then, suddenly, his eyes filled with tears. Rummaging for his pocket handkerchief, he applied it to his wrinkled cheeks. "My dear Miss Darrow," he murmured, "do please pardon me! But for just one moment, I thought I saw your poor mother, standing there."

"I'm told I much resemble her." Concerned for him, Jane crossed the room. "Mr Lloyd?" she went on, anxiously. "Are you not well?"

"I need a moment or two to compose myself, that's all. I shall be quite better by and by." Mr Lloyd glanced at the little dog. "You have a charming playmate there," he observed.

"Yes, indeed."

"Her mother's master comes here on business today." Mr Lloyd blew his nose hard. Then he put his handkerchief away. "Miss Darrow, correct me if I'm mistaken – but since your dear mother died, I understand that *you* have directed the affairs of your family's factories and warehouses in Birmingham?"

"Yes, that's right. My brother, you see, has so many cares and duties on the estate, that I felt it only proper I should assist him, where and whenever I could."

"Quite so, quite so." Mr Lloyd nodded wisely. "Well, now," he continued, "I have an idea. Since you are a knowledgeable young lady, I wonder if you might like to take an improving jaunt this morning? Mr Atkins and I go to Abersychan, to look over a small ironworks there, which we think may be able to supply us both with a particular type of machine tool. Should you be interested in coming with us?"

Jane blushed scarlet. For some unaccountable reason, the mere mention of the name had brought the hot blood rushing to her cheeks. Her heart beat frantically against her ribs, and her breathing grew harsh. Mr Atkins was going to Abersychan with Mr Lloyd, and she was invited, too. She liked the idea more than anything!

"May Blanchette come with us?" she enquired, desperately trying to sound as if it were all the same to her, whether she went or not. "She is so little, you see, and so recently parted from her mother, that I hate the thought of leaving her alone. So if she would be an inconvenience, I feel I must decline—"

"But of course! Bring the dear creature, by all means." Mr Lloyd grinned. "I shall go and fetch our travelling companion. Who, I am sure, will be delighted to welcome two such charming additions to our party today!"

The outing to Abersychan was a great success. The mild summer weather made travelling pleasant, and Jane's companions were unreservedly agreeable, including her in every conversation and constantly asking her opinions on almost everything. They were so kind to her, in fact, that she felt that this morning she was being treated by two favourite uncles, on some kind of special day.

Except that she did not wish to think of Mr Atkins as an uncle. Not at all. She blushed again as she realised she would have liked the relationship to be very much closer than that . . .

"I see you are a connoisseur, Miss Darrow," smiled Mr Atkins, as the party bowled home again, their inspection completed and orders duly placed. Still smiling, he shook his head. "I never thought to meet *any* young lady with an interest in the metal trades. Let alone one with so much good sense, and complete familiarity with everything!"

"No, indeed." Evan Lloyd nodded sagely. "But then, my dear sir, you never met this young lady's mother. Beauty, native wit, a vastly improved understanding – all were there, in one charming person combined."

"I cannot believe any woman could be more charming or quick-witted than Miss Darrow here," observed Mr Atkins, chivalrously.

"Well, Miss Darrow does her mother credit, I agree." Sniffing, Mr Lloyd dabbed his eyes. "But Mrs Darrow, sir – there was a woman! A creature so wonderful, so astonishing, that the unicorn itself is not more rare."

"Indeed?" Mr Atkins continued to smile at Jane. "I suspect, Evan, that you were more than a little in love with the late Mrs Darrow."

"You think so?" Evan Lloyd shrugged. "Perhaps," he agreed.

"Poor fellow." Patting the old man's shoulder, Mr Atkins clucked in sympathy. "But now," he declared, "we must be of good cheer. We have Mrs Darrow's lovely daughter here today, and it's disrespectful to her to be sad."

When Mr Atkins took his leave of Jane and Mr Lloyd, he once more held her hand for much longer than he needed to. Jane thought – indeed, wished – he might raise it to his lips. But then, she reflected, he was far too polite, too much the gentleman born and bred, even to think of taking any liberties like that.

All the same, the sparkle in his light blue eyes, and the smile which touched the corners of his well-shaped mouth whenever he chanced to look at her, assured Jane that he continued to find her highly interesting. He thought her company just as delightful as she found his.

"Do you ride, Miss Darrow?" he enquired, as he mounted his own black mare, and took the whip from the stable boy's hand.

"Yes, indeed." Jane smiled up at him. "At home, I have my own sorrel gelding. I also keep a little grey pony, of whom I am extremely fond."

"I have such a creature in my stables just now!" Mr Atkins returned Jane's smile, but with interest. "If you like, I could have the boy bring both the grey, and a horse for your brother, over here tomorrow. Then you and Mr Darrow could explore the countryside round about, while we old men pore over our ledgers and cast up accounts."

"That's very kind." Jane blushed. "But I couldn't possibly think of troubling you—"

"It's no trouble!" Mr Atkins positively beamed. "It

would be my pleasure, to provide some for you. Might eight o'clock be about the time you would wish to begin?"

"That would be splendid." Jane shook her head. Eight o'clock! Rayner never willingly left his bed until well past ten.

The grey pony turned out to be a pretty, docile little thing, exactly suited in both size and temperament to be a lady's mount. As she stepped lightly off the block, Jane noticed a scrap of paper tucked behind the bridle. Intrigued, she twisted it out.

'My dear Miss Darrow,' ran the note, 'I hope you will have the most pleasant day out on Perdita here. She is quiet and gentle, very sweet-natured – but also, I'm afraid, rather prone to shy. Do have a care of that. I should hate you to take a tumble on my account!

'Rest assured, my dear young lady, that I look forward to seeing you here this Wednesday afternoon most impatiently. In the meantime, please accept my very best wishes and respects.' Michael Atkins.

"What's that?" demanded Rayner, observing his sister smile, and begin to read her letter all over again.

"A note from Mr Atkins." Jane passed it across to him. "Do you wish to see?"

"My dear sister, far be it from me to spy upon your intrigues, or demand to inspect your *billets doux*." Rayner grinned. "Upon my soul – you have made the most tremendous conquest there!"

"My dear Rayner, how can you be so foolish?"

"My dearest Jane, how can you be so false and coy?" Rayner's grin broadened. "You like the man excessively. Don't deny it! Whenever his name is mentioned, you blush. As you read his memorandum just now, your cheeks seemed to catch fire. So don't pretend with me!"

In response, Jane touched her pony's flank and moved

off smartly, leaving Rayner to smirk and cackle all by himself.

Mr Lloyd always insisted on punctuality, so the dinner guests arrived at Mr Atkins's house with time to spare.

Jane had dressed very carefully that day. A pale lilac gown, rather low-necked, but modestly embellished with a mauve silk scarf, flattered her pale skin and set off her fair hair to perfection. The short sleeves showed off her slender arms, the tight bodice lifted her breasts, and the softly-draped silk of the skirt lent grace to her every movement.

Mr Lloyd told her she looked quite lovely. "I'm sure our host will think so too," he added slyly, as he bent to pat Blanchette, thus considerately sparing the lady's blush.

On arrival, the host presented Jane with an armful of flowers and a pretty, tooled leather collar for Blanchette. Then he invited her to stroll in the garden, pointedly observing to Rayner and Mr Lloyd that they would find a bottle of very fine Madeira in the study, where it awaited their appraisal most anxiously.

Rayner was about to demur, to insist that he would prefer a stroll in the garden to anything. But then, catching Michael Atkins's eye, he saw such a steely, determined glint there that he understood all argument would be a waste of time. There seemed nothing for it but to do as the master said.

"Where did you live before you came to Pontypool?" asked Jane, as she and her host walked among the apple trees in the little orchard close by the house.

"In the Vale," Mr Atkins replied. "I managed a tin plate works near Cefn Llywd, and also owned a part share in an ironworks there."

"But you did not always live in Glamorganshire?"

"No, indeed." Offering Jane his arm, Michael Atkins smiled. "As I think I may have mentioned once before, my childhood home is near Swansea. At Oxwich, to be precise, on Gower.

"It's a pleasant old house, on a headland. It overlooks hanging woods in one direction, and the wide open sea to the other side. A distant cousin keeps house for me there, and I myself visit every summer. If I can find the time, I also take parties of friends down for shooting or hunting, at other seasons of the year."

"It sounds most delightful," murmured Jane.

"It is," Mr Atkins agreed. "Miss Darrow, do you mean to see much of South Wales?"

"Alas, no. My brother intends to cross the Severn at Newport, then explore Somerset and Devon."

"Oh. I see." Sighing, Mr Atkins shook his head. Indeed, he looked so hangdog and disappointed that Jane felt wretched.

How could she make him smile again? Almost without thinking, she increased the pressure of her hand on his arm. Encouragingly, she smiled up at him.

They went into the house. At a nod from Mr Atkins, dinner was placed on the table. Now the host lost no time in engaging Jane's brother in conversation.

Having already consumed the best part of a bottle of Madeira, and meaning to become equally well acquainted with the claret, Rayner was relaxed and genial. He was disposed to be chatty, and listen with quiet indulgence to anything his host might have to say. He was even inclined to grant favours. If any were asked . . .

"I think I shall take some holiday myself shortly," observed Mr Atkins, as Rayner remarked that the weather this summer was so fine that he pitied the poor fellows shut up in factories, or labouring down mines. "I shall spend a few weeks at my house on Gower. Mr Darrow, I wonder – might you and your sister do me the honour of visiting me there? At Oxwich Bay?"

"That's a rather splendid notion." Tipsily, Rayner grinned. "When do you intend to set out?"

"Next Monday. But if I am to take a party with me,

I should let my people know as soon as possible. Then, suitable rooms can be prepared."

"To be sure." Rayner glanced blearily at Jane. "Well, my dear sister?" he gargled. Imagining he was unobserved by the rest of the company, he actually winked. "Should we accept Mr Atkins's kind invitation?"

"I think we must." Embarrassed by Rayner's foolish behaviour, Jane blushed. Her cheeks still scarlet, she turned to her host. "Mr Atkins, we are most honoured to be invited to your house. We look forward to staying there very much indeed."

The guests lingered for the rest of the afternoon, then agreed to sit down to supper, during which Michael Atkins, pretending an astonishing degree of interest in the welfare of Blanchette, remained much too close to Jane.

He kissed her hand that evening. He took it between his own, held it for a long, long moment – then raised it to his lips. The impression of them remained, an invisible scorch mark on Jane's white skin, long after she, Rayner and Mr Lloyd had taken their leave and driven off into the moonlit summer night.

From his front step, Michael Atkins watched the carriage lights gleam, then flicker, then fade, then disappear. He strode back into the house. Then, and only then, did he permit himself to laugh out loud. At last, at last, the minnows had swum into his net.

It had taken so long! First, he had had to bribe and corrupt the right people. To persuade them to sell him the most basic information. It had been exorbitantly expensive even to learn the instigator's name.

This person had turned out to be not the chairman of the Swansea bench – as might have been expected – but an obscure landowner in the Midland shires.

Puzzling indeed.

But still, he had watched and waited. Indeed, he had waited so long that nowadays he hardly expected the opportunity for revenge ever to arise. But now, at last, it had.

Sitting down at his desk, he poured himself the remainder of the Madeira. He reviewed the situation. Well, one thing was perfectly obvious. The man was a fool. Fat, lazy, and stupidly complacent, he both looked and smelled like a woman, and would no doubt squeal like one, too. When the time came.

His sister had rather more about her. But that was all to the good, for it meant she would prove more entertaining. There was little pleasure to be had in snapping straws or breaking reeds. Jane Darrow, however, seemed to be a strong, deep-rooted sapling of a girl. She would endure much, and suffer long.

"Has she been jilted?" he wondered, aloud. "Or did her lover die?" For, that gloomy cast of countenance, that dejected droop, seemed to indicate more than mere grieving for her parents. She nursed some deeper, rather more personal sorrow. He was almost sure of that.

In any case, one thing was perfectly clear. She wanted a man. As he'd looked at her today, as he'd searched her face and seen that blush rise from bosom to temples, he had congratulated himself in earnest. When he'd first met her, she had been buttoned up to the chin, encased in worsted from neck to wrists to ankles. But today, those few yards of taffeta had left so little to the imagination that it was a wonder her brother had allowed her to go out so lightly clad. It was as if the merchandise had been deliberately set out, for the inspection and approval of anyone who might care to buy.

Michael Atkins shook his head. She might be a landowner's daughter, a well-bred, elegant lady, all of that – but her dilated pupils and the urgent pulse in her neck had told him all he needed to know about Miss Jane Darrow, spinster, of Easton Hall in the county of Warwickshire.

Getting up, he walked over to the window and gazed down the valley. It was a pity the father was dead, for it was his interference and meddling where he had no business to pry at all that had spoiled everything.

No matter. His children could be tormented in his stead. They would come down to Oxwich the following Tuesday. That was time enough to prepare the banquet. To spread the feast.

Chapter Sixteen

Owen had taken to carrying Jane's letter everywhere. Creased and folded, it lived like a precious talisman deep in an inside pocket, next to his heart.

He knew it by heart, too. Down to the last stop and comma, in fact. Also, he had done as she asked. His conversations with his Creator, such as they were, always began and ended with an earnest prayer for Jane's present preservation, and future happiness.

But, as time went by, he found that praying for her was not enough. Day and night, he thought of her. Time did not heal. Every passing hour of every day, he missed her more and more.

If Isabel noticed Owen's occasional absent-mindedness and bouts of introspection, she never remarked on them. For, while he had leisure to think and reflect, she was fully occupied, managing her household and raising Honor.

Her chief concern was that the child should learn to speak pure, fluent English – which seemed increasingly unlikely, when all around her the baby heard nothing but the Celtic tongue. Honor's nursemaid would jabber away in Welsh for hours together, the other servants willingly spoke nothing else, and even Owen hung over the child's crib and called her his *cariad*, his dear little *dwt*. The poor infant was in a fair way to growing up a complete barbarian.

Not that Owen was at home very much these days. If he were not at the ironworks, it was ten to one he was visiting David Morgan at home.

“He loves that foolish old man far more than he ever loved me,” Isabel told her daughter. Whose response was a steady burble of what sounded suspiciously like the most debased sort of Saxonised Welsh ever heard.

“What’s the matter this morning, then?” demanded the apothecary, who today was carefully blending some expensive essential oils, and who did not particularly want his nephew fidgeting around his shop.

More than fidgeting. For Owen was tearing up bits of paper, leaves or flowers, picking things up and putting them down again in the wrong places, and generally distracting David from his work. “Do you have problems at the foundry?” he enquired, patiently.

“What do you say?” Sharply, Owen glanced up from his methodical dissection of a borage leaf. He stared his uncle full in the face. “Oh,” he muttered. “You mean the ironworks. No, everything’s fine there. In fact, these days the place seems to run itself.”

“Leaving you with time on your hands, and a void in your heart?”

“Perhaps.” Owen shrugged. “Maybe I need a new direction.”

“I see. So what might you try next?”

“I could go into partnership with Thomas Taliesin, perhaps. He wishes to buy some land near Bridgend, and build a domestic goods manufactory there. Perhaps I could—”

“Do you fret for her still?” interrupted David. But carefully.

“Fret for whom?”

“Come, child.” Frowning, David shook his head. “Don’t play the idiot with me! Well?”

“I miss her, certainly. But—”

“It’s almost two years now.” David met his nephew’s eyes. “*Isabel* is your wife,” he said. “She’s become a good one, too. She cares for you, and for your home, and for your child. What more could a man ask? My dear John

Owen, be circumspect. Don't destroy your own happiness wilfully!"

Stepping down from the coach, Rayner and Jane gazed all around. They were enchanted. This, surely, was the Garden of Eden. The Promised Land.

Their drive down from Swansea had been one uninterrupted delight. They'd bowled across the greenest of commons, through leafy woods decked out in their freshest summer finery, and along the most picturesque coastline art or nature could ever have devised.

But here at Oxwich, where the bay curved in a perfect arc, where hanging woods tumbled down steep, romantic cliffs, and where blues and greens and golds combined to produce the most cooling, restful, soothing effect imaginable for the weariest of travellers, here was the most spellbinding of journey's ends.

Mr Atkins stood on the steps of a large, elaborately turreted and gabled manor house. Recognising him immediately, Blanchette squirmed out of her mistress's embrace and ran to greet him, barking with joy.

"My dear Miss Darrow!" Rumpling the puppy's ears, Mr Atkins beamed in welcome. "Look at this creature! You're feeding her far too heartily."

"Indeed?" Jane beamed back at him. "But she's always so hungry! She—"

"She's greedy. Like her mother." Indulgently, Michael Atkins shook his head. "Well, no matter. She'll run off her fat on the beach. So, Miss Darrow – Mr Darrow – will you please to step inside?"

But it was Blanchette who went in first. Grinning in delight, her tongue lolling and her jaws dripping, she scrabbled and nosed and sniffed all over the entrance hall, only occasionally glancing round to make sure her mistress was still within sight.

The house was old, but well-maintained and solid. Over the centuries, numerous additions had been made to its original Norman core, so from deep, commodious cellars rose light, airy drawing rooms, sitting rooms and servants' halls, which themselves gave way to spacious bedchambers and quiet, private day rooms which were fitted up in the latest of modern styles.

The smell of fresh, lavender-scented beeswax was all-pervasive, for the ancient, Welsh oak settles and chairs and tables were polished and polished again to gleaming ebony. But, instead of the rushes on which they might have stood in days gone by, these heavy, antique pieces were placed squarely on the finest of deep-piled Turkish carpets, which cushioned even the heaviest tread.

Having been positively assured that his own servants would be delighted to wait upon them, Rayner and Jane had left his valet and her lady's maid in lodgings in Newport, to be collected when their master and mistress came back that way, to continue their travels in the West Country. So now, Mr Atkins's servants were drawn up in line, to welcome the guests.

The housekeeper and distant cousin, who proved to be a stocky matron in widow's black, was succeeded by some two or three modest girls in white caps and twill gowns. These stood next to an older woman clad in the red flannel and black homespun of Welsh women throughout the land.

These females were casually introduced as Polly, Betty, Sarah and so on – in short, they answered to the generic names of servants everywhere. But two men of about Mr Atkins's own years were formally presented. "Miss Darrow – Mr Darrow – here are Robin and Henry Corder." Mr Atkins looked from guests to servants, then back again. "If there is anything you need, any service you require, and I myself am not by, speak to either of these fellows. Your word will be their command."

"Splendid." Rayner nodded his appreciation.

"Yes, indeed." Jane smiled.

But the two heavily-made, jowly creatures who were to do their every bidding did not smile back. In fact, they met the visitors' gaze so steadfastly that Jane and Rayner were most definitely the first to look away . . .

As the guests were soon to discover, however, all the servants were anxious to please. All were deferential. Gliding in and out like silent shadows, they attended to their master and his visitors so assiduously that Jane found a dropped handkerchief was restored with a curtsey even before she realised she'd lost it. As for Mr Atkins himself – he had only to look or nod for his will to be done.

Admiringly, Jane took note. Her own domestics at home at Easton Hall, whom she had always thought well-managed indeed, were saucy and skittish when compared with these respectful creatures, who never even opened their mouths unless positively invited to speak.

Dinner was taken early, at two in the afternoon. Invited to indulge himself, Rayner made hearty inroads into both the roasts and the desserts, and drank rather more claret than was habitual even for him. So, when Mr Atkins proposed a walk, he staggered to his feet most unwillingly.

"My dear Rayner, why not stay here, and take a nap?" Shaking her curls, Jane smiled at him. "The journey down here has tired you. You need a rest, I'm sure."

"I do *not*." Squaring his shoulders, Rayner gritted his teeth. He was his sister's guardian! Her protector, too. Not to mention her dearest friend. So, if she had a fancy to go scampering along a beach, he must scamper too. "A walk would be most delightful," he said, firmly. "Exercise is exactly what I need."

So the three of them, host and guests together, set off down the cliff path. The intention was to stroll across the bay.

Soon, the wind had blown a beautiful colour into Jane's pale cheeks. Exercise brightened her eyes, and interest made her step quick and light. Living in the English Midlands, seaside holidays were a rare treat for her, and she meant to enjoy this one to the full.

So she picked up shells; she paused to examine flotsam

and jetsam, and she made mental notes on where it would be best to set up her easel the following day.

Mr Atkins strode rather than walked, but every so often he stopped, to give his visitors a chance to catch up with him. Jane always did. But Rayner lagged behind, on pretence of watching out for Blanchette, who was as delighted as her mistress to have discovered such a wonderfully fascinating place. Running into the foam, she shot out of it again. Then she hurtled back in, barking and yelping her pleasure for all the world to hear.

Waiting once more for Jane to catch up with him, Mr Atkins smiled. "My dear Miss Darrow," he began, "I observe your step has grown slow. I fear you must be tired."

"No, indeed! I stop so often because I wish to gaze, and admire." Smiling too, Jane narrowed her eyes, against the afternoon light. "You, of course, are well accustomed to – nay, you are most probably fatigued by – this magnificent view!"

"On the contrary. There is always something of interest to see – and there is an element in the view today, of which I could never tire!" Mr Atkins offered Jane his arm. "Will you walk to the end of the bay?" he enquired.

"I should love to," she replied.

For a moment or two, they strolled along in silence. Then, Mr Atkins spoke. "My dear Miss Darrow," he began, "we have been acquainted for a very short time, I admit. But nevertheless, I feel I know you well. I suspect you may feel that you also know me."

Jane blushed. "Indeed, Mr Atkins," she murmured, "I am sure you have always been open-hearted. You are also hospitality itself. In fact, my brother and I were remarking just now on your kindness. Your generosity, and your goodness in—"

"It is not of your brother I wish to speak." Mr Atkins covered Jane's hand with his. "Miss Darrow, would you permit me to call you Jane?"

Jane's cheeks were scarlet. "Well," she whispered, "I'm not sure—"

"No matter! If the idea distresses you, we will stay with Miss Darrow." Complacently, Michael Atkins smiled. "For the present, anyway."

The tide was well out, so they walked on smooth, flat sand, which made the going pleasant and easy. As they came into sight of Three Cliffs Bay, Michael Atkins sighed. "I've known so much sorrow in my life," he murmured. "But on a day like this, I can forget I ever had any cares."

"So can I." Jane smiled up at him. "Just watching the waves dance in the sunshine cheers me. At this moment, I feel sure that even the heaviest of burdens could be lightened here."

"Maybe." But Mr Atkins would not smile back. Instead, he sighed again. His sigh came from the heart.

By this time, Rayner was completely out of sight. Jane was not concerned, reasoning that he was probably fast asleep against a rock. Glancing round, to see how far they'd come, she saw the house was in the furthest distance now. A solid, reassuring pile, viewed from the beach it seemed a veritable fortress. Which indeed it was, for it was surrounded by wooded slopes on three sides, and a sheer cliff on the fourth.

But it did not look forbidding. Rather, it seemed welcoming. Comforting. Today, its glazed red pantiles glowed in the sunshine, its rosy brickwork gleamed softly, and its window panes sparkled like diamonds reflecting the light. Jane did not wonder that Mr Atkins had kept it for a holiday retreat.

Then, at long last, she admitted it to herself. She liked this man. Liked him enormously, in fact. As she had already remarked to his face, he was kind, he was generous, he was good. Blushing a little, she also admitted – but still to herself, of course – that he was very attractive, too.

Tiring now, for her little nankeen boots with their elegant pointed toes were not really designed for long rambles, Jane leaned against him. She let herself positively enjoy having this large, strong, solid man at her side, to help and guide her along.

"I hope you intend your stay here to be of some duration?" he was saying now as, sensing she was tired, he moderated his long stride to fit her short, tripping step.

"I – we would be most unwilling to take unfair advantage of your hospitality," she replied. "We would not wish to—"

"Impose?" He laughed. "That would be impossible! How could a creature who brings such sweetness and delight into my dull life even be imagined to get in the way?"

Jane looked away, too embarrassed to reply.

"Will you let me tell you something about myself?" he asked, then.

"I—"

"Don't be alarmed. It's just a short life history. Very much abbreviated, in fact. But I should so like you to hear it."

"Should you?" Feeling bolder, Jane glanced up at him. "Then of course I shall be happy to listen."

"Thank you. Well, then – I was born and bred on Gower. In fact, I was a farmer here in Oxwich until I was well past thirty. Then, my father died, leaving me some cash which I decided to invest in industry. I bought a share in a copper-smelting concern, in Swansea.

"I married quite late in life. I was thirty five. My bride, however, was but twenty. Reasonably expecting that she would survive me, all the plans I made now were based on the foundation of a wish that she and any children would not suffer after I was dead.

"But soon after our wedding, my wife became ill. We called in all manner of physicians. Each to no avail. All we could do was make sure she was rested, spared every anxiety, and kept very quiet. But all the same, she lost her baby.

"Two days later, she died in my arms. My daughter was buried by her mother's side."

"I'm so sorry." Looking up at him, Jane's blue eyes filled with tears. "So very sorry for you!"

"Are you, my dear?" Michael Atkins shook his head. "But of course, you understand. You have suffered, too."

"Not as much as you! Oh! It must have been so hard!"

"It was, at first. Very hard. But it's true, you know. Time does dull the pain." Mr Atkins looked deep into Jane's eyes. "You have a secret sorrow," he murmured. "Will you tell me what happened?"

"I was engaged to be married. The gentleman decided he preferred someone else."

"The scoundrel!" Michael Atkins's blue eyes flashed. "How dared he?"

"It was not a question of daring." Remembering, Jane bit her lip. "Looking back, I do not imagine he could help it."

"Nonsense." Still, Michael Atkins glared. "Miss Darrow," he said firmly, "I have lived much longer than you. I have by far the greater experience of the world. So I can tell you quite impartially, but also with a sincerity which comes from the heart, that the man who could see you and prefer another woman must be a fool or a blackguard. Probably both."

Jane winced. "He was a good man," she faltered. "I loved him dearly. What is more, I believe he loved me. There were reasons why he behaved as he did."

"Honourable reasons?"

"I can't answer that."

"You say you loved this creature dearly. Do you still?"

"I—

"Is your heart still bleeding?"

Jane considered. A week ago, she would have said yes. If she had consented to reply at all. But now, as she looked up at Michael Atkins, into his candid blue eyes which shone with what she could only assume was admiration of herself, she was not so sure.

It was immodest in the extreme to stare boldly at a man. She knew that very well. But now, she found she could not help but gaze! She saw that her companion's lips were parted in a half smile. His fair hair was ruffled and disordered by the wind into gleaming, golden swathes. He looked like a Viking chieftain. A Norseman, whose hair and eyes were coloured by the sun and the sea. So, was her heart still bleeding? "I don't think so," she replied.

"That's excellent," he said.

"Is it?"

"Of course. It means your heart might one day be open to me."

As a respectable, modest woman schooled from the cradle in manners and demeanour, Jane knew that she should look away. She should do so now! But, in spite of herself, she continued to gaze up at Michael Atkins. What was more, he gazed frankly back at her. In fact, he devoured her with his eyes . . .

There was a strong sea breeze that day. As she walked into the wind, Jane's light silk gown was blown so close against her body that every curve, every contour was sharply defined. Her scarf had long since blown back from her bosom, and she knew she should have caught it, pinned it, and covered herself again.

But she had not. Could not! For, she wanted Michael Atkins to look at her. Now, her colour rising, she realised she wanted something more shameful still. She wanted him to touch her. To embrace her, and kiss her on the lips.

Mortified, she hung her head.

He took her in his arms.

For a long minute, he held her close, his heart beating against her shoulder. His kissed the top of her head. "I am a very old man," he began, his voice light and humourous. "Fifty years old this All Hallows Eve, a great age to someone like you. But Miss Darrow – my dearest Jane – I hope to live many years yet. I do not wish to pass these years in solitude.

"I loved my wife dearly. Until I met you, I never even saw the woman with whom I thought I might be once again content. But now I have seen her. Spoken with her, too. My darling Jane, will you make me happy again? Will you be my wife?"

Jane's heart thumped painfully against her chest. Could she marry this man? Did she want to? For two years she had carried her misery like a burden, and by now she had grown used to its weight. She was almost afraid to lay it down.

But then, as her lover stroked her hair, as he held her in his warm embrace, it was as if something cracked open deep inside her. As if a seed began to germinate, promising the growth of hope and happiness anew.

"*Will* you marry me?" he demanded, rather more urgently now.

Jane made up her mind. "Yes, dear Michael," she replied. "I will."

"Good. Excellent." He raised her face to his. He kissed her once, twice, a third time. Meeting no resistance, he opened her mouth with his. He explored it deep inside.

As he'd suspected, she was hungry for a man. Greedy, even. Experimentally, he stroked one breast.

She drew breath sharply. But she did not pull away.

He kissed her again.

Leaving her dazed but far from satisfied, five minutes later he let her go. He took her hand in his. "Will you walk on a little?" he invited. "Along here, by the cliff?"

For a while, they strolled in silence. But then, Michael

Atkins spoke. “May I come to your room this evening?” he asked carefully, calmly, as if he asked for the time of day.

“Yes,” Jane replied.

Chapter Seventeen

Jane was so happy. So contented, so sated, so warmly relaxed, so comforted. Now, there were so many things she understood . . .

After sending a message by her maid, asking if he might wait on her, Michael Atkins had come to her room at nine that same evening. Sitting down on a chintz-covered chair, he remarked on the beauty of the dusk, then made a few general observations on the fine summer weather that year.

All the same, a fleeting glance from the master had sent the maidservant scurrying to the dressing table, where she quickly set out her mistress's brushes, combs and other requisites for the night. Then, another sharp stare sent her scuttling away.

Jane sat by the window, watching the light fade. Her lover came to stand beside her. "My dear Jane," he began, as he stroked her hair, "we agreed that I should visit you here this evening, so I have come. But I do understand that since we last spoke, you may have reconsidered. If you have, merely say the word, and I shall leave."

"I have not changed my mind." Standing up, Jane found her face was on fire. Shame and mortification washed over her, in white-hot, burning waves. For now, years of unquestioning obedience to the strictest of moral codes meant that she felt defiled, unwomanly, and unclean.

She laid her glowing cheek against her lover's chest. "I would *like* you to stay with me," she whispered, the words almost choking her. Helplessly, she shrugged. "But I can't – indeed, I don't think I *should*—"

"Poor Jane." Michael Atkins kissed the top of her head. "Don't worry," he murmured. "Your first child will not be born six months after your wedding day. There are ways to take care of things like that."

"Oh." Jane could hardly believe what she was hearing. "I see."

"So, my darling." Raising her face to his, her lover looked into her eyes. "May I take you to bed?"

Jane stared back at him. Meeting that pale blue gaze, she realised she wanted him not merely to kiss her, but to possess her completely.

Tonight, she would be a bride.

"You'll be fortunate in childbirth," he observed, as he spanned her hips, as he narrowed his eyes to measure her from this angle and that. "Your sons and daughters will never hurt you! Well, not on the day they are born, at any rate."

"Will they not?" Relaxed and sleepy, but also blissfully happy, Jane smiled. "How do you know that?"

"My dear, I'm a farmer. So of course I can tell." Her lover smiled, too. "Believe me, you were made to be a mother."

"In that case—"

"We must lose no time. We must get you with child on our actual wedding day."

"When will that be?"

"As soon as I can arrange it."

"Ah." Jane sighed. She turned her head away. "*If* you arrange it," she murmured, almost inaudibly.

"You presume to doubt me?" Catching her by the shoulder, Michael Atkins twisted her round to face him. "Well?"

That single word echoed all round the bedchamber. It made the windows rattle, and the vessels on the dressing table ring. Wide-eyed with alarm, Jane stared. "I – I do not doubt you," she whispered, fearfully. "But I was afraid you might despise me now. That you would think me shameless. Unprincipled—"

"No." Relaxing again, her lover kissed her. "How could I despise you? You have given me something precious tonight."

"Who's my precious, then?" Isabel swung her little daughter high in the air. "Who's my darling? My own dear heart's delight?"

Honor grinned and burbled, waving her fat baby fists and kicking lustily. But then, as the door of the little parlour swung open, she turned to see who had come in. "Dada!" she squealed. "Dada, Dada!"

So Isabel was obliged to hand her over.

It was as well Honor loved Owen so dearly. Again and again, in fact every single time jealousy and irritation threatened to eat her up, Isabel reminded herself that if Owen loved the child in return, he would find it impossible to disown or desert her mother. Even if, one day, he should tire of Isabel herself.

The infant was so like him. Dark-eyed, dark-haired, she was fast growing up into the prettiest of Celtic maids, with nothing of Isabel's gold and white about her at all. For Honor's hair was as black as the coal they mined here in the Welsh valleys. Her eyes were pools of cool, grey water. Her soft, baby skin was as dark as Owen's own.

"See what I've brought you today." Sitting the child on his lap, Owen rummaged around in his pockets until he found the new toy. A teething ring in the shape of a horse shoe, it was fashioned from pretty pink coral and hung with engraved silver bells. Straight away, Honor put it in her mouth.

"She likes it," observed Isabel. Having threaded her needle, she reached for the next piece of plain sewing in the basket by her side. For, these days, she was a fine seamstress, and always had some little garment to hand, which she was smocking, hemming or finishing off. "Those bells are quite secure, I hope?"

"Perfectly." Rubbing the child's nose with his own, Owen grinned. "But I had Ifan Evans cold-solder them again. Just to make sure. We don't want any accidents, do we?"

On days like today, when Honor was good-humoured and Isabel neither cross with the kitchen maid nor inclined to scold *him*, Owen found he was relatively contented. The agonised longing for Jane, while it certainly never left him, dulled from a violent torment to a mild, almost bearable ache. If he had business to transact, orders to win, and little time to consider or reflect, even that mild ache became tolerable. Like a fretful infant, it could be wrapped in a blanket, and lulled to sleep.

After a period of relative inactivity, Owen suddenly found he had a great deal to do. That spring of 1814 saw the removal of Napoleon from office, and the consequent coming of peace boosted the economy wonderfully. Business in the metal trades was so brisk that Owen found he did not have to tout for custom. Instead, it came to him. Some days, there was so much to do at the works that the master actually rolled up his own shirtsleeves and laboured in the casting shed himself, alongside his men.

He went home to his mistress and her child filthy, starving, but tired enough to sleep for eight hours at a stretch. So, after a substantial dinner of the inevitable boiled mutton and mealy potatoes, he would retire for the night. Too exhausted even to dream, he lay in his bed like a corpse in its coffin, dead to the world and certainly oblivious of Isabel, who lay fidgeting by his side.

Waking at six to the prospect of yet another twelve, fourteen, or even a sixteen hour day, he realised that soon he was going to have to contemplate the unthinkable. He would have to start turning business away.

"Could we put another furnace into blast?" he asked the foreman that following morning, as he thumbed through a fat sheaf of orders, for hundredweight upon hundredweight of best quality pig iron.

The foreman scratched his head. "Where will you find the men to charge it?" he enquired.

That was a good point. The shortage of labour in South Wales meant that Owen already employed boys as young as eight or nine, many of them on tasks far beyond their strength. "I'll advertise," he said, sticking a pencil behind his ear and looking round for his chief clerk. "I'll scour Worcestershire, Herefordshire, Gloucestershire. There are miners in the Forest of Dean who could earn twice their wages here in the Vale, working for me."

But, as Owen pondered, Isabel was thinking, too. Like him, she had reached a decision. When he arrived back at the stone cottage that evening, she dropped her bombshell. She told him she had decided to go home.

"But why?" he demanded, as she sorted linen and packed shifts and nightgowns in a brass-bound box. "What have I done, that you should wish to leave me?"

"You ignore me. That's what." Isabel threw her combs and brushes into her valise. "You get up at dawn. You gobble down your breakfast, then you go out."

"But, Isabel—"

"You come home each evening filthy, stinking and foul. You wolf down your supper, then you go to bed. You never even notice your child."

"Isabel, listen—"

"You think of nothing but that wretched ironworks. You will not miss me."

"Of course I shall!" Grasping her by the shoulders, Owen printed two sets of perfect, sooty fingermarks on Isabel's best lawn gown. "My darling Isabel! You and Honor are the dearest of all God's creatures to me. Of course I shall miss you!"

"Indeed?" Not convinced, Isabel shrugged. "Why don't you come with us, then?"

"To Warwickshire?"

"Yes. Why not?"

"I doubt if I would be welcome there." Owen bit his lip. "Do you intend to stay with your parents?"

"No, of course not. I shall travel post to Warwick, then sleep in the horse trough, in the market square."

Isabel went on with her packing. Chewing over what she'd said, Owen watched her. He supposed he ought to go with her, if only to see her safely there.

The maid set his supper before him. As he ate, he considered. Busy though the ironworks were, he could surely be spared for a week or two? The clerks knew their business. He had three excellent foremen, who were perfectly capable of overseeing things for a short space of time.

He wanted to speak to Rayner anyway, to ask if he would think about divorcing his wife. Divorce was a long-winded, expensive process, but if there was no chance of Isabel going back to him, Rayner would surely wish to marry again? If only to beget a son and heir?

Owen also wanted Isabel to be reconciled with her father. Even if he could not forgive his child, he ought to know his granddaughter. He ought to love her, too.

"I *could* come with you," he began, as Isabel strapped her bags, then began to rummage through the cupboards, looking for her light summer cloak. "We should try to come to some arrangement with Rayner, if only for the child's sake. For the sake, too, of any other children we may have."

"God forbid," muttered Isabel, shuddering. "That's another thing," she grumbled. "You promised me you'd be careful. But sometimes, you're so haphazard. You get so carried away—"

"That's not fair!" Stung, Owen glared at her. These days, he was so damned careful that there was no pleasure at all in what was supposed to be an act of love. "But accidents do happen, and—"

"Owen, please stop muttering. Do you wish to know what my Papa had to say?"

"You mean – you wrote to your father?"

"Yes. Should I have sought your permission before I even took up my pen?"

"No, but –"

"Then if you wish to be informed, don't interrupt me again."

So Owen buttoned his lip, and Isabel told him how she had written to her parents, professing her sincere repentance, begging their forgiveness, and asking if they would at least consent to receive their innocent grandchild in their home, even if they insisted her erring mother should remain standing on the gravel sweep, or in the stable yard.

She had at last received a grudging reply, offering Isabel and her bastard a roof over their heads for one week only. That Morgan fellow, however, was expressly forbidden to set even a foot upon the Graham estate. If he did, the dogs would be set upon him forthwith. He would be torn limb from limb.

Having persuaded Isabel to defer her journey for just a few short days, Owen supervised the charging of the biggest furnace, made sure his most intelligent foreman understood what was required of him, and told the men to respect and obey Mr Davies as faithfully as they would Owen himself.

Then he booked his family's passage by express coach. Isabel had written to her parents again, to inform them of her imminent arrival. But since he was well aware that the corrupter of their child would never even be acknowledged in church, let alone received in the Graham family home, Owen made other arrangements for his own accommodation in Warwickshire.

He had always been on good terms with his cousin Maria. So, now that her parents were no longer living, he did not think there would be any difficulty if he asked for shelter under her roof.

Charles Harding could hardly object. The former model of a perfect son and heir had become, on inheriting, a reprobate, gambler and fornicator of some distinction, who neglected his estate and squandered his patrimony, who drank and whored as if his life depended on the same.

But he sincerely loved his wife – and Maria, wisely, turned a blind eye to his little defects of character. Provided the amount of her personal allowance was regularly reviewed, and generously increased.

Having seen Isabel safely received by her mother, who readily took Honor into her warm embrace, but whose frightened eyes told Owen that *she* would suffer grievously if her husband learned the Morgan creature had dared to trespass on his land, Owen took himself off to Charles Harding's estate.

"My dear Owen!" Tripping elegantly down the front steps of the gracious Georgian manor house, Maria took her long lost cousin in her arms. She beamed up at him. "My *dearest* coz," she cried, "it's *wonderful* to see you again! Well? Do I deserve a kiss?"

"My dear Maria, of course you do!" Owen kissed her. Then he stepped back, to admire her. "You're looking extremely well," he said. "Extremely fetching, too."

"My dressmaker is a genius. My maid is a spellbinder of the first order. My *friseur* should be burned for a witch." Maria simpered charmingly. "You should observe me first thing in the morning," she continued, archly. "Or rather you shouldn't, for you'd scream in horror, and run quite mad. Because *then*, you see, I'm an absolute *fright*."

"Indeed?" Laughing at her, Owen shook his head. "I can't believe that. Do you not recall the day I arrived back from India? When I came striding out of the morning mist, and—"

"I ran out in my shift and curl-papers, to welcome you home?" Giggling, Maria hid her face. "How *brazen* of me! I'd never do such a thing now."

She took his hand. "Do come in," she invited. "Everything is ready for you."

Maria was such a chatterbox, such a gossip, that the day flew by. Following her about the house, inside which he had never been before, and which Maria kept done up in the latest fashion and style, Owen was entertained by a flow of ceaseless badinage and repartee. So much so that he never once managed to enquire after Rayner, or Jane.

These days, Charles Harding drank so much, gambled so hard and had so many other claims on his time that he never sat down to dinner until well past five. Not that Maria minded. It was so unfashionable to dine early, and late hours gave her all afternoon to dress.

But, because of this, it was not until early evening that Owen heard some news which almost unmanned him. Indeed, if he had not been seated, it would have felled him to the ground.

No warning was given, no ground prepared, no allowance made. Instead, "I *must* tell you, dear Owen," chirped Maria brightly, as she nodded to the butler to take the desserts away, "indeed, I should have mentioned it earlier. But no matter. The fact is, my sister is engaged!"

"Engaged? To be married?" Owen stared at her. "Your sister is engaged?"

"My poor fellow, you've turned into a parrot." Charles Harding grinned. "Yes, indeed. The old ewe is to be put to the ram at last."

"Charles! Don't be so coarse." Sighing, Maria shook her head. "Pray, my dear Owen, take no notice of him. Owen? What is it? Owen!"

"My God!" Charles Harding stared in astonishment as Owen's glass keeled over. As it dripped its scarlet contents down Maria's yellow muslin gown. As the white damask cloth was dyed a deep ruby red. "Good grief, what ails the man?"

Owen did not reply. Could not reply. His face a grey mask, he sat frozen, unseeing, unhearing, his mouth dry and his limbs useless. But then, painfully, he collected his shattered wits. "Who is the creature?" he managed to croak, as Charles Harding poured more wine, as the footman mopped at the stain. "Maria? Who—"

"Dear Owen, do bear up. Be a man!" Embarrassed for him, Maria motioned the footman away. "She writes that the gentleman is quite charming. He—"

"*Who is the creature*?"

"He is a manufacturer, in business in South Wales. He's somewhat older than my sister, but she insists he is hale and hearty, that he—"

"Has lead in his pencil yet." Maria's husband grinned again. "He'll take her by the ear without delay."

"Charles, *please*!" Maria covered Owen's hand with hers. "The gentleman's name is Mr Atkins," she explained. "He is a man of property, having a house near Pontypool, and another near Cardiff – which he uses only rarely, since his favourite home is a country estate on Gower. At present, my sister and Rayner are guests there.

"The house itself is in Oxwich. It stands in some charming—"

"I know him." Owen was still deathly pale. "I know the man, we are business associates, I supply his factories with castings, and bar iron. My God! How dare he do this? How dare he worm his way into her affections, how dare he—"

"Owen, I doubt if the poor gentleman is even aware of the connection!" Maria shook her head. "So he is a customer of yours. What of it? You and your fellow ironmasters supply half of South Wales, do you not?"

"Where – when did he meet her?"

"While she and Rayner were staying in Pontypool as guests of a Mr Lloyd, who is an old friend of Mama."

"So he sneaked into the house, trifled with your sister's affections, then stole her away."

"He has not stolen her! She is a free woman, is she not?

She may do as she chooses! This week, she has chosen to marry a respectable gentleman."

"Exactly." Charles Harding grimaced. "Owen, my dear fellow, do be rational about this. Recollect that *you* are in no position to state whom Jane may or may not marry! As a whoremaster of the first—"

"Charles!" Maria gave her husband one of her fiercest, sharpest looks. "How *can* you be so vile?"

"My dear, I speak the simple truth. I know – I am a drunk, I am a brute, I pollute the very air you breathe – but I slander no one. If this creature had kept his breeches buttoned and his hand out of the fair Isabel's placket, he would now be happily married to your sister, enjoying all the—"

"Charles, I will not hear you talk like this!" Maria rose from the table. Throwing down her napkin, she stalked from the room, calling imperiously for her maid, and leaving Owen and Charles Harding to an increasingly uncomfortable tête à tête.

Isabel's father had always loved his only child. True, her behaviour had mortified him. Her disgrace had been a blow from which he had thought he might never recover. But two or three days after the prodigal had returned, old Mr Graham was dandling his granddaughter on his knee and even being tolerably civil to the infant's mother.

Expecting to be at best ignored, abused – or at worst, physically attacked – Isabel had come home fully prepared to play the meek penitent. She was somewhat disconcerted to find there was no need. On the morning following her arrival, discovering her father still in the breakfast room, she was about to creep away again when he spoke to her. "Where is the child?" he enquired.

"In the nursery." Quaking in her little satin slippers, bravely Isabel met his gaze. "M-Mrs Stemp is dressing her now."

"When she is ready, bring her to my study." Mr Graham sniffed, then snorted, then blew his nose hard. "I have something to say to her there."

In her father's study, Isabel found a parcel addressed to her daughter, containing three dolls, several other baby's toys, and some exquisite embroidered gowns. While Isabel unpacked these gifts, the squire took Honor on his lap, let her pull his whiskers, listen to the tick of his gold watch, and dribble all over his lapels.

Isabel was relieved – of course she was – but as the week wore on she became irritable. Bored. Sitting with her mother in Mrs Graham's little sitting room, there was nothing to do but observe the summer rain slide down the panes. No one came to call. In this house, the servants saw to everything, so there wasn't even any household managing to be done.

Sighing, Isabel rose to her feet and prowled around the room. "Mama?" she hazarded.

Mrs Graham glanced up from her *petit point*. "Yes, my dear?" she murmured, absently. She'd lost count of her stitches now, and would be obliged to begin her calculations all over again. "What is it?"

"May John Groom take a note to Owen?"

"Well, my dear—"

"Please, Mama!"

"Mr Morgan is not welcome here. You know that."

"I don't propose to invite him!" Isabel plumped herself down at her mother's elegant rosewood desk. "I mean to write to him. Surely I may? Mama, I must have *something* to do!"

Owen scanned Isabel's note, and frowned. Then he stuffed it into his pocket, and sighed.

"Honor is well, I hope?" demanded Maria, carefully. "Isabel, too?"

"They're perfectly well, I thank you. But Isabel is bored." Moodily, Owen shrugged. "She says she has no one to talk to and nothing to do. She looks forward to hearing how *I* am occupying my time, in this dreary, Godforsaken corner of nowhere."

"Poor Isabel. She misses you." Maria shook her head. "I dare say Honor pines for you, too."

"What can I do about that? If I call on them, Mr Graham will set the dogs on me."

"Invite them here, then."

"To stay?"

"Well, perhaps not to stay." Maria smoothed the folds of her new silk gown. "But they are welcome to visit on a daily basis, and to take their meals with us."

Isabel glanced through Owen's reply. When she came to Maria's qualified invitation, she pursed her lips. Well, she supposed, it was one degree better than being completely scorned.

"I am the pariah of the neighbourhood," she complained, when at last she and Owen sat down together in Maria's private study, while Maria herself went to scold the cook. "We see nobody. Hear nothing. We pay no visits, and Mama will invite no one to call on *us*. Lest I infect them with my wickedness, I suppose."

"Do you not go to church?"

"Of course we do. Papa insists on that. But last Sunday, at Evensong, I was ignored completely. Even the tenants would not acknowledge me." Isabel dabbed at her eyes. "Good Christians all, are they not? No doubt they felt I defiled their holy place."

"Poor Isabel."

"Poor Honor, too." Isabel began to cry. "Oh God!" she sniffed, "I do wish—"

"What?"

"Oh, nothing."

"That you had never left him?"

"I wish it had not come to this! Owen?"

"Yes?"

"Will you build me a new house? One with large, light

casements and a gracious staircase? May we have damask hangings, and modern silver plate?"

"Certainly we may. If your father will give me the money to buy these things."

"Owen, you're rich!" Isabel pouted. "You're positively coining money these days!"

"The profits from the ironworks must be ploughed back into the business," said Owen decisively. "No one needs cannon and shot any more, so I need to develop new lines in domestic goods, for export overseas. Otherwise, Isabel, we will all starve."

"You're such a skinflint." Isabel stood up. "I'm going to find Honor," she muttered. "She needs to have her tea."

The baby had been left with one of Maria's servants, an old woman who had nursed all the Darrow infants and regarded herself as family. She was therefore very free with her tongue. Leaving Maria's room, Isabel walked along the passage towards the salon, where she found the nurse and Honor alone, save for a footman and a girl cleaning the grate.

Unobserved by them all, Isabel came close enough to hear her daughter referred to as her young ladyship's mistake. To hear the housemaid snigger, and see the footman grin. They were unabashed even when they became aware of Isabel herself, silently standing there.

By the end of the week, Owen himself had begun to tire of the sneers and smirks of the servants, the coarse remarks of Charles Harding, and the fact that he had nothing to do. But most of all he was fatigued by the querulousness of Isabel herself.

Why did she complain so much? Why did she need to grumble about everybody and everything, why was she never, ever content?

As his irritability increased, her grumbling intensified. Did she actually want a quarrel, he wondered. Very well then, he didn't mind, she could have one. As she sat in

Maria's room that rainy Wednesday morning, carrying on, her voice as shrill as a magpie's and her face inflamed, perfectly mottled with anger, he told her to shut up.

"What did you say?" she demanded, amazed.

"I told you to be quiet."

"But what if I do not choose to be dumb?"

"You will nevertheless oblige me."

"But who are *you*?" Isabel's face had become as red as her hair. "Pray, sir, who are you, that you suppose you may give your orders to *me*?"

Owen met her eyes. "I am a fornicator," he replied. "You are my whore. Accordingly, I—"

"*How dare you*!" Isabel was on her feet now. "I am a *lady*!" she screeched. "I am a gentleman's daughter, born and bred! But *you*, you're nothing but a peasant! A stupid Welsh peasant. The son of some ditch-digger, and his pox-faced drab!"

"My father was a landowner! My mother was a lady, of ancient lineage, great personal beauty, and perfect respectability." Owen glared. "I would not sully their dear names by mentioning either in the same breath as yours."

"I hate you!" Isabel glared back. "I hate you like poison, you dirty barbarian, you filthy libertine, you—"

"You harlot, you trollop, you slut." Owen turned away. "As you see, I can bandy insults as readily as any whore. But *I*—"

He got no further. Isabel attacked him. Nails clawed at his face, sharp pointed boots kicked at his shins. He let her exhaust herself, then pushed her into a chair.

She went down with a thump. Still enraged, she scowled at him balefully.

"I'm going out," said Owen.

"To walk by the lake, I hope." Isabel glared daggers. "Oblige me by drowning yourself there."

Owen strode out of the house. He walked for some distance through the park. Then, reaching the first of the open fields, he sat on a stile and thought. He could not let Jane marry Michael Atkins! Yes, Mr Atkins might be a good man. He might even deserve her, might make her happy. God knew, she deserved some happiness.

But all the same . . .

Observing a labouring man coming along the lane, Owen stopped him. "Could you take a note up to the house?" he enquired, as the man wished him a good day.

"Certainly, Mr Morgan." The man grinned. How well Owen had come to know that particular kind of grin! "Would your message be for Mrs Darrow, sir?"

"For Mrs Harding." Owen opened his pocket book. Taking out a scrap of paper he scribbled rapidly. He gave the man a sixpence. If the fellow hadn't grinned, it would have been a two shilling piece.

The message for Maria was to the effect that urgent business called him back to South Wales. Walking into Warwick, he took the evening coach to Birmingham, then the fast post service to Swansea.

As the dawn came up the following day, he was on the road to Oxwich. As the sun broke through the morning mist, Owen gazed this way and that across the ever-changing vistas of the Gower peninsula, where he had been born.

But upon which he had not set eyes since he was seven years old.

Chapter Eighteen

"Good morning, sir!" As Owen trudged along the badly-metalled road, a farmer's cart swayed level with him. Unfortunately, it was going in the opposite direction. "Looks set to be a fine one, don't it?"

"Yes, indeed." Owen nodded to the driver, but not very cheerily, because he was tired, he was hungry, and his back ached quite atrociously.

Overnight, as the coach had lurched and bumped over potholed roads, as the horses were changed and watered, as bad-tempered grooms and postboys cursed and complained, he'd wondered if he had gone mad indeed. Why else would he be tearing down to South Wales on what was nothing but a wild goose chase? Why else would he have picked a pointless quarrel with a woman by whom he had a child, who was to all intents and purposes his wife, and whom – he supposed – he loved?

But then, as the sun climbed higher, and he strode ever westwards, he began to feel better. Happy, even. Something inside him knew he was going home. That it was right to be going home. Then, he was remembering things he had thought lost forever. These greens and commons, these leafy lanes of English Gower, seemed as dearly familiar as the lanes of Warwickshire. Back there had been a village he could have sworn he had passed through once before, a long time ago.

But where had the Morgans come from? Where had Owen himself lived? He reached a crossroads. To the south was Pennard. To the west, Oxwich, Reynoldston and Llangennith. This last was the English version, surely, of a very Welsh name?

Names, names, names. He rolled them off his tongue. Bethan Davies, William Parry, Mary Gethyn. Rhosili, Port Eynon, Penrhyn Gwyr. Long forgotten, these were suddenly as familiar as his own right hand. His spirits soared.

Soon, he reached another crossroads, but this time there was no signpost. Stopping to consider, he noticed a couple of women coming across a field. Simply clad in grey cotton gowns and rough woollen mantuas, the elder wore a high-crowned black bonnet, while the younger sported a checked red scarf, which covered her shoulders but left her head bare. "Good morning," he began, as they approached.

The elder grinned. "Good morning to you," she countered, boldly. Then, behind her hand, she whispered to her companion. "*Seisnig*," she hissed. "*Jiawl du*!"

Owen was about to retort that *he* was no dirty devil of a Saxon. No indeed. But then he decided to hold his tongue. Although he was dark, he reflected, he was so tall and slim that he probably didn't look Welsh at all. "I need to get to Oxwich," he said, pleasantly. "Do I take the left fork here, or the right?"

"The left, master." The younger woman smiled. "So who are you looking for there, then?"

"A Mr Michael Atkins. I believe he has a house in the village. Perhaps you know it?"

"Yes, I know it." But now, the elder woman frowned. "I know it very well."

"Too well." Her friend grimaced. "You go down there, look," she said, pointing. "It's about half an hour's walk. No more."

They scurried away, leaving Owen somewhat mystified, staring after them.

Twenty minutes later, he arrived at the house. Gazing up at the steep gables and the landscape of red roofs above them, on which doves strutted, preened and cooed in the morning sunshine, he knew for certain he had never been *here* before. He rang the bell.

A neat but very solemn little servant girl promptly answered the door. Greeting her with a smile, Owen presented his card. "Will you please to wait a moment, sir?" she murmured. Then she tripped away into the darkness of the house.

She soon returned. "Will you be so kind as to step this way?" she enquired. All smiles now, she led him down a wide, sunlit passage towards a panelled oak door. Tapping lightly, she opened it, then ushered him inside.

"Owen, my boy!" Turning from the window, Michael Atkins beamed in welcome. He shook Owen by the hand, then motioned him towards a comfortable, chintz-covered chair. Puzzled by the younger man's sudden appearance here, but inclined to be hospitable nonetheless, he stopped the maidservant at the door and ordered tea, coffee, chocolate and fresh rolls, to be brought in without delay.

Some polite chit-chat about the weather, the beauty of the season, and the state of the nation occupied the next few minutes. Then, the maid came in, bringing what her master had ordered. Neatly, she began to set out the china and glass.

"So, my dear fellow. Is there something wrong at the works?" Sitting down at his desk, Michael Atkins gave the maid such a sharp stare that she seized her tray and practically ran out of the room. "You have a problem with the new furnace, perhaps? Well, if that is indeed the case, don't be unduly concerned on my account. I'm quite prepared to wait for my castings and spare parts."

"It's nothing like that."

"No? Then what *is* the matter?"

"Well, the fact is—"

But then, Owen stalled. He had not rehearsed this conversation at all. So now, what should he do? Come straight out with it? Say, "Mr Atkins, as I understand it, you have lately become engaged to my cousin.

But you may not marry her, for she is still engaged to me."

No. That was impossible! "I had no idea you had a house on Gower," he muttered lamely, as he played for time and searched feverishly for the right thing to say. If there was a right thing. "But this place is charming. Delightful, in fact. Do you manage to come here very often?"

"Not as often as I might wish." Idly toying with a silver paper knife, Michael Atkins shook his head and smiled. "I have been here almost three weeks. Business and duty call, but I have been unable to drag myself away. Like Ulysses, I have tasted lotus, and am most unwilling to return to the world of commerce, industry and care. So now, Owen—"

Owen decided to plunge straight in. That would undoubtedly be best, at any rate in the long run. But, as he opened his mouth to speak, Blanchette nosed open the door of the study and wriggled through the gap she had made. Feathery tail wagging, she scampered over to her former master and laid her head in his lap.

Michael Atkins stroked her muzzle. "Good girl," he murmured. "Good creature. Well now, does your mistress come?"

It seemed she did. Out in the passageway, a woman's light tread bounced off the polished boards and echoed all around. The door of the study swung open wide. His heart thudding against his aching ribs, Owen turned to see Jane and Rayner, dressed for walking, standing there.

"My God!" Narrowing his eyes, Rayner gaped, glared, grimaced – then turned away.

Jane simply stared.

Michael Atkins looked from brother to sister, then to their cousin, then back again. "Well," he began, coolly, "since it is clear you are all acquainted, perhaps you will allow *me* to learn how my friend and business associate Owen Morgan happens to know – and appears to be very well known by – my summer guests?"

"To be sure." Recovering, Jane scooped Blanchette into her embrace, then went to stand by her lover's side. "Michael, your friend comes to wish us joy. He has heard of our engagement and now intends to congratulate us in person. I hope, most heartily."

"But how did he hear? Who told *him*?"

"My sister Maria, I imagine. Just recently, he has been staying with her." Jane looked up, met her lover's eyes, and smiled. "Mr Morgan and I are closely related," she explained. "He is my cousin."

"Your cousin?" Michael Atkins's face was a mask. "But how—"

"It's quite simple." Jane shrugged. "Strangely enough, Mr Morgan's family came from this part of the world. But his parents died when he was very young. He became homeless, so my father and mother took him in.

"He was brought up by my parents, on their estate in Warwickshire. A few years ago, however, there were some differences of opinion between them, which it proved impossible to resolve. So Mr Morgan returned to South Wales, where he has family connections still. Michael, my dear? Why do you stare so? Michael?"

But Michael Atkins simply stared on. For now, the log jam shifted. The torrent flowed. Everything began to tumble downstream, and be swept into place.

Why Ellis Darrow, a Warwickshire landowner, had ever taken it upon himself to care what went on in the wilds of South Wales, to spend his presumably valuable time and money bringing an obscure part-time smuggler to justice, had always been a mystery to Michael. Certainly, he had possessed the box. But, try as he might, he had never been able to find the key.

But here it was at last. Owen Morgan! Of course! Well, there must be a thousand Owen Morgans in Wales. Several hundred, probably, in Glamorgan alone.

All the same . . .

Michael's light blue eyes grew flinty, but he said nothing. Instead, it was Rayner who broke the awkward silence. "Well?" he muttered, all the while favouring his cousin with a look of the most withering scorn, "why, precisely, *have* you come here?"

Owen drew a deep breath. "I took Isabel to visit her parents," he began. That was a mistake, for at the sound of his wife's name, Rayner flushed an angry red. "I was not welcome in her father's house, of course, so I stayed with Maria. She had just received a letter from Jane, announcing her engagement to Mr Atkins here."

"So you hastened hither to congratulate your cousin and your friend? How thoughtful." Rayner's voice was so heavy with sarcasm that Owen winced. "But could I be mistaken there? Have you perhaps come to demonstrate that most splendid of your talents? To sow discord and create misery, where there was but peace and harmony before?"

Owen bit his lip. Avoiding Rayner's eye, he now looked directly at Jane – and was distressed to observe that although she met his gaze with perfect candour, she also shrank against Michael Atkins's reassuring bulk.

More than shrank. In fact, she nestled so close that her body moulded itself against his. Incredibly, but quite obviously, these two were lovers.

Owen felt sick and ill. Furiously, murderously jealous, too. But, all the same, he managed to remain calm. "Jane," he began humbly, "may I have a private word with you?"

"No, you may not." It was Rayner who spoke. "How dare you force your way in here!" he cried. "How dare you come gatecrashing into our lives again, how dare you demand an interview with my sister – who, I am sure, hates the very sight of you, and most sincerely wishes you away!"

"Jane, I—"

"Not content with breaking her heart just once, now you are trying to destroy her happiness a second time. Well, sir – you shall not succeed. You will have no private word with Jane. If you have anything of interest to say, say it here, to me."

Owen ignored him. "Jane?" he repeated, urgently, beseechingly.

"Please, Owen. Just go." Turning away, Jane hid her face against Michael Atkins's broad expanse of waistcoat. Now, his arm was draped protectively across her shoulders. Sensing her mistress's distress, Blanchette whimpered in doggy sympathy.

"You may say anything you wish to say to Jane here. In the presence of myself and Mr Darrow, too." Michael Atkins stroked Jane's upper arm in such a proprietorial fashion that Owen wanted to kill him. "We are all friends," he continued, smoothly. "All in each others' confidence. So, you may speak as easily here as in any private chamber, believe you me."

"All the same, I wish—"

"Do you? I am sorry. It is not possible to grant any wish of yours today."

As he spoke, Michael Atkins touched a bell on his desk. At once, Robin and Henry Corder appeared in the doorway. Glancing behind him, Owen could not help but notice the look which passed between master and men. "So now," continued Michael Atkins, "please come to the point. Tell this lady whatever it is you have come so far to say."

Owen sighed. "Cousin?" he whispered. "My dearest Jane?"

Jane shrugged. But at least she turned to look at him. "Well?"

"When Maria told me you were engaged to be married," Owen began, "I was so shocked and dismayed that I fear my heart almost stopped beating. Afterwards, I was faint for hours. For days I could not eat, could not sleep, could not rest. In fact, grief and wretchedness conspired to destroy me.

"But then, I rallied. Just a little. Surely, I thought, I might at least appeal to her? Sweet, good and gentle as she is, surely she will not refuse even to hear me? So I have come here today to beg you, to beseech you—"

"How the fellow rants," muttered Rayner. "He ought to be on the stage."

"To beg you not to marry this man! Worthy and honest though Mr Atkins undoubtedly is, and far more deserving of you than I could ever be, please – in the name of God and all the saints – do not become his wife!"

"Why not?"

"Because, dear Jane, you belong to me!" Now, as Jane stared at him in amazement, Owen ploughed on. "I behaved so badly," he continued, "that whenever I think of it, I weep. I destroyed the happiness not only of the woman I love, but of her whole family, too.

"But I repent! I repent most humbly, sincerely and sorrowfully. If I could make amends, if I could resurrect the dead and restore the living, I would do so, even if it cost me my own heart's blood. Oh, Jane – darling Jane – I beseech you, leave this man. Leave this house. Come with me!"

"Go with *you*?" Jane gaped at him. Blanchette was whimpering again, so her mistress held her close. "Owen," she began, "I fear there is no hope for you. Indeed, you have run quite mad. All the same – will you try to set aside your ravings just for one moment? To consider what I have to say?

"You ask me to become your wife. But do you not already have one? Isabel lives with you. *She* shares your life! She has even given birth to your child, and she most certainly has more claim—"

"Jane, please!"

"No!" Jane buried her face in Blanchette's silky coat. "I shall not listen to any more!"

"Dearest Jane, look at me!"

"Go away, Owen!" Jane's shoulders were shaking. Obviously, she was perilously close to tears. "Please, for the love of God, leave this place!"

"Well, Morgan. You heard the lady. You had better go." Rayner took a step forward.

But it was Michael Atkins who nodded, almost imperceptibly, to Robin and Henry. Almost before he was aware of what was happening, Owen found himself standing in the sunshine once more, his hat and cane on the gravel sweep, and the doors of the house barred firmly against him.

Michael Atkins sent for cake and wine. Inviting brother and sister to be seated, he poured a glass of Madeira for each. "Well," he began evenly, "I shall confess it now. I am still confused. In fact, I am so bewildered that a simple account of events themselves, shorn of explanation, excuse or prevarication, would be of inestimable value to me."

He looked from his prospective bride to her brother, then back again. "Could one of you oblige me?" he enquired. "Jane, my dear? Alas, I fear you are yet unequal to speech. Therefore, Rayner, the task falls to you."

Rayner was only too ready to unburden himself. "As my sister mentioned," he began, "Owen Morgan was born and brought up in these parts. His father was a farmer. His parents died when he was but a little child, and his uncle and aunt – my parents – took him in."

"This uncle and aunt. They were Ellis and Rebecca Darrow, were they not?"

"Yes, indeed." Sorrowfully, Rayner smiled. "How did you learn their Christian names?"

"My friend Mr Lloyd mentioned them many a time. There was a trading agreement between him and your family. His rolling mills supplied your Birmingham factories with tin plate. I believe he had a great personal affection for the late Mrs Darrow, too."

"Ah, yes. Of course." Remembering how he had wept over Mr Lloyd's letter of condolence, Rayner sighed. "Well, then. From the ages of seven to thirteen, that creature and I were playfellows. I loved him like a brother. He affected to be fond of me. Little did I dream that he in fact hated and despised me, and would be instrumental in ruining my life!

"At thirteen, I went away to school. But although he might have gone with me, my cousin disliked the idea of receiving a gentleman's education. So he came back to South Wales, to spend some time with his paternal uncle, who is an apothecary here.

"My sister Jane, unwilling that he should lose contact with the family in Warwickshire, proposed to open a correspondence with him. She wrote to him regularly, for years."

"Did Mr Morgan write to her?"

"Yes." Jane spoke now. "Of course he did."

"To cut a long story short," Rayner continued, "this exchange of letters seemed to promote an affection which, as the years went by, grew in intimacy and tenderness. Meeting again, Jane and her faithful correspondent were delighted with one another. More than delighted, in fact. Eventually, my cousin declared himself. He asked my sister to marry him, and she consented to become his wife."

"But?"

"Three short weeks before the wedding was due to take place, Owen told my sister he could not marry her after all. He had become enamoured of another woman, and preferred her to the one he had promised to wed."

"Good God!" Michael took Jane's hand in his. "My poor darling—"

"It was worse even than you suppose. The woman my cousin had beguiled was my own wife." Closing his eyes as if in pain, Rayner reached for his glass. He fortified himself with more Madeira. Then, sighing, he nibbled more cake.

Feeling a little stronger at last, he continued. "Owen left my father's house. A matter of months later, my wife – whom I loved and was disposed to pardon, for although she had foolishly permitted Owen Morgan to declare his affection for her, she was, I assumed, too chaste and honourable to have let things go any further – came to speak with me. She was with child, she said."

"So you turned her out?"

"On the contrary. I sent her to her room, and asked that she should stay there, whilst I collected my thoughts." Rayner shook his head. "I believe I would have forgiven her everything. Had she shown any remorse, had she expressed even the slightest regret for the distress she had caused, I should have made her mistress of my heart and home once more. After all, I reasoned, her child might be her lover's. But it might just as easily be mine.

"But she did not repent. Instead, she ridiculed me, after a fashion I shall not describe here. She affirmed her affection for her seducer, and declared he loved her still."

"So you suggested she might prefer to throw in her lot with him?"

"No! Mr Atkins, I am a magistrate. A churchwarden, too. I would never have positively encouraged vice!" Rayner sniffed. "Isabel and I discussed the matter. At the conclusion of our discussion, she simply left my house. She went to her lover. She is now his whore. Her bastard takes his name and passes for his child."

"I see." Michael Atkins looked grim. "I knew he had a family," he muttered. "There is at least one child. Her mother is known as Mrs Morgan. I had assumed she was his wife."

"Why should you think otherwise?"

"Why, indeed?" Michael Atkins glanced towards Jane. "My sweetest love," he murmured, "you look so pale! I fear you are unwell."

"I am, a little." Jane rose to her feet. "Will you excuse me?" she whispered. Then, taking Blanchette, she retired to her room.

Rayner solaced himself with more cake. Michael Atkins watched him eat. He licked his fingers so greedily, and devoured slice after slice so voraciously, that he reminded his host of a fat dowager at a ball.

A professional chaperone, whose sole *raison d'être* was either to be eating one meal, or anticipating the pleasures of the next.

He was so like his cousin! But the dark good looks, the fine bone structure and athletic frame which he shared with Owen Morgan had, in Rayner's case, been obscured and submerged by layer upon layer of blubber. Sloth and easy living meant muscles and sinews had wasted. Fuel which should have powered activity and enterprise had merely been laid down as fat.

Michael Atkins fingered his paper knife. It would be exactly like killing a pig. In fact, they might do it that way. String it up by the hind trotters, perhaps. Then let it squeal for a while, to get the blood flowing, before they slit its throat.

"Why don't you go upstairs, and rest a while?" he suggested, as Rayner slurped more wine. "You've had a most unpleasant shock. You surely feel the need to recover?"

Rayner agreed that he did. He retired to his room. Then he rang down again, to ask if the rest of the cake and wine could be sent up after him, to keep his spirits from sinking any lower than they were already today.

Michael summoned Robin and Henry Corder, who closed the door behind them, then stood impassive while their master paced the floor. Eventually, he spoke. "There are arrangements to be made," he announced. "There are rooms to prepare, and work to be done."

Robin lifted one eyebrow.

Michael Atkins nodded. "The woman and her brother," he agreed. "As for the gentleman you saw off this morning – he will undoubtedly be back! I expect *him* to provide us with especially good sport."

Henry smiled a satisfied smile, which further narrowed his already thin lips.

His master did not return the smile, but went instead to stare out of the window. "We will take Mr Darrow to the cliffs," he murmured. "To one of the caves. No one will disturb us there. I'm not sure about the woman. Prepare a chamber in readiness, but leave it empty."

Turning back to his servants, the master frowned. "Well? Do you not know your duty?"

Thus dismissed, Robin and Henry left the study in silence, closing the door behind them.

Sitting down at his desk, Michael Atkins made some notes. He locked them in a drawer, then rang for a serving maid. "Ah, Sarah," he began. "Step up to Miss Darrow's room directly, if you please. Present my compliments, and enquire if the lady is well enough to receive a visitor."

As he waited for Sarah to return, Michael Atkins pondered. How much did Owen Morgan know? Anything? Everything? Nothing at all?

The child had been very small when he had been taken from Gower. Six or seven at the most. So when Ellis Darrow had begun his impertinent investigations, when he'd discovered what he evidently did, was it likely he'd have taken a little child into his confidence?

No. Of course it was not.

So, the brat grew up in ignorance. What reason would there have been to enlighten him? To cloud his days with sorrow?

None.

Obviously, Owen knew nothing. So much the better. Michael loved a good story, and would thoroughly enjoy telling this one. He would relate in detail how Owen's parents had met their respective ends. Then inform their son how he was to meet his.

"Jane, my dear?" Leading her over to the window, Michael studied Jane's pale face. "How do you feel now?"

"A little better, I think." Miserably, Jane sighed. "But

I'm so cold! I can't stop shaking, and my head aches shockingly."

"Poor darling. Shall I ask Sarah to make you a hot drink? Or would you perhaps like to walk—"

"Why did he come?" Covering her face, Jane burst into tears. "Why did he have to come here, to this beautiful place, why did he have to spoil everything about it for me? Oh, Michael! I had meant to be so happy today!"

"My dear Jane, you shall be happy!" Taking her hands in his, Michael Atkins kissed her cheek. "Listen," he murmured, "it's not yet noon. There's time enough for happiness yet."

Jane shrugged. "Perhaps," she agreed.

"Shall I stay with you for a while?" Once more, Michael kissed her, but this time on the lips. "Or would you prefer to be alone?"

"Stay," murmured Jane, as she kissed him in return. As she felt her body respond to his. As he warmed her once again.

Afterwards, she felt a little better. Hardly light-hearted, she was at least more composed. She had stopped shivering, too.

As he held her, Michael Atkins stroked her hair. "I wish to put a proposition to you," he said.

"What is that?"

"This fellow Morgan is dangerous. Mad, even. But all the same, he loves you."

"Does he?"

"I think so." Michael Atkins met Jane's eyes. "Well, my dear? Do you still wish to marry me?"

"Of course I do."

"Then, I suggest we marry soon. By special license, in the church here at Oxwich."

"That's an excellent idea."

"*I* think so. However, I hardly dared hope you would agree."

"But of course I agree!"

"That's splendid." Jane's lover embraced her. His cold, dry lips touched her forehead.

He smiled, but only to himself. Her aunt had cheated him of blood, of tears, of agony. But now the niece would pay her debt. Pay with interest, too.

Chapter Nineteen

Bruised and dusty, tired and hungry though he undoubtedly was, Owen could not be downhearted. Not in the least dismayed. For, he had seen the way his cousin had looked at him. In those beautiful blue eyes had been reproach, regret, even a little anger – but no bitterness. No hatred. In fact, she loved him still! This conviction made his heart light, and put wings on his heels.

He reached the first of the crossroads once again. Punching his hat back into shape, he jammed it jauntily on the top of his head, pushed his hands deep into his pockets, and began to whistle a lively Irish jig.

So, he and Jane would marry. Isabel would go back to Rayner, who would no doubt fidget and grumble for a while, but would secretly be glad to have her home again, where she was happiest and where she really belonged.

For Isabel had had her little adventure. As for Rayner – this actress or that harlot was surely no adequate substitute for the beautiful, cultured lady who was his lawful wedded wife?

There would be no practical difficulties about Isabel going home. No other kind of difficulty, either. Rayner was the wealthiest landowner in the district. Not to mention a magistrate, a churchwarden, and all the rest of it. If *he* chose to forgive and forget, the rest of the county would be obliged to follow suit. To accept his wife and her child in their midst, and to call them their own.

"Ah, but what about the baby herself?" asked a voice, somewhere deep inside Owen's head. "What about the innocent child?"

"Well," he replied, cheerfully, "that's no matter. On the contrary, I imagine Honor will benefit greatly, in the end. In law, she is Rayner's own daughter. Not to mention his heir."

Recalling Honor's pretty face and artless prattle, he grinned. Surely Rayner had only to see her to love her? What could be better for any child, than to have a rich, doting father – *and* an uncle more closely related, and therefore far more devoted, than the general run of uncles tend to be?

By the time he arrived in the village of Parkmill, Owen had it all worked out.

"Might you be making your way to Swansea, sir?" Now, a farmer's cart slowed down to a languid crawl, and ambled along beside him.

"Yes, as a matter of fact I am." Shielding his eyes against the noonday glare, Owen glanced up at the man who held the reins. "Could you perhaps give me a lift?"

"I was just about to suggest it, sir." The farmer grinned. "Have you been down Oxwich way?"

"Yes, indeed. I went there to pay a call."

"But your friend was not at home?"

"No, I'm afraid not."

"Never mind, sir. Better luck next time. Get up then, eh?"

Owen climbed into the cart.

As it rumbled along, he turned to look at his benefactor. He saw a broad, strong, thick-set man of thirty or so. Fair-haired and blue-eyed, he spoke not with a lilting, sing-song Welsh accent, but with what sounded suspiciously like a West Country burr. "Might you be a Gower man yourself?" he enquired, artlessly.

"That I am, sir." The farmer shook his head. "My family have lived in these parts for six, seven hundred years."

"Yet you don't look Welsh."

"*Welsh*?" The man nearly fell off his cart. "That's

because I'm not!" he cried. "Lookee here, sir. You're obviously a stranger to these parts, so let me tell you how it was. My ancestors were honest farmers. They came here in the Conqueror's time! They were granted these hills and valleys by royal decree.

"They drove the savages out. They pushed them back to the marshes and swamps of North Gower, where they belong."

"I see."

"Do you, sir? Welshmen!" The honest farmer spat. "A pack of thieving, idle, beggarly rascals, that's all those fellows are. I could tell you some tales about Welshmen, sir, that would make your hair stand on end. Have the eyes starting out of your head!

"Why, back in the last century, there was such lawbreaking, such banditry and general skullduggery over North Gower way, that we honest fellows on this side of the country slept with muskets primed and loaded, and our cudgels at the ready by our beds! When my old father was a boy—"

The farmer rambled on. By the time they reached Swansea, Owen's eyes had been opened. He'd heard all about the wicked ways and horrible habits of the barbarian Welsh, who spoke a heathen language, bowed down to graven images of their ancient Celtic gods, and had the most disgusting table manners, too.

Lounging on a settle in the snug bar of the coaching inn, waiting for the Cardiff express – for he meant to visit his uncle and tell David of his good fortune without further delay – Owen had time to cool his heels and reflect.

He was going to marry his dearest, darling Jane. That was as good as settled. He would sell the ironworks, and with the proceeds realised from this, he would buy a country estate. He would commission the building of the most beautiful house imaginable, a gracious, airy mansion in which he and Jane and their ten children would live in perfect harmony for the rest of their days.

But then, Owen remembered something else. There was going to be a loser in the case. His conscience smote him cruelly there.

For, he knew nothing but good of the man. A lonely widower, in the twilight of his years he had fallen in love with a sweet and beautiful girl, whom he meant to make his bride. But now, he was to be baulked of his dearest wish. He would be cast into the darkness of solitude once again.

Owen squared his shoulders. He would, he decided, do Michael Atkins some sort of compensatory favour. If the man were to be robbed of his heart's desire, some kind of reparation should and must be made.

"Might I have pen and paper?" he called, to a potboy idling by.

"Certainly, sir!" The boy lounged off, but a minute later he reappeared with a tray, upon which paper, two inkwells, a dish of sand and several scarlet waxen wafers were neatly arranged. With a flourish, he mended a pen, then offered it to the gentleman for inspection. Owen seized it, and began to scribble without further delay.

"I wish this to be sent immediately, by express," said Owen, as he sealed his short note.

"I'll take it to the post myself, sir," said the boy. Grinning hopefully, he pocketed the letter. Owen gave him half a crown.

Then he strolled out into the stable yard, to take the air and think. If he were to do Mr Atkins a favour, he would need an intermediary. For, he reasoned, the man could hardly be expected to accept anything from the creature who had stolen away his bride.

Frowning, Owen considered. Then, he hit upon the very fellow. Mr Evan Lloyd, a Monmouthshire ironmaster whose foundries, rolling mills and factories were famous throughout the whole of South Wales, was in the same line of business as Mr Atkins himself.

Personally unknown to Owen, Mr Lloyd was also a

friend and associate of Thomas Taliesin, and therefore by default an honest man.

At present, Thomas Taliesin's own foundries were turning out a range of castings which Mr Atkins's Pontypool works then machined and used in the assembly of steam engines which were exported to America and the Far East. The next batch of castings would no doubt be ready for delivery some time soon.

So – they could be delivered as usual, but Owen would pay the bill. Mr Atkins should have his castings more or less free of charge, enabling him to make a huge profit on his engines. Owen's bad conscience would therefore be appeased.

Changing stages in Neath, Bridgend and Newport, Owen arrived in Pontypool tired and unshaven but bright-eyed and determined, his noble purpose unshaken and his vision undimmed.

Seeking an interview with Mr Lloyd, he introduced himself as a fellow ironmaster, and was invited into the old gentleman's office. There, he got down to business. "I wish to make Mr Atkins a present," he declared. "Well, almost a present, of a batch of castings made for his factory by Taliesin and Company."

Mr Lloyd frowned. Then he shook his head. "What is that to do with me?" he enquired. "More to the point, what has Mr Atkins done for you, that you feel under such an obligation to him?"

"It's a private matter." Realising how ridiculous all this must sound, for a moment Owen chewed his lower lip. "As well as being a customer of my friend Thomas Taliesin," he continued, "Mr Atkins is a good customer of mine. But soon I am to arrange a transaction which will concern us both, and from which Mr Atkins will probably come off the poorer.

"No, don't look like that. There's no trickery or fraud involved. Mr Lloyd, I wish to do Mr Atkins a favour, without it seeming to be so. I need to employ an intermediary, or broker. I hoped that broker might be you."

Still, Mr Lloyd frowned.

Again, Owen explained.

Mr Lloyd sucked the insides of his cheeks. "This – this favour you speak of will cost you hundreds," he said. "Maybe even a thousand pounds."

"That does not concern me." Dreamily, Owen smiled. "I shall gain something worth infinitely more than gold."

"Indeed?" Mr Lloyd shrugged. He had never heard anything like it. This personable young man was either a knave or a fool. He would invite him to stay to supper, he decided, in order that he might study him more closely, and discover which.

Ringing for a servant, he offered refreshment, had his offer accepted, then told Owen that supper would be upon the table in half an hour's time. Perhaps, while he waited, his guest might like to go and wash the dust off his face and put a comb through his hair?

Owen agreed readily. Whilst he was out of the room, Mr Lloyd paced the boards. He considered the proposal which had just been made.

He had heard of Owen Morgan. He knew all about his modest, but ever-growing enterprise. In the small world which Mr Lloyd inhabited, news of bad debts, sharp practices and possible bankruptcies always spread like wildfire. But as far as he knew, Owen Morgan's business was efficiently run, his order book full, and his credit good.

Perhaps it was exactly as the young man said? He owed Mr Atkins a favour, meant to discharge the debt handsomely, and was too sparing of that gentleman's feelings to thrust any obligation back at him.

The two businessmen ate a good supper of cold souse, home-cured ham, and a fine currant pudding, which was followed by cheeses and fruit served off Mr Lloyd's own factory's splendid, world-famous lacquered ware.

"You have spent time among the heathen, I believe?" murmured Mr Lloyd, as he cut into a beautiful, ripe Stilton, then offered his guest a more than generous slice.

"Yes, indeed. I was in India for six, seven years or more." Owen accepted the proffered plate. "But how did you know about that?"

"I cannot now recall. But one hears these things." Enigmatically, Mr Lloyd smiled. The heat of India had addled many a fine brain, he reflected, and would no doubt addle many more. "You did pretty well out there?" he enquired, but casually.

"Well enough," Owen agreed. "But I missed my friends and family most painfully. I was happy to come home."

"I'm sure you were." Mr Lloyd took some strawberries, which he mashed to a delicate pulp. "I have heard," he continued, "that in the tropics, the climate is disagreeable in the extreme. The air is full of pestilence and plague."

"Indeed it is." Owen caught the old man's drift. "Many Europeans succumb, to bodily and mental infirmities of all kinds. But I myself was fortunate in that respect. I escaped with my health unbroken, and my faculties sound."

Mr Lloyd merely smiled. Nodding sagely, he ate another piece of cheese.

Some excellent port had been brought in, and three glasses of this loosened Mr Lloyd's tongue considerably. Nods and smiles gave way to comments and remarks. Filling Owen's glass once more, Mr Lloyd took up his own. "Well, Owen Morgan," he declared. "Here's to your very good health."

"To yours too, sir," murmured Owen.

"I thank you." Mr Lloyd smacked his lips. "Now there's a vintage," he murmured, approvingly. "There's a combination, too. Atkins and Morgan, I mean. Two names *I* never thought to see coupled again! Not in friendship, anyway."

"Indeed?" Owen was peeling an orange. Glancing

up, he frowned quizzically at the older man. "Why is that?"

"Oh, I don't know. Well, I do – but it's an old tale, nothing to the purpose today. Mr Morgan, you yourself spent your youth in Cardiff, did you not?"

"Yes." Owen did not wish to begin making lengthy explanations about his birth and background, not just now anyway, so he nodded. "My uncle is an apothecary there."

"Mr Atkins has connections in Cardiff. He owns a small factory near Llandaff. It came to him as part of a marriage settlement, I believe." Mr Lloyd spooned up some more strawberry mess. "But did you know his family orginally came from Gower?"

"Yes. But I learned that only recently."

"So did I." Mr Lloyd rubbed his old eyes. "I myself have several relations living there. A cousin of mine, a farmer he is – *was*, I should say. He's dead now. Died of grief, so the story goes, when his daughter lost her mind."

"Indeed?" As one who had sometimes feared he would end his own days in a lunatic asylum, Owen sighed his sympathy. "What happened to her?"

"Well, Mr Morgan." Evan Lloyd sighed too. "You should know that Gower is a backward, primitive land. North Gower especially is a lawless place. More so than most. There, thieves retreat to divide their ill-gotten gains, and smugglers ply their evil trade.

"The Excise has a hard time of it, a hard time indeed. The smugglers are desperate, wicked men, who never scruple to spill human blood. One year, in fact, one of the excisemen was actually killed.

"To restore order, and root out the malefactors in the case – or so they hoped, anyway – a company of redcoats was marched down from Swansea. The whole area was put under curfew. Poor Dilys Lloyd was a simple girl, she didn't understand that she was forbidden to be out after dusk, and one evening she went looking for a stray calf.

"The soldiers caught her. I don't know what they did to her, but when she finally got home again, they found she'd lost her reason." Mr Lloyd dabbed at his eyes. "She's still alive, I believe. But from that night forward, she never spoke again."

"The poor creature." Owen shook his head. "Can nothing be done for her?"

"It seems not." Mr Lloyd poured himself another glass of port. "But enough of that. Let me tell you a different story. Mind you, it's half gossip and the rest hearsay, but it's interesting, and it has some bearing on a remark I made earlier this evening. So – will you hear it?"

"Certainly."

"Very well. In the old days, then, there was a notorious smuggler on Gower, Morgan by name. John Morgan, that's it. A murderer, and a thief, he and his men terrorised the people of North Gower. His partner in wickedness was a fellow called Jack Atkins. A relation of our friend Michael? Possibly, but just as possibly not.

"So there were these two villains, dealing in contraband, murdering excisemen, defying the King's majesty and all the rest of it.

"Morgan was a Welshman, of course. Sometimes a farmer, sometimes a fisherman, he was always a thoroughly bad lot. Jack Atkins, however, was English. He was a respectable man, a magistrate, and a landowner of some importance. So, he was used to having all his own way. Having none gainsay him in anything! This being the case, I suppose it was inevitable that Atkins and Morgan should fall out.

"Jack Atkins had bribed some of the excisemen who patrolled the beaches of Gower, and otherwise silenced the rest, so there was nobody could touch him. After he quarrelled with Morgan, therefore, he resolved to teach the fellow a lesson. He sent to Swansea for soldiers to arrest the man, which they did. The redcoats took John Morgan away, and beat him so badly that he died."

Mr Lloyd's sight was dim. He was now engrossed in

his tale, and so well pickled in port that if Owen had risen from the table and left him, the old man would hardly have noticed, but instead would have rambled on, talking contentedly to himself. This being the case, it was not to be wondered that he failed to notice his guest had gone deathly pale.

"So anyway," continued Mr Lloyd, "this John Morgan's wife is a spirited lady. She learns of her husband's death and who was responsible, and takes herself off to Jack Atkins's house in Oxwich, where she stabs him cruelly."

Owen stared. "D-did she actually kill him?" he managed to stammer, horrified.

"Well, no." Mr Lloyd shrugged. "But she maimed him! She put her mark on him, certainly."

"Then?"

"Well, Jack Atkins's men caught her, of course. They threatened her with a fate so terrible that she turned the knife on herself. Stabbed herself through the heart, she did, and died instantly."

"Good God." Owen could hardly believe his ears. "What happened next?"

"Ah now, here's the interesting part. This lady was no plain farmer's wife. No, indeed! *She* was English, and had powerful friends in England. Her brother was a magistrate, and he—"

"What was his name?"

"That I cannot tell you. I heard he lived near Birmingham, but as I say—"

"No matter. Go on."

"When this brother heard of the fate of his kin, he had Jack Atkins arrested, interrogated, then tried for his part in the murders of all kinds of innocent men. The fellow was convicted, sentenced, and hanged for his crimes."

"But Mr Lloyd, how do *you* know all this?"

"Ah." Mr Lloyd looked crafty. He tapped his nose. "A brother of mine hired a nurse once, an old dame from Gower, and a veritable windbag of a woman, believe you me! This was one of her stories. She gave out that she had once been a servant in the Atkins household – nay, that when Mrs Morgan stabbed her master, she had treated his fever, and poulticed his wounds herself. I don't believe a word of it. But anyway—"

"There's more?"

"Certainly!" Mr Lloyd made a face which would not have disgraced a ghoul. "After Jack Atkins was arrested, his house was opened up. They found trapdoors leading to cellars stacked high with contraband – and others which had served as prison cells, and contained machines designed to serve purposes too horrible to mention."

Owen felt ill. For now, suddenly, he remembered a conversation he'd had with Thomas Taliesin on this very theme, a long time ago. "The seed does not necessarily inherit the taint of the parent plant." That was what Thomas had said. "This Jack Atkins," he whispered, fearfully, "do you think Michael Atkins may be his near relation? Perhaps even his son?"

"I don't know whose son he is. As I told you before, there *may* be a connection." Mr Lloyd tapped Owen's lapel. "This is private after-supper conversation, remember. Between you and me. As far as I'm concerned, Mr Michael Atkins is an English ironmaster, and my near neighbour. He's never been involved in anything even remotely underhand, let alone criminal. Well, not as far as I know."

Mr Lloyd poured more port. "Drink up, my boy," he invited. "You look very pale this evening. Are you not sleeping well at night?"

"Sleeping?" repeated Owen, dazedly. He wondered if he would ever sleep again.

"It's a good story, is it not?" demanded his host, grinning expectantly.

"An excellent one," Owen agreed. He felt sick to the heart. Mr Lloyd had been speaking of his own parents. How would the old gentleman feel if he knew that?

"Of course," Mr Lloyd was saying now, "these days,

the trade in contraband has virtually ceased. Since the peace came, the coastguard and the Excise have so many vessels and extra men available that it's not worth anyone's while to attempt it."

"No," Owen murmured absently. "I suppose it's not." He stood up. He found he was so unsteady on his feet that he was obliged to clutch the table, to support himself.

"Are you sick?" enquired Mr Lloyd, staring at him in astonishment. For he didn't look like the sort of young man who could not hold his liquor, and in any case, he hadn't actually drunk very much. "My dear young fellow, are you indisposed?"

"No, no." Owen took a deep breath. "But I do need some air."

"Then, a short walk in the garden—"

"Yes." Owen turned to his host. "I thank you for supper," he said. Taking out his gold hunter, he glanced at it. "It's very late. I really must go home."

"Stay here!" The hospitable Mr Lloyd beamed. "My dear sir, you are more than welcome to a bed for the night."

"Thank you, but I must go." Wildly, Owen stared around him. "The works," he went on, gibbering now. "The new furnace. We must have it put into blast by Wednesday, so we—"

"Ah, yes." Immediately, Mr Lloyd understood. "Well, then," he rumbled, staggering bravely to his feet, "that business about the castings. You will be in touch?"

"Yes, of course. Thank you again."

Owen walked into Pontypool. At the livery stables, he hired their strongest, fastest mare, for the first stage of what would be a gruelling journey. For he must get to Swansea, and soon. He refused to think about what might happen if he did not.

He did not *know* Michael Atkins was a villain. He had no proof of criminal activity, no concrete evidence whatsoever, of even the most trivial misdemeanours or misdeeds. But all the same, he was sure Jack and

Michael Atkins must be connected. That they were almost certainly father and son.

He had to get Rayner and Jane away from that man. He felt it instinctively and it chilled him to the bone.

Chapter Twenty

Owen put up at a coaching inn near Bishopston, a village well inside the confines of English Gower. Still bemused by Mr Lloyd's astonishing story, and bone-weary from his long journey, he nevertheless forced himself to assume a relaxed and carefree air. He sauntered round the room he'd been offered, smiling and nodding his satisfaction. Then he tipped the chambermaid handsomely. Going downstairs again, he asked the landlord to open a bottle of his best claret, then invited the fellow to take a glass himself.

Drawing the cork with an expert hand, the landlord grinned his appreciation. "Thank you, Mr Ellis," he said. "That's very civil indeed. I'll join you in a few minutes' time, if I may."

The inn was quiet that evening. The landlord had spent the past hour polishing all his pewter tankards, which were now gleaming softly in the candlelight. Sighing, he looked around for something else to do. There was nothing, except to talk to his solitary guest. So, waddling over to where Owen sat, dozing off to sleep, he plumped himself down on the settle opposite.

"Sorry, sir! I didn't mean to startle you." For Owen's eyes were suddenly open wide, and he regarded the landlord with what looked like stark terror. Shaking his head, the man grinned. "You're a stranger here, sir?" he enquired, genially.

"Yes, indeed." Ever since his arrival back on Gower, Owen had been at pains to purge his accent of even the slightest hint of a Celtic lilt. "I'm originally from

Hereford. But these days I live in Birmingham most of the time."

"What brings you down here, to Gower?"

"I am an ironmaster and coppersmith. My partners and I own a factory near Wolverhampton, and another in Dudley." Blandly, Owen smiled. "But we wish to expand our operations into South Wales. We hope to develop a site near Swansea, and go in for copper-smelting and tin-plating there."

"I see." The landlord refilled Owen's glass. "Well, Mr Ellis – in my considered opinion, you couldn't have fixed on a likelier spot. Swansea's a fine place! A splendid town, up hill and down dale! You certainly won't lack opportunites there."

"I'm sure I shall not." Again, Owen smiled. "Anyway, Mr Langford – leaving the town behind me, I decided to explore the area round about. You can imagine my delight when I discovered Gower! To find this jewel of a place – this little corner of paradise, abutting a great industrial metropolis – was a pleasure indeed."

"It's a beautiful spot." Complacently, the landlord shook his head. Then he leaned towards his guest, confidentiality personified. "It's an English paradise, too!"

"Indeed?"

"Oh, yes! Why, sir – this part of Gower has been a Saxon stronghold for centuries. Since William the Conqueror's time, in fact."

"You astonish me."

"I see that." Sagely, the landlord wagged a stumpy forefinger in Owen's face. "My own ancestors came from Devon," he declared. "But my great-grandmother was a Fleming. Born and bred in the Low Country, far across the sea. That accounts for my poll and whiskers, you understand." He nodded his blond head, and grinned.

Obligingly, Owen grinned back. Red-faced, blue-eyed, Mr Langford was certainly no Celt. "Do not any Welshmen live on Gower these days?" he enquired, artlessly.

"Oh, yes. But they keep to the north." Disdainfully,

the landlord sniffed. "A rascally, beggarly crew they are, as well. Gethyns and Morgans, Lloyds and Llewellyns – pirates, thieves and villains all, sir. To the very last man.

"In the last century, they were smugglers and wreckers, too. But little of that goes on now. The Excise has grown too clever for ignorant Welsh vagabonds. So – they stick to their cockle-gathering and sheep-farming mostly. They don't give us much trouble nowadays."

"I see. Well, that's fortunate for trade, anyway."

"Indeed it is, sir."

"Tell me a little about the old days." Pouring the last of the wine, Owen motioned to the landlord to drink up. "Tell me some stories about what went on here, long ago."

"You want tales of piracy and pillage, do you sir?" The landlord grinned. "I'll tell you some to make your hair stand on end and your eyes start out of their sockets, believe you me."

So the landlord began his first story. Growing thirsty, he called for some ale. Soon he was reaching for the jug with impressive frequency, all the while rambling on about dirty Welsh peasants who were always outsmarted in their knavery by clean, brave English lads, invariably from Bishopston or the area round about.

Owen remained sober, for he was making plans. As the landlord came to the end of one particularly tall story, he touched his sleeve. "Do you have a boy here who could run an errand for me?" he enquired.

"Yes indeed, sir!" Raising his snout from his tankard, Mr Langford glared blearily all around. "Anthony?" he bellowed. "Anthony!"

Eventually, a tow-headed lad appeared. His face flushed and his eyes watering, he had evidently been turning a spit or lighting a fire. "This gentleman wants you to do him a favour," muttered the landlord, as he applied once again to his tankard.

"Could you take a message to Oxwich?" asked Owen, as the lad looked at him enquiringly. "An acquaintance of mine is staying there for the summer, and I wish to let him know I am here in Bishopston. Tomorrow morning will do," he added loudly, praying that the landlord's pride in his establishment would mean he'd insist the message was delivered that evening.

"He'll go tonight, sir." As if jerked by a string, the landlord's head shot up. "The evening is clear, the moon will be up later, and he knows the way."

"Excellent." Handing the boy an envelope with Rayner's name on it, Owen tipped him a shilling. "Give this into the gentleman's own hand, mind," he adjured him, as he gave him directions to the house. "Let no one take it from you but Mr Rayner Darrow himself."

"From a Mr Ellis, you say?" Frowning, Rayner tore open the envelope, then skimmed through the letter inside. It was signed by his obedient servant, John Ellis. Rayner had never heard of John Ellis, in all his born days.

But the tone of the note, which had apparently been written at the behest of his stockbroker, was urgent. So – if Mr Green had seen fit to send his new clerk all the way to South Wales, perhaps the man ought at least to be granted an interview? Rayner took a keen interest in his financial investments. He had a horror of losing so much as a brass farthing in unwise speculation, and Mr Green was very much aware of the fact.

"There's no reply." Dismissing the boy with a shilling, Rayner walked back to the drawing room. He made up his mind. While Bishopston wasn't within walking distance of Oxwich – not for Rayner, anyway – it was not too far to go on horseback, on a clear, moonlit night like this.

Especially like this. For, this evening, Rayner was bored. The lovers sat together whispering and laughing, presumably making plans which had nothing to do with him. He disliked reading, and there was no one with whom to play cards.

His host and sister had glanced up curiously when the maidservant came to summon Rayner to the door, but neither had remarked on the fact. They were too wrapped up in one another, he decided sourly, to be even remotely interested in him.

He coughed, to attract their attention. "My dear fellow," he began, wishing Michael Atkins would stop ogling his sister for just one moment, and have the courtesy to pay some attention to *him*, "you may think this is a rather singular request – but the fact is, I have a fancy to take a short evening ride. May I borrow a pony from your stables?"

"Certainly." Michael Atkins turned from his contemplation of Jane's pretty white neck, and how it would look stretched, to ring for a servant. "I would suggest you take Domino," he murmured, absently. "I know your preference is for Cassandra, but I fear she is a little lame today."

As Rayner left the room, Michael turned back to Jane. For the second, the third time that week, he felt his resolution wavering.

When he had first met her and learned who she was, he had hardly thought of her as a woman at all. She was a creature, on whom he meant to take a terrible proxy revenge, and he had spent many a happy and inventive hour planning the torments of the damned for her.

But now, alas, he knew her. In fact, he felt he knew Jane Darrow better than he'd ever known anybody, in all his long life.

Shaking his head, he sighed.

She was sewing tonight. Something small, white and gauzy moved beneath her nimble fingers, fluttering like a butterfly's wings. Could it be a baby's christening robe? A nightgown? Yes – it must be something like that, for she had mentioned only yesterday that an acquaintance in Warwickshire had recently been confined.

As she bent her head over her work, her profile outlined against the candlelight, he watched her. She was so tranquil. So relaxing. She was the kind of woman whose mere presence warmed and comforted a man. Dear Jane, he thought, she could soothe even the most savage breast.

As he gazed at her, he felt contentment washing over him, in gentle, calming waves. He caught his breath in dismay.

"Michael?" Smiling, Jane glanced up. "Did you say something?"

"What?" He blinked, rapidly. "No, my dear," he muttered, turning away. "Not I."

"But I'm sure you – dear Michael, is something the matter tonight?"

"No. Nothing is wrong." He turned back to her. "Jane?"

"Yes?"

"Do you love me?"

"Of course I love you!"

"Good." He narrowed his colourless eyes against the candle's light. "Do you also fear me?"

"I don't think so." Jane put her sewing to one side. "Should I?"

"Perhaps." Michael Atkins shrugged. "Most women seem to be afraid of me."

"Indeed?" Jane shook her head. "Now you mention it, I have noticed that one or two of the housemaids seem rather wary of you."

"Quite."

"Yet you are not a harsh master." Considering, Jane covered her lover's hand with her own. "The maids are very young," she observed. "Sarah and Polly especially are timid country girls, anxious to please but nervous of giving offence to those they see as their elders and betters. Perhaps what you call fear is merely respect?"

"Do you respect me, then?"

"I love you." Jane kissed his cheek. "So, of course I respect you, too. Love comprehends respect, admiration, affection – all good things."

Michael Atkins could bear no more. Standing up, he

excused himself, saying he had an urgent letter to write. Some business matters needed his attention, too.

Rayner mounted a pretty grey mare and rode off into the twilight. Arriving at the Three Feathers, he enquired for Mr Ellis and was shown up to a private chamber on the first floor.

The room appeared to be unoccupied. Glancing round, Rayner observed a large, old-fashioned tester bed, a washstand, a couple of chairs – but no sign whatsoever of human habitation. Then, however, a sudden movement alarmed him, and he spun round to see Owen standing against the door.

"Don't cry out!" Owen's own voice was anxious. Urgent, and desperate too. "For the love of God and your sister's preservation, don't shout for help!"

"You again!" Too angry to be afraid, Rayner glowered at him. "Fiend from hell!" he hissed. "Spawn of Satan! Of all the horrible, ungrateful, churlish abominations, *you* are the most disgusting, revolting—"

For a minute or two, Owen simply let him rant. But then, sensing his cousin was running out of steam, he drew up a chair. "Please," he said quietly, motioning towards it. "Please, Rayner. Sit down."

"I'll never sit down with you. Never!" Furious, Rayner glared daggers. "Tell me why you sent for me," he muttered.

"I am afraid for your sister," said Owen. "Rayner, Jane is in the most terrible danger. Even as we speak, she is—"

"Stuff and nonsense." Still Rayner glared. "She is with the man she means to marry," he growled. "She could not be safer anywhere."

"She is under the roof of a madman! She is in the company of a creature so cruel, so villainous and so evil that I am sick to the heart whenever I think of it!"

"On the contrary. She is under the roof of a gentleman born and bred, who has recently made honourable proposals towards a lady whom he loves. The madman is here, in this room, with me." Rayner picked up his hat, which had fallen off as Owen surprised him. "I am going now," he muttered. "Do not obstruct or attempt to follow me."

"Oh, Rayner!" Owen was in despair. "Please listen to me!"

"Why should I?" Rayner would not look at him. "I hate you. I—"

"I deserve your hatred." Meekly, Owen hung his head. "But we both love Jane."

"One of us does."

"Rayner, I would give all I have, down to the last drop of my blood, to save Jane even a moment's distress! For her, I would endure the cruellest torments man could devise, I would suffer—"

"If you could only hear yourself." Rayner curled his lip in scorn. "This cant of yours disgusts me. Have you anything of interest to say?"

"Certainly! I—"

"Then say it. I find it close in here, and am anxious to leave."

"Hear me in silence, then. If not for my sake, for that of my poor aunt, who loved me – and who, if she could speak to you now, would implore you to listen to me—"

"Do get on!" Exaggeratedly, Rayner yawned. "I am missing supper on your account."

Chapter Twenty-One

"You cannot go back there tonight." Getting up from his chair, Owen stirred up the fire which had died down while he had told his cousin the facts, for Rayner was shivering now. In fact, he looked positively sick and ill. "Rayner, you must not! Instead, we must decide how to get Jane away."

"But we – oh, God! I don't know what to do!" Trying to pull himself together, Rayner clenched his fists. He glanced towards his cousin. "How do I know *you're* not telling me a pack of lies?"

"Dear God, I wish I was!" Owen shook his head, both in frustration and despair. "Rayner, believe me, I—"

Just then, there was a sharp tap at the door. Even that, however, was enough to make Rayner start, and grow pale. "It will only be the chambermaid," soothed Owen. "I asked for more coals to be sent up. Come in!"

But it was not the chambermaid who entered, but a middle-aged, fair-haired man. Dressed like an upper servant, he wore a good cloth coat, stuff waistcoat, and the ubiquitous knee-breeches and stockings which were still favoured in the countryside, despite the fact that in towns and cities most men wore trousers nowadays. His linen was clean, his cheeks neatly shaven, and he looked every inch a respectable, trustworthy fellow. "Mr Darrow?" he enquired. "Mr Rayner Darrow?"

"Yes." Rayner scowled at him. "What do you want?"

"May I come in?"

"If you must. Well?"

"Well, sir. I am Mr Atkins's head groom. I—"

"Indeed?" Rayner's glower intensified. "*I've* never seen you in the stable yard."

"I do have other duties, sir." The man shrugged. "As general custodian of the place, it is not my job to clean the stalls, or lead the horses to the mounting block. Instead, I go—"

"Very well, very well." Irritably, Rayner waved the explanation away. "What do you wish to say to me?"

"It's to the other gentleman I actually need to speak." The man turned to look at Owen. "I saw you at the house, sir," he began. "I watched you that day, I observed your coming and going, but I recognised you at once. You're John Rhys Morgan's son."

"I'm sorry?"

"Please, sir. Don't dissemble!" Beseechingly, the man met Owen's gaze. "I received word of your return two hours ago. I wished to speak to you then. To warn you, in fact. But I could not get away any sooner, so I—"

"Could you not have sent a message?"

"No, sir. That would have been too dangerous, both for the messenger and for me. But I have a good friend here in Bishopston, who looks out for me. It was he who sent to tell me you were back on Gower."

"But why should my presence be of interest to you?"

"Oh, sir!" The man had grown pale. Indeed, he was shaking now. "I have served that family since I was a child. Since before I knew what evil was! But then, growing older and – I hope – becoming wiser, I learned to shut my ears and close my eyes to what went on in that house. Indeed, had I not, I should have run mad!

"Just recently, however, I have seen and heard things which make me fear for my own safety. For the safety of others, too."

"What have you heard?" demanded Owen.

"It is a wicked servant who betrays his master. But I have no choice but to do so now. Sir, Mr Atkins knows who you are! He knows how Mr Darrow's father – your uncle – was instrumental in the death of his own! He means to make you and Mr Darrow here pay for it.

"He *will* do it, sir! He will have you and Mr Darrow killed! He will have Mr Darrow's sister abused and tormented for the rest of her days!"

"What absolute nonsense." Rayner shook his head, in scornful disbelief. "Mr Atkins would not hurt my sister. Not for the world. For God's sake, fellow! The man is in love with her!"

"He's not, sir." Heavily, the man sighed. "Mr Atkins could never love anybody. Except, of course, himself."

"What do you mean?"

"He was married once. To the sweetest, prettiest young woman you ever saw. She came of a good family. Her father was a manufacturer and mine-owner, with a country house and other property, near Cardiff I believe. This lady brought my master beauty, accomplishments, and a handsome dowry, too."

"What happened to her?"

"She died." The man shrugged. "Sir, I know women and children are fools, who must needs be corrected. As a child must be weaned from the breast, a woman must be weaned from her folly, and it's her husband's bounden duty to perform the task.

"But Mr Atkins used his wife cruelly! He beat her. He burned her. He had her locked in her room for weeks on end. He starved her, he—"

"If this is indeed the case," interrupted Rayner, "why did her friends and family do nothing about it? Why did they stand idle while she suffered?"

"They knew nothing of it. She was too afraid of him even to hint, let alone to speak of it. Of course, the burns and bruises were always out of the way. Very well hidden, in fact. But her maidservants talked of what went on, as servants will."

"Did Mr Atkins behave like this when he was sober? Or when he was in liquor, and too drunk to know what he was at?"

"Mr Atkins never takes spirits. He has no great interest in even the finest wines." The servant sighed. "The man is cruel, sir. He loves to torment, and he does it for cruelty's sake alone."

"So, continue. What became of his wife?"

"She learned to endure. She studied how to please him, and sometimes she was successful in the attempt. She was pregnant, and happy to be so, when one day she made a foolish mistake. I don't know what she did to upset him, but whatever it was, it angered him dreadfully.

"He went too far. He beat her regularly, it's true, but this time he beat her half to death. She miscarried of a dead child, and three days later she died herself."

Owen stared, both in horror and in dread. "He is known to be a widower," he whispered, fearfully. "He makes no secret of the fact that his wife died in childbirth. Is it possible that you might be mistaken about the circumstances of her death?"

"I wish that might be so, sir. But it is not."

"Why have you come here?" demanded Rayner, curtly. "Why have you sought us out? If your master discovers your treachery, surely you will suffer the torments of the damned?"

"Indeed I shall." Again, the man shrugged. "My master keeps two men in his employ, who are used for just that evil purpose. They are known throughout the whole of Gower as his lieutenants. I ought to say, his executioners. For there is blood on their hands, murder in their eyes, but mere empty voids where human hearts should be."

Owen was convinced. "We must get Jane away from that place," he said.

"Must we?" Rayner stared into the fire. "May I ask why?"

"*Why*?" Owen gaped at him. The word coward was already formed, and hung ready on his lips. But now, he turned to the servant. "Go and ask them to find me a pony," he muttered. "I'll be downstairs directly."

The man went.

"Rayner, will you not come with me?" demanded Owen, as he reached for his coat.

"No. Yes. No!" Rayner wrung his hands. "I don't trust him!" he wailed.

"Him?" Owen met his cousin's eyes. "Tell me, Rayner. What do you mean? Whom don't you trust? The servant? Your host? Or both?"

"The servant, of course!"

"You think he is lying? To what purpose?"

"I don't know!" Rayner paced the floor. "I don't understand any of this. But I don't trust that servant. Not at all. I think he's here to spring a trap."

"Nonsense." Owen regarded his cousin with scorn. "The man was sickened by his master's behaviour towards his first wife, and is reluctant to see another poor woman suffer the fate of her predecessor. So, will you come back to Oxwich with me?"

"No," replied Rayner. "I never wish to enter that house again."

The servant stood at the foot of the stairs, waiting. "I'll smuggle you in, sir," he said, as Owen clattered down the last few steps. "Have no fear on that score."

From the window, Rayner watched his cousin and the servant depart. Fetching a deep sigh, he sat down again. Ringing the bell, he told the chambermaid who answered his summons that Mr Ellis had been urgently called away, but that Rayner himself would settle that gentleman's account. "I need to drive into Swansea later this evening," he continued, smoothly. "Does this inn keep its own chaise?"

"Yes indeed, sir," replied the maid.

"Then please see that it is made ready for me, without delay." Rayner gave the girl a new half crown. "In the meantime, might I have paper and a pen?"

Owen's path lay through the kitchen garden, past the laundries and across the stable yard. Here, the servant motioned to him to be silent, and keep his head down low. Finally, they reached a row of offices, where the stud books were kept, where the farrier stored his instruments and where medicines for sick beasts were prepared. A light shone dimly from underneath the last door.

"In here, sir." The servant tripped the latch.

"Mr Morgan? You come betimes!" Flanked by Robin and Henry Corder, Michael Atkins sat calm and relaxed in a battered elbow chair. He spread his hands in welcome. "But now that you *are* here, do please come in."

Owen simply stared. But Michael Atkins grinned. "So my suspicions were justified after all," he murmured, pleasantly. "I was right to send Dennis after the fat fool – who disdains all daytime exercise entirely, but suddenly has a fancy to take a twilight ride!"

He turned to the groom. "Well done, Dennis," he said. "Very well done indeed. You shall have a reward."

"Thank you, sir." Dennis smirked.

"Actually, I was expecting *you* to arrive rather later in the day," continued Michael Atkins, as he eyed Owen up and down. "But where one cousin comes, I daresay another will soon follow. So tell me. Where is the greasy simpleton just now?"

Owen said nothing.

Michael shrugged. "He'll doubtless be back for a late supper," he murmured. "Dennis, go and fetch the lady. Do so directly, if you please."

Five minutes later, the door opened, and Jane entered the room. In her nightdress and a light silk robe, for she had been fast asleep, now she smothered a yawn.

Roused from her slumbers by Sarah, whose agitation and terror had been written only too clearly across her innocent little face, Jane had asked for her robe and slippers. She had reassured the maid and then, her puzzlement growing, had followed the servant to the stable yard, across the cobblestones and into the office, where she expected to find – she knew not what.

When she observed her lover sitting at his ease, his two faithful servants flanked like bookends on his either side, she frowned. But when she glanced to her left and saw Owen Morgan there, she stared in blank astonishment. "Owen?" She gaped in disbelief. "What are you doing here?"

"He's come to seek his fortune." Michael Atkins still grinned, but now his pale blue eyes became as hard as flints. "I would imagine he means to seek a lady's favours, too."

Jane stared from her cousin to her lover, then back again. "I don't understand," she began. "I don't see what—"

"Be silent." Michael Atkins glared at her. "I've had enough," he muttered. Then he turned to Owen. "Mr Morgan, I've a score to settle with you, and tomorrow I shall call you to account.

"As for you, Miss Darrow – you have taxed my good nature to its limits. Indeed, I have been generous and indulgent to the point of imbecility! But in this, the fault was mine. For I never thought the day would dawn, when a woman would try to make a fool of *me*."

"What?" Her bewilderment growing by the second, still Jane stared. "My dear Michael, how—"

"But now," interrupted Michael Atkins, sourly, "you have tried my patience long enough. You have imposed upon my hospitality. You have betrayed my confidence and abused my trust. In my more charitable moments, however, I am ready to believe you are more stupid than cunning. So for you, it will be quick."

"Quick?" Her pupils dilating, Jane gaped at him. "My dear Michael, what can you mean? I never made a fool of you! Owen and I were engaged, it is true. But I—"

"He came back for you." Michael would not look at her. Instead, he produced a letter, its seal broken and its cover torn. "He loved you once, and he loves you still. This letter proves the point. As for you, his dearest Jane, his own heart's darling – I can hardly doubt that you return his regard!"

"No! Michael, please—"

"It is of no moment." Fingering Owen's letter to Jane, a short note written in haste in a Swansea coaching inn, but in which the tenderest sentiments were most movingly expressed, Michael Atkins hesitated only a moment longer. Then he tore it to pieces, and dropped these into the candle's flame. "Dennis?"

"Master?"

"Take these two lovebirds upstairs, to the room prepared for them. See they are kept close."

Chapter Twenty-Two

Robin, Henry and Dennis were used to this kind of thing. Expertly taking their captives into custody, they hustled their master's guests into the house and up three flights of stairs to a convenient attic room which had been specially prepared for an occasion such as this. Pushing Jane and Owen inside, they locked then barred the door.

"But I don't understand!" Bewildered, Jane stared all about her. "What can be the matter with the man? He must have run mad indeed!"

"He has." Owen shook his head. He made as if to take Jane's hand. "My poor cousin! You don't know even one half of what he—"

"*Don't dare to touch me*!"

"Sit down quietly, then. Listen to what I have to say. Then, dear Jane, make your peace with your Creator. Repent of your sins, if you've ever committed any, which I doubt—"

"But what *is* all this?" Jane looked astonished, horrified and incredulous, all at the same time. "Owen, are you telling me he intends to kill us?"

"I think he must."

"I don't believe you." Jane turned away. "I can see why he might hate you," she muttered. "But why should he wish to hurt me?"

"Because I wrote to you, to tell you that I love you."

"Why should your demented ravings matter to a man like Michael?" Jane shook her head. "In any case, I never saw any letter."

"He intercepted it. He read it. You watched it burn."

Owen longed to embrace her, yearned to comfort and reassure her. But there was nothing reassuring to say. "Jane," he murmured, "since you will not pray, try to sleep, instead. If we are to acquit ourselves well tomorrow you will need all your strength of body, and of mind."

"This is a nightmare. I shall wake presently." Turning back to her cousin, Jane pulled her wrap close about her body. "But before I wake, entertain me. Explain yourself. Tell me what this is all about."

So Owen did. Haltingly, stopping every now and then to recover his equanimity, he told his cousin the whole wretched story. Leaving out the most unpleasant details, and skimming over the rest, his tale was nevertheless a horrible one.

"Oh, God." As Owen spoke, Jane had grown pale. Then, as he concluded his narrative, she began to shudder and shake so violently that she was obliged to sit down. Slumped in a corner, she covered her face with her hands. "Dear God in heaven," she cried, "can there be such a man?"

"It would seem so."

"Seems is the word." Looking up again, Jane met Owen's eyes. "You were ever a romancer," she muttered. "I wonder now if you've just spun me another of your foolish tales."

"Why should I do that?"

"I don't know!" Her face working, Jane looked ready to burst into tears. "Why, Owen?" she wailed. "Why did you come to this place? What did I ever do to you, that you should wish to destroy *me*?"

"How can you say that? All I've ever done is love you!"

"I think you're mad." Jane massaged her eyes. "It must run in this family. Your mother was deranged, and so are you."

"But – what do you know of my mother?"

"Enough." Jane shrugged. "After you left Easton Hall, and my own mother died, my father became unwell.

That's to put it mildly. In fact, he was distraught. Positively beside himself with grief.

"He spoke to me of matters to which he would never ordinarily have given utterance. He told me things he perhaps ought never to have told his daughter at all."

"What did he say?"

"Owen, do you honestly not know why my father and your mother quarrelled?"

"No. Do you?"

"Yes, indeed. Shall I enlighten you?"

"Provided you do not break a confidence, or betray a trust."

"What? You're a fine one, to speak of breaking confidences and betraying trusts!" Jane closed her eyes. "The truth of the matter is, your mother tried to kill mine."

"She did what?" Owen stared. "Jane," he began, "I know you're upset. But what foolishness is this? My mother would have been incapable of such an act! She would have scorned—"

"Would she?" Jane opened her eyes again. Angrily, she glared. "Only two minutes since, you told me how she tried to murder Michael's father!"

"But that was an act of desperation! Do but recall the facts! Her husband had been done to death, in the foulest, most treacherous fashion imaginable. His widow was smarting with the injustice of it. Half out of her mind with grief, and despair—"

"Just as she was when she burned Easton Hall to the ground?"

"When she did what?" It was Owen's turn to glare. "My dear Jane, have a care what you say. I will not hear slander or lies. Not even from you. I will never believe—"

"I do not care what you believe." Wretchedly, Jane sighed. "The fact is, your mother was jealous of mine. She loved her brother dearly, you see. So, she would probably have been a difficult sister-in-law towards any woman who usurped her place in my father's heart. But my mother was not only beloved, she was low born.

"In consequence, your mother hated mine from the start. When my mother presumed to conceive a child – something, apparently, that your own had been anxious to do for years, but without success – her anger knew no bounds. So, whilst my father was away from Easton Hall, she paid two ruffians to fire the place, with my mother inside it."

"Nonsense." Owen scowled. "You've listened to too much village gossip. You've been taken in by old wives' tales."

"As I said before, it's of no interest to me whether you believe me or not." Shivering, Jane hugged her knees. "Call me a liar, if you wish. It's of no account now."

"I never called you a liar!" Too late, Owen realised he had been too harsh. "I merely wondered aloud if you had been misled."

"Perhaps I have." Jane's lower lip began to wobble. Unshed tears stood shining in her eyes. "After all, I've been misled about everything else, for almost the whole of my life."

"Oh, Jane! I'm so sorry!" Observing how his cousin trembled, Owen took off his coat, and covered her. Then he went to sit by the window, to watch for what he feared – no, was quite certain – would be his last dawn.

Jane remained silent. Half an hour later, when Owen glanced towards her, he saw that her eyes were closed. Her body relaxed and her breathing regular, she appeared to be fast asleep.

"Good morning!" Booted and spurred, Michael, Robin and Henry stood on the threshold of the attic room. Freshly shaven, his linen immaculate and his riding clothes cut to a perfection rarely seen out here in the back of beyond, Michael Atkins beamed at his guests. "We will take him with us," he said, nodding towards Owen.

"Sir." Henry Corder grinned.

"But what of the lady?" demanded Robin, looking meaningfully at Jane. "Sir?"

"I don't know." Irritably, his smile fading, Michael Atkins shook his head. "Maybe. Maybe not."

On her feet now, Jane stared at him. Meeting that incredulous blue gaze, he turned away. "I know," he muttered, as if to himself. "She's young. She's pretty. She could provide us with some most interesting entertainment. But I have decided against any of that."

Jane looked dazed.

Owen thought it prudent to keep silent.

Michael Atkins considered further. "Take her downstairs," he said at last. "We can—"

"No." Breaking away from Henry Corder, Owen stood between his cousin and his host. "Do whatever you wish to me. But let Jane leave this place."

"Let her go?" Michael Atkins's pale blue eyes became glassy. "My dear fellow, thanks to you she knows enough to have me hanged in chains, on Swansea quay! Yet you talk of letting her go."

"Marry her, then." Owen shrugged. "You are already engaged, so make an end of it. Then, when Jane has become your lawful wedded wife, you are secure. Married, she cannot be forced to bear witness against you."

"After what you told her last night, I doubt if she would allow me to take her by the hand. Let alone lead her to the bridal bed." Michael Atkins sighed. "You signed her death warrant in earnest, when you spun her that fine tale."

Owen closed his eyes. He should have remained dumb, he saw that now. But all was not lost. Rayner was bound to return, for his sister's sake if not for Owen's own. In the meanwhile, Owen must buy time.

He drew a deep breath. "I don't care what you do to me," he began. "Believe me, it's true. Yes, I know what goes on here. I've heard stories about you and your family to chill the marrow and freeze the heart's blood."

Owen looked at Robin. "You, sir," he murmured. "A past master, are you not? The ladies are your favourites, I believe. But I've heard you do a very neat line in the flaying of either sex. A strip at a time, is that right? A whole day's labour? Perhaps we should begin without delay?"

He glanced back towards Michael. "I'm young," he went on, "I'm healthy, and I'm strong. My heart and lungs are sound. I'd give you splendid entertainment, lasting a very long time. Surely, given that, it would not hurt you to spare Jane?"

"But I think it would," Michael Atkins replied. "You see, in sparing her, I should be denied a pleasure particularly precious to me."

"But why must you have such a pleasure, when you can torment me instead?"

"He does not understand." Michael Atkins shook his head. "He's a fool," he muttered, talking to himself. "A braggart, a simpleton, and a fool. In fact, he's a Welshman, through and through."

The master pulled on his gloves. "Well, my lads," he said, briskly. "It's time we were on our way."

Owen met Michael Atkins's colourless eyes. "Before we go," he said, "as you are a gentleman, at least give me a guarantee that Jane will not suffer."

"A guarantee that *what*?" Michael Atkins grinned. "My God. You're even more of an idiot than I first believed."

But now, Jane spoke. "If Owen is to die," she whispered, her face pale and her eyes hollow, "at least let me go with him. Let me suffer your pleasure, too."

"You mean to expire in one shared breath? How loverlike. How touching in the extreme. But no. It cannot be." Michael Atkins picked up his whip. "For the present, my deceitful, dissembling lady, you stay here."

Chapter Twenty-Three

As Owen Morgan's sturdy little Welsh pony was cantering towards Oxwich, Rayner finished his letter, which he gave into the landlord's safe-keeping. Then, he climbed into the inn's old-fashioned, creaking chaise, shook the reins, and drove off into the warm, summer dusk.

The moon was full, the night cloudless and the going dry. Making much better progress than he had dared to hope, by midnight Rayner was in Swansea.

"Hey, you! Yes, my good fellow, you. Come here." Thus accosting an elderly night watchman, who was glumly trudging up and down the High Street, Rayner enquired where the lodgings of the town's chief magistrate were to be found.

Directed there, he hung on the bell until a maidservant in a dirty flannel wrap and a headful of curling papers finally answered the door. Apologising for disturbing her sleep, and acknowledging the dreadful lateness of the hour, Rayner asked if she would go and wake the chairman of the Swansea Bench.

"Well sir, I don't know about that." Doubtfully, the maid eyed Rayner up and down. "The thing is, Mr Grandison must be up betimes tomorrow. It's the assize, you see."

"Here." Rayner handed her a gleaming half-crown. "So now, Betty – go and rouse your master. Tell him a gentleman wishes to speak to him most urgently. I shall make it worth your while, never fear."

The girl accepted the silver. Then, shutting the door

in Rayner's face, she disappeared into the darkness of the house.

But soon enough, the half-crown worked its magic. The street door opened again, the maid ushered the visitor into the vestibule, and two minutes later Mr Grandison himself came clumping down the stairs.

Clad in an ancient powdering gown, on which the smears and stains of many a breakfast in bed were stickily evident, his slippers flapped on the polished boards, while his smoking cap sat right on the back of his head, crazily awry. "If this is some stupid knavery," he muttered crossly, "I shall deal with the fellow severely. You may tell him now. It shall go hard with him!"

But then, as Rayner came into his line of vision and he observed a fine gentleman, rather than the ruffian drawn from the ranks of the Watch whom he had confidently expected to see, he stopped grumbling. In fact, he became civil. Genial, even.

"Will you come into my study, sir?" he invited, as Rayner stood silent, trying to arrange his ideas, and wondering how he could possibly cudgel the farrago of absurdity, which he'd brought with him from Gower, into a coherent, believable narrative. "Sit down, sit down. Now, sir. Before you say anything, will you take a pipe of tobacco with me?"

"Thank you, no." Motioning the proffered jar aside, Rayner sank gratefully into an easy chair. "Mr Grandison, I'm sorry to have woken you at such an unearthly hour, but you see—"

"Just one moment." Mr Grandison lit his pipe. Coughing, choking, and wheezing like a pair of rusty bellows, he grew purple in the face and wattled about the neck. But then, as the stimulant began to take effect, he relaxed. He leaned back in his chair. "Well, sir?" he enquired.

"Well." Rayner cleared his throat. Then, he made his deposition.

"I am aware it all seems wholly preposterous," he concluded lamely, as the magistrate regarded him with narrowed, bloodshot eyes through a haze of fragrant smoke. "Indeed, my dear sir, I can well appreciate that – to you, at any rate – this whole story must sound perfectly ridiculous, from beginning to end! But I assure you, I—"

"My dear Mr Darrow, calm yourself." A dragon in padded silk, the magistrate exhaled more blue fumes. "Your anxiety is most understandable, and I sympathise wholeheartedly. But please consider. You are tired and upset. You have unburdened yourself to me, which I hope has given you at least some relief. What you need now is a bed."

"A *bed*? But, sir!"

"Nothing can be done until morning. Then, however, everything will be set in train." The magistrate rang the bell. "Molly will attend you, and show you the way."

"But—"

"Molly? Molly! Where *is* the girl?" Mr Grandison glared all round for the maid. "Make up a bed in the blue room," he rapped, as she finally appeared. "See Mr Darrow has all he requires.

"Sir, I wish you a very good night. We will meet again tomorrow morning, at breakfast time."

After seeing Rayner lighted upstairs, Mr Grandison called for a glass of brandy. He drank it down, allowed the consequent fit of coughing and choking to subside, then began to pace the floor of his study. He rubbed his hands in glee.

At last! At long last, he had an excuse to issue a warrant. He, George Frederick Grandison, would live to see the inside of that house on the headland. To take its owner into custody.

Rayner slept fitfully. He was, however, glad of the rest. Summoned to an early breakfast, taken at the ungodly hour of seven o'clock, he ate fresh rolls and hard-boiled eggs while his host swallowed ham, cold sausage, and a fair-sized beefsteak with onions and gravy, too.

Mr Grandison's clerk sat at his master's side. Gulping scalding coffee, he took rapid dictation in a fine, legal hand.

For, everything had to be done properly today. Learning that back in Warwickshire, Rayner was a magistrate himself, Mr Grandison meant to show this fine gentleman from the Midlands that here in South Wales, the officers of the law understood their business as well as any university-educated, Latin-spouting Englishman.

The paperwork seemed to take an eternity. As the clerk's quill flew like a shuttle, backwards and forwards across whole acreages of clean, white paper, Rayner's already very limited patience was even more sorely tried.

Surely, he thought, there was no need to be quite so scrupulous? But it appeared there was every need. More letters were written now. Then, a whole regiment of post boys was sent off to deliver them, all around the town. *Then*, a minute was taken of all that had been done so far.

Finally, however, Mr Grandison was satisfied. He dismissed the clerk. Summoning his valet, he rose to go and dress.

This also took time. But, by eleven o'clock, Rayner and his host were booted, spurred and mounted on a pair of fine grey geldings, and ready to leave the magistrate's house. They would not travel unescorted, for a company of soldiers drawn from the local militia had been detailed to accompany them.

When he saw the redcoats, Rayner was impressed. Calling out the militia was a serious business, in the process of which endless strings needed to be pulled, and unlimited favours promised. "My dear Mr Grandison!" he cried, now ashamed of his earlier impatience, "I see you have worked miracles this morning! I thank you most sincerely for your trouble. I hope I shall be able to repay your care."

"My dear sir, think nothing of it." Complacently, the magistrate grinned. "The destruction of this particular nest of vipers is long overdue, believe you me."

"Indeed?"

"To be sure." Mr Grandson shook his head. "You may think nothing of it in the Midlands. Indeed, why should you? But here in South Wales, your dealer in contraband was ever a lively beast."

Rayner frowned. "You believe Mr Atkins to be involved in that wicked trade?"

"Sir, I know he is!" The magistrate sniffed. "He's a clever fellow, certainly. He needs to be. For the coastal waters nowadays are far more effectively patrolled than they ever were during the last century.

"But Oxwich is remote. The family exercises such authority there that no man, however sorely used or abused by them, would dare inform on them to the powers that be. For this would court the visitation of yet more cruelty, on him or upon his kin."

"But how can this be?" cried Rayner, horrifed. "How can a man behave like a feudal baron – and get away with it, too – in this modern age?"

"I doubt if he *will* get away with it, after today." Mr Grandison pursed his mottled lips. "Pray sir, batten down your anger. Conserve your strength. There will be time enough for indignation, when this day's work is done."

"Mr Grandison, sir? I think we're approaching the house." The captain of militia, who had ridden alongside Rayner and his host, had said nothing the whole length of the way. But now, he was anxious to have his orders. "Sir? I need to instruct my men."

"Please, Mr Grandison. Be circumspect!" Catching hold of the magistrate's bridle, Rayner looked his entreaty. "I am already afraid for my sister. If this man is as dangerous as you suspect, a soft question—"

But Rayner's anxious pleading fell on deaf ears. Mr Grandison had dreamed of this day and, thanks to Mr Darrow, it had finally dawned.

He gazed towards the house on the headland. A lady was

being held there, against her will. So, he had the perfect excuse to search her gaoler's den. To ransack the hideout of a creature who had been a thorn in his flesh for half a lifetime. But whose day of reckoning was come.

Soon, the magistrate, his companion, and the captain of militia were cantering up the rhododendron-lined drive, towards the ogre's lair. Ten minutes later, a company of armed redcoats stood easy on the neat gravel sweep.

Dismounting, the magistrate rang the bell. When there was no response from within, he gave the order to batter down the door.

As the wood began to splinter, there was a sound of bolts being drawn. As the soldiers hammered harder, the chain came off the hasp. The captain gave the order to shoulder muskets just as a frightened little maid put her nose round the edge of the door.

"Sarah?" Recognising her, Rayner dismounted. He walked up to the door. "Sarah, my dear? Don't be afraid. In spite of appearances to the contrary, these gentlemen mean you no harm. But now, I wish to speak with my sister."

"Your sister, sir?" The maid was white-faced. She trembled like an aspen leaf. "I'm sorry, but I don't understand."

"There is a lady here, Miss Jane Darrow by name, who is being detained against her will." Mr Grandison fixed the servant with his most magisterial frown. "Come, child. Where is she to be found?"

"There's no lady in this house!" Sarah began to sob. "Please, sir! Don't cause any more damage! If you do, they're sure to have me whipped. Or worse!"

But, as the maid pleaded, Rayner heard it. A dog barked, whimpered in distress, then barked again.

"Blanchette!" Elbowing the servant aside, Rayner ran into the darkness of the hall. His fear for his sister generating a surge of energy most uncharacteristic of this heavy, ungainly young man, he tore up one flight of stairs, up another, then up another still.

As he reached the landing from which a dozen attic rooms led off in all directions, he saw the dog. Blanchette was beside herself. Crying like a human baby, she nosed helplessly at a firmly closed door.

A key hung on a hook nearby. Seizing it, Rayner pushed it into the lock, turned it, then flung the door open wide.

"Rayner!" The creature who started up from the bare wooden floorboards looked like something from the nether world. It was a ghost, perhaps, which had lost its way, one dark Hallowe'en. Its hair undressed and tangled into a mass of elf-locks, its face blanched far whiter than its gown, it was hollow-eyed, staring and bloodless.

As Rayner gazed in horror, Jane sprang to her feet. She threw herself into his arms. "They've taken Owen!" she cried, as she burst into floods of tears. "They mean to kill him! Oh, Rayner! You must make haste!"

"Must I?" Relieved beyond expression that his sister appeared to be unharmed, Rayner was not in the least inclined to risk his hide in any more madcap escapades. Especially not in an attempt to rescue his cousin from what was probably a richly-deserved fate.

Observing his sister was clad only in a thin cambric nightgown and a hardly more substantial wrap, he was more concerned to shield her from the impertinent gawping of the soldiers, who were now milling around on the stairs. "My dearest Jane, had you not better get dressed?" he enquired, somewhat testily.

"Oh, God!" Disengaging herself from her brother's embrace, Jane turned to the window. Gazing blankly out, she fought to compose herself. To stem the flow of her tears.

Then, turning back to Rayner, she took him by the shoulders. She looked deep into his eyes. "He offered to die," she said, her voice now calm and controlled. "Do you understand me? He told them that, if they would only spare me, they could do as they pleased with him."

"Indeed?" Rayner shrugged. "Well, perhaps the creature has found his conscience at last."

"What do you mean?"

"He repents of his sins, and is prepared to accept the punishment he deserves."

"Rayner, those villains mean to kill him! Slowly and painfully, too. How can you stand there, muttering of sins and repentance, when a man is—"

But then, Mr Grandison intervened. "Excuse me, Miss Darrow," he began. "I am sorry to interrupt this tender interview between brother and sister, but I have the King's business to transact here. I wish to speak to Mr Atkins. Do you know where he is to be found?"

"I do not." Mistress of herself once again, Jane met the magistrate's gaze. "I therefore suggest you begin a search without delay."

"Madam, I mean to do exactly that." But then, observing the state of undress Miss Darrow was in, Mr Grandison looked politely away. "Take the lady to an inn," he said, to no one in particular. "See she is breakfasted, then put to bed."

"I'm coming with you!" Drawing her wrap close about her, Jane tied the belt. "Only find me a pony, a nag – a mule or donkey, even – and I shall join you without more ado."

"Madam, you are not dressed!" Shocked, the magistrate gaped at her. "In any case, the roads are bad. We mean to search the whole of Gower, and will doubtless be traversing marsh and moorland. Mountain and valley, fen and fell. We—"

"This is of no account whatever." Jane's eyes flashed blue fire. "I wish to accompany your party. In fact, I am firmly resolved to do so, whether you say aye, or nay."

Thus challenged – thus defied, in fact – by a wild-haired, wild-eyed termagant, Mr Grandison considered his options. "Do you ride, madam?" he enquired, somewhat nervously.

"Of course I ride! As well as any man here, I dare say. Better than many, I expect."

"That's as maybe. But you see, we have no lady's tack. We have no side saddle, no—"

"I can ride astride. I will go bare-backed, if need be." Finding a ribbon in one of her pockets, Jane tied back her hair. "I shall not be denied. When you leave this place, I am coming with you."

Mr Grandison sighed. His wife had a mind of her own. His two daughters were as obstinate as their mother. So, he was expert in determining at what point discretion became the better part of valour, particularly when there was a lady in the case. "Find Miss Darrow a pony," he muttered to the captain of militia. "Do so now."

Mounted on a pretty bay mare, which she had ridden several times before, Jane took her place in the column which now wound its way down the drive, then fanned out into the open countryside. The search for Michael Atkins began.

The day wore on. A lovely morning gave way to a deliciously golden afternoon. It seemed no creature stirred. Even the soft whispering of the light summer wind was hushed. The whole of Gower lay in slumber, under a benign summer sun.

Escaping from its ribbon, Jane's fair hair tumbled down and lay upon her shoulders. In order to ride astride, she had tucked her voluminous nightgown up to her knees. So now, clad only in the flimsiest of night attire, her sleeves rolled up to the elbows and her ankles on public display, she looked like the most abandoned, most forward sort of hoyden imaginable.

Rayner was embarrassed for her. The glances of the soldiers, who were evidently considering the merits of her calves, would have been offensive to any woman – but were doubly insulting to a lady of his sister's rank. When all this was over, he meant to report the creatures to their captain, and demand that they be flogged.

"I hope there is some method in this peripatetic madness," he muttered to Mr Grandison as, hot and perspiring, but too much the gentleman even to consider taking off his coat, Rayner sought to relieve his irritation by grumbling. "In spite of appearances to the contrary, I trust you have some scheme for the apprehension of this villain in mind?"

"To be sure." Mr Grandison grinned. "Do but look behind you, and you'll see."

Rayner did as he was bidden. To his astonishment, he saw that the column had doubled, or even trebled its length. From every village, from every tiny hamlet, every labourer's cottage and every beachcomber's den – from everywhere, in fact, that Mr Grandison had stopped to make enquiries – help and encouragement had been forthcoming. A little army of farmers, fishermen, cockle women from Penclawdd and cattle drovers from Penrice trailed after the soldiers. For all the men on Gower – Welsh and English, too – were united in one thing. In their hatred of the Atkins family.

They searched the caves, they searched the woods. Energetic, agile lads found ropes and scaled the mysterious Culver Hole – an ancient columbarium, so legend had it, but more probably a smugglers' lair – built into the cliffs at Port Eynon, burrowing into its slimy recesses and malodorous depths. All the caverns, all the sheepcotes, all the secret, hidden dells – all those places, in fact, where men who had fallen foul of the Atkins family had met with unlucky accidents – were investigated thoroughly. But of the quarry these hunters sought, there was no trace.

It would soon be evening. The enthusiasm of the search party was flagging. Murmuring could be heard among the soldiers too, to the effect that taking part in a wild goose chase, with no Welsh heads broken nor any English villains handed over into military custody, was not their idea of a good day's work.

But then, as Mr Grandison was debating the wisdom of continuing this rummage round Gower, in search of a person who might now be anywhere in the whole of the British Isles, a villager pushed through the muttering throng and shook the magistrate's sleeve.

A Welshman, his English was halting, laboured and on the whole unintelligible to the average Saxon, so Mr Grandison heard him with growing disgust. Finally, having had enough of listening to gibberish, he elbowed the creature aside. He glared round the villagers. "Can anyone tell me what this fool is saying?" he demanded. "Come along. There must be somebody here who understands both the King's good English and your own barbarous tongue!"

There was indeed. A native speaker of Welsh, who had once been in good service in a Swansea copper-smelter's family and there learned to speak the Saxon language fluently, now conferred with the poor labourer. "He says," he reported, "are you truly searching for John Rhys Morgan's son?"

"*I* don't know!" Mr Grandison scowled. He turned to Rayner. "This fellow your sister says was taken away by Atkins and his men," he rapped. "Your cousin, is he not? What's *he* called?"

"Owen Morgan. His father was John Rhys Morgan, of Llangennith. Or so I believe."

Hearing those names, the old labourer's eyes brightened. He fell to muttering with his bilingual neighbour, other people joined in, and soon a regular pow-wow was going on.

The magistrate shook his head. Then, his patience finally exhausted, he coughed loudly enough to attract the peoples' attention. He pointed his whip at the labourer. "What's that fellow's name?" he shouted, above the din.

"William," replied the copper-smelter's man. "William Ifan Parry, of Llangynnydd. He and his ancestors have worked for the Morgan family since time immemorial, and he is the last of his line to—"

"Yes, that's all very well." Mr Grandison glowered. "But what does he have to say to *me*?"

A further indistinct conversation took place. Then, the

copper-smelter's man turned back to the magistrate. "He says to try the marsh," he declared.

"The marsh?" echoed Mr Grandison sarcastically. "So – does he have a preference for any particular marsh, or must we investigate all five hundred tracts of swamp in this God-forsaken place?"

"He means, the estuary of the River Loughor. The north shore."

Those on horseback spurred their tired beasts and arrived on the banks of the river just as the tide was beginning to flow. Gazing across the broad expanse of the estuary, they realised a search would be impossible tonight.

The moon would be up, it was true. But treacherous quicksands and quaking mires, into which a man on horseback might stumble and be swallowed up in ten minutes flat, made the business of combing the area a hazardous one.

They sought one man. But a whole army could have taken cover amidst the waving reeds, and the undulating banks of marram grasses which lay piled one upon the other in this place.

The tide was lapping the smooth, silver sands. The moon hung in the sky, the softer flame of its lantern kindled, ready to light the night. Flowing fast, the tide would soon cover all the flat marshland across which the searchers gazed.

If Michael Atkins and his men had indeed taken refuge there, they had a very hard choice before them. They could give themselves up to the soldiers – or to the sea.

Jane was almost in tears now. Fatigue and disappointment had weakened her earlier resolve, and she was so bone-weary that as she had jogged along at her brother's side, her eyes had closed of their own accord.

Hopelessly, helplessly, she stared into the setting sun. But then, she saw it. A shadow on the sands. She blinked, then blinked again. Surely it was a trick of the fading light? She turned to Rayner. "Do you see anything?" she demanded.

"What had you in mind?" Bored, cold and hungry, Rayner wanted a hot bath, a good supper, and a soft bed for the night. "I see reeds," he muttered, crossly, "I see water, mud, sand—"

"Look over to your left." Jane stood up in her stirrups. "There!" she cried wildly, turning this way and that. "Mr Grandison, Captain Denham! Look there!"

"The lady is right!" A fisherman on a donkey, his night vision far better than likely, peered into the twilight. "There, masters! On the sands!"

"Yes!" An Englishman from Reynoldston, mounted on a fleet-footed little pony, spurred his mount forward. The rest of the party followed him.

Owen lay on his back, staked out like a starfish. The tide was lapping his ankles. Teasing him, it ran up to his knees, then retreated. Then lapped again, this time encroaching further. Further still.

Sliding from her pony, Jane ran across the shining sands. Falling on her knees, she examined her cousin anxiously, all the while bracing herself for what she might see.

Fear and terror had fuelled her imagination all day long. So, scanning his face, she was prepared for gouged-out eyes, a tongue ripped from its moorings, a nose hacked off, temples stove in . . .

But, to her unspeakable relief, there seemed to be no damage. No permanent damage, anyway. Apart from some red and purple bruises on his forehead and cheeks, and two magnificent black eyes, Owen's face looked exactly the same as when she had last seen it.

"Owen?" As the men cut the ropes biting into his wrists and ankles, Jane spoke to him. Encouraged him, too. "Owen, my dear? Don't despair. You are saved!"

But Owen was barely conscious. If he heard Jane's voice, he could make no reply. If he knew she knelt beside him, if he was aware of the Englishman from Reynoldston hacking through the ropes and helping him to his feet, he could neither acknowledge this nor mutter any thanks.

Those people who had had to go on foot were gradually gathering on the river bank. William Parry elbowed his way to the front of the crowd. "John Rhys Owen." The tears stood in his eyes. "John Rhys Owen Morgan, your father all over again!"

Turning to the people, he shook his fist in the air. "They killed his father!" he cried. Now, his anger made him fluent, even in the language he despised. "They did away with his poor mother, and to this day no man knows how! Today, they tried to murder him!

"For years, they've robbed us. Insulted us. Used us, cheated us, both Welshmen and English alike! I say it's time we made them suffer! I say the hour of reckoning has come!"

A murmuring arose from the crowd. Like angry bees, they buzzed and muttered, in both Welsh and English.

Then, they swarmed.

That night, the house on the headland, together with everything in it, was destroyed. There was no looting, for anything of value was systematically defiled, then broken into as many pieces as could be. For the people meant to take a terrible revenge on the family which had held them in thrall for so long.

But finally, their orgy of breaking, smashing and wrecking over, they all left the house. Burning brands were brought across the cobbles, tossed through broken windows, and soon flames licked out of each and every casement, making the night sky bright.

"Leave them to it." The magistrate heard the news of the blaze with indifference. "We'll say it was an accident, if anyone enquires."

Recovered enough to sit slumped on a saddle, Owen rode between his cousins. Anxious to know what had happened to him, they realised he was hardly equal to conversation, but still they plied him with questions.

Eventually, he roused himself sufficiently to make a few halting replies.

"They were going to put my eyes out," he muttered, as he rubbed them, as if to make sure they were still there. "But then Henry suggested it might be more interesting for me, if I could actually see the water lapping all around. If I could gaze up despairing, and know I would soon die. So they contented themselves with beating me, then tying me down."

"Poor Owen." Jane looked at him. "I think – I am afraid your nose might be broken," she said.

"Maybe," he agreed. "It's very sore."

Owen and Jane met one anothers' eyes. The flesh around hers was almost as discoloured by fatigue as his was by ill-treatment. But each thought he or she had never seen a lovelier face. Each knew the other thought so, too.

Jane wanted to take Owen to the nearest inn, where he could rest and have a surgeon examine his injuries. Her brother, however, flatly forbade it. He was not going to leave Owen and his sister alone at any inn. Ill and exhausted though Owen Morgan undoubtedly was, there was no knowing what the fellow might get up to unsupervised, and Rayner was taking no more chances that night.

But Mr Grandison stepped in now and invited – or rather, ordered – all three cousins to go back to Swansea with him, to his own house, where their various needs could readily be met.

Rayner and Jane made their depositions that same evening. Owen, however, was put straight to bed. As for his tormentor – although more soldiers were drafted in, and the whole of Gower searched with the most meticulous care, they found no sign of Michael Atkins, or of his men.

Chapter Twenty-Four

A week went by. Rayner and Jane recovered completely from their individual ordeals. Their cousin, however, still lay abed. As Mr Grandison sagaciously remarked, *his* road back to health and strength would be a long and weary one.

"He'll get there in the end, however," added the magistrate cheerfully, giving Jane a very arch look. "After all, he receives only the best of medicines. The most gentle care. A glance from Miss Darrow's bright eyes, moreover, a smile from her own cherry lips, must work their own miracles. Indeed, what more wholesome tonics could a man desire?"

"You seem destined to enchant all the old men," muttered Rayner sourly, as Jane blushed at these compliments, and smiled in spite of herself.

Mr Grandison grinned back. But then, heaving himself to his gouty feet, he excused himself and stumped ponderously out of the breakfast room into the hall. Soon, he could be heard bellowing for his coat and gloves, and calling his valet all the names under the sun.

Jane met her brother's eyes. "You still don't believe me, do you?" she asked.

"I suspect that your recollections of those forty-eight hours will always be somewhat confused." Rayner shrugged. "It's not to be wondered at. Indeed, my own are hazy in the extreme."

"But mine are as clear as day. Rayner, you must give me credit for some powers of recall! Some degree of understanding. Everything I've told you is absolutely true."

"So you continue to insist."

"You don't *want* to believe me. Do you?"

"Anything *I* want is of no consequence. No consequence at all." Rayner added more sugar to his chocolate. Reflectively, he began to sip.

Wrapped in a warm, quilted robe, that dull Tuesday morning Jane had been sitting at the breakfast table for an hour or more, drinking dish after dish of sweetly fragrant best Ceylon, and warming her hands round the cup. For, these days, she was cold all the time. So cold that she doubted if even the hot sun of the tropics could have warmed her blood again.

Here in South Wales, the fine summer weather had been succeeded by cooler nights and days. Chilly winds blew in from the Atlantic, and rain poured down out of a grey, leaden sky. "They meant to kill us both," she murmured. "They would have murdered him, then come back for me."

"Indeed?" Determined not to be convinced, Rayner sniffed his disdain. "He was ever one for the dramatic gesture," he muttered. "The flamboyant declaration. The boastful aside.

"In any case, Atkins can hardly have meant to injure *you*. For God's sake! The man was in love with you! He would never have harmed his future bride."

"On the contrary. He would have tormented me cruelly, and delighted in the act." Shuddering, Jane pulled her robe close about her body. "As for Owen – he did what he did not out of bravado, but because he loves me. He would have endured the most brutal tortures man could devise, and borne them bravely too, had he known I was safe."

"I never heard such nonsense." Disgusted, Rayner shook his head. "Jane, you are not yourself these days. In fact, I sometimes fear you have run a little mad."

"I think not." But, all the same, Jane changed the subject. "Is there any word of that creature?" she enquired, evenly.

"I'm afraid there is not. I spoke to Mr Grandison's clerk

only this morning. He fears nothing new will emerge for some time yet.

"I see."

"But don't worry." Grimly, Rayner smiled. "They *will* be taken. Mr Grandison will not rest until that day dawns, for he considers it a matter of honour that they should be captured, loaded with chains, then put on trial here. In Swansea itself."

"Good." Involuntarily, Jane shivered. "I shall not rest easily in my bed until they have all been hanged. Preferably from the highest gallows in the land."

"Do you intend to see it done?"

"I do." Jane's blue eyes grew flinty. "Now I comprehend the full extent of that man's wickedness, it is my favourite ambition to see him expire. In that, I imagine I shall be but one element of a great, angry multitude."

Jane motioned to the maid, to refill her cup. "Rayner," she continued, "I so often wonder what became of my poor Blanchette."

"Ah, yes. Blanchette." Rayner grinned. "I have at last made successful enquiries. After the fire, it seems she was found wandering and crying in the grounds of the house. A local villager has taken her in. So – do you want her back?"

"I don't know. She's good and innocent herself, of course. But if I take her back, she will constantly remind me of that time." Jane glanced up. "Yes, Sophie? Did you wish to say something?"

"I do, ma'am," replied the maid. "I beg your pardon for being so forward – but did you know Mrs Grandison's pug has lately died? Mistress was beside herself for weeks. But I think that now—"

"She might wish to consider making another friend?" Jane smiled. "Then I shall ask Mrs Grandison if she would like to meet Blanchette. Thank you, Sophie. You may go about your business now. Rayner, I meant to mention this earlier. I have written to Isabel."

"Why ever did you do that?"

"To assure her we are all safe and well, of course."

"Why should she care?"

"I also took the liberty of asking her to come down here. You see, when she heard you were married, Mrs Grandison was most insistent that I invite your wife to stay. She declares Mr Grandison will certainly not object to a fourth – or even a fifth, *little* guest! If Isabel should wish to bring the child, I mean."

"It's of no moment whether he objects or not," retorted Rayner, flatly. "Isabel will not come to see me."

Jane and Rayner were sitting in the parlour taking their mid-morning coffee when, a week later, Isabel arrived. Looking very well and dressed in the height of fashion, she carried an equally modish Honor in her arms.

"Good morning, Jane," she began, nervously. She glanced towards her husband. "Rayner?"

But Rayner merely looked away.

"Good morning, Isabel." Smiling, Jane rose to her feet. Realising her sister-in-law was horribly embarrassed, she took her hand, then relieved her of her daughter, who had been squirming to get down. "Come, Honor," she went on. "If we look in the jar here, I think we may find some sugar candy, just for you."

While Jane busied herself amusing Honor, Isabel was left to observe her husband, who sat sullen and uncommunicative over his coffee, no doubt wishing her away. Having nothing else to do, she glanced round the room.

"He's upstairs," muttered Rayner, sourly. "He can't walk very well. His ankles were damaged, you see."

"Broken?"

"No. But the sprains are severe. The ligaments are all torn."

"What other injuries does he have?"

"Three ribs are cracked, his nose is broken, and his neck is twisted quite awry." Rayner's own face twisted now. "But his manhood is intact," he went on. "His bruises will fade. In time, all his wounds will heal themselves."

"I'm glad to hear it."

"I'm sure you are." Rayner grimaced. "Ladies are always glad to hear good tidings of Mr Morgan. He was ever the favourite of the fairer sex, and so he remains to this day. The females in this house flock about him constantly."

"Oh, Rayner!" In spite of herself, Isabel wanted to laugh. "I do believe you're jealous!"

"Not at all." Dismissively, Rayner shrugged. "My sister wrote to you, did she not?"

"Yes, she did."

"No doubt she spoke at length of my cousin's valour? Of his bravery, nobility and unflinching self-sacrifice?"

"To be sure, but she also—"

"*I*, of course, did nothing. Mr Morgan, on the other hand, is the hero of the hour."

"Yes." Isabel nodded agreement. "My dear Rayner, you must admit that Owen appears to have acted most courageously."

"Of course he did. My sister prates of his heroism constantly, and sings his praises all day long." Rayner glanced towards where his sister sat, playing with her little friend. "She is reluctant to leave him even for a moment. In fact, I'm surprised she has spared these few precious seconds in order to greet you."

"Oh, Rayner! I—"

"I should warn you, he's not very pretty just now. But I'm sure he'll be delighted to see his mistress once more."

Isabel, however, did not take her cue. Instead, it was Jane who now excused herself, and was heard to run lightly upstairs.

Rayner reached for his newspaper. "The maid will show you and Honor up," he muttered. "The bell is there, on the desk. Be so good as to use it."

"Rayner, I wish to speak with *you*." Moving to the sofa, Isabel called Honor to her side. "I came—"

"To visit your paramour."

"No, Rayner. Owen and I have nothing to say to each other. Nothing at all." Isabel bit her lip. "I came to show you your child."

"My bastard, you should say. Or shall we be even more correct, and refer instead to my legitimate incumbrance, got upon my wife by another man?"

"No, Rayner. We shall refer to your own dear daughter. To your child and mine."

"Then we shall be talking the most deliberate nonsense ever heard." Rayner turned away. Now, bitterness drew lines on his face which would not appear of their own accord for another ten years or more. "Isabel, you're a drab. I am a cuckold. Do but accept these sordid facts. Cease to persist in this ridiculous lie forthwith."

"My dear, it is not a lie. I speak the simple truth." Isabel edged closer to her husband. "My dear Rayner, will you not even look at me?"

Rayner would not. Could not. It hurt him beyond endurance to recall their time together. To remember how much he'd loved her, once.

So Isabel talked on. "My dear," she continued, "do you recall the fact that your mother had a birthmark? A little mole shaped like a half moon, just above her left eyebrow?"

"What of it?"

"Maria remembers her saying it was something which had run in her family for generations. Your grandmother Searle had it, and doubtless *her* mother bore it, too. Honor, my dear?"

The baby, who had been earnestly sucking a stick of barley sugar, looked up. Sure enough, the mark was there, plain for all to see.

"I thought she had scratched herself," continued Isabel. "Then, when the place did not heal, I realised I was seeing one of those – strawberry marks, I believe they are called – which are not present at birth, but which appear when the baby is five or six weeks old.

"I thought no more of it until Owen took us to visit

Maria, and I entrusted Honor to the care of a nurse who had formerly worked for your family. She remarked on it at once. She called it a witch mark, and said it was a sign Honor will be gifted with the second sight."

"What foolish nonsense."

"Maybe. Maybe not." But now, somehow encouraged, Isabel dared to lay her white hand upon her husband's cuff. "Rayner," she cried, shaking him, "look at her! She's dark, it's true, but look at her eyes! Her grandmother Darrow's were shaped exactly thus – large and round, long-lashed and heavy-lidded, just like these. Her mouth, her nose, her high cheekbones, all are your own poor mother's. Rayner, my dear, this child is yours."

"Perhaps." Rayner shrugged. "But the fact that she is – or might be – mine, does not excuse her mother's disgraceful conduct. Not in the least."

"No." Justly rebuked, Isabel hung her head. "But Rayner, consider. You are not guiltless yourself."

"What do you mean?"

"I mean, husband, that you were often unfaithful to me. Do not deny it, for I am certain it is so. You and Charles Harding—"

"I did not bring my harlots home! I did not expose you to ridicule and infamy, I did not hurt—"

"True. But you encouraged other disreputables to visit you. My house was a sanctuary for all the card sharps, strolling vagabonds and miscellaneous spongers in the Midlands!"

"May a man not have friends?"

"My dear Rayner, your actresses were more than friends."

"Isabel, such talk does not become a woman."

"Rayner, such conduct does not become a man!"

"How dare you! I never once compromised you, nor did I—"

"Please." Isabel looked down at her finger nails. "Please, Rayner, let us not quarrel in front of the child, and in a stranger's house."

"You are the one who seeks to quarrel. Not I."

"You are mistaken. I seek a reconciliation. But I do not come here in the spirit of one who must supplicate. I do not grovel, begging bowl in hand."

"You intend to live on fresh air, I suppose? Or has your father relented? Has he forgiven your trespasses indeed, and made his will in your favour once again?"

"Neither." Isabel shrugged. "But eighteen months ago, an aunt of mine – a spinster lady, living in Virginia – was taken ill and died. She left me a little competence, entrusted and disposed in such a way that my husband – if I should chance to have one – could make no use of it. After *my* death, anything that remains becomes my daughter's own.

"Rayner, the income I shall derive from this inheritance is very modest. But since you and I parted company, I have learned the value of money, and come to understand what it can and cannot buy. I could live on an amount which I would have considered mere pin money before."

"Indeed? That gown you are wearing today was not cheaply bought."

"It was a present on my birthday, from my mother. I have no others like it. Rayner, do you understand what I'm telling you? Even if my family were to cast me off again, and my father should decide I must pay for my errors for the rest of my life, I shall not starve to death.

"So, if you will not take me back as your wife, nor accept Honor as your daughter, I shall find myself a little house to rent, somewhere in the countryside. I shall give out that I am a widow, and try to bring up my child as her father would have wished. Rayner, my dear, may we walk together a little? The rain has given over, and I feel the need of some air. The girl here will mind Honor, I dare say."

So Isabel and Rayner, saying nothing but beginning to feel his spirits lift, went into Mr Grandison's garden.

* * *

"I suppose we may try. Merely to see how we go on, you understand." For Rayner was by no means ready to forgive, nor to forget.

But he was still fond of his wife. He could see she was penitent. More to the point, he accepted that her daughter must be his child.

They had walked all round the rather sooty rose garden and were coming back towards the shrubbery, when they noticed a servant looking this way and that.

"Mr Darrow, sir! My master wishes to speak with you." The man was excited. In fact, he was fairly bubbling over. Impatiently, he hurried Rayner and Isabel towards the house.

"What's the matter?" Never one to run where he could walk, Rayner puffed along. He caught at the servant's sleeve. "Well, man?"

"Sir, they are apprehended!" The man grinned, hugely. "My master had word by special messenger, not half an hour since! It seems Mr Atkins and two of his followers were taken in Holyhead, whilst trying to arrange passage on a ship to Ireland. Also, the body of the man Dennis has been found."

"The body?" Rayner frowned. "What happened to him?"

"It seems he was in hiding for a few days, but then his friends became anxious to be rid of him. So they launched a boat from Port Eynon Point.

"A storm blew up in the night and he was capsized. Then battered to death on the rocks of Penrhyn Gwyr. Oh, sir! Good news, is it not?"

"Excellent news indeed." Rayner himself grinned then. For now, he hoped, the nightmares would cease. But even if they did not, from tonight he would at least have someone in bed with him. Someone to hold on to. Someone warm and soft and human, someone whose simple presence alone must surely help to frighten the demons of his imagination away . . .

* * *

As soon as Michael Atkins was known to be safely behind bars, the gossips' tongues began to wag in earnest. Everyone from Swansea to Rhosili Bay, Welsh or English, had a story to tell against him or his family, hinging on their rapacity, their cruelty, their arrogance or their greed. This was strange, for at the trial of his father hardly anyone, from Gower or Swansea or anywhere else, had been prevailed upon to testify against the old man.

Owen and Jane heard the news from the woman who made the beds and emptied the commodes. When they were told, they nodded their satisfaction, but declined to learn any further details. So the servant went away shaking her head, reflecting that she'd never seen anything like it in her life. Mr Morgan and Miss Darrow were interested in nothing and no one – save one another. They were missing the sensation of the decade!

As the woman collected her basket of cleaning things and prepared to go on her way, Jane began to tidy the medicines, the ointments, the balms – all paraphernalia of the sick room, in fact.

"The sun is actually shining today," she observed drawing back the curtains and pulling up the blinds. "Owen? Do you see?"

"I see." Narrowing his eyes, Owen winced. "Don't look at me!" he cried, covering his face. "I'm hideous enough in the dusk. I shall hardly repay scrutiny by the light of day."

"Indeed you will not." Looking at him anyway, Jane laughed. "I remember when you fell out of the great oak at the end of the drive, back at Easton Hall. You looked terrible for a fortnight then."

"Not as terrible as I do now, I'll be bound."

"Dear Owen, you will mend."

"Slowly."

"But surely."

"I hope so."

"Don't fret." Jane smoothed the covers on the bed. "Be

glad you are alive. Be grateful no permanent damage was done. Rest, and allow nature to take its course."

That was all Owen *could* do. His broken ribs made breathing painful and exertion impossible. He was sore all over, in fact, from the top of his head to the soles of his feet. His wrists and ankles were scarred and crusted with weeping sores. His face was still a mess of purples, yellows and blues. His chipped or missing teeth, broken nose and puffy eyelids ensured that these days he resembled nothing so much as a gargoyle. One of the water spouts which adorned the gable ends at Easton Hall.

"I had a letter this morning," said Jane, sitting down on the edge of his bed. "It was from my sister. She says my house is ready at last."

"*Your* house, Jane?" demanded Owen. "Do you actually own a house?"

"I do. It is called The Ash Grove." Recollecting, Jane smiled. "It is very secluded, very small, but extremely neat and pretty. It has a charming garden, where I mean to grow raspberries and currants, tend roses, and keep a row of hives."

"Indeed? That sounds extremely dull."

"Does it? My dear Owen, dullness is exactly what I need these days!" Jane shook her head. "I have had enough adventure. From now on, I seek a quiet existence."

"A rural idyll, free from care?"

"Precisely," Jane agreed. "You'll see, I shall play the part of village gossip brilliantly. I shall positively rejoice in the title of old maid."

"But *you* can't be an old maid!"

"Can I not?"

"No! You must marry me."

"Marry a monster?" Jane shook her head. "Marry a creature so hideous that he could frighten a little child into a fit, or cause its mother to miscarry? My poor Owen, one glance from you would curdle milk at once, and send the dairymaids fleeing in panic, to sanctuary!"

"I dare say." Wincing, Owen laughed. "We would be beauty and the beast indeed. All the same—"

"Owen, before you ask me to marry you again, tell me just one thing."

"What is that?"

"Do you still love Isabel?"

"I—"

"Don't dissemble."

"I shan't." Owen looked into Jane's eyes. "So here is the truth. You'll hate me for it, I know. But, the fact is, from the moment I saw her again, I wanted her."

"Why?"

"Oh, she was – is – so beautiful! So lovely. When she made a play for me, I was overwhelmed. Flattered out of my senses, in fact. I imagined myself desperately in love. So much so that I simply didn't care if I hurt you.

"There. Now you know. Now, you'll despise me forever."

"No." Jane stroked his hair away from his battered forehead. "She *is* beautiful. Had I been a man, I think it likely that I myself would not have been proof against her charm. Thank you for being so honest with me."

"Now tell me you hate me."

"I don't hate you at all. I never have. Even when you – when you and Isabel—"

"Don't say it." Reaching for her hands, Owen took them in his own. "Jane, listen to me. As far as I am concerned, you are the only woman in the world. I love you, certainly. But I also like you. I admire you and respect you, too.

"You say Isabel is beautiful. But so are you! Admittedly in a less obvious, quieter way."

"I am *too* quiet."

"No! You are serenity personified. You—"

"I mean, I did not understand." Jane bit her lip. "I

should have seduced you myself, before Isabel even thought of it."

"Jane!" Owen was shocked. "My dear cousin, a respectable woman does not even consider—"

"Oh, don't talk such stuff! We were engaged to be married! We had been lovers at least in the abstract sense for years. But I would never open even my mouth for you. Let alone my legs."

"What?" Astonished, Owen stared at her. Had she taken leave of her senses? "Jane, my dearest," he began gently, "I don't think you're well. Those coarse expressions, that language of the gutter hardly becomes—"

"Please, Owen! Let your tongue rest." Jane looked away. "I was so afraid you would think I was forward," she muttered. "I was so jealous of my good name! But now, when I recall those polite little kisses in the rose garden, those timid embraces on the terrace, I feel such a fool I could weep for shame."

"Jane, please—"

"But you were a fool, too! Dear God! How delicate you were! How careful, lest you might frighten or upset me, lest you should inflame my virgin's cheeks with a blush! You never touched my breasts. You never once stroked my hair.

"For, I was the squire's daughter. I was your elder sister, in everyday custom if not in fact. In a word, you were in awe of me."

"No, Jane. I—"

"So, I should have taken the initiative. But I was too staid and prim. Too much the simpering hypocrite to let you begin to understand how much I needed you."

"Don't!" Owen could keep silent no longer. "You conducted yourself like a decent, respectable, modest woman. You—"

"I conducted myself like a tease and a flirt. Like a coy, precious, ignorant simpleton, who pretended she had no desires, no longings – nay, no feelings, even – of her own."

"I'll never accept that," said Owen. "Jane – dearest Jane – I don't expect you to say you'll be my wife. Not today, anyway. But please, give me a little time. Let me learn how to deserve you!"

"You will need nursing for several weeks yet." Leaning towards the invalid, Jane kissed his cheek. "I'll write to Maria and ask her to make the necessary arrangements.

"So, you shall have the best bedroom. We'll have Charles Harding's Ferguson to valet you, and borrow Maria's own Mrs Bradley, to sit with you when I can't be there.

"Oh, darling! Please hurry up and get well, or at least fit to travel! Then we can go home."

"To Warwickshire?"

"Of course." Jane kissed him again. "The Ash Grove is waiting for us. Maria has been in to look things over. But I am still anxious lest the maids should not have scoured the kitchen, and aired all the beds properly."